A
Dinah Harris
MYSTERY

Pieces
OF LIGHT

Julie Cave

First printing: May 2011

ISBN: 978-0-89051-608-9
Library of Congress Number: 2011928273

Cover by Left Coast Design

Scripture taken from the HOLY BIBLE, NEW INTERNATIONAL VERSION®. Copyright © 1973, 1978, 1984 Biblica. Used by permission of Zondervan. All rights reserved. The "NIV" and "New International Version" trademarks are registered in the United States Patent and Trademark Office by Biblica. Use of either trademark requires the permission of Biblica.

Scripture quotations marked (NLT) are taken from the Holy Bible, New Living Translation, copyright © 1996, 2004, 2007 by Tyndale House Foundation. Used by permission of Tyndale House Publishers, Inc., Carol Stream, Illinois 60188. All rights reserved.

All characters appearing in this novel are fictitious. Any resemblance to real persons, living or dead, is purely coincidental.

Please consider requesting that a copy of this volume be purchased by your local library system.

Printed in the United States of America

Please visit our website for other great titles:
www.masterbooks.net

For information regarding author interviews,
please contact the publicity department at (870) 438-5288.

Master
Books®
A Division of New Leaf Publishing Group

Acknowledgments

I would like to thank Dr Georgia Purdom, who once again provided generously of her time to read the manuscript, make suggestions and ensure accuracy. Her dedication and attention to detail is more appreciated than words can say. I have grown to rely on and trust her instincts when it comes to creating the best possible manuscript.

I must also thank my husband, Terry, for the sacrifices he makes to ensure that I have the time and space needed to write. Thank you for the many times you have given up a weekend or an evening so that I can immerse myself in the world of Dinah Harris. Thank you for sharing a passion to reach out to others with the good news of Jesus Christ, and for being a Godly husband and father.

For my children, Jasmine, and the precious baby who is due to be born in August: I love you both so dearly. I pray that you will grow to love God and serve Him with joy your whole lives.

This book is dedicated to you – the fans who keep buying my books, the people who read these books and blog about them, who follow me on Facebook, who talk to their friends and family about them, who leave me supportive and encouraging comments, who allow me to speak to at their churches or events, and who generously give up their time and energy to support the vision of my books. You will never know how much you all mean to me, and how grateful I am for you. To say thank you seems woefully inadequate. In any case, I say thank you from the bottom of my heart.

All glory, honor and praise goes to God.

Contents

Sussex 1 State Prison
Waverly, Virginia
Prisoner Number: 10734
Death Row

I am on death row and they say I deserve to be here. I suppose I agree. I
don't really know. I don't have any feelings about it. I know I killed
some people, and that's why I'm here.

I live in a cell that feels like the size of a postage stamp, but at least I'm
by myself. I have my books, a television, and some paper on which to write.
I have my thoughts, which are strangely muted as though they have jumped
into someone else's head and I'm eavesdropping. They've been that way ever
since they arrested me. Before that, my thoughts were all mine and I could
hear them just fine.

Apparently, this didn't help me during the trial. The prosecutor called
me a "cunning, cold killer who took great pleasure in planning the details
of his innocent victims deaths." The judge told me that my unemotional
response to the guilty verdict read out by the jury foreman "chilled him to
the bone." Even the newspaper, brought by my family when they visited the

first time, had a picture of my blank face with the headline: "No Remorse Shown by Bomber." Why didn't you show any remorse? my family asked me. Why not at least apologize?

Because I don't feel remorse. I don't feel guilt. I don't feel sorry. I feel nothing. Somebody has hit the mute button on me and I no longer can communicate the way I used to.

I've heard the rumors about me — that I'm a sociopath, that I'm angry and hatred-fueled, that I'm mentally impaired because I have no conscience.

I have felt anger, hatred, frustration, guilt, and even love before all this happened. I used to be a fully functioning, reasonably normal human being. I think that pieces of me are dying slowly, so that by the time my execution date rolls around, I'll be almost dead anyway. There are pieces of light inside of me, slowly extinguishing themselves, one by one.

I don't blame this prison, or the police, or the jury or the judge. It is my fault — the dying process started the day I set the first bomb. When it exploded, something inside me let go and seems to be irreplaceable. It was then that the numbness began to creep over me the way the deadly cold slowly claims the life of those lost in the snow or at sea. The more bombs I set off, the worse it got. Perhaps, then, I'm a suicide bomber, only by slow degrees rather than all at once.

But I was caught, and sent here to death row. My lawyer told me he'd appeal until there were no appeals left. I've probably got 15 years of life in a lonely cell ahead of me. I have to live here 23 hours a day. The 24th hour I go outside to a special yard for death row inmates and stare at the sky, wishing that my spirit could be free. My family visits me every 90 days, as per the warden's regulations, but they are not allowed to touch me. They can only speak to me through glass. I eat when they push a tray into my cell and I sleep when they dim the lights. At least I get to choose the method of my execution — lethal injection or the electric chair. Another death row inmate told me I should make up my mind now: by the time they get around to executing me, it's likely I'll have lost the mental capacity to make that decision.

I haven't yet lost the ability to dream.

I dream of silence. Here, it is never quiet. When awake, death row inmates yell at each other, scream at the guards, make demands of God, and vent their frustrations. When asleep, they weep, cry out, howl, or whimper, depending on which nightmare they're having.

I dream that I have a normal life — loving parents, perhaps a wife and kids. Not the dysfunctional mess of a family I currently have to deal with.I dream that I have the freedom of a bird, to fly where my heart desires, unfettered by the judgments of men.

I dream of being stuck in traffic, waiting on a delayed flight in an airport, being unable to find a parking space, and a thousand other little grievances because it would mean that I was free.

I know there aren't many who would feel sympathy for me. What about the lives of the victims? They didn't get to choose the circumstances of their death. I, a convicted killer, have more rights in that regard than they ever did.

That's true. I don't have a reply to that.

So why on earth did I do it? I hear this frequently from my mother, who considers herself an abject failure in the parenting department because her son grew up to be a convicted murderer and death row inmate.

I have no reply to that either. I don't know. I just don't know.

Someone is coming who might be able to help me understand why. Her name is Dinah Harris. She used to be an FBI agent and she wants to write a book about people like me. She helped to track me down and arrest me but I'm not angry with her. I don't feel anything.

Actually, I'm looking forward to it. She has black hair and pale skin and eyes that are haunted. I can see that she has pain in her past, like I do. I can tell that she is a complex woman, with deeds she wishes were left undone and words left unsaid.

When she visited me the first time, to ask me whether I'd be willing to participate in her book, I told her that I would. She smiled and suddenly I saw that my initial impression had been a little wrong. Yes, she'd been haunted and hurt and regretful. But when she smiled, all of that was stripped away and I saw compassion, peace, and understanding.

So I guess the truth is that I've agreed to do these interviews with an ulterior motive. I want to question her as much as she wants to question me. I want what she's got — compassion, peace, and understanding so powerful that they have somehow defeated despair, bitterness, and judgment.

How did she do it?

ONE YEAR EARLIER

The funeral service had finally moved to the graveside, following the traditional church ceremony. It had been a moving service, at least for the mourners who didn't make up part of his immediate family. The eulogy was heartfelt and tear-jerking. It was a direct reflection of his life: flashy and impressive, soulful and well-loved. Yet it left an empty feeling in the deepest parts of the hearts of his children and a dark scar on the heart of his wife.

The mourners were now few — his wife, Rosa, his adult children, Isabelle and Michael, several long-standing family friends, church friends, and some old work colleagues. The small group stood around the casket, staring down at the incongruously glorious spring flowers that adorned it, avoiding eye contact with each other.

The day was still and hot, an Indian summer's day with a venomous thick humidity that settled on the shoulders of the mourners. The officiating priest's forehead was slick and shiny with sweat, and he looked distinctly uncomfortable in his black attire. Isabelle thought that everybody attending this funeral looked desperate to be elsewhere, though not because of the weather.

Isabelle had been asked to give a eulogy and had refused. What would she have said about her father? *He ruled us with an iron fist. He didn't come to any of my piano recitals. He pushed my mother against the wall when his shirts weren't ironed. He broke my wrist. What a guy. Is it irreverent to remark in his eulogy that I am glad he's dead?*

Isabelle tried to gather her unruly thoughts, reminding herself that she had only one more day to pretend her family was fine. She glanced at her mother, a tiny woman with veiled eyes. Surprisingly, Rosa's grief seemed genuine. Isabelle then darted a glance at Michael, wondering what he was truly feeling behind the freezing blank glare trained at the ground. Beside her, her husband, Scott, fidgeted impatiently, his irritation at having to be here oozing from every pore.

Isabelle wondered what the other mourners were thinking. Had they really known Reginald McMahon? There had been the public persona: charming, witty, kind, thoughtful. He had been the first to volunteer to help another family, to paint the church, to give money where it was needed. Those outside his family had not known of the explosive temper, the controlling behavior, the acidic tongue. Yet it was clear from the small number of mourners that he'd never really had a close friend.

Finally, the priest finished his brief remarks and invited those present to say a few words before the casket was lowered into the grave. In awkward silence, the attendees shuffled and desperately avoided looking at the priest or at each other. After a few moments, the priest began the last rites, throwing handfuls of dirt over the casket. He encouraged everyone to follow suit.

Rosa lingered over the grave and wiped away tears. Isabelle marveled at the depth of her mother's delusion, even on the very day she became free from her husband's tyrannical rule. Michael sauntered over and tossed in a handful of dirt carelessly, the contempt curling his upper lip the only indication of the emotion he was feeling. Isabelle was quick, glad that the whole sorry day was almost at a close.

The small crowd dispersed, leaving the family to watch the burial in silence. In the still air, the rhythmic thud of the shovels of dirt being tossed into the grave was hypnotic. Isabelle wondered whether her family could now begin to heal, now that he was dead.

"What am I doing to do?" Rosa finally spoke, her voice a low keen. "What am I doing to do without him?"

"How about throw a party celebrating the fact that he's dead?" suggested Michael, his voice hard and tight. "Then we could burn his clothes and try to pretend he never existed at all."

Rosa gasped, turning to Isabelle to defend her.

"Michael . . ." started Isabelle.

Michael waved his hand dismissively. "Yeah, I know. Now is not the time or place. Whatever. It's *never* the time or place."

"Well," interjected Scott, with perfect timing, as usual. He looked meaningfully at his watch. "I've wasted too much time here already. I've got to get back to the office." He looked at Isabelle, eyebrows raised, as if daring her to challenge him.

Isabelle didn't want any confrontation, particularly in front of her mother. She smiled. "Of course, I'll see you at home," she replied and watched Scott stalk away. For a moment, she wondered at her ability to deeply care about how everyone else was feeling when they so often didn't seem to return the favor. She hoped fervently that Scott would return home that evening in a much better mood.

She turned to Michael. "We can discuss it anytime you want," she said. "I just don't think the funeral is the most appropriate venue."

"Don't speak ill of the dead," added Rosa, which didn't help the inflammatory situation at all.

"Mom," said Isabelle with a touch of frustration.

"Okay, okay," her mother relented. "We're all upset, I understand."

We are, but for different reasons than you think.

"Let's have dinner tomorrow night at home," Rosa continued. "Will you both come home?"

Michael glanced at Isabelle, who knew that if she didn't accept the invitation, then he wouldn't either. "Sure, sounds great, Mom," she said, with a long look at her brother.

"Sure," he agreed. He didn't raise his eyes from the ground, where he was scuffing the toe of his sneaker in the dirt.

They began the walk to the parking lot in silence, Isabelle wondering when this agonizing day would finally be over.

* * * *

He had been told that he looked like Billy Idol, the eighties rock icon, and he'd been pleased with that. So now, when he was in combat mode, he thought of himself as Billy Idol. As he worked, he hummed some of Idol's songs and changed the words to suit himself. Instead of singing, *It's a nice day for a white wedding,* he sang: *It's a nice day for some blood shedding.*

As he sang, he built the bomb.

He'd spent yesterday preparing for his target. There were a number of prerequisites: an older building was preferable, plenty of space at the front or side of the building, and the possibility of little collateral damage. It was important to him that surrounding buildings, like family homes, were not impacted by the blast. That's why he was tailoring the bomb not to ensure maximum payload but simply to damage the target building. He absolutely didn't want a child sleeping in her bedroom to wake to shrapnel peppering her curtains.

It was important that people knew that he wasn't a monster. He wasn't interested in causing maximum harm. He just wanted to make his point.

After about two hours, he'd found one that fit his criteria and then had begun looking for a vehicle to steal. There, too, were prerequisites for the vehicle. It had to be tough, big, unremarkable, and disposable. Therefore, he'd discounted a van with baby seats in it, a van filled with gardening equipment, and one he'd observed belching blue smoke as its driver pulled up to the curb.

He didn't really know why he was applying moral values to the mission he was trying to complete. To an outsider, it would have seemed ridiculous. But how could he in good conscience build a bomb in a car with baby seats?

Humming under his breath, he carefully inserted dynamite in the industrial plastic bag and checked that it was surrounded equally by the slurry mixture of ammonium nitrate and fuel oil. Then he meticulously attached the fuse, which he intended to set on a time delay.

When his back started aching from bending over, he stood up and nearly smacked the top of his head on the roof of the van. It was far easier to build the bomb in the van in which he intended to detonate it, but it made for cramped quarters. The fumes were also getting a little too pungent, which was the biggest problem with building a bomb in a small space. And it was hotter than a commercial oven inside the vehicle. He checked that both windows were open and wiped his sweaty forehead.

There was suddenly a pounding at the door of the van and his heart dropped to his feet. "What?" he yelled, fear hammering in his throat.

"You okay in there, man?" a familiar voice yelled back.

The bomb maker ground his teeth in frustration. It was his neighbor Randy, who was simple and harmless, if a little too curious for his own good. He flung open the door and quickly exited the van, almost stepping on Randy as he did so.

"Just bought some fertilizer," he explained. "For my garden."

Randy glanced around the weed-choked yard, but if he was surprised by this revelation he didn't show it. "Cool, man," he said with a shrug. "You were just in there a while."

There was an awkward silence. "So did you want something?" the bomb maker asked finally.

"Oh, right," said Randy. "Just wanted to see if you wanted to hang out."

"Uh," said the bomb maker, throwing a glance back at his tools. He thought quickly. He'd timed the tasks he needed to do today to perfection, and he couldn't afford a break. But he didn't want Randy to become suspicious. He'd always been pretty happy to hang with Randy in the past, mostly because his neighbor never noticed whether the company was bad. The bomb maker wanted to scream with indecision.

"I'm sorry, Randy," he said finally. "I sort of committed today to getting this chore done."

"Oh," said Randy, nodding. But he didn't move. The silence stretched out.

"Randy?"

"You want some help?" offered Randy. "Man, it *really* stinks in there!"

The bomb maker wanted to start pounding the side of the van with his fists. Instead he laughed, a brittle noise that sounded forced even to his ears.

"I'm good," he said. "Thanks though. No point both of us passing out from the smell."

Finally, it seemed to sink into Randy's thick skull that he wasn't wanted. He languidly waved goodbye and sauntered away.

The bomb maker glanced at his watch and thought about all of the things he still needed to get done before his self-imposed deadline.

Feeling his stress levels rise, he began humming to calm himself down. An anxious bomb maker often made for a dead bomb maker. He *had* to have steady hands and a clear brain.

He thought of a Billy Idol song, in an effort to settle his mind. Instead of humming *In the midnight hour, she cried more, more, more,* he changed the words to *In the midnight hour, the bomb roared, roared, roared.*

Feeling calmer, he got back to work, attaching the time delay to the fuse. By design, he was working with explosives that were reasonably stable. He didn't have to worry about heat, bumps, fumes, or anything else that would set the bomb off prematurely. The payoff was that the bomb would lack the power of its more unstable cousins. The bomb maker's intent was not to take as many lives as possible, or even to cause the maximum damage. There would be collateral damage, of course. Lives probably would be lost; destruction would certainly be wrought.

But in the end, he simply wanted to send his message.

Pieces of Light

* * * *

Dinah Harris glared at the oscillating fan as though one of the hottest summer days on record was solely the fan's fault. She lifted hair damp with sweat from her neck and twisted it up on top of her head. She was perusing notes for her book idea and had spent last night writing down every random thought that came into her head about it. Now she was sorting through them all and wondering at some of the nonsense she'd clearly thought sounded lucid last night.

She'd gotten the idea from a friend at home group during the week. There were two funny things about that statement, she suddenly thought with a grin. One, that she had a friend, given her profound instinct never to let anyone get too close; and two, that she was going to a church home group. The idea of it had been awful, but the reality had been a lot better.

Dinah had been telling the women in her group about her current job as a freelance crime consultant, and her previous job as an FBI agent. They had all been so interested that one of them suggested she should write a book about her experiences.

It got Dinah thinking, but down a different line. She wanted to write about the *people* she'd encountered along the way. There were many stories worth telling — gang members with the courage to walk away, everyday heroes, and even the backgrounds of violent criminals.

Her thoughts were interrupted by the shrilling of her cell phone. "Hello?"

"Hey, Harris, it's your old partner in crime," said a familiar voice.

Dinah felt a rush of delight at hearing the voice of her old FBI partner, David Ferguson. They'd worked closely together for years, until Dinah's drinking problem had gotten her fired from the Bureau. He had always been her greatest champion, even when at her lowest point she had turned up for work drunk or hung-over. Their relationship was one of bantering rather than deep and meaningful discussions, but they were still as close as a professional partnership could be.

"What's up, Ferguson?" she asked. "Why are you bothering me on a Sunday?"

"Oh, I don't know," said Ferguson breezily. "I just thought you'd be pretty thrilled to talk to the new Assistant Special Agent in Charge."

Dinah grinned. "You? Didn't they have anyone else? Are things really that bad at the Bureau these days?"

"I really miss that sarcastic sense of humor, Harris," said Ferguson. "You really know how to build a guy up, don't you?"

"Seriously, you're the new Special Agent in Charge?" asked Dinah. "That's really something. Congratulations."

"You haven't asked me what department," said Ferguson, sounding like the proverbial cat with the cream.

"What department, Ferguson?" Dinah asked impatiently.

"Domestic terrorism!"

It was a prestigious gig. The Bureau appointed agents to high-profile positions only if they had a long, scandal-free history of clean cases and a good solve rate. Her own presence notwithstanding, Ferguson had been a longtime and loyal servant for the Bureau and deserved his promotion.

Dinah couldn't help but feel an edge of jealousy. She had been one of the Bureau's brightest stars, brilliant at her job in the Violent Gangs department, extracting high-ranking gang members in exchange for intelligence. She'd enjoyed almost legendary status, at least until she lost her husband and son in a car accident, began drinking heavily to cope, and made a series of spectacular mistakes. Finally, her alcoholism had led to her firing from her beloved Bureau.

"Ferguson, you are totally awesome," she said sincerely.

"Listen," said Ferguson, suddenly serious. "The best part about being in charge is that if I need an external consultant, I can hire one."

Dinah smiled. "You don't have to keep saving my butt, Ferguson."

"Yeah, I know. But just so you know . . . if I need you, I'll call you. I heard you did some good work with the serial killer and the Metropolitan Police."

Dinah thought of the last case, a serial killer bent on removing victims he decided were not worthy of life based on his own crazy eugenic agenda. It had been the first case she'd worked in a long time completely sober, and the gratifying thing was that she'd done some good work.

"Thanks, Ferguson. I'll always take your calls," said Dinah.

"Well, stay tuned," said Ferguson. "Listen, is everything going okay with you?"

Dinah knew what he was talking about. He wanted to know if she was still sober and if she was coping. "Ferguson, I've been clean for close to six months," she said proudly, one relapse notwithstanding. "I feel optimistic and hopeful. I have my faith in God and joy in the redemption that He's offered me. I honestly feel the best I have in a long time."

"That's really great, Harris," said Ferguson.

"Listen, could you do me a favor?" Dinah asked.

"Sure thing. What?"

"Do something about this ridiculous heat, will you?" Dinah grinned. "It's killing me here."

Ferguson laughed. "I hear you. You'll have to put a word in to the man upstairs about that, if you know what I mean."

Dinah hung up and made herself a cup of coffee. While she inhaled the bittersweet aroma, she stood by the window, looking down at the street. The heat was intense and it had brought people outside: kids in paddling pools, parents on loungers in the shade, older children enjoying the luxury of a cold ice cream. Dinah smiled at the activity and wondered what her boy Sammy would be doing today had he still been alive.

It had been three years since his death along with his father, Dinah's husband, in a car wreck. He would be six now, going to school and the emergency room in equal measure, given his adventurous spirit.

Dinah noticed that the ever-present sadness filled her heart, but at the same time, she was smiling at the fond memories. This was a big step, she thought. She'd never been able to attribute any positive emotions to the memory of Luke and Sammy. Perhaps, finally, she was dealing in reality rather than alcohol-numbed delusion.

Still with a smile on her lips, she walked to the kitchen and began to poke around in the refrigerator, searching for something to eat.

For one of the first nights in a long time, she didn't think about alcohol.

* * * *

The sun, a belligerent orange disk, took its time to sink down to the horizon, as if petulant that it could no longer terrorize the inhabitants of D.C. during the night. The bomber had hoped for a cover of darkness but eventually conceded that long-shadowed twilight would have to do.

He drove the van carefully. Although it wasn't unstable, the cargo in the back was heavy and he didn't want the bags to topple over. He also drove carefully to ensure a passing cop wouldn't pay him any attention.

He wore high-visibility work clothes so that wherever he stopped, he looked like he had work to do. He'd even brought some tools and temporary fencing with him. If questioned, he planned to say that he worked for the city and had received an urgent call-out.

Finally he arrived at the chosen target. Our Lady of Mercy Catholic Church, on Fourth St. NW, had been built in the late 19th century of red brick and stained glass windows. It was not large and occupied a grassy corner block. At the moment, a steady stream of people arrived at the church for evening mass.

The bomber parked his van up on the curb illegally and immediately pulled out his temporary fencing and placed it around the fire hydrant. It would look to passersby like he was conducting emergency repairs of the hydrant, and in any case, he didn't plan to be here long. He busily inspected the hydrant, tapping it and casually producing tools as if he knew exactly what he was doing. He bent down and stared hard at a bolt, as if it were offensive in some way. He stood up, scratching his head. The final scene in this grand charade involved pretending to receive a cell phone call, glancing at his watch, and walking rapidly away.

With his heart making a staccato rhythm in his throat, he waited for someone to yell at him or stop him. At the end of the street, still pretending to have a conversation on his cell, he turned around and scoped out the street. All the visible pedestrians were too busy to take notice of the van and hurried by without a backward glance.

The bomber then looked at the buildings around the church, where somebody looking out of a window might have seen him and wondered what he was doing. The bomber had taken precautions: he had a stolen van, he wore unremarkable, working-man's clothing, and the broad-brimmed high-visibility hat he wore low so that his face was partially obscured.

Everything had gone according to plan.

Now the bomber made his way to a nearby shopping mall, where he would buy a drink and sit at a table facing the street. From here, he couldn't see the church, but he'd be able to see the detonation.

At 5:30 precisely, evening mass began at Our Lady of Mercy Catholic Church. The usual Saturday evening attendees were there.

At 5:42 the bomber, seated at a bench overlooking the street, pretended to take another cell phone call. Except this time, he pressed the "receive" button.

The explosion could be seen before the loud rumble reached his ears, and the seat beneath him shook a little. A smoky orange ball rose above the rooftops and the bomber had to suppress a smile at its beauty.

Loud exclamations erupted around him. Instinctively, people began to leave the mall quickly, fearing being trapped among tons of steel and concrete in the event of a second blast. The bomber, a look of blank panic upon his face, did the same, except he made for the men's room rather than the exit. There, he ditched the high-visibility work clothing, underneath which he was wearing casual chinos and a T-shirt. He wandered out onto the street, where bewildered people were milling as sirens grew louder in the dusky air.

"What happened?" he asked a young lady standing nearby. "Do you know what happened?"

"Something's been blown up," she said, her voice high-pitched. "People are saying a church has been blown up!"

"What?" he said, faking incredulity. "Who would do such a thing?"

"Terrorists," she said gravely.

He shook his head as if he couldn't believe his ears.

As he'd known it would, his bomb shut down the city. Trains stopped running immediately and buses and cars stalled in a severe traffic jam. Police were in the process of setting up roadblocks near the bomb site to check vehicles.

The bomber walked the 15 blocks home. It was hot and tiring, but he was keyed up anyway and needed to exercise off the adrenaline. By the time he reached his little bungalow, the bomb had made it to the major news stations. Like a pyromaniac watching his own fire with glee, the bomber watched the newscasts late into the night, eventually falling asleep on the reclining armchair.

By morning, the news would be able to paint a clearer picture. Two people were dead, 35 were injured. The church looked like a listing, stricken warship, one entire wall missing and the roof leaning precariously to one side. A burning, acidic odor wafted pungently over the bombsite.

It was immediately apparent how the church had been attacked: only ten feet away from the collapsed wall sat the smoking remains of a vehicle.

The bomber couldn't have been happier. His reign of terror had begun, and it filled a gaping, desolate part of him with an elation and arrogance he'd never felt before.

Pieces of Light

Everyone in the city whispered to themselves and each other: *Am I in danger as I kneel to pray? Will I be blown up as I raise my voice in praise during morning prayers?*

Mostly, they wondered, *Who did this and why?*

The air was an iridescent green as Isabelle emerged from her house, already running 15 minutes late. The afternoon was eerily still and expectant, waiting like a pregnant mother for the big event as the thunderstorm building from the west approached with ominous warning in its growling thunder.

Isabelle made it to her car, her over-stuffed handbag making her left shoulder ache. She found her keys and unlocked the door. She noticed her hand shaking with dread expectation at her next appointment as she inserted the key into the lock.

It was even hotter inside the car and Isabelle started the engine, turning the air conditioning up and waiting expectantly for the blast of arctic air. Her entire body felt slimy with sweat and she sat still for a moment, enjoying the cold air. The tinny car radio voice gravely issued a severe storm warning for the D.C. area, and then brightly announced that the Yankees were up two games in the World Series.

Then she looked at her watch and realized that it was 7:20 and she was going to be extremely late for dinner at her mother's house.

Isabelle drove out of the staff car lot just as the first fat drops of rain fell, intermittently at first and then with a thunderous roar as the heavens opened. She looked nervously through her windshield as her visibility dropped away and all she could see was a thick blanket of rain. Thunder grumbled in a heavenly temper tantrum, and lightning hissed with a pout. She realized with a sinking feeling that the traffic would be absolutely horrendous and she would be even later for the family dinner.

Tonight was the family dinner arranged at her father's funeral. Isabelle had been dreading it all day, anxiety building steadily inside her like steam in a pressure cooker with no release valve. Now it was here and she was thankful that she had only one class to teach today.

Her cell phone rang, and the ring tone was almost drowned out by the deluge drumming on the roof of the car. "Hi, it's me," Scott said unnecessarily. Isabelle could barely hear him.

"Where are you? We've got dinner at Mom's tonight," Isabelle reminded him.

"Yeah, I can't make it," Scott said. "I've got a meeting with the mayor tonight."

She sighed. "I would like it if you were there."

"I'm sorry, but this is the only chance I've got to meet with him." Scott didn't sound the least bit sorry. "I can't put it off."

A slow flush rose in Isabelle's cheeks. She ignored the anxious roller coaster in her stomach. "Fine," she said. "I don't care."

There was a pause on the other end of the phone. "This isn't one of those episodes where you tell me you don't care and then sulk for a week, is it?" he said, his voice hardening. "I really don't have the time or energy for that kind of nonsense."

Don't start anything, she warned herself. "No, of course not. It doesn't bother me," she lied. She didn't want to antagonize him. She put a smile in her voice. "I'll see you later at home. Don't work too hard."

Mollified, Scott said, "Okay. Have a good night."

Isabelle focused on driving in the deluge, trying to ignore the stress of the upcoming dinner together with worrying about whether Scott was angry with her.

The storm had diminished in fury by the time Isabelle arrived at her mother's house. The battered pickup Michael drove was already parked outside and Isabelle pulled her own car up behind his.

The house smelled wonderful as Isabelle made her way down the hallway to the kitchen. Her mother had no doubt cooked up a feast for the occasion. The pungent aromas of garlic, parmesan cheese, and freshly baked bread gently massaged her nostrils.

"Hi everyone," she said, announcing her arrival.

Michael had been staring out of the dining room window and spun around to greet his sister. Rosa had her head in the oven checking on the dinner. She withdrew to announce, "It's been ready for half an hour. Go and sit down. I'll serve it in the dining room." Isabelle heard the reproach in her mother's tone for being late.

Michael and Isabelle did as they were told. The dining room was an old-fashioned formal room with an oval table made of polished wood, draped with a starched damask cloth. The room was lit with smoky, diffused light from an elaborate chandelier. Overlooking the proceedings were two large pictures of the virgin Mary, her face a picture of serenity and the hint of a halo above her head. An antique sideboard held all of Rosa's precious crockery, and atop the sideboard was a small shrine to the late Reginald McMahon. Various framed photographs jostled for position amid some of his favorite things — a family portrait when Isabelle and Michael had been kids, their phony smiles portraying a happy family, his gun license, and a Yankees pennant.

Wonder where the leather belt is, mused Isabelle, remembering distant and shadowy times when a night of drinking inevitably led to the loosening of her father's belt. She could still hear the eerie whistling it made as it flew through the air before it made contact with bare skin with a resounding slap.

Michael sat and scowled at the shrine. He looked at Isabelle and she read the conflicting emotions in his eyes. His entire body was strung as tightly as a lute, his fingers tapping and feet bouncing. They did not speak, but Isabelle took his hand and squeezed it in solidarity.

Rosa swept into the room with plates of freshly baked garlic bread, lasagna, honey-glazed baby carrots, and broccoli with roasted almonds. After she had served the food and poured wine, she said, "Let's pray."

Isabelle and Michael bowed their heads and Isabelle kept a tight hold on Michael's hand. She knew what was coming and that it would agitate Michael even more.

"Dear Heavenly Father," began Rosa. "Thank You that we could gather tonight to remember Daddy. We intercede for him, Lord, please take his soul into heaven with You. Have mercy on him, Lord, for he was a good man on this earth. He provided for his family and protected us, Lord."

Michael's large hand tightened on Isabelle's, the pressure causing her fingers to go numb.

"Please show him Your grace and mercy. Lord, You know he was a good man. Amen."

Isabelle extricated her hand from Michael's and tried to rub some blood flow back into her unfeeling fingers.

Michael began to eat, concentrating his nervous energy on the mechanics of chewing.

"So how is work, Michael?" Rosa asked.

"Good." Michael didn't even raise his eyes to acknowledge his mother. Isabelle briefly closed her eyes, knowing it was going to be one of *those* nights.

"Are you busy?" persisted Rosa.

"Yeah, you know."

Please drop it, Isabelle silently begged.

"Is there something wrong, Michael?" Rosa asked.

"Mom, how was your day today?" interjected Isabelle, brightly.

Rosa glanced at her with a frown, clearly misunderstanding her daughter's intent. "Michael?" she repeated.

"Can you leave me alone?" he snapped. "I'm trying to eat."

"I understand if you're missing your father," Rosa said.

Isabelle massaged her temples.

Michael gave a short, contemptuous laugh. "Believe me, I'm not missing him."

Rosa was taken aback.

"You wouldn't believe what happened in class today," Isabelle said. "I have this student who. . . ."

Abruptly, Michael stood and walked over to the sideboard, looking at the mementos of the father he had been pleased to bury. He picked up one of the earlier photos, where Reginald McMahon had been in the prime of life and lord over his small kingdom. Isabelle saw the shudder that traced down Michael's spine as he looked at the photo.

Rosa kneaded her hands together anxiously and asked, "What are you doing, Michael?"

Michael gave a brittle laugh that belied humor. "I'm just remembering our dear departed father."

Isabelle stood and looked between her mother and her brother, unsure of what she should do.

"I wish you would show more respect," Rosa said plaintively. "He was your father, after all."

Michael turned to look at his mother. "You're right," he agreed. His voice was ominously quiet. "He was my father, and I did respect him, particularly in the emergency room at the hospital every few months."

Rosa drew in a sharp little breath. "Well, I know he wasn't perfect. He did his best, he loved us all, and he provided for us. He had a very stressful job, you know, he. . . ."

"Don't make excuses for him!" snarled Michael, suddenly vicious. "He was nothing but a wife beater and a child abuser. I was *glad* when he died."

"Michael!" Isabelle moved toward him, her cheeks burning with disquiet.

"Don't say that!" cried Rosa. "Don't disrespect him so, Michael! He was a *good* man!"

"Mom, please, sit down," pleaded Isabelle, but her voice was lost in the crackling electricity of emotion in the room.

"*I — hated — him,*" Michael said through clenched teeth. "When he was sober, when he was drunk, when he was watching TV, when he was hitting me with an electrical cord, I hated him all along." He advanced on his mother, his six-foot frame towering over her tiny one. "How can you defend him? It makes you no better than him!"

Silence reigned, a heavy blanket settling over the room. Rosa was shocked, her dark eyes enormous and shiny with tears. Michael was struggling to get his temper under control, and Isabelle could see the torrent of emotion he was trying to suppress.

"I tried my best," Rosa said, defeated.

Michael let the photo slip from his fingers to the floor, where the glass in the photo cracked with a sharp report. Without a word, he walked out of the room, slammed the front door shut, and was gone in the night.

Rosa bent and picked up the photo frame, stroking the picture it contained. She looked at Isabelle, her guilt and shame naked in her eyes. "I tried my best," she repeated, tears slipping down her cheeks. She had learned to cry silently many years ago, an age ago.

The two sat in silence, Rosa thinking about long-past memories and failures. Finally, Isabelle told her mother that she had to go.

Rosa said imploringly, "I did my best. You know that, don't you?"

Isabelle was thinking of herself when she replied, "Sometimes your best isn't enough."

* * * *

Dinah Harris was sipping her first heavenly coffee of the morning and watching the newscast of the church bombing the night before when her cell phone rang.

"Hello?" she said absently.

"Harris, you busy?" Her old partner Ferguson spoke in his professional voice, and she snapped to attention.

"Go ahead," she said.

"I've caught the church bombing case," he told her. "You want in?"

"You don't even need to ask," Dinah said.

"Okay. You had breakfast?"

Dinah laughed. "Still having eight square meals a day?"

"Absolutely! Meet me at the Emporium Deli, downtown. You know it?"

"Yeah, I remember. You still their best customer?"

"They insist on selling spinach and feta pastries," complained Ferguson. "What's a guy to do?"

"I'll be there in 30 minutes." Dinah hung up and quickly found something professional to wear — gray pin-striped pants and a black blouse with black pumps. She gave her straight black hair a brush and applied some mascara, the only concession she made to makeup.

Rush hour thwarted her attempts to arrive at the deli on time. Dinah, who was spectacularly impatient, found sitting in traffic impossible. She was the one who weaved in and out of lanes, trying to somehow outwit the traffic. This usually made her more irritated than before, so she was trying to curb this behavior. Nevertheless, when she strode into the Emporium Deli near the J. Edgar Hoover building on Fourth St. NW, she was rattled. She spotted Ferguson sitting in a corner and made her way over, after ordering the biggest coffee the deli could provide. "Ferguson, how are you?" she said, then realized that he was sitting with another man.

Ferguson's companion turned around and Dinah was hit with a bolt of electricity. Her hair stood on end and she stood stock still, momentarily stunned. Ferguson sat with one of the most gorgeous men Dinah had ever seen. His hair was blue-black, like hers, his jaw line and cheekbones were perfectly sculpted, and he possessed brilliant, silver-blue eyes that were locked onto her.

Ferguson stopped tucking into his breakfast to see Dinah's expression and he smiled to himself. "Dinah," he said. When there was no response, he said louder: "Dinah!"

Dinah shook herself and realized she was behaving embarrassingly. "Sorry. Hi, Ferguson."

"Nice to see you can join us," he said. "May I introduce you to Special Agent Aaron Sinclair?"

The gorgeous man stood up, and Dinah noted that he was also very tall, and that he filled out his sober black suit very nicely. He held out his hand to shake. When she shook it, she observed that his hand was large, strong, and gave a firm handshake.

"This is Dinah Harris, consultant," said Ferguson. "Normally, she can speak for herself quite well."

Dinah gave herself a mental slap. She was acting like an infatuated teenager, for Pete's sake. "Nice to meet you," she said, sitting down. She didn't dare meet his eyes again. They seemed to possess the ability to rob her of the power of speech.

"Sinclair is a bomb expert," explained Ferguson. "He'll be working with me." Addressing Sinclair, he said: "Harris used to be my partner and has always been a pretty decent investigator. So it'll be the three of us working on the church bombing case."

"What do you know about it so far?" asked Dinah, trying to kick herself into professional mode.

"ANFO bomb," said Sinclair, his ice-blue eyes turning to her. "That means an ammonium nitrate-fuel oil bomb. It's an extremely easy bomb to make, and the current favorite among suicide bombers in Iraq and Afghanistan. It's a dry slurry mixture made up of nitrate — usually extracted from fertilizer — and diesel fuel, for example. The bomber used dynamite and an electric blasting cap to detonate the bomb. The blasting cap was detonated remotely."

Dinah nodded. "Any CCTV near the area?"

"No, we didn't see anything," Ferguson said. "No witnesses either. The van was pulled up on the curb, near a fire hydrant. We found the remains of the temporary fencing that city workers use when they're repairing roads, for example. So it's possible the bomber used the fencing to pretend he was a city worker, so that nobody would question the presence of the van on the sidewalk."

"Any organization claimed the credit for this?" asked Dinah.

"The usual fundamentalist nut cases," said Sinclair. "But nobody plausible."

"The news said the casualty list was two dead, 35 injured," said Dinah. "Is that right?"

"Yes. The deceased are a junior priest who was helping with the service, and a member of the congregation, a middle-aged woman."

"Anything about those victims that would suggest they were specifically targeted?"

"Not yet," said Sinclair. "But I'm not convinced that would be the case anyway. The ANFO bomb wasn't big enough to damage the entire building, and the bomber would have known that the payload wouldn't be big enough to kill many in the church."

"Can I take a look at the bombsite?" Dinah asked.

"No," said Ferguson.

Dinah frowned at him. "Why not?"

"I haven't finished breakfast."

Dinah rolled her eyes and noticed Sinclair smirking at her. Her heart flipped.

Ferguson shoveled the remainder of his breakfast down his throat, threw the keys to Sinclair, and said, "Let's roll."

* * * *

The whole block, the corner of which the church had once occupied, was roped off by the police and would be until the investigation was complete. Dinah drank the scene in, noting the bitter, burnt smell of ammonia that hung over the church; the charred remains of the vehicle used in the bombing; the leaning, precarious position of the church; and the enormous hole that had been blasted through one wall.

It was immediately obvious why the bomber had chosen this church. Dinah had been given a crash course in bomb making by Sinclair in the car on the trip over. An ANFO bomb was reasonably powerful but didn't have the payload of a more sophisticated bomb made of Semtex or other military grade explosives. This was of particular importance when the bomb was not actually inside the target building but adjacent to it. A modern building with reinforced concrete and steel would not have sustained as much damage as the old church, built of bricks and mortar.

The three investigators climbed out of the car and Sinclair led them to the remains of the van. "This is where most of our evidence will occur," he explained. "This is where our perp has been, physically and emotionally. All you'll get from the church is an indication of how much damage was done and who the victims were."

The van had essentially been reduced to an engine block and chassis, surrounded by twisted scraps of metal and shards of glass. One of the cabin seats was torn in half and resting on the nearby sidewalk, and Dinah had to pick her way past all kinds of debris from deep within the van's construction.

The engine block had not been badly damaged and Sinclair wrote down the vehicle's identification numbers. "If you can believe it," he commented, "when bombers use a vehicle as the primary blast site, some have been stupid enough to rent the car in their own names, build the bomb in it, and then detonate it. A day later, they wonder how we found them so fast."

"Let's hope this bomber is that dumb," said Dinah, peering absently through the debris.

Sinclair went through what was left of the glove box but found only what looked like a map of D.C.

"So who responded to the scene last night?" Dinah asked.

"Emergency 911 was flooded with calls, so uniforms and paramedics were first to arrive," explained Sinclair. "There were two deceased victims and 35 injured. Due to the nature of construction of the church, extraction of the dead and injured was relatively easy. Nobody was trapped underneath a steel beam or layers of concrete, for example."

Dinah nodded, trying to concentrate but distracted by the bomb expert's deep and melodious voice.

"Metropolitan police then sent in sniffer dogs to determine whether any further devices had been placed in the vicinity," continued Sinclair. "A security perimeter was established and the FBI notified. It was obvious to all concerned that this was an incendiary device, thus falling under the jurisdiction of domestic terrorism."

"You speak like a true Feeb," Ferguson told him, appearing alongside Dinah. "Cut out the jargon and speak like a normal person, will you?"

Dinah hid her smile. "Were there any witnesses?" she asked.

"I have some preliminary statements taken by MPD uniforms," said Sinclair, shooting his boss an injured expression. "We'll need to check those out ourselves and interview the victims."

"Did the forensic lab technicians come through already?" Dinah asked.

"Yes, including bomb investigation specialists," confirmed Sinclair. "They were looking for trace explosive residue, the appearance of chemicals, materials used in the construction and transportation of the bomb, fragments, and your standard list of blood, hairs, fibers, and so on."

"Materials used in the construction of the bomb?" Dinah echoed. "Didn't you tell us that it was made of fertilizer and fuel oil?"

"Yes," agreed Sinclair. "But there are other markers which narrow down who might have made the bomb. The type of fertilizer and how readily available it is for sale, for example. Or how the bomb was built and what it was stored in."

Sinclair crouched down and pointed to the corner of what had once been the back of the van. "Here's something," he said. "The lab people will have already documented this, but it's good to have for our records, too." He picked up a scrap of thick plastic.

"This looks like the type of plastic used to make thick industrial bags," he continued. "The type used to store agricultural grade fertilizer or pesticide. I wouldn't be surprised if we find trace amounts of ammonium nitrate on this."

"What would the perp have built the bomb in?" Dinah inquired.

Sinclair pursed his lips. "Because the main ingredients are stable and dry, it doesn't really matter. He could have used a barrel or a thick plastic bag, like this scrap here. The most important thing is that it must be contained to achieve maximum force."

He stood up and stretched. Using a camera he'd been carrying around his neck, Sinclair snapped more than a dozen photos of what was left of the van.

Then he moved to the area between the van and the church. "Now I'm looking for blast effects," he explained. "That means structural damage to buildings, bent signs, fragmentation, and so on. We can see the structural damage pretty clearly." He pointed at the church, tilted away from the van as if trying to escape the deadly blast. "However, I wouldn't think there is much damage to surrounding buildings other than windows blown out or walls peppered with debris. If the bomb wasn't powerful enough to bring down the church, I doubt it was powerful enough to substantially harm other buildings."

The three investigators walked toward the church.

In silence, they observed their surroundings as they approached the mortally wounded building. Glorious stained glass windows now lay in shards around their feet, lethal weapons in themselves. Red bricks were torn in half, as if no more substantial than foam. Wooden pews were splintered into matchsticks, and severed electrical cables twisted and danced like dying snakes.

The damage was incredible, and Dinah wondered how only two people had been killed in the midst of such carnage.

Sinclair said softly: "The deceased victims were both standing close to the impacted wall. One was a priest, the other a member of the congregation."

Dinah sighed and rubbed her arms as a chill ran up her spine. "Who would target a church during evening mass? Are we looking at Muslim radicals?"

"This *is* the bomb of choice for insurgents in Iraq and Afghanistan," conceded Sinclair. "I wouldn't rule out anything yet."

Dinah shook her head, wondering why she was surprised by the destruction and bloodshed wrought on each other by human beings.

* * * *

The bomber, unable to invent a nickname for himself, decided it was time to check out his next target. He knew from the newscasts that the Catholic Church he'd bombed was still roped off by investigators and that nobody could get within a block of it. That was okay. His new target would have nothing to do with that part of the city and nothing to do with the Catholic Church.

He drove a stolen Impala, a car that would fade in a person's memory like no other. He made a habit of using a different stolen vehicle every time he went out on a mission so that any wily witness might be foiled.

He headed in the opposite direction of Our Lady of Mercy Catholic Church on Fourth Street, which is to say he didn't want to be anywhere near the center of D.C. but out in the suburbs. He drove through the suburbs toward the beautiful, rolling countryside of Virginia, where residential developments were continuing to spring up at a rapid pace.

Eventually he rolled into the town of Manassas, Virginia, a city of about 35,000 souls that was part of the D.C. metropolitan area. Manassas had gained notoriety in 2002 when the 11th Beltway sniper attack killed a man pumping gas near Interstate 66.

The bomber intended to make it more notorious. As he rolled into town, he knew that he'd found the right spot. His research told him that Manassas was a place where families lived, and where there was a gathering of families there was usually a good sprinkling of churches.

It was now close to noon and the suburban streets were quiet. Parents were at work and children were at school.

A few blocks later, he stopped the Impala to look at his target. The First United Methodist Church of Manassas was built in the style of a community hall. It was modern and large but looked like it was constructed more of glass and pre-fabricated concrete rather than steel beams. A spacious car lot at the back of the building provided plenty of car parking for the congregation and provided an excellent position for the bomber to park his dangerous load.

He drove around the block several times, looking for landmarks that would disqualify the hit: the presence of a close-by police station or fire station, for example. However, the coast was clear and the bomber could not help but smile. It was working out perfectly.

Next, he drove straight back into the depths of D.C., searching for a vehicle in which to build his next bomb. The police would be suspicious of vans; they were likely to implement road blocks and roadside traps for any poor soul driving a van so that they could search it. So he intended to mix it up.

He drove toward one of the elementary schools in the inner city, where a fleet of yellow school buses were parked in the lot, waiting for their afternoon run. The bomber ditched the Impala and slipped into the lot. It was poorly supervised. The bomber bet there would be one or two security guards tasked with watching the lot, but since they didn't believe anyone would want to steal one, he wasn't concerned.

He slipped between the buses, his eyes and ears sharp. He waited several moments for a shout or for footsteps but heard nothing. He glanced at his watch and saw that it was almost time for the fleet to move out. He pulled on a cap that resembled the uniform the bus drivers wore.

When he saw movement in a nearby bus, he hot-wired the ignition and pulled the cap down low over his eyes. In the rear vision mirror he caught sight of a figure dressed in a bus driver uniform. He gave a quick wave and began to drive the bus out of the lot.

His ears on high alert, he listened over the noise of the rumbling engine for shouts or running footsteps. He didn't hear anything, and only saw a line of yellow buses behind him, lined up like bees waiting to exit their hive.

Feeling more relaxed, he drove the bus sensibly through the city before peeling off toward swanky Georgetown. From there, he drove a circuitous route around the inner city, with no particular destination in mind except to appear like a normal school bus driver who had finished his duties for the day.

Finally, when he thought it was time, he drove the bus toward his home. It was here that he assumed the most risk: it would take only one nosy neighbor to wonder what he was doing with a school bus.

He drove it into his workshop and left the door open. In case anyone was watching him, he promptly jacked up the rear of the bus, took out an impressive toolbox, and eased himself underneath the vehicle. When an appropriate length of time had passed, he made sure some grease was smeared on his hands and face and rolled out from underneath the bus. Then he closed the workshop door and headed inside, ostensibly to fix some dinner.

Inside, he waited with bated breath for someone to hammer at his front door and demand to know why he had a school bus in his workshop. But the street was silent, and eventually the bomber relaxed. Everything was going according to plan. While the police sent out bulletins regarding stolen vans, he remained a step ahead. He smiled.

He hummed a Billy Idol song to himself. Instead of singing *It's hot in the city, hot in the city, tonight* in his head, he sang, *I'm smart in the city, smart in the city, tonight.*

Sinclair wanted to start with the van. Dinah wanted to start with the victims and witnesses to the bombing, but Sinclair won. He was the bomb expert, after all, and Dinah found it hard to argue when he fixed his blue eyes upon her.

Tracing the vehicle identification number showed the van was registered to Mr. Maximilian Lowe, currently residing in the suburbs of North Virginia.

The sun was still hot and beat down on Dinah's face through the glass window of the car as they drove to Mr. Lowe's house. On the way, she learned more about Aaron Sinclair's rise through the FBI, his interest in explosives, and his blinding ambition to continue climbing the promotional tree.

Dinah felt a stab of envy as he spoke, thinking of her own rise and fall at the Bureau, both as spectacular as each other. She had at one time extracted high-ranking violent gang members into witness protection, hoping to dismantle the leadership of the gang in the process. Her ability to achieve this monumental task was unique and brilliant. When rookie agents began their training in Quantico, her name had been touted in the training program of the success one could achieve within the FBI. She bet they'd now stricken her name from the record, unwilling to highlight the fact that one of their brightest had fallen into a deep well of alcoholism.

Suddenly, she realized that the car had stopped and that both Ferguson and Sinclair were staring at her. "Sorry!" she said. "I was too busy thinking."

They had arrived at the house of Mr. Lowe, and Ferguson took the lead, rapping on the door loudly.

Mr. Maximilian Lowe was a short, gnarled man in his early sixties, the kind of man who looked like he'd done hard labor all his working life. His face was tanned and seamed, his hands large and callused, and his eyes weary but bright.

"Yes?" he said suspiciously.

"We're Special Agents Ferguson and Sinclair from the FBI," announced Ferguson. "And this is our consultant, Ms. Harris. We'd like to speak with you about the van you reported stolen last week."

Lowe waved them into the small house, into a vintage 1960s living room resplendent with lime-green shag carpet and brown paisley wallpaper.

"Must be serious," Lowe observed. "I reported the theft to the police last week. Must have been Tuesday I think. It went missing on Monday night."

It wasn't uncommon for criminals to report their own vehicles stolen and then use them in illegal activity, Dinah knew all too well. But this man looked entirely too honest to have been the church bomber.

"What were the circumstances under which it went missing?" inquired Sinclair.

Lowe turned bemused eyes upon the agent. "The circumstances are that the van was here when I went to bed on Monday night and gone when I woke up Tuesday morning."

Sinclair nodded. "Did you hear anything during the night?"

"Nope," said Lowe. "But then, I sleep like a log and snore like a wounded bear, apparently."

"Was anyone home with you at the time?"

"Nope. My wife died a few years ago, so it's just me here now. She could've told you all about my snoring, and she would've heard the van, too. She was a light sleeper."

"Did you leave the keys in the ignition?"

"Please," snorted Lowe. "Do I look like an idiot? No, I didn't."

"You do any agricultural activity around here, Mr. Lowe?" Sinclair asked.

Lowe laughed. "This is suburbia, in case you haven't noticed. Didn't you notice the herd of cows in my front yard?"

Dinah couldn't help but smile at the old man's sarcasm.

"No fertilizer on the property?" Sinclair asked, still completely serious.

"You mean other than a few slow-release pellets for my pot plants? No."

"Got any fuel on the property?"

"Nope." The wily old man's eyes looked from one agent to another. "My van was used in that church bombing, wasn't it?"

"I'm afraid I can't provide any particulars to you at this time," said Sinclair, which drew a roll of the eyes from Mr. Lowe.

"Mind if we take a look around your home, Mr. Lowe?" Sinclair asked. "We won't take long."

Lowe narrowed his eyes at them. "Don't you need a warrant?" Without waiting for a reply, he shrugged. "Well, I got nothin' to hide, so help yourselves. Just try not to make too much of a mess."

Inside, Sinclair quietly explained what they were looking for: materials that seemed out of place, like a soldering iron in the bathroom; Internet activity on bomb-making; a room that might look like a science laboratory.

While Sinclair quickly looked through Mr. Lowe's desktop computer, Ferguson and Dinah looked through the little house. They found nothing suspicious. Mr. Lowe lived like a bachelor, although traces of his wife's decorating touch remained. Several large photos of the Lowes when she was still alive adorned the living room wall. The kitchen was sparse and looked like Mr. Lowe subsisted mainly on macaroni and cheese and chili.

It wasn't just about what she saw that made Dinah feel the unspoken truth of the house — it was lonely here, and too quiet. Perhaps there should have been the quick laughter of grandchildren or the old records of a woman who loved swing music. There should have been evidence of a lovingly tended vegetable garden, a half-finished knitted scarf, a book almost read. Dinah felt compassion swell in her as she drank in the atmosphere. She knew what it was like to be entirely alone, with no parents, children, or spouse.

Sinclair motioned to them. "I'm done here," he said. "You finished?"

"Yes," said Dinah quietly. "We found nothing. You?"

"Nothing."

Mr. Lowe looked at them from his recliner. "I told you, I got nothin' to hide."

"Thank you, Mr. Lowe, for your cooperation," said Sinclair gravely. "We appreciate it and we'll leave you to get on with your day."

"Will I be getting my van back?" Mr. Lowe asked.

"Uh . . ." said Sinclair. "No. Sorry."

"It didn't survive the bombing, huh?" Lowe's eyes twinkled shrewdly.

Dinah smiled and shook the old man's hand. "Thanks, Mr. Lowe," she said. "Is there anything you need?"

He looked into her eyes. "There are many things I need, mostly my wife back," he said. "So nothing you can help with." He turned away before she could see the grief consume him.

In the car, driving back into the city, Ferguson called the office. "I want you to scour the stolen vehicle registry for any van," he said. "Let me know of the most recent ones."

He hung up and sighed. "Shame our bomber isn't as dumb as some of his predecessors," he remarked. "He could have made our lives a lot easier by renting the van in his own name."

"There's no challenge in that," said Sinclair. "I'm glad it's not that easy."

Dinah smiled to herself in the backseat. As an agent, she would have thought exactly the same thing.

* * * *

Isabelle McMahon lugged a pile of student files from the garage to her dining room table, and then wiped the sweat from her face. *Why is it so hot?* she demanded of no one in particular. She noticed that the house was quiet and filled with shadows, which meant that her husband Scott wasn't home yet. She was instantly filled with relief. It meant she had time to quickly clean the house up and start dinner. Scott hated coming home to a messy house.

She spent half an hour tidying and dusting, making sure everything was in its correct place. She washed her face and hands and applied some lip gloss.

In the kitchen, she marinated steaks in a red wine and oregano jus, and popped into the oven a potato rostii made with cream and cheese. While she grilled the steaks, she lightly steamed a vegetable trio of broccoli, corn, and peas.

Scott liked to eat quality food, which meant that Isabelle constantly scoured cookbooks for new recipes and found sources for expensive food from farmer's markets and organic food stores. She had learned very early in the marriage that bland food would not cut it with Scott, and so now her repertoire was impressive. In those early days, food he didn't like was thrown in the bin untouched, usually with a scathing comment. He would then go out to eat, making it perfectly clear that she wasn't invited and she was quite welcome to eat her own tasteless food if she wished.

It didn't take long for Isabelle to understand what Scott wanted: creamy risottos, herbed roasts, marinated steaks, spicy chicken, and tasty sides, all thoughtfully served with a matching wine. She had learned quickly.

Tonight, Scott still wasn't home by the time dinner was ready, and Isabelle left the food to stay warm in the oven, waiting for him. An hour later, she was so starving that she decided she wouldn't wait any longer. She would probably catch trouble from Scott for not waiting for him, but that was a risk she was willing to take.

An hour after she'd finished her meal, Isabelle began feeling worried. She wondered if Scott was okay. She called his cell phone, which rang and rang. She roamed around the house, passing by the front windows often to watch for his headlights turning into the drive.

She saw nothing but darkness. She called his cell phone again, and he didn't answer. Anxiety built in her rapidly.

She cleaned the kitchen and threw out Scott's meal, now thoroughly ruined. She tried to look through the papers she was supposed to be marking from her health economics class. She couldn't concentrate; her anxiety was too great.

She called Scott for the third time, and got no answer. An insidious thought wormed its way into her mind. *You'll feel better,* it promised her.

As if guided by an unseen presence, Isabelle made her way upstairs, to the en-suite bathroom she shared with Scott. She hid thin razor blades in her personal toiletries, a place Scott wouldn't look.

She ran a deep, hot bath, stripped, and climbed in. The heat took her breath away for a few seconds and then she relaxed as the steam rose above her.

She took a new blade from its packaging and tested the edge. It was coldly sharp.

Her left arm palm up, resting on her knee, she used the razor to slice into her upper forearm, watching the bright red blood blossom.

Almost instantly, she felt her anxiety begin to release, as though it had been trapped in her skin and now it could escape. She made another cut, a twin to the first one. Blood dripped into the bath, turning the water a rosy pink. Isabelle watched as her blood and the water mingled and marveled that she felt very little pain.

She made two more cuts on her right arm, near the crook of her elbow. The anxiety seemed to rush out, like air from a balloon, until there was nothing left of her except shriveled skin. She didn't care, as long as the worry that ate her up had gone.

The relief was so great that she actually felt sleepy, lying there in the bathtub. For a moment, she allowed herself to drift, thinking of a life without fear. Perhaps she could spend a year in Australia, swimming with sharks, wrestling crocodiles, daring the snakes to come get her, sky diving into the isolated outback so that she could fear nothing. Perhaps she could trek to the North Pole, unafraid of the desolate landscape or the freezing wind or frostbite. Perhaps she could cross the Sahara Desert on motorbike, or climb Mount Everest, or dive into dark, underwater caves. If she survived all these things, would she have conquered her fear? Would she be able to live completely confidently within herself, with no room for anxiety?

With a start, Isabelle came back to the present: a steamy bathroom, stinging cuts on her arms, and a husband who would go ballistic if he caught her. With familiar dread caught in the back of her throat, she quickly dried off and dressed, bandaged her arms, and ensured that the bath contained no telling pink residue.

She looked at her watch. It was almost midnight, and Scott wasn't home. Feeling completed drained, Isabelle fell into bed and was quickly asleep.

She woke at three in the morning when Scott rolled into bed, and registered the alcohol and cigarette smoke on his breath. She tried to forget about it, at least until morning. She slept fitfully, tossing and turning until five, when she finally admitted defeat and rose, red-eyed and exhausted.

In the early morning cool, when each day began with a promise, Isabelle could almost convince herself that her life was the one she wanted to be living.

* * * *

Senator David Winters enjoyed the finer things in life: a fine bourbon, a hand-rolled cigar, and clothes crafted in Italy. Unfortunately, such things cost money, and Winters' trust fund had all but dried up.

That was why he did deals with lobbyists that weren't entirely legal. More than his love of fine things was the burning fire of his ambition to be the president. This was another reason he did shady deals: to obtain financial backing to enable him to run. It also assured him the support of whichever group he'd dealt with, which would result in tangible votes during the election. In the meantime, he used his power and reputation to achieve things that the groups themselves would have had trouble doing.

The most recent case was the inclusion and passing of an assisted suicide provision in the Health Reform Bill, on behalf of a group of people who believed in the ideals of eugenics. Prior to that, he'd removed a secretary of the Smithsonian who'd converted to Christianity and had wanted the biblical account of creation included in the museum, on behalf of an organization devoted to atheism and the purity of science.

Winters himself didn't particularly care for the agenda of any group he dealt with, except with one caveat. Equal to his love of money and power was his hatred of religion, particularly Christianity. If the group he supported was sufficiently cashed up and opposed in some way to Christianity, then he was your man.

This morning, he had arranged a meeting with a man named George Cartwright. The man represented an organization devoted to the separation of church and state, and in Cartwright's opinion, the divide was not deep enough in the United States of America. He needed the influence of a powerful senator to champion his cause, and in return, his wealthy backers promised half a million dollars to the bank account of Winters.

Whistling to himself, Winters arrived at the exclusive restaurant close to Capitol Hill, where discretion was guaranteed. He was shown to his usual table, a private table where discussions couldn't be overheard.

A few minutes later, George Cartwright arrived. He was a tall, well-built man who looked like he'd once been a college quarterback and was now tending toward fat. He favored conservatively cut suits and managed to blend into the background effortlessly, which was precisely what he sought to do.

He shook Winter's hand and sat down. "Have you ordered yet?" he asked.

"I got us both steaks," said Winters. Without preamble, he added, "So tell me what you're thinking."

Cartwright nodded. "There is a high-profile Christian group that has spread around the country, working with high-risk teenagers or something. You know, drugs, teen pregnancy, gangs, that stuff. They all receive some level of local government funding. We had a recent case in Vermont, where we tested the validity of government contributing to a religious organization under the First Amendment of the Constitution. The court found that such an arrangement contravened the Constitution and declared the funding unlawful."

"I see. That's impressive. Your group funded the lawsuit?" Winters paused as the waiter brought red wine.

"Yes." Cartwright tasted the wine. "Nice drop. The lack of funding meant that the Christian group had to cut services. That's what they call it, anyway. I call it brainwashing vulnerable teenagers."

Winters smirked. "So what do you want from me?"

"To have this decision in case law is good, but it stands only in the state of Vermont. I'd like to take the case to the federal court, and if need be, to the U.S. Supreme Court. I understand that you have an acquaintance in the U.S. Supreme Court by the name of Maxwell Pryor."

Winters only smiled as the steaks arrived. He was impressed by anyone who'd done their research thoroughly. Then he asked, "So what specifically do you want me to do?"

"Well, we're going to make it a big deal," explained Cartwright. "The person lodging the lawsuit is a very good-looking, articulate woman who is completely backed by our group. We intend to raise up loud supporter bases in as many major cities as we can who can demand media attention. We expect to lose, whereupon we'll appeal. That's where you can help. We need Justice Pryor to agree with us, for a start. Secondly, we need him to influence other justices in the Supreme Court."

Winters pursed his lips, thinking. "I see. I can't see a problem with having Justice Pryor on board. I happen to know him pretty well, and I know that he agrees with me on topics such as this. However, to ask him to influence other justices is difficult. For one thing, I don't have any power over that. Second, the group of people you're asking him to influence aren't stupid and they'll know if they're being manipulated. Most, if not all, are staunch liberals or conservatives and won't be easily swayed."

Cartwright nodded. "Sure, I understand that. The only guarantee I'm after is Pryor's unconditional support. Whatever else he can do is a bonus."

"I can get you Pryor's unconditional support," promised Winters.

"Great. We also need your presence in the media where possible," continued Cartwright. "I'm sure you won't have a problem with that."

Winters thought for a moment. He was a senator from California, a state that contained a flourishing community of liberals but also bastions of conservatism. He walked a thin line, trying not to deeply offend either group. He would have to choose his words carefully. Ultimately, if the half-million dollars were contingent upon him speaking to the media, then he would do it. And Cartwright knew it.

"That'll be fine," said Winters. "But I will need to speak carefully, as I'm sure you can appreciate."

"Sure," said Cartwright agreeably. He finished his glass of wine. "I feel very positive about our partnership, Senator."

"As do I," said Winters.

Cartwright stood and shook the other man's hand. "Watch in the news for the lawsuit launch," he said. "I'll be in touch."

Winters watched him go. When he was president, men such as Cartwright would be groveling for his support, not making demands. And he would take great pleasure in being the most powerful man on earth.

* * * *

Sinclair finally agreed to visit the victims of the bombing in the hospital. Dinah got the feeling he was more comfortable working with the mechanics of the bomb than with the people that the bomb had impacted.

The three investigators arrived at George Washington University Hospital where 6 of the 35 injured were receiving treatment. Thankfully, most of the injured had received only minor abrasions and burns.

However, Trevor Martin had not been so lucky. A flying shard of glass had cost the man his right eye, and he'd also sustained burns on the right side of his face and arm. He was a squat middle-aged white man with a reddish crew cut, and he was not happy to be stuck in the hospital.

"Never been in a hospital my whole life," he grumbled to the detectives. "Never been sick either. Now look at me."

"I'm sorry you were hurt, Mr. Martin," said Dinah. She perched herself awkwardly at the side of his bed. "We're going to find the person responsible."

"I hope so," scowled Martin. "Coward. Who was it? A terrorist?"

"At this stage, we're not thinking terrorists," Dinah said. "Can you tell me what happened that day?"

"I missed morning mass," explained Martin. "What a mistake, huh? I went to the evening instead. I had an early dinner with my wife, who *had* been that morning, thank goodness. Then I drove over and parked in the lot."

"Did you see anything unusual when you arrived?" Dinah asked.

Trevor Martin was silent for a few moments. "I don't think so. I mean, I just wasn't really paying attention."

"Did you see a vehicle that didn't belong, or someone loitering around the church?" Dinah pressed.

"There is one thing," Martin said. "I don't know what it's worth, but we were in the middle of prayers when I heard a guy working outside. It annoyed me, so I looked out of the window. There was a city worker hammering at the fire hydrant."

Dinah glanced at Sinclair and Ferguson, her heart quickening with excitement. "What did you notice about him?"

"Not much," said Martin. "He was dressed like a worker, had a toolkit, and a van. . . ." His voice trailed off as he realized what he'd just said. His ruddy skin went pale. "Oh . . . was that the guy?"

"Possibly," said Dinah. "What did the worker look like?"

"I don't know," admitted Martin. "He was wearing normal worker clothes, a big hat, a toolkit. I don't even know if it was a man, to tell you the truth."

Dinah was disappointed, but not surprised. The bomber, if even a little bit smart, would know to disguise himself.

"I was sitting there listening to the prayer," Martin continued. "Suddenly there was a huge bang, a flash of light and" — he faltered for a moment — "like, a wall of air. It picked me up and threw me to the ground. I didn't know how badly I'd been injured until later. And afterward, the most terrible smell, like acid burning or something."

The investigators knew that chaos had erupted at that point and that very few people would have noticed what the bomber had done in the midst of dying and injured victims, the acrid pall of smoke hanging low over the scene, and the panic that had likely risen in the throats of anyone who'd witnessed the event.

As it turned out, Trevor Martin had seen the most out of the six seriously hurt victims, and they gleaned nothing further from interviews conducted in the hospital. However, they were pleasantly surprised to see the senior priest, Father Angelo Ribbardi, sitting next to one of the victims. The father looked shaken and drawn, like he hadn't slept or eaten since the blast. This was an accurate observation, he told them gravely. Ferguson asked him if they could speak to him privately.

Father Ribbardi agreed to speak to them in the hospital chapel. He was round and short, with a shock of black hair and an expression that once might have been jolly. "I don't know how to get through this," he admitted, once in the privacy of the chapel. "They didn't train me to expect disasters at my own church." He blanched. "Or that a junior priest would die, right in front of me."

"I'm so sorry for your loss," said Ferguson gently. "I hope this isn't too painful, but the more information we can get, the sooner we can put the person who did this behind bars."

Father Ribbardi sniffed and nodded, appearing to mentally pull himself together.

"Did you have any inkling that your church might be in danger?" Ferguson asked.

Ribbardi snorted. "Most of my congregation is over 50 and some of the least violent people you are likely to meet," he said. "I had no idea something like this could happen!"

"Have you received any threats or hate mail recently?" Ferguson pressed.

"Well, I receive those on a semi-frequent basis," said Ribbardi. "Most of them seem pretty random. They're aimed at the Catholic Church in general, rather than me or my parish."

"What do they say?"

"Oh, just blowing up about our stance on abortion or euthanasia or stem-cell research," said Ribbardi. "I'd tell them to send their complaints to the Vatican, but the cowards don't leave their own names or addresses."

"Nothing personal or specific?" Ferguson asked, sounding almost disappointed.

"No. I can tell you, nobody was more shocked or devastated than me that this happened," said Ribbardi gloomily. "I still can't believe Julian is gone."

"What do you remember about it?"

"I was reading from the prayer book," the priest said. "Occasionally I look up, to see if anyone's asleep. Something flickered in the corner of my eye, I still don't know what it was, and then I heard a huge noise, so huge I couldn't even comprehend what it was. Then the wall to the left of me disappeared. I dived to the floor. When I looked up, there were people running everywhere and smoke and this horrible smell. My first thought was to get out of the building, but then I saw Julian — the junior priest. Something . . . had gone through his chest. I knew it wasn't good." Ribbardi stopped, eyes glistening with tears. "Who could have done this?"

Ferguson touched the man's arm briefly. "We'll find out, Father. I promise."

* * * *

Sussex 1 State Prison
Waverly, Virginia
Prisoner Number: 10734
Death Row

Today is our first meeting.

I have been awake most of the night; which isn't unusual. It's hard to sleep with the light and noise that blankets death row 24 hours a day.

However, this time I've been kept awake by nerves and excitement. I wonder what Dinah Harris will think of me. Will she like me? What will she write about me in her book? What sort of questions will she ask me?

I know that I'll never taste freedom again, and so I see her book as a way of liberating my spirit, to live on once they execute me. I don't want to be remembered only for my crimes, but for the other unspeakable parts of my life. Maybe people won't be so quick to judge me once they know the full truth.

I force down some breakfast. All the food in here is rubbery and tastes like cardboard. Frankly I don't know how it keeps us alive, but miserably, it does. Before I lived here, a death row inmate started a hunger strike. He spent a week or two wasting away in his cell before they hauled him off to the infirmary and force fed him with a tube. When he was well enough to return, they brought him back and gave him notice the next day that his execution date had been set.

They are determined that we will not die on our own terms. They do not allow hunger strikes, drug overdoses, or self-harm of any kind. But they will kill me quite happily when my allotted time is due.

It seems like a century passes as the time between breakfast and my visitor slowly ticks by. Finally, a guard appears at my cell and barks: "You got a visitor."

Meekly, I submit as I am thoroughly searched and shackled in preparation to see my visitor. I don't want to do anything that might jeopardize our time together.

I am led to a small, gray room without a window. It is lit by a harsh fluorescent bulb. The metal table and chairs are bolted to the floor. Still, I am grateful that they have allowed us to be in the same room. I guess they figure Dinah Harris can look after herself if I freak out and become violent.

They sit me at one end of the table and tell me that the room is monitored by cameras and any misbehavior will result in harsh punishment. Although I can scarcely think of anything worse than death row, I have heard rumors of solitary confinement called the Hole, and that all inmates are deeply afraid of it.

Finally, the door at the other end of the room opens and Dinah Harris walks in. She is a tall woman, wearing a masculine suit and no makeup. She is attractive in a standoffish way: I wouldn't want to mess with her.

"Good morning," she says, approaching the table. Although I'm happy to see her, I keep my emotions well under control.

"I'd shake your hand," I say, holding up the shackles. "If I could."

She gives a brief smile and sits down. "Thank you for agreeing to speak with me," she starts. "I've already spoken to you a little about the purpose of the book, so that you in turn can understand why I'm asking certain questions. If you don't feel comfortable answering a question, please tell me and we'll move on. Basically, I'd like to get an understanding of who you are outside of the crime you committed, and whether you have any insight into the crime itself. Are you okay with this so far?"

I nod. She puts a recording device on the table with a notebook and pen, and asks, "Are you ready to start?"

I nod again, hoping I'll find my voice soon.

"Where shall we begin?" Dinah asks. "Can you tell me about your childhood?"

I shift uneasily. That's the place I want to finish at, not begin with. "Can we leave that until later?" I say. "It's not a comfortable topic."

"Sure," says Dinah. "Let's start with the first bomb."

I'm happy to talk about that. I explain how I built the bomb in the van, using a mixture of fertilizer and diesel fuel. I tell her that it's easy to learn how to build bombs like these. I worked for three years in a granite mine in Vermont and they dislodge the granite with explosives almost identical to mine. I explain how I stole the van and lie about why I chose the little Catholic Church — it was old, built of bricks and mortar.

"But why did you choose that church?" Dinah pressed. "It wasn't just for the way it looked. Do you have a problem with the Catholic faith?"

"Yes," I say. "I have a problem with all faiths."

"Why?"

I don't want to talk about that just yet.

"Not very many people are religious these days," I inform her.

"Not many people declare it by blowing up churches," Dinah returns.

Well, that's true. We sit in silence for a moment.

"We can talk about that later, if you like," she says.

"Okay," I say gratefully. It's not that I don't want to talk; it's more that it's hard to talk about. I need time to organize my thoughts into words, and to build up the courage to say them.

"Did you intend to kill people?" she asks.

It sounds funny, but actually, I didn't think about it. It was an abstract concept to me. I built the bomb to express how I felt about the church, not with the intent of killing people. Of course, I guess I knew that I might hurt someone. If that was my intent, I would have made it bigger, used more dynamite as the primary explosive, tried to get it closer to the church. I still managed to hurt and kill people, though. I guess it's an occupational hazard when detonating a bomb.

Our hour had passed too quickly, and I heard the guard opening the door to get me.

"You'll come again?" I ask, suddenly anxious.

"Of course," says Dinah. "Next time we'll talk about the second bomb."

Knowing this gives me time to prepare, to think through my answers carefully for her.

I don't want to disappoint her.

ONE YEAR EARLIER

The next morning, Dinah received a phone call on her cell from Ferguson. A cleaner had found something odd in the trash can in a mall near the church, he told her. Dinah told him she'd meet them there in an hour.

It would only take half an hour to get there, but Dinah had a morning routine she held dear to her heart. It was then she spent time in devotion to God, reading her Bible and praying. She had learned to treat her faith like a treasured relationship: it required quality time. There were things she read in her devotion book and the Bible that seemed to have been penned specifically for her. There were other times when what she learned stretched her comfort zone — like giving over her control freak nature to God and allowing Him to be in command. The hardest thing of all was allowing God to deal with the vast amounts of shame and guilt she felt for a myriad of things: that the last time she'd spoken to her precious son, she'd shouted at him in anger; that she'd driven her husband away into the rainy night; that she wasn't the one killed, though she was surely more deserving; that she had numbed her soul with alcohol and silenced her spirit with thoughts of suicide. There were so many mistakes, so much brokenness in her life, so much to be sorry for. She found it hard sometimes to believe that God would accept her pathetic self anywhere near Him. This was a hard lesson learned each day, and would be for a long time to come, Dinah suspected.

She arrived at the mall a little late and met Ferguson and Sinclair at the service entrance. When her eyes fell upon Sinclair, her stomach did a strange, queasy flip. *Those eyes,* she thought, *those eyes are just spectacular.*

The supervising janitor led them through the bowels of the mall, while Dinah brought herself under control and assumed some level of professionalism. His name was Nate, and he explained as they walked that a team of janitors worked at night to mop floors, clean windows, empty trash cans, polish banisters, and otherwise ensure the place was spotless for opening the next morning. The mall had been closed the day after the bombing, given its close proximity to the church, and the cleaning team had been given a night off. Upon their return the following night, one of them found something odd in the trash.

The location of the bin was near the food court. The mall was reasonably new and the food court featured an outdoor balcony where diners could eat their fast food outside if they wished. Dinah immediately noticed that the food court faced the direction of the church, and although the church itself couldn't be seen, it was possible the detonation could have been.

It would have been a perfect vantage point for a voyeuristic bomber.

Inside the trash can, the cleaner showed them the bright yellow work clothes that had been stuffed inside. There was a broad-brimmed hat, perfect for pulling low over the face, a long-sleeved shirt, and long pants.

"Did you touch these?" Sinclair asked the cleaner, who glanced at his supervisor and shook his head.

"No, sir."

Using a fresh evidence bag, Sinclair carefully placed the clothes inside for evidence. There was little else of value inside the trash.

They thanked Nate and drifted into the food court. There, they split up and asked each food vendor if they remembered seeing a person in high-visibility work clothes around the time of the bombing. Nobody seemed to have seen anything. Most could have described the exact moment the bomb exploded with startling detail, but nothing about who had been hanging around the food court at the time.

Their final destination was the Public Safety Office, from where the security guards worked. The supervisor, a bulldog of a man named Oliver with small eyes and weathered skin, explained what had happened on the day. They didn't know where the bomb had detonated or whether there were more bombs timed to explode. The policy book requires that shoppers and vendors be evacuated with minimum panic from the building to a safe zone in the event of a disaster.

Oliver and his guards had done just that. With efficiency, they'd organized the terrified shoppers into some semblance of order and helped them out into the street. Next, they'd rounded up the shop owners and workers, who had quickly locked up to safeguard their goods. Then they'd had another quick run-through of the building to ensure it was empty and locked it up until further notice.

"It seems strange," Oliver admitted. "We made sure everyone was on the street, but we couldn't be sure there was no danger out there. We could have been sending everyone into harm's way."

"It's an impossible choice," said Dinah. "You couldn't have known. If you'd let everyone stay inside the mall, a bomb there might have hurt people, too."

"Anyway," said Oliver, "it turned out okay. But I have to say that I didn't notice one person from another. My main concern was getting everyone out, whether they were male, female, black, white, young, or old. I wanted them safe."

"What about surveillance tapes?" Sinclair asked. "Specifically, we're interested in the food court area."

Oliver barked an order to one of the security guards. "It probably won't be the resolution you're after," he said. "High-resolution cameras are inside the stores to help with shoplifting, but in the general areas we only have a few."

They crowded around a small screen and watched as the guard rolled the footage. It was long-distance and grainy, and though they could see people's movements, distinguishing characteristics was impossible. The images weren't in color either, and if someone wearing the high-visibility work clothes had entered the mall, it wasn't evident on the tape. Dinah was disappointed that they wouldn't catch a glimpse of the bomber.

Ferguson, Sinclair, and Dinah thanked Oliver and his guards, and strolled back up to the food court for lunch.

"So what do we know so far?" Sinclair said, a little dismally. "A person who wore high-visibility work clothes, who stole a van, who built a bomb."

"Cheer up," said Dinah. "We might get some DNA from the clothes, or some information from the lab about how the bomb was built. Don't give up yet!"

Sinclair smiled lazily at her and she suddenly felt dizzy and flustered. *What is going on?* she wondered. *Start acting like a woman your age, for goodness' sake.*

Ferguson just watched them, a paternal knowing smile on his face.

* * * *

It was mid-morning by the time Scott lurched into the kitchen, looking decidedly worse for wear. Isabelle made him a coffee and placed it in front of him. Her hands were shaking with anxiety — that he would notice the long sleeves she wore to hide her bandages, even though the day was blisteringly hot; that he would be in a terrible mood because of his hangover; and that she would make his mood worse by asking questions.

"How was the meeting?" she inquired.

Scott grunted. "Good."

"I imagine it must have gone very well," she continued. "You were out for a long time."

Scott rolled his eyes. "Are you going to nag me all morning? I have better things to do."

"I'm just saying a phone call would have been nice," Isabelle said, trying to make her voice sound placating. "I was worried about you."

Scott ignored that comment and took his coffee upstairs. Isabelle retreated to the deck, staring at her favorite view, feeling utterly invisible.

She didn't have any classes that day, due to the light summer semester workload, so she spent the morning cleaning the house. She found cleaning therapeutic, and anyway, hadn't she always been taught that cleanliness was next to godliness?

It was the day for her monthly lunch date with her mother and the location was an Italian restaurant downtown. The food was impeccable, and more importantly, up to Rosa's standards. Rosa also liked to see if any power brokers came to lunch there, and if she could eavesdrop, there was no happier woman alive.

"How are you?" Rosa asked as they sat down to their table.

"Fine. How are you?"

"You look tired." Rosa looked at Isabelle critically. "Have you been sleeping well?"

"I'm okay. I didn't sleep well last night."

"You should try some warm milk," advised Rosa. "Or take a bath. It'll relax you."

Warm milk and a bath aren't going to fix what's wrong.

"Right. I'll give it a try," agreed Isabelle, if only to change the subject. She decided not to tell Rosa about Scott's late night. It would only upset her, and Isabelle would be fending off a dozen phone calls a day, checking up on her and dispensing advice. This irritated Isabelle, because she hated that her mother tried to pretend that her marriage had been perfect.

"What have you been up to?" Isabelle asked. The waiter came and took their order — ravioli with snow peas and calamari for Isabelle, and gnocchi with pine nuts and white wine sauce for Rosa.

"Just the usual — the garden is looking good after the storms. I've been swimming every day," replied Rosa, who had been diagnosed with osteoporosis several years ago and now followed a regimen of exercise to ward off further deterioration in her bones. "What about you?"

"Work mostly. I work on my thesis when I get the chance." The food came with a plate of hot garlic panini.

They had been eating companionably for several minutes, when a high-pitched voice sounded: "Rosa! Great to see you! Mind if we sit down?" Two women in their sixties stood above their table, one with steel-gray curls and the other with a frosted bob. Both women were lightly made up and dressed expensively in linen. They were vaguely familiar to Isabelle.

"Hi, ladies. Please pull up a chair," invited Rosa. "You remember my daughter, Isabelle? This is Hazel and Heather, from the church."

"Gosh, we haven't seen you in *years*," said Hazel, she with the blond bob. "Since you were a young girl. How are you?" Without waiting for a reply, she turned to Rosa. "It was a lovely funeral, Rosa. How are you coping?" Her tone was pleasant and concerned, but Isabelle detected the slightest hint of gossipy glee in the other woman's voice.

"It's been hard," admitted Rosa. "We all miss him terribly of course."

"I'm sure you do," said Heather, of the gray curls. She turned to Isabelle. "Your father was just a *saint*, wasn't he? You must just miss him *awfully*."

"Oh yes," agreed Isabelle, her voice heavy with sarcasm. The two older women didn't notice.

"Reginald did such a lot for the church and parish," said Hazel. "He organized the fundraising and building of the new building for the parish primary school. Nobody else wanted to take on that task. We haven't found a replacement for him that even comes *close*."

"And he always organized the church fete every year," chimed in Heather. "It all ran *so* smoothly while he was in charge."

"Remember all the work he did around the church?" added Hazel. "He was *such* a handyman. He could fix anything. One year the church roof started leaking after a bad storm and the father didn't know who else to call. Reginald came out in the middle of the night and fixed the roof. He saved the church an *awful* lot of money."

"Such a dear man," said Heather fondly. "The church misses him in *so* many ways."

"Yes, we all do," Rosa said very quietly.

Isabelle savagely speared a piece of calamari and stuffed it into her mouth to squash the alarming wellspring of tears that had surfaced.

"And how is Michael?" asked Hazel, suddenly remembering the younger sibling.

"He's doing very well," Rosa said. "He's a paralegal at a law firm here in D.C., and he also does some writing in his spare time."

"Oh, I bet he inherited his father's altruistic streak, too," said Heather. "Good for him. Does he feel the loss of his father very badly? It's hard for boys to lose their father, don't you think?"

"It hit Michael very hard," said Rosa. "He still misses him very much."

"Are there any grandkids yet?" asked Heather, winking at Rosa.

"No, we're taking precautions," replied Isabelle acidly. The two ladies looked taken aback and uncomfortable, literally drawing away from Isabelle as if her sin might be contagious. Isabelle enjoyed their awkwardness. Rosa glared at Isabelle.

"Well," said Hazel brightly, after the silence had dragged on for longer than was polite. "We'll leave you to your lunch. *Lovely* to see you, Rosa. Do call if you need anything, won't you?"

They teetered away, heads close together, no doubt gossiping about Rosa's condemned daughter.

"So you've been lying to them for a while now, have you?" Isabelle said, before she could help herself.

Rosa put down her fork. "Pardon me?"

"Dad was a saint, was he? A wonderful, caring man even. They have absolutely no idea what Dad was really like, do they?"

Rosa sighed. "Isabelle, do we have to go into this?"

"I'm just curious. I assume you've known Hazel and Heather for a pretty long time. They never even guessed at Dad's true nature?"

"Please don't speak ill of him," said Rosa sharply, but Isabelle ignored her.

"I would've thought the church would help you," she continued. "Surely you could've asked them for help, and we could've gotten away from Dad."

Rosa shook her head. "Isabelle, divorce is a sin. What do you think the church would have done?"

"Are you serious?" Isabelle asked, feeling old resentments boiling away inside her. "The church would rather you stayed with an abusive husband than get divorced?"

"It is my family," Rosa said quietly. "It's not their business. If we had problems, it was up to me to solve them."

"Well, you really did a fine job of it," muttered Isabelle.

Rosa flinched as if she had been slapped, her eyes shadowed and wounded. Isabelle immediately felt awful. "Mom, I'm sorry," she said.

Rosa pushed her plate away. "Are you finished? I'd like to go home now."

They did not speak as the bill was paid and they walked downstairs to the parking lot. As Isabelle drove home, she was haunted by conversations that should never have been voiced.

* * * *

Ferguson had received a phone call during lunch from the FBI lab, where technicians had been working around the clock to identify the components of the bomb. After lunch, where Ferguson had eaten an impressive plate of nachos, they headed to the lab. Dinah looked forward to seeing Zach Booker, the unique and irrepressible crime scene technician.

He came to meet them in the lobby. Instead of one mohawk, he had three — one down the center of his head and one on either side. The middle mohawk was dyed platinum blond and the side mohawks were dyed bright green. His facial piercings — eyebrow, nose, and lip — were all tiny little pirate flags.

"Well, if it isn't the good pirate," commented Dinah, shaking his hand. "Yo ho ho and all that?"

"It may interest you to know, uncultured one," said Zach, loftily, "that today is International Speak Like a Pirate Day."

Dinah laughed. "Your lab report should be interesting then, m'hearty."

Zach grinned. "Well, I wouldn't put you through that. I'm just showing a little solidarity." He quickly stuck out his tongue, which was also pierced and which also sported a pirate flag.

The three of them followed Zach into his lab, which was appropriately adorned with skull-and-crossbones for the occasion.

"So, the bomb," Zach began. He'd identified the components using a mass spectrometer and had the results on his computer screen. "It was a very typical ANFO bomb, made up of fuel oil and ammonium nitrate. Easy to source the ingredients and easy to make."

He clicked the mouse and the screen changed. "The fuel oil is diesel. Diesel fuel is cheap and readily available. You can obtain it to use to fuel trucks, for example, or heating oil. They have slightly different chemical compositions. In this case, your man obtained diesel fuel used to operate trucks and machinery. About five and a half percent of the bomb was diesel fuel."

"Hard to trace," said Sinclair knowledgeably. "He wouldn't have needed staggering amounts to make the bomb, and thus wouldn't have triggered suspicion."

"Right," agreed Zach. "The remaining ninety-four and a half percent of the bomb was ammonium nitrate, or fertilizer. The fertilizer is synthetic nitrogen made in granular form, used extensively in the agricultural industry. Here is where you might find some leads. A person needs a reason and a license to obtain this type of fertilizer."

"Or have stolen it or have a contact who can get it for you," added Sinclair.

"Sure," said Zach. "Now the bomber used old-fashioned dynamite as a booster, which was set off with a remote detonator. A time-delayed fuse was attached to the blasting cap, which detonates the dynamite, which in turn causes the ANFO to explode."

"Where did the dynamite come from?" asked Sinclair. "Is it traceable?"

"It was actually quite old dynamite," said Zach. "The kind they used in quarrying or mining a while ago, I believe."

Sinclair nodded, deep in thought.

"All told, the bomb was pretty small," Zach continued. "My guess is about five hundred pounds. Compare this to the Oklahoma City bombing, for example, which was about five thousand pounds."

"I guess the fuse and blasting caps were all pretty generic?" Sinclair asked.

"Yeah, I'm afraid so, though I'd hazard a guess and say that they may have been obtained with the dynamite," said Zach. "Maybe from a quarry or mine? I believe the ANFO mixture was probably mixed in the heavy plastic bags in which the fertilizer is sold. I can't find traces of plastic or metal that would indicate the bomber used barrels or crates."

They stood in silence for several moments, contemplating what they had learned. Dinah thought about the type of person the bomber would be — he or she would have to be reasonably organized and methodical, given what they knew about him. There had been great attention to detail in the type of vehicle used and stolen, the materials obtained, the scene set up, and the disposal of the identifying clothes.

"There's only one other thing that might be of some help," Zach added. "If the bomb was made off-site, which is probable, he wouldn't have wanted to drive the van very far with the fuse and blasting caps attached. The ANFO mixture is stable, but the blasting caps are somewhat volatile. I would think the bomb was built easily within the city limits."

"How much fertilizer are we talking about?" Sinclair asked.

"I'd say about eight 50-pound bags," said Zach. "Before you do the math and tell me I can't add up, you have to add the weight of the fuel oil and dynamite to the fertilizer to get the five-hundred-pound weight of the overall structure."

Sinclair nodded. "Thanks, Zach. You've been helpful. I guess you didn't find any identifying markers?"

Zach shook his head. "No useable fingerprints. Plenty of DNA, as you'd expect from a scene where there were multiple injuries and fatalities, but nothing of any use."

Ferguson sighed. "What are your thoughts on the guy or group who did this?"

"My first thought is that it's not a group, at least not in the way you're thinking," replied Zach. "I don't think this is the work of a terrorist group, for instance. They would usually target a much more symbolic address, like an embassy or a government building. They like to target people and buildings that cause maximum shock value around the world. This is a little too low key. Second, I'm not even thinking a radical right-wing extremist like Timothy McVeigh, for example, because the bomb was so small. People who are hardened by years of hatred and contempt often try to cause a lot of damage, but again, this isn't the case."

"So, any ideas on who might be behind this?"

"My gut feeling, which is based on nothing except instinct, is that it's a lone person, with a specific agenda," said Zach. "The agenda may be against the Catholic Church, but I don't think it includes killing as many people as possible. I think it's an agenda fueled by desperation, rather than ideology or hatred."

"That's a very interesting viewpoint," commented Sinclair. "I tend to agree with you."

"Of course you do. That's why I'm the *man!*" joked Zach.

"Oh, Zach," said Dinah, shaking her head sadly. "What a crazy, deluded world you must live in."

* * * *

When Dinah opened the doors to her church that evening, she couldn't help but cast an eye around for suspicious people before entering the building. She was here for her weekly Bible study with four other ladies from the church. For a brief, chilly moment, she imagined that she would be in this church when the bomber blew it up.

Don't be ridiculous, she chided herself. *For one thing, he'd probably wait for a Sunday service, not your little study group. For another, this is one of hundreds of churches. Why would he choose this one?*

Dinah forced the thought from her head and found the little room where they held their weekly Bible study. On weekdays, it was used for playgroup and senior citizens' meetings. On Sundays, it was used for Sunday school. It was a busy, thriving church, but now Dinah couldn't help but worry that it was also a target.

They were studying the life of King David, and Dinah was enjoying it immensely. She loved how the Bible told the history of his life with such candor. King David had been a great king, a godly man, yet he had also plumbed the depths of sin. It was comforting, in a way, to know that even the greatest men in the Bible struggled with their sinful natures, just as she did some two thousand years later.

Dinah glanced around the little group as they opened the study in prayer. Ruth was the unofficial leader; Alicia was a young woman with an infectious laugh; Sara was a harried mother of four; and Deborah was a stately, well-dressed wife of a Washington dignitary. There were times she still couldn't believe that she was here, sharing her life and faith in an intimate setting. Dinah shied away from close human contact after the death of her husband and son, certain that it only led to heartbreak. She'd built effective barriers of sarcasm, alcoholism, and anger, designed to keep people at bay. It had taken the love and persistence of a Christian couple, Andy and Sandra Coleman, to start the process of dismantling the walls.

Inch by inch, they came down. Where once she would have found the concept of a study group ludicrous, now she was participating in one and actually looked forward to it each week. Where once she hated talking about herself to anyone, she now found herself sharing her thoughts and problems with these ladies. Where once she hadn't cared if she lived or died, she now loved life fiercely and was beginning to think about what the future held for her.

Most perplexing was the fact that she found Special Agent Aaron Sinclair attractive. She and her beloved husband Luke had been college sweethearts and they'd known, almost from the instant they met, that they were meant to be together. After his death, men could have been green aliens with six tentacles for all she cared: she wasn't interested and she couldn't imagine ever allowing herself to love again. Nor could she contemplate betraying Luke's memory by sharing her life with another.

Now she wondered whether it was okay to feel attraction toward someone else. Did it mean that she would be disloyal to everything she and Luke had shared, including their precious son Sammy? What would Luke have wanted her to do?

Then she started to think about what a new relationship might actually mean. She would have to explain the fight: the fateful night where she'd screamed at her husband and son, driven them out into the dark rain, where they'd lost their lives; her descent into depression and self-medication with alcohol; her deep yearning to end her own life. How could she explain her lifelong battle with addiction? What sort of man would want to start a relationship with her, knowing all of her history? He would have to be nothing short of a masochist. Any normal man would run screaming for the hills once he'd heard her story.

It's just an attraction, Dinah decided. *That's all it is. It'll never be anything more. I won't see him again after this case. Then I can forget all about his beautiful eyes and strong hands and deep voice and. . . .*

"Dinah!"

Suddenly she was aware of four pairs of eyes staring at her.

"Oh!" she exclaimed, startled. "Sorry, I was on another planet!"

"Is everything okay?" Ruth asked.

"Yes," said Dinah, weighing up whether to tell the woman about Sinclair, her late husband, and the complex, twisted tale that involved them. "Everything's fine. I'm just a little preoccupied with the case I'm working."

She might bring it up at a later date, she decided. She needed some time to sort out how she felt before she sought their counsel.

The four women knew that they couldn't ask for details about the case, but Ruth seemed to sense that Dinah wasn't telling the whole truth.

"How is everything with you personally?" she asked.

"I'm doing well," said Dinah. "I feel like I'm on an even keel at the moment."

"What can we pray about for you?"

"Wisdom," said Dinah instantly. She had no idea why she said that but it seemed right. "I've made some stupid and selfish decisions in the past. I need God's help in making the right decisions now."

Ruth nodded. Eager to turn the attention away from herself, Dinah asked, "What can we pray about for you?"

Ruth began talking about her son, who was almost grown up but still involved in the usual teenager angst. Dinah relaxed slightly, thankful that she didn't have to talk about herself any further.

When it was time to pray, Dinah quickly sent one for herself.

Dear Heavenly Father, I am confused about how my past and my future will fit together. Am I supposed to be alone for the rest of my life? Should I think about re-marriage? What is Your will for me? Please give me Your wisdom in figuring this out. I don't trust my own judgment and I only want to do Your will. Thank You for Your everlasting mercy, grace, and love. Without You, I have nothing. Amen.

The next morning, the three investigators had decided to meet at the office of the FBI medical examiner. Dr. Paul Campion was the long-serving coroner for the Bureau, and embarrassingly, Dinah remembered turning up there during the Smithsonian case, still drunk or hung over. Dr. Campion had never said anything to her, but he would have known. It was just something else, thought Dinah, in a very long list of humiliating moments that she would have to forgive herself for and move on.

Dinah was the first to arrive and waited in the parking lot for Ferguson and Sinclair. She had no desire to begin an awkward conversation with Dr. Campion and preferred to sit in the relentless heat.

Sinclair arrived and Dinah felt her heart speed up a little when she saw him. He dressed sharply, and today wore a tie that was the same deep azure of his eyes. Dinah liked the way his eyes crinkled warmly when he smiled.

"How are you?" he asked, striding over to her.

"Great. How are you?"

"Good. Did you work on the case last night, or take the night off?" Sinclair asked, turning his back to the sun.

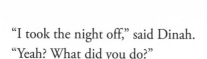

"I took the night off," said Dinah.

"Yeah? What did you do?"

"Nothing. Just chilled out at home." Dinah felt an instant flush of shame. Why was she lying to Sinclair about going to a Bible study group? Didn't she want him to know she was a Christian? Why was she trying to complicate her life?

"What about you?" she asked after a stilted silence.

"Oh, much the same," he said. "I lead a pretty boring life, to be honest."

Dinah stole a glance at his left hand: no wedding ring. "Do you . . . have a girlfriend?" she asked hesitantly.

He glanced at her with a tiny smile. "No. Do you have a boyfriend?"

"Uh . . . no."

Ferguson's car squealed into the lot and as he parked his car badly, Sinclair leaned his head closer to Dinah. "Well, perhaps we should talk more about that," he suggested. "Want to get a drink after work?"

"Sure," agreed Dinah, before she thought it through properly. As Ferguson, already sweating in the hot sun, materialized before them, Dinah thought of all the issues she now faced, simply by agreeing to meet Sinclair after work. They were going for a drink, which she couldn't have, because she was an alcoholic. She'd have to explain that to him. Then she'd probably have to explain why she had become an alcoholic. No doubt he'd mention that she had been fired from the Bureau, and be curious about why. The painful topic of Luke and Sammy would eventually surface. What a disaster!

This, thought Dinah, giving herself a mental slap, *is why it is much easier just to be alone. Trying to have a relationship is going to be too difficult.*

With a sigh, Dinah tried to concentrate on the task at hand. Dr. Campion had wheeled out the bodies of the two victims of the church bombing. Julian Nolan was the junior priest who'd been helping run the service, and Melissa Cousins had been the parishioner who'd been in the wrong place at the wrong time.

Dinah couldn't help but shiver in the cold, bare room as Dr. Campion uncovered the bodies on the steel trolleys.

Dr. Campion began: "I have to start by saying that this was not a pretty job. You can see that both victims sustained significant injuries, typical of a bomb blast. Julian Nolan died almost instantly when a sheared part of the wooden window frame pierced his chest. You may also notice some minor burns and shrapnel wounds from flying debris."

"I have to admit," said Ferguson, "I would have expected greater injury."

Dr. Campion nodded. "You can't see it, but there certainly was greater injury. There was extensive internal bruising and bleeding that would have been fatal. This is what killed our second victim, Melissa Cousins."

Cousins seemed to have borne the brunt of the blast. One of her arms had almost been torn from her body, and she had also suffered minor burns and shrapnel wounds.

"As required, I completed a full body x-ray," continued Dr. Campion. "This will determine the composite of the shrapnel. Sometimes, the maker of the bomb will fill it with nails or ball bearings, to inflict greater damage."

"We didn't find evidence of that at the scene," said Sinclair with a frown.

"Nor did I," agreed Dr. Campion. "There was glass, brick, wood, and concrete, mainly from the construction of the building."

"That seems to support one of our theories," mused Sinclair thoughtfully. "It seems the bomber *didn't* want to inflict the greatest damage. He built a relatively small bomb, used small amounts of primary explosive, and didn't fill it with nasty ingredients."

"A morally conscientious bomber?" Dr. Campion smiled.

Sinclair sighed. "Something like that!"

"Well, I'm sorry I can't be more helpful." Dr. Campion gently re-covered the bodies.

The three investigators stripped off their plastic protective clothing and left the building. Outside, the blinding sun seemed incongruous to the chilly, gloomy morgue.

Squinting, Dinah waited for Ferguson to walk ahead of them before she said quickly to Sinclair, "I just remembered something; I can't do tonight."

Sinclair looked surprised. "Oh. Okay. Maybe some other time?"

"Yeah, maybe." Dinah couldn't look at him. She really wanted to spend time with him, but the complexities involved seemed to be too daunting.

"Is everything okay?" Sinclair touched her arm lightly.

Her skin burned and it spread to her face. "Yes, fine," she mumbled. "I just forgot I have plans for tonight."

"Are you two coming?" yelled Ferguson impatiently.

Almost running, Dinah headed for her old partner, desperate to leave the awkward conversation with Sinclair behind.

* * * *

It was Saturday, which meant Scott was home. When he was in a good mood, Isabelle enjoyed having him there, given they often didn't see much of each other during the week due to Scott's work schedule. When he was in a bad mood, she knew she had to keep out of his way.

Unfortunately, today he was in a bad mood. And it got worse when he discovered Isabelle's brother would be visiting. "What is wrong with your family?" he demanded. "Do you have to live in each other's pockets? Can't you go one day without seeing them?"

Isabelle decided not to point out that she'd only seen her mother twice since the funeral and that it had been almost a week since she'd seen Michael. Instead, she said, "Given the fact that my father just died, I think it's important to make sure Michael's okay."

Scott narrowed his eyes. "I thought you were all happy that he's dead."

"Relieved might be a better word," replied Isabelle. "It's not as simple as you think."

"Whatever," said Scott. "I'm going to be in the study."

Isabelle sighed. "I thought you were going to have lunch with us."

"Listen," said Scott. "I can take your family in small doses. Michael creeps me out."

"*Creeps* you out?" Isabelle was incredulous. "What do you mean?"

"He's just so . . . needy and damaged," said Scott. "He needs to get over it and move on."

"That is a really insensitive thing to say," said Isabelle, trying to control her anger at his comment. Provoking Scott would only make things much worse. "You don't know what Michael has been through."

"I wouldn't expect him to understand."

Both Isabelle and Scott jumped. Michael had suddenly appeared in the kitchen, and had apparently heard every word. He stared at Scott with contempt.

"Great, so you just let yourself into other people's houses now?" Scott snapped.

"Scott, he's *family*," said Isabelle, feeling the tenuous control she had over the situation disintegrating. "It's not a big deal."

"It's a big deal when it's my house!" said Scott. He hadn't taken his eyes from Michael.

"Don't be so melodramatic," said Michael, knowing full well such a comment would enrage his brother-in-law.

"Okay, that's enough," said Isabelle, quickly hoping to avoid an escalation.

"*What* did you just say?" Scott took a step toward Michael.

"You heard me."

Isabelle wrung her hands. How had this gotten so out of control?

"We've decided to go out for lunch," she announced. "Michael, let's go."

"Just so you know," Michael added, for good measure, "you might be able to bully Isabelle because you're a coward, but you don't scare me."

"If it weren't for your sister, I'd whip your butt out of here in five seconds flat," said Scott, lifting his chin belligerently. "Just like your dad did."

That did it. Michael completely lost it and punched Scott right in the nose. Isabelle screamed, suddenly transported back in time to nights of violence, where her father was the aggressor and the victim his wife or children. The metallic smell of blood immediately brought back the fear, loathing, and confusion she felt for her father. She remembered cowering in fear in the corner, trying to protect Michael with her own body, listening to her mother cry softly. She remembered lying in bed, stiff with fear as her father made his way drunkenly up the stairs, looking to release his frustration on one smaller and weaker than himself. She recalled bruises, covered-up and lied about; broken limbs, explained away; shattered hearts, carefully hidden.

Thankfully, Scott had gotten what he wanted and he smirked at Michael while wiping away blood. "I'm going to press charges for assault," he declared. "My wife saw everything and she'll testify against you."

"Scott, come on," said Isabelle desperately. "There's no need to call the police. We're not going to press charges. I'm not going to testify against Michael."

"You will do whatever I tell you to do," snapped Scott, glaring at her. Isabelle shrank back fearfully.

"Go ahead," taunted Michael. "Tell the police you're a coward who won't fight back."

"Michael," interjected Isabelle. "I think you should go. Scott, why don't you cool down and then make a decision about what you want to do."

Michael finally wrenched his eyes away from Scott and nodded. He left the house as silently as he'd arrived.

Isabelle tried to help Scott staunch the blood flow from his nose, but he shook her away. "Don't touch me!" he said coldly. "I see where your loyalties lie."

"I'm not on anyone's side," insisted Isabelle. "I just don't want to fight."

Scott pushed her away forcefully, and she almost stumbled. Shaking his head with disgust, he stalked away to his study and slammed the door. Moments later, Isabelle heard the lock slamming home. It was a clear message that she was not wanted.

Anxiety seemed to replace the blood in her veins, pumping around her body, visiting upon her a crushing headache and a sick feeling in her stomach.

She took the stairs two at a time and locked herself in the en-suite bathroom. There, she found her package of trusty razor blades. She sat in the empty bathtub and made the first incision on her left upper arm. The moment the blood oozed, Isabelle felt relief start to wash over her. She cut again and again, until it seemed the stress and fear inside her escaped with the blood and trickled down the drain.

When she'd made enough cuts for the roaring sensation in her head to abate, she drew her legs up to her body and rested her head on her knees. One single sentence reverberated around her skull, bouncing like a ball, uttered by Michael only a few months ago: *You married your father. You married your father. You married your father.*

* * * *

The press had been notified. At the appointed time, a stunning woman in her early thirties appeared on the steps of the District of Columbia Federal Court. She was beautifully dressed in a knee-length black skirt, black high heels, and a gray and black striped shirt with gold cufflinks and diamond earrings. Her blond hair was mid-length, stylish, and neat, and her makeup flawless.

In one hand, she held an important-looking legal file. Next to her stood distinguished United States Senator David Winters, smiling beatifically as if what they were about to do would change the world.

The woman, whose name was Elena Kasprowitz, waited for the media throng to settle down and then announced, "Today marks an important day in the social and political direction of our great nation. Our founding fathers sought to create a nation built on liberty, justice, and freedom for all. One of the most fundamental tenets of liberty and freedom is the separation of church and state, sanctioned in the First Amendment. Yet we still see the influence and power of religion in almost every facet of life, most regrettably in government."

She paused, for dramatic effect. "Today, we're demanding more of those in power: we demand freedom from the religious agenda! We demand freedom from religious propaganda and indoctrination! We demand the freedom to *choose* where we hear religious instruction — we don't want it in public places but in churches where it belongs!"

Her voice swelled impressively, captivating her audience. "Today, we file a lawsuit demanding that the government immediately withdraw financial support from religious organizations. Why should I, a taxpayer, fund organizations in which I have no personal belief? How can there be satisfactory separation of church and state when the state provides financial assistance to the church? This is a direct violation of the First Amendment and we demand that the government cease this activity immediately!"

Her beautiful brown eyes implored the cameras. "Please support our cause. Do you want to live in a country where religion is forced upon you; where your freedom to live peaceably without religion is impinged? Then help us in our fight, for we have a lot of work ahead of us. Our adversaries are powerful and well-financed, make no mistake about that. *Your* government provides them with financial backing! Today, we fight for justice and freedom, and we will not be intimidated!"

She held the legal file up high, as if it were a hard-won trophy. The press was enthralled and flash bulbs popped like fireworks. After a couple of minutes, Senator Winters took Elena by the elbow and motioned for her to walk up the stairs of the courthouse.

Though the courthouse was busy and filled with harried lawyers and clerks, it was a place where they could talk without interruption. "Nicely done," said Winters in a low voice. "A call to arms is always a good strategy."

Elena smiled, showing perfect teeth. "Are you happy that I didn't mention you in my speech?"

"My presence was enough," said Winters. They waded through distracted lawyers on cell phones, clerks with armfuls of paper, and thoroughly confused citizens attempting to find their way through the maze of corridors and small rooms.

"What is the plan once the lawsuit is filed?" asked Elena.

"We gather support," said Winters. "We need noisy people willing to march, gather, and yell on our behalf. The media will love it. We need sponsors to fund the lawsuit and we need prominent people to support it in the media."

Elena nodded as Winters' cell phone shrieked. "Hello?"

"It's Cartwright," rumbled the humanist's voice. "Nice job. I told you she was good."

"Agreed," said Winters, glancing over at his companion. She was pretending not to listen to his conversation.

"Prepare for a media blanketing of the issue," continued Cartwright. "We are endeavoring to have the lawsuit become famous before it even goes to trial. We'll have experts on talk shows, radio interviews, bloggers, and everyone in between talking about it. You'll be sick of hearing about it."

"I have no doubt about that," said Winters dryly. "What do you want me to do?"

"Continue lending moral support, as you did today," said Cartwright. "Enter into discussions with your friend." He didn't need to say Chief Justice Pryor's name for Winters to know who he meant. "Find out if there are other senators or congressmen who might feel strongly about the subject."

"Right," said Winters. He didn't often take orders from anyone, but there was no harm in letting the other person believe he was in control. For half a million dollars, he could keep his mouth shut — for the time being.

He hung up and Elena looked away. "You'd better prepare yourself for the onslaught," he suggested. "You're the face of this lawsuit."

"What will happen?" she asked curiously.

"I suspect you'll be in great demand," said Winters. "The media will love you. You'll have all kinds of anti-religious groups wanting to talk to you. They'll probably ask you to support some of their agendas, but I'd stick to this one if I were you."

Elena nodded and seemed to be fantasizing about being famous. Winters wanted to roll his eyes. "Be prepared for the hostility, too," he added. "Not everyone is going to be receptive to your message; there are many who disagree with you. They can be loud and insistent."

"You mean the religious organizations whose funding we're seeking to strip?" Elena asked.

"Yes, but they'll have lots of support from groups that aren't even necessarily religious," said Winters. "And, as you said, they are well-funded and powerful. Let me know if you get any death threats."

"*Death* threats?" Elena suddenly looked shocked. "Are you serious?"

Winters enjoyed the fear on her face. "Sure. Did you think this wouldn't be controversial?"

"But . . . what do . . . I mean . . .," stuttered Elena, suddenly realizing her mission.

"You'll work it out," said Winters, tiring of the game.

He turned and strode from the courthouse, leaving Elena in his wake.

* * * *

On Sunday morning, as venomous heat spilled over the eastern horizon, the bomber drove the school bus containing four hundred pounds of ANFO explosives carefully toward Manassas. He took a risk and left in daylight, hoping that his neighbors would take no notice of him. He knew that when the media reports came flooding in, if they'd seen the bus, they might connect him to the bombing. However, their houses were quiet and still and he was relieved when he left his neighborhood behind. He wore mechanic's overalls, in case he was stopped for any reason.

He'd timed the drive perfectly. He didn't want to be pulled over by the cops, so he obeyed the road rules impeccably. He didn't want anyone to remember him, so he was careful not to engage in road rage or make a mistake. He wanted to arrive at the church after the morning service had commenced, so that there would be nobody in the parking lot wondering why a school bus had stopped there.

However, on the journey toward Manassas he realized he'd made a critical error. A yellow school bus, driven on a Sunday morning, was bound to generate interest. It was not a common sight, and he caught a few curious stares as cars passed on the freeway. He cursed himself for his oversight. It made perfect sense when he'd stolen the bus during the week, but he hadn't thought through the plan to its end. Now he would have to hope that anyone who saw the bus wouldn't take any notice of *him*, at least not enough to be able to describe him to the police.

Everything went according to plan, despite his apprehension. Early on a Sunday, traffic was light and the bomber arrived in Manassas at 8:40. The morning service started at 8:30 and he allowed 15 minutes for latecomers to straggle into the church.

The parking lot was situated behind the church, so none of the congregation would see him park there. Pulling his baseball cap low over his eyes, he drove as close to the church as he dared and quickly shut off the engine.

Tense as a cat stalking a hapless mouse, he waited for footsteps or a voice, asking why he was there. But he heard nothing except the faint sound of music and singing coming from the church. When he dared to look around, he didn't see a soul.

He walked out of the parking lot, using SUVs and minivans as shields, just in case someone caught a glimpse of him. At the edge of the church property, he stopped and listened hard, taking one last look. There was no indication that anyone had seen him, so he continued walking down the street and into an alleyway behind several alfresco cafes. A Dumpster stood in the deserted alley, servicing the cafes. He eyed the dumpster, thinking about whether to take off the overalls now. He didn't want to waste time now, so he continued to a sidewalk table at the café nearest the church.

Again, the vantage point was crucial. He wouldn't see the blast, but he'd see the acrid plume of smoke rise above the buildings. He ordered a cappuccino he knew he wouldn't drink, found a complimentary copy of the *Post*, and settled back in his chair. When the waiter had left him, and there was little activity nearby, he took out the cell phone and pressed the TALK button.

It seemed to take an eternity, but finally a slight rumble made the cheap aluminum tables clatter. The noise of the explosion arrived several nanoseconds later, a deep, throaty roar that caused everyone to stop and swivel their heads. Seconds after that, a dark ball of smoke rose into the sky.

As several other patrons did, the bomber jumped to his feet with a startled cry. He looked wildly around, wondering whether people would flee or run toward the explosion to help. Self-preservation seemed to be the order of the day, with many cups of coffee left un-drunk on the tables.

After several moments, the bomber followed the crowd. When they had dissipated, he slipped into the alleyway behind the café, stripped off his mechanic's overalls and baseball cap, and discarded them in the Dumpster. A few blocks over, he hailed a cab and traveled to the nearest shopping mall. There, in the vast parking lot, he stole an unremarkable Ford sedan and drove back to D.C., keeping to the speed limit despite his overwhelming desire to put his foot down.

He ditched the stolen car a few blocks away from his house and trotted home, eager to watch the newscast of his bombing. As expected, the Sunday morning talk shows were interrupted as the networks sent cameras and reporters to the blast site as quickly as possible. When the first pictures came through, he felt a thrill break out goose bumps all over his body.

The blast had left a crater in one wall, which was still standing despite the damage. Many of the stunned survivors, preyed upon by the reporters, told of a horrible burning smell that blistered their nostrils and made their eyes water. Many experienced breathing difficulties.

What of the casualties? the bomber asked, flicking from one network to another.

A tentative count came through about 15 minutes later — 1 confirmed dead, 2 critically injured, 21 with an assortment of non-fatal wounds.

The bomber felt the thrill cascade over his body again. The media had already begun to talk about the similarities between this bombing and the Our Lady of Mercy Catholic Church bombing, despite the police department's best efforts to downplay the connection.

Contentedly, the bomber allowed himself to take the rest of the day off. The tension in his body had leaked away and he felt almost happy.

His work here had been done.

Dinah enjoyed Sundays. She went to church for the service at nine o'clock, spent time with the friends she was making there, immersing herself in the teaching of the Word of God, and then treated herself to a sumptuous brunch at a deli nearby. She luxuriated in reading the newspapers, drinking coffee unhurriedly, and thinking. On Sundays, she allowed herself to think of Luke and Sammy, the lost loves of her life. She reveled in good memories, even if they brought her to tears. When the bad memories surfaced, she closed them down like a steel trap in hunting season and wouldn't allow any further contemplation until the following Sunday. The staff at the deli seemed to have become used to her, a solitary figure who would sometimes weep into her coffee and sometimes smile with exquisite joy. Dinah thought wryly to herself that they had probably decided she was quite mental, in a harmless kind of way.

Today, her third cup of coffee was interrupted by a call from Ferguson.

"We've had a second bombing," he told her without preamble.

Dinah immediately shifted into work mode. "Okay," she said calmly. "Where?"

"Up in Manassas," Ferguson said. "The First United Methodist church was hit during their morning services. Where are you?"

"Just finished a late breakfast," said Dinah, giving him the address of the deli. While she waited for him to pick her up, she visited the bathroom to check her hair and re-apply her lip gloss. A few minutes later, she laughed at herself in the mirror. *You've never checked your hair or makeup for Ferguson. Who are you trying to impress? Stop being ridiculous. You're acting like a schoolgirl.*

Ferguson screeched up to the curb and Dinah climbed into the back seat. Inside the car, the atmosphere was professionally charged with the desire to catch the bomber before he hurt anyone else.

"How many killed and injured?" Dinah asked as they sped toward Manassas.

"One dead, two critically injured," said Sinclair, twisting around in the front seat to lock his stunning eyes on hers. She looked away, pretending to think.

"You're not going to believe what vehicle he used to deliver the bomb," continued Sinclair.

"What?"

"A school bus."

"A *what*?"

"A bright yellow school bus."

Ferguson snorted. "Makes our investigation a little easier, don't you think? Someone was bound to see a school bus driving around on a Sunday morning."

Dinah nodded. The bomber had made a critical error, one that might lead to his capture. Excitement shot through her at the thought of arresting him.

When they arrived at the church in Manassas, the scene of devastation was similar to the one at Our Lady of Mercy church. The burnt-out shell of the school bus was obvious, and the force of the explosion had destroyed the cars that had been parked nearby. Some had been tossed on their roofs as if no more substantial than a toy. The damage to the building looked less severe, with a hole blasted in one wall. The structure overall seemed to be standing up well, like a stoic warrior with a flesh wound.

The choking, burning smell that hung over the bombsite was still pungent and immediately signified that it had again been an ANFO explosion. The scene was littered with debris, from twisted pews, destroyed hymnals, and the smoldering remains of a cross to the remnants of the pre-fabricated concrete wall.

The uniformed police officer in charge of the scene spotted them and waved them over. He looked somewhat relieved to be able to hand the details of the case over to them. "We received the call at about 9:45 this morning," he explained. He was the spitting image of a small-town country sheriff, with a thick moustache and sideburns, stiff, formal carriage, and a slight drawl in his voice. His name was Robert Dawes.

"An explosion had been detonated at the First United Methodist Church during the morning service," he continued. "Upon arrival, we discovered that a hole had been blasted in the wall of the building, apparently from a bomb placed inside a bus parked nearby. We searched the premises for further bombs. Once cleared, we assisted the paramedics with casualties and then secured the perimeter."

"Good job," said Ferguson. He glanced over at a throng of media, jostling for the best position. "Could you have your men keep them under control? We'd like to go through the scene carefully, if you don't mind."

"Of course," Dawes said. "We've been taking statements from witnesses and survivors, which I'll provide to you once you've finished."

"Good man," said Ferguson. "Thanks." He smiled as the policeman marched over to the media and explained in ringing tones that they were not welcome to come any further toward the crime scene.

Sinclair was already searching through the remains of the bus. It had fared a little better than the van used in the first bombing, but not by much. The windows, including the windshield, were blown out. The tires had melted. The internal structure of the bus — the seats, instrument panel, steering wheel, and side panels — had all been ripped from the vehicle and lay in various twisted poses in the debris. The engine block had been torn from the nose of the bus and lay, still virtually intact, several feet away.

Sinclair quickly took care of writing down the identification numbers from the engine. Then he moved to the body of the bus, where the bomb was built.

"Would the bomber have driven the bomb here?" Dinah asked.

"He certainly wouldn't have made the bomb in this parking lot," said Sinclair. "So he had to drive it from somewhere, but it wouldn't have been too far. As we already know, ANFO is relatively stable, as far as explosives go. The bomb wouldn't have been too heavy and the bus wouldn't have had a problem carrying its load. Unfortunately, there are plenty of places within 30 minutes' drive of here from which the bomber could have driven."

Sinclair picked up a scrap of heavy industrial plastic and eased it into an evidence bag. "I thought I might find this," he said. "My theory continues to be that he mixes the ANFO inside the bags that the agricultural-grade fertilizer comes in. Exactly the same plastic was discovered at the Catholic church scene."

The crime scene technicians had arrived and looked like white ghosts in their protective suits, dusting for fingerprints in the wreckage, combing through the debris, and photographing the scene from every angle.

Dinah, Sinclair, and Ferguson moved into the building. The wall that had sustained the damage was the back wall, and thankfully there had been a gap between the wall and the congregation. If attendees had been crammed right up against the back wall, the number of those killed would have risen dramatically.

"Again, this was not a big bomb," said Sinclair softly. The wreckage of the church was somehow sacrilegious and Dinah felt a strange, maternal sadness, the way she used to feel when Sammy was sick and she would have done anything to have him well again. "He could have built a much larger bomb, given the space available in the bus. Yet for some reason — perhaps he is limited by his own ability — the bomb size has to be about five hundred pounds or less."

"Do you find significance in the fact that this is a Protestant church rather than a Catholic one?" Dinah asked.

Sinclair thought for a few moments. "Interesting. I don't know. If he has a specific agenda, it's not aimed solely at the Catholic church."

They stood in silence, surveying the wreckage of the building and its contents.

"Come on," said Ferguson at length. "We've got to talk to the witnesses."

* * * *

Some of the survivors who had not been injured and witnesses had stayed at the scene, giving their statements to the police. Ferguson, Sinclair, and Dinah now began the task of asking them to repeat everything they'd already said.

One lady described the huge noise and rumbling sound. She had been lifted out of her chair and flung to the floor. Dazed, deafened, and confused, she lay there for a few moments before an overwhelming desire to evacuate overcame her. It was very dark inside; the power had gone off and she couldn't see much. She heard people groaning and crying. She had crawled toward daylight.

Another man expressed a similar experience: the air had literally moved around him, he said, picking him up as if it had formed powerful hands. He remembered the sensation of sudden, bright light, and then total darkness. When he had collected his thoughts and realized he wasn't hurt, he began helping those around him to get out of the building.

Every survivor talked about the bitter fumes that hung over the wounded church. Their eyes burned, their noses scalded, their lungs struggled to find oxygen. Apparently, some of the victims taken to the hospital had suffered minor burns to their skin.

Their tales were eerily similar to those from the Catholic church bombing.

The next witness was a middle-aged man named Strickland who'd been walking his dog around the block. The church was in his sights when the bomb exploded.

"I literally watched the whole thing," he said. His hands were still shaking from shock; his dog had broken the leash and bolted for home. He shook his head. "It's the weirdest thing. I actually remember seeing the school bus in the parking lot and thinking that it was odd. Why would a bus be at church? In the next instant, the bus vanished in the explosion. I saw a flash of fire and heavy gray smoke. I saw cars being thrown into the air and then I saw stuff falling *out of* the smoke, like debris I guess. I was so scared, I didn't know what to do. I just stood there, staring. I couldn't believe my own eyes. As the smoke started to lift, I saw a hole in the church wall and then I saw *people*, crawling out of the hole."

Tears formed in his eyes. "It was pitiful, seeing that. Then I called 911."

"Did you see any movement around the bus before it exploded?" Sinclair asked. "Someone walking away from it or out of the parking lot, for example?"

"No," said Strickland. "It was pretty quiet this morning. I just remember the bus because it was hard to miss."

"While you were out walking," continued Sinclair, "did you see the bus driving around?"

"No, sorry," said Strickland, shaking his head.

Other witnesses had only heard the explosion and come running from their homes. Frustratingly, nobody had seen the bus arrive at the church nor who had been driving it.

"He had to get out of the bus and walk away," said Dinah, after what seemed like the millionth useless interview. "He had to drive the bus into the lot. How is it that nobody saw him?"

"Somebody saw him," said Sinclair confidently. "Someone had to see him. They just haven't put it together yet, or they haven't seen the news yet. Once they hear that a bus was used in the bombing, it'll click."

The final interview was with the pastor of the church, Reverend Warren Unger. He was clearly shaken and disturbed by the bombing. His skin was pale, his eyes red and raw, and his voice raspy. Dinah wondered if he shouldn't be at the hospital himself.

"I was leading the music," he told them. "I play the guitar. It was just another Sunday, everything was going so well."

His lower lip quivered and it took a moment for him to compose himself. "Right in the middle of the third song," he continued, "I looked up for a moment. Something caught my eye, I think, and I saw a fireball tear through the wall. I heard a loud, roaring noise; so loud I couldn't hear anything else for a while. All the lights went out and in the dark I saw the wall collapsing, and people being hurled forward. The noise seemed to go on for ages — when it finally stopped, I could hear people coughing and moaning and crying. Then I just tried to get people out. I thought the building might collapse, I don't know why."

"Do you have any idea why someone would want to bomb your church?" Ferguson asked.

"No, I don't. This is crazy! It's like a scene from a war zone," said Unger, shaking his head.

"Have you received any threats or is there anyone you know who wishes you harm?" Ferguson pressed.

"No. We're just a peaceful group of people," said Unger. "We try hard not to be controversial. I just don't know who would want to do such a thing!"

"Any disgruntled congregation members? People you've had to kick out or something like that?"

"Nothing like that for at least a couple of years now," said Unger. "Although there was one person to whom we refused membership."

"Really?" pounced Ferguson. "How long ago was this?"

"Only about two months ago," said Unger, scratching his head thoughtfully. "His name was Andrew Cochrane. He was a young guy, maybe late twenties? He'd been coming regularly for six months, claimed to be a new convert to Christianity."

"But?" prompted Ferguson.

"My gut instinct told me there wasn't something right about him," said Unger. "I thought I might be reacting a little harshly, so I gave him the benefit of the doubt. The problem was, he didn't follow any of the rules."

"What do you mean by that?"

"He struck up a friendship with a young couple, just newly married. Several months later, he tried to entice the woman to have an affair with him. He also treated the children in the church badly, losing his temper with them and calling them names if they got on his nerves. We think he was the source of gossip between several families, causing a rift between them. In short, he was a troublemaker. When the young lady told me he'd suggested an illicit affair, I interviewed him about it and explained the Christian standards of our church. I gave him the opportunity to confess and repent, but he refused. He thought that he'd done nothing wrong, so I told him he was no longer welcome and asked him to leave."

"How did he take it?"

"Not well. He lost his temper, shouted at me, and called me all kinds of names," said Unger, shuddering at the memory. "Luckily I'd arranged for several of the elders to be there and together we managed to remove him."

"Did he threaten violence toward you or the church?" asked Ferguson.

"Not explicitly, as I recall," said Unger. "But I might have missed it. The whole scene was quite an ordeal."

"Did you obtain contact numbers or an address from him while he was with your church?" Ferguson asked intently.

"Yes, thankfully in my work laptop, which is at home," said Unger. "I can send them to you."

The three investigators thanked the reverend and moved away to discuss the possibility of Andrew Cochrane being the bomber.

"It doesn't make sense to bomb another church first," admitted Ferguson. "But he's the strongest lead we have so far."

"It won't hurt to pay him a visit," agreed Dinah.

Sinclair grinned. "Bring it on!"

* * * *

As the bomber watched the evening newscasts, a pall of melancholy settled down on him like a fine sheet of silken cobweb. He glared at the television and wondered why. Usually, on the day of the bombing he was elated. At least, he had been last time. Before that feeling could wear off, he'd start looking for a new target, and the anticipation was almost as good as the elation. What was going on?

He paced behind his chair, listening to vapid newscast after newscast. None of them had anything new to report, so they rehashed what they did know in different words and scrambled to find interesting experts to voice their opinions. Nothing they said led him to believe that the police had any idea who was behind the bombings.

So why was he so dissatisfied?

He rehashed the day in his mind. In retrospect, the bus idea hadn't been great. It had been a brilliant scheme when it came to stealing it, but a yellow school bus on a Sunday morning had turned out to be a pretty stupid plan. There were any number of people who might have seen the bus, but none of them could have seen *him*. On the freeway, they might've had a few moments at best. What could they have told the police? A man, wearing a baseball cap? They couldn't have seen his hair color, eye color, or any distinguishing feature from their vantage point.

What about once he'd parked the bus? He'd been so careful. He hadn't seen a soul, but that didn't mean someone hadn't seen him. Some bored soul might have been nosily watching through their windows for gossip. Surely, though, if that was the case, an artist's rendition of him would be plastered across the news. No, he was pretty sure that he hadn't been seen.

Suddenly, it occurred to him. None of the newscasters were *getting it*! Not one of them was asking the question *why*! He stopped pacing and sat down. That was easily fixed, he thought. He could send a message to the television networks so that they understood the reason behind the bombings. Then they'd have something to actually report!

He sat at his computer and began to compose a letter.

It was important to word the letter just right. He deleted the first attempt and pounded his fist on the desk in frustration. It was too vague. It needed to start with a bang, to get their attention. A threat, perhaps? Yes, that was a good idea, a threat.

The second attempt was somewhat better but ran out of steam at the end. He glared at his computer, as if it were its fault that inspiration was lacking.

He realized that he was humming out loud — a Billy Idol song, of course: "Don't You (Forget About Me)." What a perfect way to end his letter!

Instead of singing, *Don't you forget about me, don't, don't, don't, don't, don't you forget about me*, he changed to the words to *Don't you underestimate me, don't, don't, don't, don't, don't you underestimate me.*

This time, he was inspired to go further than simply the chorus. Instead of singing *Would you recognize me? Look my way and never love me/Rain keeps falling, rain keeps falling, down, down, down*, he changed to the words to *You won't recognize me! Look my way and never see me/ Bombs keep falling, bombs keep falling, down, down, down.*

He sat back, grinning to himself. He'd set them a challenge: they would never find out who he was, even if they were looking right at him. He looked so normal.

He reviewed the letter. He'd started with a threat, to get their attention. The middle was concerned with his motivations, most of which he hinted at without being too obvious, and the ending was a taunt, hidden in Idol lyrics. It was perfect. It would make them scramble and think, investigate and worry, and that was precisely the outcome he sought.

Suddenly, he felt elated again. He was glad he'd found a reason for his agitation and a solution to soothe it. He again felt like he was top of the food chain: the craftiest, smartest, most cunning predator of them all.

His thoughts turned to the next target, a bombing due in a week. He had learned from the bus fiasco that he needed to find a new vehicle that would attract less attention. He needed a vehicle that looked like it belonged, in any scenario, under any circumstance, a vehicle that engendered immediate trust, a vehicle that nobody would look at twice.

When the idea struck him, it was immediately brilliant, but this time he thought the plan through from inception to execution. The more he thought about it, the more he became convinced that it really was a perfect plan, far better than his school bus idea.

First, he would hand-deliver his letter.

Then, it was time to hunt, to stalk, to find his prey and destroy them.

* * * *

The air was still and heavy and expectant, waiting for the storm that had been building to break. The clouds that had gathered on the western horizon were purplish and pregnant, the air thick enough to touch. The sun had been blotted out by thunderheads indifferent to its efforts to light the city beneath.

Ferguson, Sinclair, and Dinah sat in an Italian restaurant that catered to the young family crowd, and tried to ignore the gangs of small, rowdy children engaged in the destruction of the immediate area. They had skipped lunch and so decided on an early dinner while they waited for the storm to pass. Dinah marveled as Ferguson wolfed down an impressive plate of pasta, while Sinclair, who apparently ran half-marathons for fun, ate a salad. Dinah had zoned off a little, watching the little kids run around with amusement, thinking of Sammy's delighted roar when other kids and mayhem were concerned.

Finally, Ferguson heaved his body out of the booth and explained that he needed to call home. The atmosphere seemed to electrically charge the moment he left.

"Listen," said Sinclair, when his boss was out of earshot. "I hope I didn't freak you out earlier. I didn't mean to come on so strong."

"Oh," said Dinah with an embarrassed laugh. "Don't worry, it's not you. It really has more to do with me."

"I only want to be your friend," said Sinclair, eyes gleaming like blue steel. "I just approached it the wrong way. If nothing else, I have a profound professional respect for you."

Dinah chewed on her lip and thought about how *she* ought to approach it. "It's a little complicated," she began, "which means, *I'm* a little complicated. It's a long story. I'm not sure you'd be so keen to be friends once you hear it."

"I don't know," mused Sinclair. "I like complicated. It's a challenge."

"That's one way of putting it," laughed Dinah. Her stomach felt strange, light, and fluttery. She wondered if she could further humiliate herself by throwing up.

"All I wanted to suggest," said Sinclair, "was some time away from the job, just to talk. That's all."

Relax, Dinah told herself sternly. *You don't have to treat every situation like it's a crisis. It's just a chance to talk!*

"Okay," she said. "Sure. I'm warning you, though. You probably won't be able to leave fast enough once you've heard my story."

Sinclair's eyes bored into hers and she looked away, flustered. "Stop denigrating yourself," he said. "Everyone has a past, a story."

Just how much do you know? Dinah wondered.

"Anyway," added Sinclair with a playful smile, "I also happen to think you're pretty cute."

Dinah immediately turned as red as a beet, and despite valiant efforts her brain couldn't think of a reply. She had clearly completely lost the ability to converse with the opposite sex about anything other than work. How could he find her interesting when she had nothing to say?

Don't get your hopes up, anyway. Once he finds out that you are a widow, mother to a lost son, disgraced FBI agent, alcoholic, formerly suicidal, and a Christian, he will be so uninterested you may as well be a rock.

Ferguson happened to return at the moment, just as the awkward silence stretched. He glanced between them both and sat down.

"Dessert?" he suggested.

"How can you fit in dessert, after all you've eaten?" said Dinah, relieved to be back in familiar territory.

"Second dessert stomach," he said, waving over the waitress. "It never fails me."

She shook her head and laughed.

The storm broke outside and Dinah watched nature unleash its fury. While Ferguson somehow managed to eat a banana split, she was spellbound by long tongues of flickering lightning, thunder raising its voice in protest, and raindrops assaulting the earth. She'd always loved storms, but now when she watched one she was reminded of the awesome power of God. Storms were untamable, unpredictable, and completely indifferent to the whims of mankind.

Ferguson's phone suddenly burst to life and Dinah was jolted back to reality, only to see Sinclair's eyes twinkling at her. "Welcome back," he teased. "Nice trip?"

She flushed and burned and desperately tried to think of something to say.

If anyone else had said that, I would have had a smart comment snapped back in a nanosecond. What is it about this guy that makes me forget how to talk?

Thankfully, Ferguson started talking. "That was the night editor from the *Post*. Apparently they've received a note from someone claiming to be the bomber."

Dinah was instantly alert. "Is it a fake?"

"He thinks it's real," said Ferguson. "I said we'd drop by and check it out."

They stepped outside tentatively. The thunder and rain had moved on, leaving behind a soft, steady rain that would vanish later in the night. The sun was trying to make a comeback in the early evening, light weakly breaking through the clouds left behind.

Ferguson tossed the keys to Dinah. "Want to drive?"

"You sure you can handle it?" she shot back.

"I figure we'll get there quicker if you drive," he said. He patted his stomach. "I want to have a little nap."

To Sinclair he said, "She's a maniac behind the wheel, but she's fast."

"I'll make sure my seatbelt is tight," laughed Sinclair.

Behind the wheel of the dark FBI car, rain hissing beneath the tires, to Dinah it almost felt like old times again.

The offices of the *Washington Post* reminded Dinah a little of a casino: with no windows and plenty of feverish activity, there seemed to be little regard for the time of day or night. However, the newspaper was fond of clocks and several large ones dominated the floor, constantly reminding the harried reporters below of deadlines.

Night had finally claimed the city as the three investigators were met at the door by the night editor, Ralph Haywood. He was short and bulky with thick black hair. Beetling eyebrows made him appear menacing, and he spoke in short, sharp sentences, as though he were a walking newspaper article. "Hand-delivered at about six," he told them, leading the way to his office. "Didn't read it until about seven. Got my attention then."

The office resembled the aftermath of a tornado. Dinah could barely make out the chairs in which visitors would sit amidst piles of paper, newspaper copy, and assorted junk. "Sorry about the mess," Haywood said, pushing aside some litter to reveal two swivel chairs. "It's how I work."

"Right," said Ferguson, exchanging an eye roll with Sinclair. "You got the note there?"

"I touched it," said Haywood, handing over a folder. "Before I knew what it was."

"Okay," said Ferguson. He opened the folder and the three of them hunched over it. Ferguson and Dinah had taken the chairs and Sinclair stood behind them. Dinah was patently aware of the close proximity of Sinclair's head as he leaned over to read the note. It was typed on a computer and the writer was fond of italics and capital letters. It read:

Dear Media,

You should *listen* to me. I am the church bomber. I am responsible for bombing the Catholic Church and the Methodist Church. If you don't take me seriously, I *will* take out other civilian targets. If you don't report the existence of this letter by Wednesday at the latest, I *will* bomb an elementary school. You don't want to test me.

YOU PEOPLE ARE NOT GETTING IT! You haven't asked why I'm doing this. Don't you think it would make a good story? Let me give you a hint. I don't like *hypocrites* and *thieves*. I don't like people who *always let others down*. They spend their time JUDGING others but they should be JUDGED more harshly than anyone!

Don't you underestimate me,
Don't, don't, don't, don't,
Don't you underestimate me
You won't recognize me!
Look my way and never see me
Bombs keep falling, bombs keep falling,
Down, down, down.

Sinclair whistled softly. Ferguson frowned and Dinah pursed her lips. There was nothing in the letter that hadn't been reported by the media outlets, but it seemed to ring true nevertheless. In any case, thought Dinah, it wasn't worth risking an elementary school just to engage in a game of pride. However, the Bureau might feel differently and there wasn't much she could do about that.

"We'll need to take this with us," said Ferguson.

Haywood shrugged. "Am I reporting it?"

"We'll let you know," Ferguson said. "Stay near your phone."

The three had barely left the office before Haywood began yelling at someone on the phone.

They found a Starbucks nearby and sat down in the brightly lit store. There was silence as they took turns reading the letter again and again.

"So do you think it's real?" Ferguson asked at length.

"I'm inclined to think so," said Dinah. "But it's only a hunch."

Sinclair nodded. "I can't see anything that makes me doubt the letter. Equally, there is nothing in the letter that some random person couldn't have picked up from the media coverage."

Ferguson sighed. "I tend to agree." He stirred his coffee for a few moments. "The Bureau has a policy of refusing to negotiate with terrorists."

Dinah's heart sank. "You won't agree to report the letter?"

"I didn't say that," said Ferguson with a wink. "I think I can find a way around both the bomber's demands and the Bureau's requirements."

"How is that?"

"The bomber didn't ask for the letter to be reprinted," said Ferguson. "Only that its existence be reported. I think we could get away with a small article under the guise of asking for public help."

Dinah was relieved. "I definitely think you could get away with that."

"What are your thoughts on the person who wrote it?" Ferguson asked.

Dinah nodded. "My first thought is that there aren't any spelling or grammatical errors," she said, trying to organize her ideas. "This would indicate to me that the writer is reasonably well educated, even perhaps with a college degree. I sense the feeling that he thinks he's on a mission — the tone of the letter is fervent and passionate. He cares about wanting the public to know why he's bombing churches. Whatever hatred or anger he feels toward the church is very deep and very strong."

"What do you make of the lyrics?" Sinclair asked.

"Do you know whose lyrics they are?" Dinah asked. They were vaguely familiar to her, but the tampering with the words meant she couldn't quite figure it out.

"I think it's a Billy Idol song," said Sinclair. "You know?" He suddenly began to sing the song: "*Doooon't you forget about meeeee, don't, don't, don't. . . .*"

"That's enough," said Ferguson, clapping his hands over his ears. "Please make him shut up!"

"Well, I'm offended," said Sinclair. "I happen to think I have a good singing voice."

"You'd be the only one," grumbled Ferguson. "Don't ever do that again."

Dinah couldn't suppress her laughter anymore and was almost bent double with glee.

"Et tu, Brute?" said Sinclair, pretending to take a knife from his back. That caused all three investigators to completely lose it and all that could be heard throughout the Starbucks were peals of laughter.

* * * *

Scott had made it home in time for dinner but had taken his plate to the study to eat there. Isabelle sat by herself at the dining room table wondering why she expected anything different. She watched an episode of *American Idol* without really seeing it. Instead, she was lost in her thoughts.

She knew better than to confront Scott about his withdrawal from her. That would only serve to upset him even further. She needed to find a way to placate him. The tense atmosphere of their home was too much for her; she knew that it barely affected Scott.

The truth was, she couldn't muster up the courage to go to his study. Ultimately, she knew that he was likely to tell her to get out or some other equally nasty scene. At the moment, she just couldn't face the coldness in his eyes or the contempt in his voice.

She had gone up the main bedroom when she heard Scott's study door open and his footsteps on the stairs. Her heart quickened as she scrubbed her face.

What's wrong? she wanted to ask. *What is troubling you?*

Fearing the inevitable cutting reply, she kept her mouth shut.

In fact, Scott didn't speak until Isabelle changed into her pajama top. Without thinking, she allowed the cuts on her arms to become visible, if only for a few seconds. "What is that?" he demanded, and Isabelle's heart turned to dead-weight ice in her chest.

"What's what?" she asked lightly. *Please don't have seen my arms.*

Roughly, Scott yanked up the sleeve of her top. He'd never asked why she wore long-sleeved pajamas or shirts even in the unbearable heat of this summer.

He could now plainly see the scars of old cuts and the pink edges of recent cuts that were healing. He stared at them for several seconds, and Isabelle felt every single internal organ turn icy cold.

"What is this?" he asked, gritting out the words from between clenched teeth.

"Nothing, just an accident," she said, trying to cover up.

"Did you do this to yourself?" The anger in his eyes dared her to lie.

"Yes, but it's nothing!" Isabelle was full of sick dread, and fear thrummed through her.

"Nothing!" shouted Scott. "What is wrong with you? Why are you doing this?"

Isabelle didn't know how to reply and Scott took a step closer. "Tell me why you're doing this," he said, each word dripping with a threat.

"It makes me feel better," she said lamely.

Scott shook his head in disgust. "Why do you need to feel better? What is so wrong with your life?"

Again, she was lost for words.

"Tell me what's wrong with your life!" shouted Scott, veins standing out starkly in his neck.

"Nothing, it has nothing to do with you," Isabelle said.

"Don't I provide everything for you?" Scott continued, apparently not hearing her. "You don't have to go to that pathetic job at the university. You want for nothing! I never question you about your shoe collection or what you spend *my* money on. All I ask for in return is a *normal* wife!"

Isabelle felt tears threatening but she suppressed them viciously. Tears only angered Scott further.

"I am normal," she gasped. "I am."

"No normal person I know attacks themselves with a knife," snapped Scott. "Are you trying to completely humiliate me?"

Isabelle didn't know what he meant but she couldn't meet his eyes.

"Remember the charity ball?" Scott said. "The two-hundred-bucks a plate charity ball? The one in a week?"

Suddenly, she remembered.

"So you're planning to turn up to the ball with all your scars on display, are you? Everyone will be talking about you, pitying you and worse, pitying me! But I suppose that's exactly what you want, isn't it?"

"I can use makeup," she protested. "No one will know, I swear!"

Please stop, please stop, you're hurting my heart, you're crushing my soul.

"I had no idea what a useless freak you really are," Scott said, his voice quiet again. "Who cuts themselves, causes themselves *pain*, to feel better, for pity's sake?"

"You don't understand," said Isabelle. "Please, I don't know what else to do."

"Here's a thought," said Scott, voice like acid. "Try acting like a normal person." He shook his head in disgust. "So you got attention? That's what you really want, isn't it? You want me to notice and worry about you and take care of you?"

Shame was like a torrent of water, pouring over her until she was completely drenched in it.

"Well, it's not going to work," he continued coldly. "You're an adult, you can sort this stuff out yourself. I'm not going to tiptoe around your precious mental status, hoping that everything is okay."

Scott suddenly took her wrist and squeezed.

"You listen to me carefully," he breathed. "If I see one more cut on your arm, I'm going to kick your butt to the curb, you understand? I'm sick of this drama and I'm not going to put up with it. One more cut, you're out. Get it?"

And all Isabelle could think, dripping with humiliation, was: *He didn't say anything about my legs! It'll be okay, I can still cut my legs!*

Scott stormed downstairs and Isabelle was left alone, her body filled with stress. If ever there was a time she wanted to release the pain inside her, it was now. She wondered if she dared to do it. Scott's threats were never empty — if he said that he'd kick her out, he meant exactly that. She just couldn't take the risk of Scott finding her, doing it now.

She had to make do with digging her fingernails into her own skin, into her hairline, as hard as she could. The pain wasn't enough, not as good as the sweet song of the razor blade, but oh, it still reminded her she was alive.

* * * *

The bomber, at peace with himself again, used a stolen Toyota to scout for a new church. It was important that he never be seen in the same vehicle twice, in case he was identified. Every time he left the house, he stole a different car and dumped it after he'd finished with it.

The heat hung in the air, almost visible, and the humidity climbed with each passing hour. Soon, in the old Toyota with no air conditioning, he was sweaty, hot, and miserable. He wouldn't let it deter him, though; he had an important task to do.

He had in his mind what he wanted to find, but it was proving difficult in reality. He realized his mistake halfway through the morning, as the relentless sun climbed toward its zenith. He needed to look in more affluent suburbs for the type of church he wanted. The poorer suburbs wouldn't have been able to afford to build such a structure.

He turned the car around and headed south, toward Kalorama Heights and Columbia Heights. He needed a wealthy parish, one that would have spared no penny in building their church.

He found it off Wyoming Ave. NW, and when he laid his eyes upon it, he knew that it was the one. An Episcopalian church, it was actually a cathedral. It was Gothic in design, intricately carved with stone, and magnificent as it rose into the sky. The small surrounding gardens were immaculately tended. There was no parking lot, but a strip mall next door provided parking spaces right up to the side wall of the church.

He drove around the site several times, trying to judge it from every angle. He could park the bomb reasonably close to the side wall. The stone structure would be reasonably strong, and certainly as well built as any 19th-century building, but it would not withstand the power of a fertilizer bomb. He envisaged the wall missing, a great smoking wound right in the heart of the church.

This time, he had a daring plan. He was becoming more comfortable in his role as the bomber, and this time he intended to pretend to be a parishioner. He understood the power of the bomb, and he knew how to protect himself from it. This time he wanted to experience his own bombing.

It was risky, it was audacious, it was crazy. Nobody would suspect someone who went to the church as the bomber. He would be a victim, along with everyone else.

He couldn't keep the smile from his face. Sometimes his own genius surprised even himself.

He cruised around the quiet suburb until he found a shopping mall, where he ditched the old Toyota. Then he started looking for a new vehicle, the one in which he would build his bomb.

It wouldn't be as obvious as a school bus this time. It wouldn't be a white van either. He had to pass himself off as a family man, a quiet church man who worked hard at his job during the week and spent time with his family on weekends. He needed a big SUV.

He trotted around the parking lot of the mall for seemingly endless hours, growing hotter and sweatier by the moment. Then he spotted it, a lovely deep-red Ford Expedition, with plenty of room. He knew that it could seat up to eight people, but what he wanted to do was make sure that it could transport a four-hundred-pound bomb.

The bomber had to wait for a mother nearby to load the groceries into her car, which seemed to take an age. At one point, he wanted to help her if only to hurry her up, but it would mean that she would remember him. Finally, when she'd driven off and the parking lot was empty again, he set about stealing the Expedition.

It was a lovely ride, he thought. It was big and sturdy, perfect for his purposes. As he drove it home, he knew that he'd made the right choice.

Once at home, he drove the car into the garage and found the newspaper. He wanted to know whether his letter would appear in the paper and whether, therefore, he would be required to scout for an elementary school. He fervently hoped he wouldn't have to — he didn't want to target children.

The authorities, thankfully, had acquiesced and allowed the paper to run a story. It was front-page news, actually, which made the bomber very proud. He read it several times.

The story didn't print the contents of the letter but did mention that the bomber had called his targets hypocrites and thieves. It was a good start. Most people would get the implication: that he believed churches to be sycophants, drawing congregations and their money in with promises of inclusion and redemption.

People would probably also get that he was angry — very, very angry — with churches and that the hatred he felt in his heart toward them was deep and ingrained.

Carefully placing the newspaper on the coffee table, he turned his thoughts to the bomb that would mortally wound the grand cathedral. It was time to gather his supplies and to turn his attention to creating that which destroyed.

* * * *

As the three investigators finished their lunch, Ferguson took a call from the Manassas Police Department. They'd found something interesting near the church bombing site and they thought the FBI might be interested.

Ferguson, Sinclair, and Dinah climbed into the unmarked car and drove back to Manassas. Now that the initial flurry of activity had died down, the church cast a mournful figure. Crime scene tape fluttered around the building, cutting it off from the rest of the world, and it looked lonely as it gamely stood, even gravely injured. Dinah could almost feel its silent suffering.

Robert Dawes, the chief of the Manassas Police Department, met them at the site. "We made a few discoveries," he told them, his face very serious. "I wanted to walk you through them, one by one, and then have you draw your own conclusions."

"Right," said Ferguson. "Lead the way."

"Keeping in mind the location of the church," began Dawes, walking down the street. "I'll first take you to a small café, about a block away. It is here that a café worker remembers serving coffee to a man in overalls on Sunday morning, just before the blast."

It was a quick trip, only about five minutes' walk away from the church. The sidewalk café was small and busy. Dawes waved over a young man in a long black apron, who was balancing several coffee cups in one hand. "This is Vincent," said Dawes. "He was working here on the day of the bombing. Vincent, meet Special Agents Ferguson, Sinclair, and Harris of the FBI."

Dinah thought about correcting the notion that she was an FBI agent but decided it wasn't worth getting into.

Vincent set down the cups and smiled. "Hi."

"What can you tell us about the day of the bombing?" asked Sinclair.

"I was working here, doing the morning shift," explained Vincent. "It was a pretty busy day. Lots of people like to have brunch here on a Sunday morning."

He glanced at his audience before continuing.

"I remember this one guy, for some reason. He was wearing work overalls, like he was a mechanic or something. Most of the people who come here on a Sunday are in casual clothes, know what I mean? It stood out."

"That's an odd detail to remember," commented Sinclair.

Vincent shrugged. "I'm a painter and a sculptor. I notice things. When I saw him, I had an idea for a painting of a working man surrounded by richer folks, laughing, living it up."

"What did this guy do exactly?" asked Sinclair. Dinah pursed her lips. If she'd been questioning him, she might have tried to put the young man more at ease, express a little interest in his art.

"He came only a few minutes before the blast," said Vincent. "I took his order, he sat at a table, and I had barely gotten it to him when we heard the explosion. There was a rumble, like there was electricity in the ground, and then we all saw the smoke in the air."

"Do you remember his reaction to the blast?"

"Not really," said Vincent. "It wasn't out of the ordinary. We were all shocked. Most of our customers left; I guess they thought there could be another explosion. My boss wasn't too keen to hang around either, so we locked up the café and went home."

"The guy in overalls disappeared with everyone else?"

"I guess so. I didn't see exactly where he went, but he didn't drink his coffee and I didn't see him again."

"What did he look like?"

"He was kind of tall, like about six foot?" Vincent chewed on his lip as he tried to recall. "I couldn't see his hair, he was wearing a baseball cap. I think maybe dark eyes. He was pretty ordinary looking."

"Any distinguishing features, tattoos, an accent?" Sinclair asked.

Vincent shook his head. "No, definitely not."

"Thanks, Vincent," said Dawes, shaking the young man's hand. "You've been very helpful."

He turned to the three investigators. "Now, I'll show you why the overalls and baseball cap are important."

He led them to an alley behind the café where Vincent worked. Dawes pointed at a commercial-sized Dumpster. "That's where we found the discarded clothing."

In plastic evidence bags, Ferguson, Sinclair, and Dinah could see a set of beige work overalls and a baseball cap. Both looked reasonably new and unused.

"So what's your theory?" Ferguson asked Dawes.

"We know that the bomber remotely detonated the bomb," explained Dawes. "I believe he walked to this café, which is not too far away but certainly well out of harm's way, ordered his coffee, and detonated the blast. Amid the confusion, he dumped his overalls here and left, thinking that nobody would remember him."

"Why would he wear overalls and a cap?" Sinclair asked.

"Because he was driving a school bus," chimed in Dinah, glancing at Dawes. He nodded at her. "He was driving an obvious vehicle on a day you usually don't see school buses. If he is wearing mechanic's overalls and he's noticed or stopped, he can explain that he's fixing the bus and making sure it runs well."

"He stands out in overalls in this neighborhood," added Dawes. "This is a family suburb, where most folks have the weekend off and either go to church or relax. He was in working clothes, a bit of an oddity, and it just happens that the young man serving him coffee has an eye for detail."

"I guess if we find bomb detritus on the clothing, your theory will stack up," admitted Sinclair.

"There's one more thing," said Dawes. "We received a phone call from a woman who saw a school bus driving toward Manassas on the morning of the blast. I just can't think of any other reason a school bus might have been out that day except for the bomber, so I took her call seriously. She said that the driver was wearing a baseball cap, but that's all she could see. She was going toward D.C. at speed, so there wasn't a lot of time to catch a good look at him."

"I knew somebody had to see that stupid bus," said Dinah. "There must be others."

"Anyway, her brief description fits the cap we found here in this Dumpster," continued Dawes.

"You and your guys have done a great job," said Ferguson. "Thanks for the hard work you've done."

Dawes shrugged. "Glad to do it. Nobody comes here, kills my folks, and takes out a church without me being all over it. I kind of take it personally."

Ferguson smiled. "We'll take the clothes down to our lab and we'll let you know, okay? We'll also send some lab people up here to search the Dumpster. Could you tape it off so that there's no contamination in the meantime?"

"Sure thing. I'd appreciate that," said Dawes. "When you catch him, I'd like to take a few minutes with him. Let him know about my displeasure."

"I think we all would," said Ferguson. "Thanks again, sir."

As the three investigators approached their car, Dinah asked, "What's next, boss?"

"Time to pay a visit to a certain man who was kicked out of this church," said Ferguson, sliding behind the wheel. "Let's see what he has to say for himself."

Pieces of Light

* * * *

Sussex 1 State Prison
Waverly, Virginia
Prisoner Number: 10734
Death Row

Dinah is always on time. I like that. I've always valued punctuality.

Even the freedom of punctuality has been taken away from me. I have lost the ability to decide when I'll do anything. I eat when they say I should, sleep when they say I should, and exercise when they let me out of my cage.

Even when I greet my visitors, I am dependent on guards to ensure I'm on time. You think the guards care about my love of punctuality? They do not.

Slowly, I am memorizing every detail of Dinah Harris: the sweep of her black hair, the crinkle of warmth at her eyes, the precise way she has of speaking, and the crackling luminescence of her mind.

Today, she asks about the second bombing.

"Why did you decide to use a school bus?" she wants to know.

I shake my head regretfully. "It was a tactical error," I admit. "It seemed like a smart idea when I stole it, but I didn't think about how obvious I would be driving around on a Sunday morning. I realized too late that people had noticed me."

"Was the bomb you built similar to the first one?"

"Exactly the same," I say. "I didn't want to deviate from my comfort zone too much."

"You know that one person died in that bombing," says Dinah. "Two more were hurt badly and will suffer their injuries for the rest of their lives. Did you think about those people when you detonated the bomb?"

I can only be honest: I did not think of this. Will she ever understand that my pain is so great, so encompassing that I cannot see other's suffering? It is strangling me, like a great python; consuming me, like a flesh-eating disease; suffocating me, like a dark, airless room where even tiny pieces of light cannot penetrate.

I say nothing and the silence stretches.

"Why did you choose the United Methodist Church?" Dinah asks finally.

"It was really more about the style of building than the people in it," I insist. "I didn't care what denomination it was."

"Why didn't you choose a Jewish synagogue or Muslim mosque?" Dinah presses. "Is it the Christian faith you hate?"

To be honest, it didn't occur to me to choose a synagogue or mosque, I think to myself.

"I have experience with the Christian faith," I say carefully. "I suppose that's why I chose Christian churches. I've never stepped foot into a synagogue or mosque."

"What was your experience with the Christian faith?" Dinah continues.

I don't really want to talk about that just yet, but I owe her some kind of explanation. "Well, it's simple really," I say. "I hate it."

"Why is that?"

"It is hypocritical and judgmental."

"Of you, specifically?"

"Yes."

"Do you want to talk about why?"

"Maybe. Not yet."

"Do you subscribe to any faith now?" Dinah changes the angle of the subject.

I shrug. "I guess I believe that we all determine our own fate. I've heard that some people think God is a giant puppet master, that we have no control of our own destiny."

"Is that what you believe?"

"I don't believe in the supernatural," I say. "I believe what I can see, hear, touch, and taste."

"If you're the master of your own destiny," says Dinah carefully, "you must have intended to end up on death row."

"Subconsciously, I must have," I concede. "I chose to engage in an activity with severe consequences."

"Is this how you envisaged your life?"

Oh, how laughable. Does anyone envisage that they'll live in a cage awaiting execution like a condemned turkey at Thanksgiving? Yet I could never imagine normal life, of a wife and kids and white picket fence. It was as if I knew that such simple pleasures would be denied, and that I would live on the outside, watching those on the inside enjoy what I could not have.

"No," I say.

"Did you think you could continue to bomb the churches and never receive punishment for it then?"

I consider this. Had I planned to continue bombing churches for the rest of my life? Probably not. That sounds exhausting.

"I don't think so," I admit.

"Then, if you don't mind me saying," says Dinah, her stare forthright and disconcerting, "if you are in control of your own destiny, yet you end up living your days in a way that you didn't intend, you're not doing a great job, are you?"

Stupid logic. "No," I agree.

"So we're back to my original question," says Dinah. "Why?"

I think I know why, but I'm not telling just yet. It's painful. It takes time to gather up the courage to talk about that.

So, Dinah Harris with your clear eyes and logical mind, you'll just have to wait.

ONE YEAR EARLIER

Andrew Cochrane, the man who'd been refused membership at the Manassas United Methodist Church for his indiscretions, now lived in a loft in Adams Morgan, a suburb of D.C. that had become more gentrified by day but was still a little scary at night. It was late afternoon when the three investigators arrived at his address, and it appeared that he'd just gotten home from work.

He opened the door with a beer in his hand and a scowl on his face. "What?" he said rudely.

"Special Agents Ferguson and Sinclair, FBI," said the boss brusquely. "Special consultant Harris. Got a minute to talk?"

Cochrane was in his late thirties, with sandy, tufty hair, blue eyes that were aggressive and bloodshot, and a big attitude problem. He glared at them. "What about?"

"We'll tell you, if you'll let us in," said Ferguson.

Cochrane sighed loudly. "Fine, come in."

His loft was a typical bachelor pad — sparsely furnished with only the necessities. He took an armchair, which left only one other chair

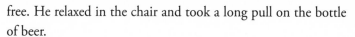

free. He relaxed in the chair and took a long pull on the bottle of beer.

Ferguson, Sinclair, and Dinah all chose to continue standing. Perhaps they could intimidate some respect into the man, thought Dinah.

"We want to talk to you about a bombing," said Sinclair. "The bombing of the First United Methodist Church of Manassas."

Cochrane stared at them. "What? I hadn't heard about that."

"The bomb was set on Sunday morning, during their services," continued Sinclair. He started to pace around the room, turning to look at Cochrane occasionally. "One person died. Two people were critically injured. Do you know anything about that?"

"No," said Cochrane. "I don't." He stared at Sinclair belligerently.

"Really? Are you upset to learn of the casualties? Does it bother you to know that one of the church walls was destroyed?"

"Well, it's not my church, so not really," said Cochrane.

Dinah raised her eyebrows at Ferguson.

"Didn't you try to make it your church?"

Cochrane drank some beer and shrugged. "Don't know what you're talking about."

"Apparently, you tried to join the church and they refused membership to you," said Sinclair patiently. "Remember?"

Cochrane narrowed his eyes. "Oh yeah. My misguided attempt to find religion."

"Why were you refused membership?"

"They were uptight," said Cochrane dismissively.

"Because you tried to seduce a married woman? Or because you were abusive to the children in the church?"

Cochrane snorted. "Whatever. They were just uptight. I was glad to leave."

"So you feel a bit of anger toward the church, since they were so uptight?"

"I don't feel anything," said Cochrane. "They don't rate a mention in my thoughts."

"Really? The rejection didn't get to you?"

"It wasn't *rejection*," snarled Cochrane. "I didn't want to join that stupid church."

"Did you visit any other churches during this period of time?" asked Sinclair. "Any other denominations, for example?"

"Nope. I only tried one."

"Don't suppose you've got any fertilizer lying around?" Sinclair threw a new angle in.

"Fertilizer? Obviously you've seen my enormous back yard," said Cochrane sarcastically.

"What about the Internet history?" pressed Sinclair. "Would we find instructions about how to build a bomb?"

"No," said Cochrane. "You wouldn't. Go ahead. Have a look." He shook his head and drank some beer.

Dinah was starting to get the feeling that Cochrane wasn't who they were looking for. Despite his other social problems, she doubted that he was smart enough to plan and execute the attacks. In any case, there was no credible reason that Cochrane would also bomb a Catholic church.

"What's with the attitude?" Ferguson demanded.

Dinah knew. She could see the humiliation in the man's eyes — he'd gone to an organization that preached inclusivity and love, and had been rejected. She guessed that Cochrane had been rejected many times before. It had made him angry and isolated, like an injured bear waiting to lash out.

She walked over and crouched down near Cochrane as he finished his beer.

"I get it," she said quietly. "That church had it coming, didn't it? It deserved what it got. You don't care what happens to the people, because they didn't care about you. Am I right?"

"You're right about one thing — I *don't* care about that church or its people," agreed Cochrane. "But I sure didn't blow it up."

Sinclair began drifting around the room, glancing through the meager bookshelf and papers on the cheap desk before moving onto the desktop computer. Surprisingly, Cochrane didn't object. Perhaps it was the glassy-eyed effect of the beer calming him down.

In any case, Dinah didn't think he was the bomber. He might have held a grudge against the United Methodist Church, but there was no connection to the Catholic church, and he showed no anxiety at having the FBI crowded into his loft.

They waited in silence as Sinclair cast a cursory eye over the computer. Finally, he straightened up and shook his head. "Thank you for your cooperation," said Sinclair, pulling his business card from a sleek steel holder in his pocket. "If you can think of anything that might be useful to our investigation, please contact us."

Cochrane barely glanced at the business card as it was handed over, and he tossed it onto the coffee table. "Sure," he said carelessly.

Outside, Dinah asked: "What did you find on his computer?"

"A few disturbing websites that single, lonely men sometimes visit," said Sinclair. "There was nothing at all to do with a bomb. Another dead end, I'm afraid."

The three lapsed into silence as they considered their next avenue of investigation. "Go home and get some sleep," said Ferguson at length. "We'll reconvene tomorrow and see what we've got."

* * * *

Senator David Winters almost leaped from his own skin when he arrived the next morning at his office, expecting silence and solitude, only to find someone standing at the window gazing thoughtfully at the view below. "What are you doing here?" Winters demanded.

The person turned around, and Winters saw that he was only a young kid, tall and gawky in what was probably his first suit, anxiously clutching a briefcase.

"I'm Connor Eastleigh?" he said, his nervousness making everything he said a question. "Your new intern?"

Winters frowned. "Was I supposed to get a new intern?"

"I think so?"

Winters sighed and pinched his nose. He vaguely remembered conducting interviews, which seemed like an age ago. He'd been so caught up in his extracurricular activities that he'd forgotten about the more mundane things, like staffing.

"Well, Caleb," he said. "I. . . ."

"Connor, sir."

"What?"

"My name is Connor. Not Caleb?"

Winters paused, let the kid squirm for a few moments. "Right. Well, *Connor,* welcome to my office. I suppose you are doing some sort of degree in political science?"

"Yes, sir," said Connor eagerly. "And forensic accounting."

This young man would be about as interesting to have around the office as a can of paint, thought Winters. However, on the other hand, it would be handy to have an office lackey whose sole focus was pleasing the boss.

"Are you interested in a career in politics, son?" Winters asked.

"Oh, yes," said Connor. "I hope to be a United States senator myself someday."

"Not the president?" asked Winters with a wry smile.

"Perhaps," said Connor. "One goal at a time, I guess."

"Take a seat," said Winters. "I guess I should tell you about the issues on the table at the moment. How are you at researching case law?"

"I can do anything you ask, sir," said Connor with a slight frown. "But I thought law clerks usually worked with case law."

"First rule of this office," said Winters. "There is no black and white. Everything is gray. So if I need case law researched, then that's what you'll do. Understand?"

"Yes, sir."

"Great. I want you to dig out every constitutional challenge with regard to separation of church and state," said Winters. "I want to know every precedent, every opinion, and every argument."

"Yes, sir," said Connor. "Which side of the argument is your preference?"

Winters looked at the young man shrewdly. Perhaps this wouldn't be so bad, after all. It had been a long time since he'd molded a person into his likeness, influenced his behavior, and crafted him to become just like himself. Sadly, his last protégé had become expendable and Winters had had to arrange for his assassination. Now, perhaps it was time for a challenge again. "Well, Connor," he said, "I happen to be championing a legal challenge to require greater separation of church and state. You know, our great nation was founded on that very principle. You know why?"

Connor wisely shook his head.

"Because when the church and state are linked, religious freedom is compromised, including the freedom to have *no* religion," said Winters, warming up to his subject. "Why should people who don't believe what the Church teaches be forced to live by their rules? Why should Christian-driven legislation be enacted that infringes on people's freedoms if they choose not to believe in Christianity? I believe in a society that is free from religious dogma, where I don't have to hear about religion at all unless I choose to walk into a church."

"Okay," said Connor. "I see."

"Federal courts are our last line of defense to protect our constitutional rights," continued Winters. "That's why I want you to research case law. I am championing a legal challenge at the moment, and I want to know the background of every case before it."

"Is that the government funding religious charities case?" Connor asked. "I saw it on the news."

"Right," said Winters. "I want you to research this topic thoroughly. I want to know what Congress has said about the issue, what judges have said, what presidents have said. I want to know who is with us and who is against us."

Connor nodded, obviously pleased to have an important task to do. Meanwhile, Winters would be free of his young charge.

After Connor had left, Winters rang his secular humanist friend, Cartwright. "How is the media attention for the case going?" Winters wanted to know, without preamble.

"I'm happy to report we now have the support of the two big humanist organizations in America," said Cartwright. "Both the American Humanist Co-operation and the Secular Humanists of America have agreed to support and fund the court case."

Winters heart warmed when he heard the word "fund." "What does their support entail?"

"Both groups have a significant online presence," explained Cartwright. "We can expect them to generate a lot of Internet traffic with regard to the issue. They publish blogs, magazines, and articles relating to the issue all over the web, in addition to the usual Facebook and Twitter pages. They also have a YouTube channel on which they post videos pertaining to humanist issues."

Winters didn't fully understand the power of the Internet, but he was glad the humanist organizations did. "What else?"

"Both have extensive contacts in the traditional media," continued Cartwright. "Press releases will be sent out regularly, and there are many experts and speakers who can be called upon to argue the case on radio or television. They have a very professional, savvy public relations department that has been very successful in saturating the media with the humanist agenda."

"Great," said Winters, actually starting to feel impressed. The professional power of these groups was making his previous association with a eugenics group look like a roomful of preschoolers.

"Finally, they have a network of activists and lobbyists who campaign heavily on Capitol Hill," said Cartwright. "You should look out for them. They have also been successful in educating Congress and the Senate on the humanist viewpoint and strive to ensure they are represented."

"What do you want me to do?" Winters asked.

"Sit tight for the moment," advised Cartwright. "Soon our campaign will be rolled out on a national level, with a coordinated effort between the online world, traditional media, and lobbyists. Elena Kasprowitz will be the face of the campaign, but she'll have the backing of these two powerful humanist groups. Our fight is to win the hearts and minds of Main Street, and there is one message in particular that will do that."

"What's that?"

"Separation of church and state is fundamental in ensuring religious freedom," said Cartwright. "Nothing scares our religious opponents more than the idea that their freedom to go to church and homeschool their kids could be taken away. Our message is that if they oppose separation of church and state, then they are limiting their own freedoms."

"A scare tactic," summarized Winters.

"Whatever works," laughed Cartwright. "I've done it before, in several European countries. It's worked brilliantly. I see no reason why it won't work here. In the meantime, I'll contact you when we need your support in the media."

After Winters had hung up, he reflected on the sleek humanist juggernaut that was about to be unleashed on the American public and smiled to himself. *This* is how you change the world. You manipulate the media, blanket the web, and scare the public into believing your message. Then it is only a matter of time before Congress and the courts cave in to public opinion.

Then, you elect a president utterly committed to eradicating religion. *Like me.*

* * * *

The elementary school from which the yellow bus had been stolen had contacted authorities, Dinah learned. It was an inner-city school and they thought the bus had been stolen just as the afternoon run had begun.

The principal of the school was an African American woman in her early forties with an aura of stern authority named Anna Spoker.

She let the three investigators into her office, a space adorned with school achievements. For a poor, inner-city school, it had certainly accomplished a great deal.

Spoker watched Dinah glance around at the walls and said, "I require a great deal from my students. They may come from poverty, abuse, addiction, and neglect, but I insist that they rise above it."

"It's very impressive," Dinah said. "Do you have problems with gangs here?"

"Yes, big problems," admitted Spoker. "That's why I've set up programs before and after school, trying to keep my students so busy they'll have no time for gangs. It's a constant battle."

She leaned back in her chair thoughtfully. "It's been said that a gang offers a person security, a sense of belonging, and a family. When I see where many of my kids come from, I can see why that's appealing to them. So I've tried to replicate the idea of security, belonging, and family in school programs. Our success rate is pretty good, but it could be better."

"What sort of programs do you run?" Dinah asked.

"For example, the gangs will offer kids a chance to earn money by dealing drugs," explained Spoker. "I offer them a chance to earn money doing other things, like washing cars, mowing yards, helping elderly folks. I spend a lot of time asking for donations to fund such a program, but it does work. Or if kids are passionate about theater or dance or singing, we encourage them to explore that and look for opportunities for them to perform."

"You're doing an awesome job," said Dinah. "I only wish all of our schools were so committed to the welfare of our kids."

Spoker smiled briefly. "I have motivation: my 14-year-old son was lured into a gang and shot dead during a drug deal. No parent should have to experience that."

Dinah nodded, knowing only too well the sharp and exquisite pain of losing a child. "I'm very sorry," she said.

"Anyway," said Spoker briskly. "Enough about me. You're here to find out about the stolen bus?"

"Yes," said Sinclair. "Can you tell us when you realized it was missing?"

"It didn't take long," said Spoker. "The drivers arrive about half an hour before the afternoon run commences. When the kids are let out, the buses are ready and waiting to take them home. We realized we were one bus down when we still had kids waiting, a bus driver, and no bus to take them."

"Did anyone see the bus being stolen?" Sinclair asked.

Spoker shook her head. "No. Unfortunately, nobody looked twice at a school bus being driven away from a school right around the time the afternoon run starts. We have 15 or so. The drivers themselves don't really take notice of each other, either."

"What run would that bus usually have taken?" Dinah asked.

"Northeastern suburbs," said Spoker. "I think I know why that particular bus was stolen, though. It's pretty simple."

"Yeah?" Sinclair said.

"It was the last bus in the row," explained Spoker. "They're lined up in the parking lot like a row of soldiers. Whoever stole it took the one closest to the gate."

"Ah," said Sinclair, glancing at Ferguson. "That does make sense."

She shrugged. "I see a lot of criminal activity around here, Special Agent. Over the years I've grown to understand a little about how criminals think. If *I* wanted to steal a bus, that's what I'd do."

"Do you have surveillance cameras around the lot where the bus was stolen?"

"No."

"Anyone call the school or district about a bus that was out of place, or in an area it shouldn't have been?"

"Not that I know about."

"Anyone report a bus being seen on a weekend?"

"I don't think so."

There was silence as the investigators realized there was very little information that could help identify the person who'd stolen the bus.

Spoker realized this too and sighed. "Sorry I can't be more helpful," she said. "It's such a chaotic time of the afternoon, and my main concern is that my kids don't get run down in the traffic."

"That's okay," said Dinah, smiling at the other woman. "You've been very helpful. Thanks for your time today. I wish you luck with your programs here, by the way."

"Thank you," said Spoker, standing up to show them out of her office. "I wish you luck in finding the guy who stole the bus. I guess since there are three FBI agents standing in my office, it's not just about the bus, is it?"

Sinclair smiled and Dinah had to look away as her heart fluttered at the sight. "I'm not at liberty to say, ma'am," he said. "I think if you watch the newscasts tonight, it'll become pretty clear."

Outside in the relentless heat Ferguson said, "All we've got on the guy in the bus is an eyewitness, who happened to be traveling at the speed limit in the opposite direction. Is our guy a ghost or something?"

"No, he's just an average guy," said Dinah. "A very average-looking guy at whom you wouldn't look twice. I'm willing to predict that he would have come to the school dressed similarly to the other bus drivers. He plans methodically. We just have to be patient and smart."

"I'm glad you mentioned smart," said Sinclair, with a wink at Dinah that made her stomach dive and roll. "That's where I come in."

Ferguson rolled his eyes and groaned. "Why did I think having two smart alecks on my team would be a good idea?"

The three investigators made their way in the car back to the FBI lab, where Zach waited with the preliminary findings from the Manassas church bombing. The pirate paraphernalia was gone, but Zach had coordinated his facial piercings to be twinkling green jewels, which almost matched the color of two of his mohawks.

"Greetings, defenders and protectors of the free world!" he said brightly.

"And you wonder why you can't get a girlfriend," muttered Ferguson, while Dinah stifled her laughter.

Zach pretended to be insulted. "The only reason I don't have a girlfriend is because of all the hours I'm putting in trying to catch your bomber."

"Okay, calm down," said Ferguson. "What have you got for us?"

"Well, your guy is putting together a few distinguishing trademarks," said Zach. "Apart from choosing churches to detonate his bombs, of course." On his computer screen, he showed a three-dimensional figure of both the van used in the Catholic church bombing and the school bus used in the Manassas church bombing.

"We can see a pattern emerging," explained Zach. "We've had two small bombs, both built within the heavy plastic bags in which agricultural fertilizer is sold — or at least similar to those types of plastic bags. I have estimated that he would use about eight 50-pound bags and he lines them up in two rows of four, very symmetrically."

"How did you ascertain that?" Ferguson asked doubtfully.

"We can tell by the blast pattern within the vehicles," said Zach. "We can see where the individual charges were detonated. There is plenty more room in both vehicles, by the way, to stuff more explosives. He could have put in twice as much."

He paused as the three investigators nodded.

"He has used exactly the same type and brand of fertilizer," continued Zach. "The dynamite and blasting caps were also exactly the same, including their age. I mentioned last time that these were not brand new."

"Therefore, probably stolen from a stockpile, like a mine," added Sinclair.

"Right. Now we know that an individual cannot purchase large quantities of this type of fertilizer without a license," said Zach. "You have to prove that you are a farmer, for example. I checked as many databases and search engines as I could to find out if there have been any large scale thefts of fertilizer of this type, but to no avail."

"You think he faked a license?" Ferguson asked.

"That's one possibility," conceded Zach. "But one that's fraught with risk. My guess is that he probably bought the fertilizer in small quantities, from many different suppliers, over a period of time."

"Wait a minute," frowned Dinah. "Aren't 50-pound bags pretty large?"

"Well, to you and me, perhaps," agreed Zach. "But when you need them for their proper purpose — farming or horticulture — a 50-pound bag is nothing. I'm talking about orders of a thousand pounds at a time."

"You believe he's been planning this for a while?" Sinclair asked, eying the technician quizzically.

"I do," replied Zach. "Here's why. Although instructions on how to build an ANFO bomb are readily available on the Internet, you still need to have some idea about explosives to detonate them. The mixture of ammonium nitrate and fuel oil, for example, must be mixed in the correct ratios or else the bomb will fail. Too much ammonium and there is a deficiency in oxygen, resulting in a bomb that is inefficient. Too much fuel oil and the bomb will probably fail to explode at all. You need a lot of practice or a good teacher. This guy *could* have spent a year in the wilderness somewhere experimenting with the bomb until it was just right."

"Or . . . ?" Dinah prompted.

"He was taught by someone."

"We strongly believe our guy is working alone," said Sinclair.

"Agreed. His teacher doesn't have to be of the illegal variety though, does he?"

"Just get on with it, will you?" said Ferguson, exasperated.

"Anyone who works in a mine or quarry might have gained an expert knowledge, for example. Or someone in infrastructure, who has to blast a tunnel underground or through a mountain in order to build a road or railway line."

Dinah thought about that. "If that's true, he could have stolen *everything* from his place of work — the ammonium nitrate, fuel oil, dynamite and blasting caps — little by little, over time."

"And his boss wouldn't have known," added Zach. "But that's just a theory. I have no way of proving that yet. It's just something to keep in mind."

"Okay," said Sinclair. "Any fingerprints, hair, DNA that doesn't belong?"

"No," said Zach. "It takes a lot of tedious work to come up with that disappointing answer, by the way. There was plenty of DNA and hair from our victims, from people who go to the church and from people who work at the church. None of it was flagged."

"What about the bus?"

"We looked carefully at the instruments our guy *had* to touch — the steering wheel, the dashboard, the pedals, and so on. We found nothing. He would have been wearing gloves and shoes. If, on the slim chance he left a hair or fragments from his shirt, there is every chance it vanished in the explosion." Zach shrugged. "Sorry I don't have better news."

Dinah wasn't surprised. Nor was she discouraged. The bomber had already shown that he was capable of making errors and of being seen by witnesses. It was only a matter of time.

While Ferguson visited the men's room, Sinclair and Dinah waited in the foyer of the lab. Sinclair tilted his head toward Dinah and asked, "How about that drink sometime?"

"Shall we make it coffee?" Dinah suggested.

"Sure. When?" Sinclair asked.

Oh, I have such a busy social calendar. I'll have to check for openings.

"After work sometime," said Dinah, after a brief pause. "If we get the chance."

"I look forward to it," said Sinclair, his lips close to her ear.

Dinah's whole face turned hot and red, and her ear burned where his breath had touched her.

How she would actually carry on a conversation with him, she did not know.

Late afternoon turned to early evening and the sun hid behind a bank of thunderheads. Isabelle waited on the back deck, wondering if Scott would come home tonight. He seldom bothered to tell her.

Isabelle thought of her childhood years, when she and her family had waited for her father to come home. The underlying fear was always whether he'd be in a good mood or a bad mood. If it happened to be a bad mood, things usually went downhill from there.

Generally though, her father had simply been an unpleasant man at home, and became worse when he'd been drinking.

She recalled her first piano recital. She had been desperate for her father to recognize her, to praise her, to even acknowledge her. She'd chosen her outfit several weeks beforehand. She had played well and had earned several accolades. At the end of the recital, when she joined her parents, she had turned her glowing face up to look at him, urgently seeking his approval.

"Glad that's over," he'd muttered. "Nearly fell asleep."

He hadn't needed to say anything else: Isabelle had been crushed. Although her mother had fussed over her and complimented her, nothing could have made up for the devastation she'd felt at the hands of her father's cruel remark.

She remembered dreading the weekends. On Friday and Saturday nights, her father would watch sports — it didn't matter what — and steadily drink bottles of Coors. The more he drank, the colder and quieter the house became as his wife and children realized what this meant. It didn't matter that Rosa put the kids to bed earlier than usual. Isabelle would lie awake listening to the TV being switched off after the game.

He would start on Rosa, picking a fight, finding fault with something. It didn't matter how she reacted, whether with tears, silence, or assertiveness, it always ended with a sharp slap or dull thud and a muffled cry of pain. Rosa could escape with no more than a backhand across the face if he hadn't had too much to drink. When he was very drunk, though, she would usually cop a vicious punch to the small of her back or stomach. Many times, she would sport a black eye or swollen lip for the rest of the weekend.

Then the heavy footsteps would sound up the stairs and Isabelle would start sweating, knowing that he hadn't yet finished for the night. He would choose between her or Michael, depending on who he imagined had been naughtier. He knew they were both awake, waiting. Isabelle would curl herself into a ball as small as possible, wondering how she would ever escape him.

"This hurts me more than it hurts you," he always began regretfully, "but you need to learn your lesson." Isabelle and Michael never knew what the lesson was, or what they had done wrong. She just remembered the leather belt descending on her legs and back with ruthless efficiency. Crying or yelling always resulted in a longer thrashing, so she learned to keep silent, bite back the pain, and hold back the tears until he had gone.

Isabelle remembered the guilty relief she felt when she heard her brother's door open. After it was over, Michael would sneak across the hall and crawl into bed with her. He would lie shaking next to her, his small body shuddering with sobs until he fell asleep.

There were times when the children would make legitimate mistakes and their father would fly into a temper. In many ways, this was more frightening that the weekend thrashings because he was so volatile when enraged that they could never be sure he wouldn't go too far. Once when Michael had spilled a full carton of milk, his father had thrown him clear across the room and broken Michael's collarbone. When he had caught Isabelle in a white lie, he had dragged her by the hair and she had ended up with a bald patch where he had torn her hair out.

Yet in public, at church, at work, and with friends, Reginald was the most charming, thoughtful, and attentive man. He treated Rosa with tenderness and respect. He pretended to be great friends with Michael and Isabelle. There was nothing he wouldn't do for someone in need. He volunteered hundreds of hours a year at church, helping to run services or maintain the grounds and building.

Isabelle knew that most people had no idea what went on behind their closed doors. With the hindsight of an adult, a nagging question played at the back of her mind: did they *really* not know? Could they *really* not see Rosa's black eye or bruised face? Did they *really* not notice that his children flinched every time he made a sudden movement?

With a start, Isabelle realized that she hadn't fixed dinner, and that if Scott *did* come home, he would be very upset with her.

She made Spanish chicken paella, a rice dish with chicken pieces and broth, peppers, onions, garlic, tomatoes, and plenty of spice. Once again, she ate sitting alone at the dining room table, listening for the sound of a car in the driveway.

Then she cleaned up the kitchen, just in case Scott caught sight of the mess. As each hour passed, her agitation grew. Her skin seemed too small for her, like she was a fat sausage about to burst out of its casing. Her blood was too hot. Her head pounded with the pressure. Her fingers itched with the desire to release her fear and disquiet.

Yet what would happen if Scott came home and found her in the bathtub with a razor blade? Even if he didn't see the cut, he'd know by the pink-tinged water what she'd done. She knew he'd make good on his promise to kick her out of the house. His wrath would be terrible to endure.

What about a shower? her treacherous mind suggested. *The evidence is washed right away.*

Her need to unfetter herself of tension outweighed her fear of her husband. Isabelle found herself in a hot shower, making cuts high on the front of her thigh. Again, the relief was almost instantaneous. Then, knowing Scott could get home at any moment sent adrenaline flowing through her veins.

She didn't start to relax until the plasters had been applied across her thigh and she was dressed in pajamas, ready for bed.

Several hours later, when she went to bed, she wondered why she'd been so fearful of Scott finding her out. In fact, the following morning, when pale sunshine revealed that Scott hadn't slept in his bed at all, she wondered how she could continue living this existence, this twin rollercoaster of fear and release, for any longer at all.

* * * *

Safely ensconced in his workshop with the stolen SUV, the bomber began assembling his new bomb. The beauty of building a bomb in a soft casing, such as plastic bags, was that he didn't need to worry about stripping the inside of the vehicle. He could just place the bags wherever he pleased.

He ensured that although the workshop doors were closed, the windows of the building and of the car were all open as far as possible. Even so, the fumes were harsh and he had to stop periodically to poke his head out of the window and breathe some fresh air.

It was during one of these breaks that he stuck his head out and immediately caught sight of his neighbor, Randy, skulking down the back fence. Randy saw him and lifted his hand in a wave.

The bomber cursed, knowing he couldn't let the other man inside the workshop. He left behind his work and shut the workshop door firmly.

"Yo, Randy," he called, trying to hide the nervous shake in his voice. "What's up?"

"Hey, dude," Randy replied languidly. "Not much. You?"

"Same." The bomber hoped the other man would leave.

"You been in your workshop?" Randy asked.

"Yeah, just messing around, you know."

"You got a car in there?" Randy's eyes lit up. "I love workin' on cars. I could help you out."

"Uh . . . ." The bomber tried to think quickly. Randy could have seen the SUV arrive, and a lie would make him even more curious. "There was; I just finished it. Sorry, dude."

"Oh," said Randy, looking disappointed. "You want to hang out?"

Don't you have a job? the bomber wondered, and then thought that people could well say the same thing about him.

"Maybe later," he said. "I've got some errands to run. Gotta clean up my workshop."

Randy nodded and looked around. "Well. Okay. See you later?"

"Okay, Randy."

The bomber went back inside his workshop and spent several minutes watching Randy from his window. His neighbor took his time going back inside his own house, and this made the bomber frown. What was Randy up to?

The bomber wondered if he would have the nerve to kill Randy, if it came to that. His neighbor seemed harmless but was too curious for his own good. If it meant preserving his own freedom, then it was something he would have to consider.

The bomber checked the windows more often than he'd planned, hoping Randy wouldn't come back. As a result, it took longer to complete the bomb, which put him in a bad mood. He had his days scheduled to precision and he hated it when those plans went awry, for whatever reason.

As his dark mood descended, Randy was apportioned a great deal of the blame for the upset in his schedule. He decided that it wouldn't be a problem to take Randy out, particularly if he appeared at the front door right now. The bomber almost willed his half-witted neighbor to ring the doorbell. Killing Randy would probably make him feel much better. The doorbell remained silent and so the bomber turned to the task of writing his second letter to the newspaper. This time he wanted to make it more purposeful, to deliver a more precise message.

It took several attempts to get the wording just right, but eventually he was satisfied with the result. Leaning back on his chair, he opened a bottle of soda water to celebrate.

Soon he would sit in a church, waiting for the inevitable explosion. The thought of infiltrating the parishioners was exhilarating. Imagine that: the *actual* bomber, sitting in their midst. Perhaps afterward he could give interviews to the media or to the police. The thought made his scalp prickle with excitement. He might even, for the sheer thrill of it, sustain a minor injury. It would be so authentic that the police wouldn't for a minute suspect him.

He envisioned himself as an angel of justice, wielding a great and angry sword, dispensing punishment on those who deserved it. Who was more deserving than those who privately imbibed and publicly denounced? Who warranted destruction more than those who refused to practice compassion? Who could invite wrath more than those who spoke shiny words with hearts as black as tar?

He dozed in his chair. The image of a Gothic cathedral bearing fire and destruction became a dream, where he saw the congregation fleeing in terror. He saw people willing to set foot in a church dwindle, because of fear. He saw entire denominations collapsing under the weight of his judgment.

He dreamed of flames and heat, of wrath and justice, of revenge and cruelty, of a present-day Sodom and Gomorrah.

* * * *

Dinah met the two FBI agents at a Starbucks the next morning, a place that had become their regular haunt to debrief about the bombing case. Ferguson seized the opportunity to have a second breakfast, usually choosing a hot, buttery croissant to have with his grande latte.

Today they were joined by Zach, the lab technician who wore more bling than a rapper. Faux diamonds winked from his ears, fingers, and eyebrow. While they waited for their drinks to arrive, he absentmindedly rubbed his mohawks.

"I'm thinking of getting rid of them," he confided.

"In favor of what?" Dinah asked.

"I want to shave designs into my head," explained Zach.

Seeing he was completely serious, Dinah asked, "What kind of designs?"

"Constellations."

Dinah exchanged a look with Sinclair, who was trying to hide his laughter.

"Of the stars?"

"Yeah. Why not? Wouldn't it be cool to have the Big Dipper in my hair?"

"Very few people would get it," warned Dinah.

Zach shrugged as Ferguson arrived with the coffees balanced precariously in his arms.

"Zach wants to get the Big Dipper shaved into his head," announced Dinah.

Ferguson stared at the young lab technician. "Of course you do," he muttered. "Now, can we get down to business?"

"Sure," said Zach, pulling out a thin file. "You wanted me to analyze the clothing found near the two crime scenes. First, the high-visibility work clothing found in the trash at a mall; second, overalls and a baseball cap found in a Dumpster behind a cafe."

"Great," said Ferguson around a mouthful of croissant. "What did you find?"

"I have good news and bad news," explained Zach. "The good news is that whoever was wearing these clothes is our bomber. The bad news is that I have no idea of the identity of that person. Both the high-visibility clothing and the overalls contained particles of ammonium nitrate and some evidence of fuel oil, both of which match exactly the evidence taken from the bombsite. There were no hair strands, skin fragments, or fingerprints left in any of the clothing, however."

"So our bomber is risking being seen," mused Sinclair. "He's gone to a public place after placing each bomb, to detonate the charge and possibly to obtain some voyeuristic pleasure out of seeing people's reactions to the blast."

"In his favor, he looks very average and could be almost anybody," added Dinah. "It could also be a disguise. If he has distinctive red hair, for example, he might always wear a brown wig so that nobody notices this characteristic about him."

"True," agreed Zach. "It *is* odd to get no hair strands from a baseball cap. Most people shed their hair all over the place and don't realize it."

"What about the ammonium nitrate and fuel oil?" Ferguson asked. "Can we trace that to a particular source?"

"I think so. I mentioned to you that both the ammonium nitrate and fuel oil aren't brand new, which leads me to suspect they've been stockpiled. It's much easier to trace new orders for ammonium nitrate in particular, because we keep close tabs on who is obtaining it and why."

"The Oklahoma City bombing was in 1995, and the laws surrounding obtaining fertilizer were tightened up as a result," said Dinah. "Surely our guy can't have been stockpiling since before then. That was an awfully long time ago."

"I wouldn't think he's been stockpiling since before 1995," agreed Zach. "I would say only that he has a source for the stuff, and he's been quietly taking small amounts that may not be noticed over a period of time. He'd probably be aware that moving large quantities of fertilizer is going to arouse suspicion."

"So we should look for thefts?" Ferguson asked.

Zach was silent for a moment. "Maybe. It'll be a large net, though. I mean, I can't tell you whether the fertilizer came from a farmer, a plant nursery, the city's Parks Department, or a mine. I don't know whether it came from Virginia or California. I don't know whether the theft would even have been noticed or missed."

"We're fast running out of leads," said Ferguson with a sigh. "I think we have to chase down every possibility."

He turned to Dinah with an imploring smile. "If I give you my remote codes for the FBI computer systems . . .," he began.

"You want me to do your boring, monotonous work, don't you?" Dinah said, pretending to be insulted.

"Well, it's just that Sinclair and I have to go to a department meeting," Ferguson said. "And you can work at home without any interruptions."

"Okay, okay," she said. "Stop begging. You're embarrassing yourself."

Sinclair snorted.

"Good to see you haven't lost your attitude," commented Ferguson, with a quick glare in Sinclair's direction.

"Of course not. It's one of the things you like most about me," rejoined Dinah.

Ferguson rolled his eyes and heaved his girth out of the booth. Zach joined him, and while Sinclair and Dinah had a moment together, Sinclair leaned across the table.

"Do you want to meet up this weekend?" he suggested in a low voice.

Dinah's heart galloped. "Okay. Sure, okay. Can we get a coffee, rather than a drink?"

He nodded and smiled. Dinah felt like a piece of petrified wood.

"I'll call you later," Sinclair said, getting up to leave. "I'm looking forward to it!"

Dinah swallowed. "Me too," she said, which came out as a croaking whisper that he probably didn't hear.

Now that she had committed herself to a course of action, the anxiety kicked in. A thousand thoughts fought for traction in her head. *What if he doesn't like me and we still have to work together? What if he is disgusted by my past? How could he possibly want to get involved with someone with so many issues?*

She slapped the table and sighed. She would just have to concentrate on work for the day, and then worry about the date afterward. She was imagining the worst; what if it turned out to be an amazing date? What if they discovered they liked each other?

Dinah thought about this as she headed home. The truth was that she just couldn't see how a man would want to get involved with a woman as messed up as she. Once Sinclair realized it, she knew he would run screaming in the other direction, hoping to get away from her as quickly as possible.

* * * *

In the quiet of her apartment, with only the television providing some background noise, Dinah used the codes Ferguson gave her to access the vast computer networks of the FBI. She had never lost her proficiency at using them, and so she set to work immediately.

First, she did some general industry research. She wanted to know who would use ammonium nitrate in the highest concentrations. She quickly discovered that it was used in agriculture and mining almost exclusively.

The next question was, from where did the agricultural and mining industries obtain their ammonium nitrate? Farmers bought it from rural supply stores in large quantities, for which they had to have a license. Mining companies bought it directly from the manufacturers and also were required to have a license.

Many of the manufacturers were overseas companies subject to strict customs controls. It would be very hard, thought Dinah, to bypass customs for anyone who wanted to import a large quantity into the United States without a license. That would be at the top of their terrorism watch list.

It was more probable that the bomber had stolen the materials from a continental supplier or consumer.

Dinah checked the database for reports of the thefts of combustible materials. Just as she had expected, there were no reports of large quantities of ammonium nitrate being stolen from anywhere in the country.

As for fuel oil, there were no legal requirements to report large purchases. Dinah's only recourse was to search for thefts of a decent supply, and she found nothing. She couldn't even see a relevant case for siphoning, which might indicate someone stockpiling the fuel. With a sigh, she pushed her chair back from her desk and glanced up at the television.

An ad caught her eye. It was obviously brand new — she didn't recall having seen it before. The screen filled with an artist's rendition of God in the sky, with a long beard, surrounded by fire. An outstretched hand and pointing finger rained down fire upon a village of people, from which ran tiny figures, on fire and in agony. Thunderous music accompanied the scene. Words scrolled across the screen: "I punish children for the sins of their parents to third and fourth generations: Exodus 20:5."

The scene changed to a modern-day humanitarian effort, of choppers dropping food, wells being dug in poor villages, Western doctors treating the afflicted, children receiving gifts. The words across the screen now read: "Ensure that the child is protected against all . . . punishment on the basis of status, activities, opinions, or beliefs: Convention on the Rights of the Child."

The screen faded to black, and then white words appeared in stark relief on the screen. Accompanied by a rich baritone, it said: "What would you prefer your tax dollars supported: judgment or freedom?" A website then appeared, with an appeal to donate or volunteer.

Dinah stared hard at the television, unable to believe her eyes. Of course she had come across opposition to Christianity before, but not on a scale so organized and widespread. There had to be a reason behind it. She began to type in the website name on her computer when the doorbell rang. A courier waited outside with a thick envelope.

Curiously, Dinah signed for it and took it back inside her apartment. She checked the return address and saw that it was from the office of Senator David Winters. He just happened to be her nemesis, a psychopath who took delight in arranging the murders of those who got in the way of his ambition. During her last case, he had sent her a bottle of vodka, knowing that she struggled with alcoholism.

With caution, almost expecting it to be a letter bomb, Dinah opened the envelope to see a thick stack of paper. With a frown, she quickly looked through it.

It appeared to be a lawsuit, duly filed in the Federal court. It was entitled *Kasprowitz v. United States*. Although Dinah had trained as a lawyer, the prospect of looking through the thick stack of paper to find out what the lawsuit was about was unappealing. Senator Winters had not made any notes anywhere on the document, and so Dinah carefully put it back into the envelope. It could wait for another day, when she didn't have a bomber threatening churches all over D.C.

She was suddenly struck by another thought. What if the bomber had stolen the ammonium nitrate and fuel oil mixture *after* it had been mixed? She had already discovered that many mines bought the dry mixture pre-mixed, and only had to attach their primary explosives. It streamlined the whole process, allowing mines to more efficiently blast through rock.

Her database search yielded a frightening amount of pre-made ANFO slurry being stolen from mines all across the United States. Despite high security, mines regularly reported the disappearance of bags of pre-made ammonium nitrate and fuel oil.

Dinah shook her head in wonder. She couldn't help but feel a thrill of excitement. Her gut instinct told her that she was on the right path. Pre-mixed ammonium nitrate and fuel oil came in heavy, industrial-grade plastic bags, just like the ones found at both crime scenes.

Quickly, she sent a text message to Sinclair, knowing that he'd be in the department meeting by now, telling him of her theory.

She waited impatiently for a return text, getting up for a glass of water and pacing around the room, her thoughts spinning in her head.

Finally, her phone beeped and she read Sinclair's message. "Gr8 theory. Check mines closest to D.C. first."

Dinah couldn't help but pump her fist in the air. She was on the trail of the murderous bomber, and she was closing in. *I'm coming for you,* she told the bomber silently. *I'm coming for you and I'm going to get you.*

It was a beautiful Sunday morning, although the temperature was tipped to soar above one hundred degrees again. Already the heat shimmered above the blacktop as the bomber drove the SUV laden with the bomb carefully through the strip mall parking lot.

The Gothic Episcopalian cathedral had been built on a beautiful lot, with green lawns and shady trees. During tough economic times, the parish had sold the spare land next to the church and it had become a boutique strip mall, with a gourmet deli, beauty salon, café, and bookstore. It was in the parking lot of the mall that the bomber intended to set the bomb.

The mall had been set back from the road, with plenty of landscaping to impress the well-to-do suburbanites. It meant that the parking lot abutted the church, which was built forward on its lot.

The bomber parked the SUV at the farthest end of the lot, backing in so that the payload was closest to the church wall.

He climbed out of the vehicle, looking around to see whether anyone had noticed him. There were few people around this early in the morning; the church congregation wouldn't begin arriving for another half-hour.

Chapter 10

To make it look like he had legitimate business in the mall, and to kill time, the bomber browsed through the bookstore, which also sold gifts and home wares. Once he'd had his fill, he ordered a coffee at the cafe and sat at a table that offered him a partial view of the cathedral.

The reverend had arrived, together with volunteers who obviously helped to open up the church and prepare for services. Slowly, the church began to spring to life.

He sipped his coffee as the parishioners slowly began to appear, like ants coming home to the nest. Ten minutes before the service was scheduled to begin, the bomber stood and casually made his way over to the church.

He was dressed smartly, in the style of an upper-middle class churchgoer, and he was greeted with a smile at the front doors of the church.

"Welcome to our service," a middle-aged woman said through a practiced grin. She gave him several pieces of paper at which he barely looked. He was too busy scanning the seating, to make sure he would sit as far away from the doomed wall as possible.

Inside the church, the air was slightly cooler and still. Overhead fans heroically tried to create a breeze. Hushed chatter created a low buzz in the cavernous space.

The bomber found a seat on the opposite side of the church, and he made sure he was well away from the windows. In this cathedral, the windows were high and narrow, in intricate stained glass. Because the glass was probably as old as the church and therefore weak, he was expecting all the windows to shatter, not just the ones in the wall destined for destruction. He wanted to ensure he was well away from the spray of glass when that happened.

A man in the pew in front of him annoyingly tried to strike up a conversation with him. He was too tense and edgy to carry on a meaningful discussion, and his one-word replies eventually encouraged the man to give up.

The service began. The bomber heard nothing of it, but he could see there were plenty of latecomers. He decided to wait them out.

His original plan had been to detonate the bomb early in the service. Now he decided he would sit through most of it to ensure the majority of the congregation was there.

While he waited, he looked around at the faces of the parishioners, listening with rapt attention to the reverend. He felt no pity for them, only resentment.

They were wealthy. He could see by the diamonds sparkling on fingers, the expensive leather shoes, and the exclusive handbags. Theirs were comfortable lives, filled with charity balls, lunches with friends, summer houses near the ocean, European cars.

Angrily, he wondered if any of them had set foot in a soup kitchen or domestic violence shelter. If they thought about the poor and downtrodden at all, they had probably given money to them instead, not wanting to dirty their hands. Did they realize that across the city, people were living in desperate circumstances, not sure how they would feed their children or keep them warm in the coming winter snows?

They were all the same, thought the bomber, trying to control his rage. They were supposed to love and take care of the poor and less fortunate. They were hypocritical and judgmental, probably blaming the poverty-stricken for their own problems. They sat in their beautiful church, with their expensive clothes and perfumes and accessories, thinking only about how they would spend their pile of disposable income.

Oh, he'd enjoy detonating this bomb. He would watch their terrified faces, smug prosperity wiped off in an instant, replaced with panic and fear. He would enjoy this day of judgment, when he would punish them for their sins of hypocrisy and ignorance. He would rain down upon them fire and brimstone, fury and penalty, fright and wrath. He would enjoy every moment of it. They deserved it. They had ignored him when he needed them. And now they would pay.

Pieces of Light

* * * *

Elena Kasprowitz and Senator Winters had decided to kick off their campaign in Washington, D.C., on the streets in front of the Federal Court. The first wave of the advertisements had hit the airwaves three nights ago, and had generated a great deal of attention.

Winters surveyed the crowd in front of them and was pleased to see several representatives from the news media in attendance.

The American Humanist Association had handed out banners and signs to the crowds, which were now being unfurled.

He nodded at Elena to begin proceedings. She took the microphone and called: "Attention those of you who seek honesty and transparency in our government!"

There was a loud cheer and the crowd focused its attention on Elena, who wore black pants, a white silk blouse, and pearls. She looked beautiful and powerful, and that was enough to control the rally.

"Today we rally against *our* tax dollars being used to fund organizations with whom we fundamentally disagree! Shouldn't I have a say in how my tax dollars are being used?"

"Church and state — sep-ar-ate!" chanted the crowd.

"The church seeks to conceal its influence over the government. They try to hide the pressure they place on our lawmakers! We are here today to tell our government that we do not accept this!"

"Church and state — sep-ar-ate!" cried the crowd, waving their signs and banners furiously.

"We require truth from our government! We require them to uphold the sacred tenets of our Constitution! We demand that they bring to light all agreements with religious organizations that use taxpayer funding!"

"Church and state — sep-ar-ate!" they yelled.

"Do *we* as a humanist organization rely on government funding? Do *we* require handouts? No! We raise our own funds and our own support! We *demand* that religious groups are required to do the same!"

"Church and state — sep-ar-ate!" The crowd was delirious.

"Our great nation was founded on the principle that church and state should be completely separated. Yet we have Christian groups in the pockets of our government, obtaining funding to proselytize! They seek new converts using *our* money!"

"Church and state — sep-a-rate!" screamed the crowd.

"Today, we say enough is enough! We will seek all avenues to remedy this situation. We will file lawsuits, we will demonstrate, we will picket, and we will use the power of our votes, to ensure that our government is called to account for its actions!"

Having whipped the crowd into a frenzy, Elena handed the microphone to Winters and stepped back.

"I want to implore you, my good friends," he began, his tone rich and mellifluous. "We cannot do this on our own. Even I, in a position of responsibility and power, cannot do it on my own. We ask you for your support, but also for your advocacy. Spread our message to your families, friends, work colleagues, and churches. Yes, I did say churches. It's important that you know that even churches recognize the need for separation of church and state. It is a rogue few who refuse to respect our Constitution! The more support we can get, the louder our voice will be. Cast your votes wisely during elections! Refuse to elect anybody with loyalty to these religious groups. Let your Congressman know that you and your electorate won't stand for such subterfuge. Speak the truth loudly and often!"

"Church and state — sep-a-rate!" agreed the crowd.

Elena took the microphone back and cried: "Let us march to Capitol Hill, where they must take us seriously!" With a roar, the crowd began to inch down the street, spurred on by enthusiasts positioned in the throng by the American Humanists Association.

Elena turned the microphone off and rolled her neck backward with a sigh. "Are you coming with us?" she asked.

Winters rolled his eyes. "Are you kidding me? I'm a United States senator," he said contemptuously. "I don't march for anyone."

"Oh. Right." Elena looked awkward, not sure what to say.

"I'll do some media spots," he said, so that she felt he was still on her side.

In truth, Winters couldn't wait to get away from the throng. As a rule, he avoided the unwashed masses wherever possible.

A zealous reporter materialized in front of him and shoved a recorder in his face. Winters was tempted to break the man's arm.

"Senator, can we get a few words on today's rally?"

Winters held the reporter's gaze for a few moments, an icy look that conveyed his disapproval of the man, his family, his profession, and his life. When the reporter dropped his eyes, Winters said, "Certainly. I'm happy to lend my support to this cause. I am a wholehearted believer in the Constitution and the freedoms it affords our citizens. One such freedom is religion — in this case, the lack of religion. We guarantee the same freedoms to people who choose *no* religion. That is why it's a requirement of our First Amendment that church and state be separated. It's something that is not being observed as it should be."

"You agree that it's not acceptable for governments to fund religious organizations?" the reporter asked.

That's what I just said, moron. "Right. I have no problem with citizens who support such organizations to use their private funds to bankroll their programs. Public money categorically should *not* be used."

"Do you. . . ."

Winters was thoroughly sick of the reporter. "I have finished commenting," he snapped, and walked away.

When the reporter tried to follow, two large men in suits and earpieces stood in his way.

The rally continued to snake through the streets, toward the bright dome of Capitol Hill.

* * * *

The service in the Gothic cathedral had almost reached its zenith, as bright as the noonday sun. The bomber chose a moment during the penultimate hymn, as voices soared toward the ceiling, to detonate the bomb.

He pressed the button and it seemed to take an age. In reality, it was only a moment.

With senses hyper-alert, he felt it before he saw it or heard it. A giant wall of hot air lifted him and then let him fall. As he was slammed down on the floor on his back, he saw the wall blow. It was an awe-inspiring sight.

A great battering ram of fire forced itself through the stone, obliterating the blocks in its way. Other blocks, broken but not crumbled, were flung like pieces of Lego into the church. The sound came a nanosecond afterward, an earth-shattering sonic boom. The glass windows imploded with a high-pitched shriek, as if in agony themselves.

The bomber, still dazed, watched people catapulting into the air. He saw fire licking at pews and hymnals and limbs. He heard screaming, moaning, and wails of sheer terror.

Seconds later, the debris began to fall — chunks of glass, blocks of stone, materials from inside the walls and roof. Some of the wooden pews near the blasted wall had been splintered into long, sharp fingers.

The explosion had finished, and in its place, an acrid smell hung in the air, as heavy as the smoke that obscured his vision. Despite light spilling into the building through the devastated wall, it seemed murky and dark due to the ammonia and smoke. There were sounds of the injured, groans and cries of pain. And somehow, surrounding these noises like a heavy cloak, shocked silence reigned.

The bomber eased himself into a sitting position, acknowledging that despite his attempt to escape the bomb, he still managed to hurt all over.

He suspected he'd have a very large bruise on his back, where he'd slammed into the floor. His head hurt, his throat burned, and his eyes watered. His head pounded viciously and he could feel sticky wetness on his face.

Gingerly, he stood and surveyed the damage. He'd gotten off lightly, compared to some of the poor souls he now saw. He didn't feel remorse or sorrow at their plight; only the satisfaction of a job well done.

He managed to get himself outside, grateful for the fresh air. Outside, traffic had some to an abrupt halt. People had climbed out of their cars, some still in the middle of their 911 calls on their cell phones. Others were gamely approaching the church to render assistance to the stunned survivors.

After what seemed like an eternity, ambulances arrived en masse, screeching to a halt outside the cathedral, paramedics spilling out with stretchers and equipment bags. One paramedic approached him. "Are you injured?" she asked.

"No," he said. "There are worse inside. Don't worry about me."

"Sit down and take deep breaths," she advised him. "Don't move. I'll be back to assess you for shock."

The bomber saw that those who hadn't been badly injured were sitting on the ground in disbelief or wandering aimlessly. Adopting their shambling walk, the bomber wanted to see how much damage had been done to the wall.

The entire wall was missing, and part of the roof that it had supported had collapsed. The bomb had performed admirably.

Police cars were now arriving in waves of flashing lights, which sent a rush of adrenaline through the bomber's body. Did he look guilty? Would they know?

It became obvious that they didn't have any idea about him. They spread out like a swarm of blue ants, some checking through the rubble and assisting with rescues, others talking to the survivors.

In fact, the bomber had to admit that the paramedics and police were well-organized and efficient. Though, he supposed, they were getting used to it.

The police were instructing survivors to stay, so that they could take statements and so that the paramedics could assess them. The bomber knew it would be suspicious of him to attempt to get away, so he found a clear patch of grass and sat down.

Eventually a paramedic found him and began cleaning up a wound he'd sustained near his hairline. While she did that, a police officer decided to take his statement.

The bomber was proud of himself for holding it all together. He described his arrival at the church a few minutes before the service started, how it all went very smoothly until the second to last hymn. He described the explosion, how he saw it from the opposite side of the church. No, he had no idea who would want to do this. No, he hadn't noticed anything strange or anyone loitering around the building.

The cop nodded and moved on, while the paramedic suggested he go to the hospital for observation.

"No," he said. "I just need to go home and have a good sleep."

After being cautioned on the dangers of concussion and symptoms to watch out for, he was allowed to leave.

He drank in the scene one last time, savoring it and memorizing it for posterity.

Still elated from his success, the bomber walked several blocks, then stole an old Ford Escort to drive home. He knew the newspaper would receive his note that evening and print it the following morning. In the meantime, he would watch every newscast with voyeuristic pleasure.

* * * *

Dinah Harris had taken special care with her outfit and makeup that morning. She wore a dark blue beaded top with cream-colored pants and kitten heels. For work, she normally pulled her black hair into a ponytail, but today she let it flow loosely around her shoulders. She'd inexpertly applied mascara and lip gloss and tried valiantly in church to listen to the sermon with a strange queasy feeling in her stomach.

All because she'd arranged to meet Sinclair for a date after church at her favorite cafe. The queasy feeling got stronger the closer she got to the date.

He was waiting for her, at a table that overlooked the street. She smiled at him and approached, struck again by how good-looking he was. His blue eyes were electric, she thought, like bolts of lightning somehow contained.

He stood to greet her and leaned over to kiss her cheek. "You look lovely," he said. "You look much younger with your hair down."

"Uh . . . thank you," she managed to reply, through stammering lips.

"Care for some brunch?" he asked. "I haven't eaten yet."

Too nervous for breakfast, neither had she. "Sounds great," she agreed.

"So what have you been doing this morning, on a rare day off?" he asked. She marveled at his ability to ease into conversation.

"Oh, I went to, uh, church," she explained.

He smiled. "I should have gone, too."

"What did you do instead?" she asked.

"Went for a ten-mile run," he said.

The waiter arrived to take their order, but Dinah hadn't even looked at the menu.

"A few more minutes?" she asked. To Sinclair, she said, "Wow, that's impressive. I'm up to about five miles."

"Let's go running sometime," he suggested casually. "I'll run five miles with you."

"I couldn't keep up with you!"

"I'll slow down. We can have a cool drink and lunch afterward."

"Well . . . it'll be a rather leisurely pace for you," conceded Dinah.

"Actually, I don't care about the running. I'll take any excuse to spend time with you." Those blue eyes bored into her own, intense and spectacular.

She turned red and couldn't reply.

"Why is it so nerve-wracking for you to believe I'd want to spend time with you?"

Dinah realized she'd forgotten she was in a conversation with a man trained in the nuances of interrogation: he could tell when she was nervous, anxious, dishonest, fearful, and uncomfortable. Obviously, she wasn't doing a great job of hiding the caldron of emotions bubbling away inside her.

"I don't know," she said, instinctively trying to protect herself. A moment later she admonished herself to be honest. "Well, I suppose . . . I find it hard to believe that you *would* want to spend time with me."

"Why?"

Dinah dared to look at him. "I'm sure you've heard the stories about me. The Bureau is hardly discreet."

"I've heard gossip," admitted Sinclair. "But gossip doesn't matter to me. If there are things you want to tell me, I'll believe you. But I won't buy into water-cooler rumors."

"Right. Well. It's a long story for a first date," Dinah said. "I don't want to bring the mood down."

"I'm just glad you referred to it as a date," said Sinclair, grinning, blue fire in his eyes.

Dinah desperately wanted to hold onto the hope of a first date, before it was ruined by the truth of her life. So she changed the subject.

"Tell me about your family," she suggested.

He spoke of a quiet childhood in a sleepy small town in West Virginia. His mother and father were both hard-working people who hadn't been able to go to college, but fiercely believed their children ought to. Sinclair and his older sister Carmen had been encouraged by their parents to excel in school in order to obtain scholarships to college.

Carmen had won a full scholarship to Amherst College in Massachusetts, an elite college with an outstanding academic record.

She had almost completed an undergraduate degree in science when she'd been killed in a car accident three weeks short of graduation.

Shocked, Dinah said, "Oh, Sinclair, I'm so sorry."

"First," he replied, "call me Aaron. Sinclair is my work name. Second, thank you. It was the worst time for our family. My father particularly had adored Carmen. She had been accepted into medical school — she wanted to work in research, to understand more about how to treat epilepsy and Asperger's syndrome. They were so proud of her."

"So all the pressure fell to you?" Dinah asked softly.

The waiter appeared again, at precisely the wrong moment. Dinah asked him to come back.

"Yes," said Aaron. "I felt I had to honor her memory by achieving everything she no longer could. I did law at George Mason University in Virginia before I joined the FBI. Graduation was difficult — I felt that my parents were wishing Carmen had been able to graduate, too."

"I'm sorry," said Dinah. "I know what it's like to lose someone close to you."

Aaron covered her hand with his. "I know."

She felt a rush as his skin connected with hers. It seemed she could have stayed in that exact position for hours.

The waiter appeared again, now somewhat annoyed.

Aaron took away his hand to point at the menu, and Dinah felt an inexplicable anger at the waiter for ruining her moment. She ordered an omelet, willing the waiter to leave them alone.

"*Do* you know?" she asked, curiously.

"I've heard about it," said Aaron. "I don't know how accurate it is."

"I lost my husband and son in a car accident," Dinah said forthrightly. *Oh, the exquisite pain*, she thought, *it's still there*. "Three years ago. I didn't handle it very well."

"I'm sorry," said Aaron. "Losing a child must be about the worst thing I can imagine."

"It is," agreed Dinah. "I miss him every day. I loved him so much."

She felt the sudden tightening of her throat, signaling tears. Trying to fight it, she looked down at the empty table.

She felt warm pressure on her hand again as Aaron leaned forward. "I'm sorry," he said. "I didn't mean to upset you. I'm so sorry I brought it up."

Dinah took a deep breath. "It's okay," she said. "Really. It's just still, after all this time, so hard to talk about."

"If I didn't think you'd run away from me a thousand miles an hour," said Aaron, "I'd give you a hug."

"One day," whispered Dinah. "I'd like that."

"Someday . . . soon?" Aaron asked, his voice soft.

Dinah smiled in spite of herself. "Someday . . . soon."

Then suddenly, both their cell phones rang. Their eyes met, and they both knew, instinctively, that another church had been bombed.

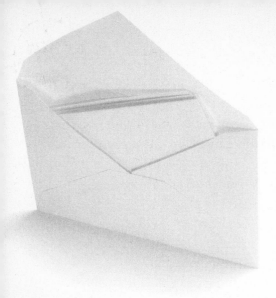

The moment broken, Sinclair and Dinah immediately made their way to the church, using directions given by Ferguson, who was already there. Even a few blocks away from the church, chaos had filled the streets. Police were trying to control traffic around streets that were closed down, while pedestrians who wanted to rubberneck were trying to get past police blocks.

Eventually, they made it to the bombsite, where the vision of the damaged cathedral was tragic. Like the churches before it, it still stood, albeit minus one wall and half of the roof. Dinah could imagine at the head of the great structure, where the spire stood tallest, she could see tears slipping down the stone, tears of pain and sorrow.

Ferguson met them and began talking immediately. "The bomb was blasted from the mall parking lot, right over there," he said, pointing. "It was built in an SUV and detonated toward the end of the service."

"What are the casualties?" Dinah asked.

"Four confirmed dead, another who has been rushed to the hospital but likely won't make it," said Ferguson. "It's the worst so far, probably because the roof collapsed. We haven't seen that happen so far."

Chapter 11

Sinclair wanted to see the vehicle in which the bomb had been built first. The SUV's destruction was almost complete. Around it, four other cars had sustained significant damage as a result.

Wading through the debris, Sinclair picked up a piece of heavy plastic. "Same plastic," he said.

"You know my theory about the plastic bags?" asked Dinah.

"No, what?" Ferguson asked.

"While I was doing your grunt work, I discovered that mines and quarries use ammonium nitrate and fuel oil to blast away rock," she explained. "To save time, they buy the mixture pre-mixed, in heavy plastic bags, called dry slurry. All they have to do is attach the primary explosives, blasting caps, and fuses. Dozens of mines and quarries all over the country have reported thefts of the mixture."

Ferguson raised his eyebrows. "Does that fit the evidence you've seen here, Sinclair?" he asked the bomb expert.

"Absolutely," said Sinclair. "I had thought that our perp had mixed the fuel oil right into the plastic bag of ammonium nitrate. As I've said, to get the mixture exactly right requires specialist knowledge. It is much easier for someone to get the pre-mixed slurry and simply attach explosives. It still takes a rudimentary knowledge to affix the dynamite, fuses, and so on, but anyone could find a website to find out how to do that."

"Can you keep looking at these thefts of the ANFO mixture?" Ferguson asked Dinah.

"Sure," said Dinah. "Here is another theory for you — what if our perp picked up his knowledge of bomb making while working in the mine or quarry?"

Sinclair nodded thoughtfully. "It could well be an inside job," he agreed. "He might have managed to siphon the slurry mixture and dynamite away from the employer over time."

Ferguson nodded. "It's a theory we'll run with," he said. "Let's take a look inside the cathedral."

Inside, the church seemed quiet and solemn, having witnessed a great tragedy. It was immediately apparent why more people had been killed in this attack. When the roof collapsed, tons of heavy stone blocks had fallen with it, from a good height. Those unfortunate enough to be directly underneath would almost certainly have been crushed.

"The bomb didn't look to be any bigger than its predecessors," said Sinclair softly, as if able to read Dinah's mind. "But this building wouldn't be as strong. That's why the roof caved in."

Dinah nodded. The paramedics had finished tending to the wounded, and few victims remained.

"Why do you think he's targeting these churches?" Dinah wondered, as they looked through fallen stone, twisted debris, and shattered pews. "Why did he choose these particular ones?"

Sinclair took some time to consider his answer. "I don't know," he said at length. "I think he's chosen some buildings that wouldn't withstand the blast he'd planned. He hasn't targeted one of those big, brand-new, steel and reinforced concrete buildings."

"Right, that makes sense," agreed Dinah. "But there must be four or five cathedrals similar to this one around the District. Why this particular one?"

"At the moment, all I can theorize is that he chooses them based on the ability to detonate a blast reasonably close to the church," said Sinclair. "The first one, he was able to park on the street; the second, in the church parking lot; this one, the mall parking lot."

The lieutenant of the police who had overseen the disaster response trotted over to the agents. His name was Peyton Spacey, a tall, lean man with a buzz cut and shrewd, dark eyes. "We've taken a lot of statements this morning," he began. "None of it helpful to the investigation, I'm afraid."

Ferguson folded his arms across his paunch. "Nobody saw the bomber or anyone near the SUV?" he guessed.

"Right. All of the statements relate to the bomb exploding," explained Lieutenant Spacey. "You know, I-saw-this and I-heard-that. Very similar to the Catholic church bombing, and from what I understand, the Manassas church bombing."

Ferguson sighed. "Our guy is making mistakes, but not enough to identify who he might be," he vented.

His cell phone chirped, and he turned away to answer.

"My uniformed police will fan out, asking questions," Lieutenant Spacey told Sinclair and Dinah. "We'll let you know if anything comes up."

Ferguson returned, a frown on his face. "That was the editor of the *Post*," he said. "They've just received another letter from the bomber."

Dinah reached out to take the keys from him. "I think you'll want me to drive," she said. "I'll get us there faster."

Ferguson allowed himself a smile. "Alive, too, if it's not too much trouble."

* * * *

Ralph Haywood, night editor of the *Washington Post*, had instructed the staff to call him immediately if they received a note purporting to be from the church bomber. He would normally be asleep at this time of day, he informed the FBI agents and Dinah. That explained his gray pallor and bloodshot eyes. Furthermore, he continued, it was his responsibility to take care of the letters and liaise with law enforcement.

Cynically, Dinah wondered whether Haywood simply wanted the credit for the story. He took them to his mezzanine office and made a show of carefully producing the letter. Again, it was carefully typed on white paper and read:

I am the church bomber. I have just judged and punished a cathedral at Kalorama Heights. Remember, if you do not print this letter, I will bomb innocent children. Their blood will be on your hands.

Note these figures well:

$24,950

$88,400

$55,000

Have they gotten their hands dirty? Do they understand what it's like to be poor, homeless, destitute, afraid? They are concerned with their own comfort, their own happiness, their own prosperity. For this, I make them pay. Vengeance is mine, says the bomber.

If I looked all over the world
These churches are all the same.
Oh, their empty eyes,
They pass the poor by.
I'm left to judge them by myself.
So let's sink another church
Cause it'll give me time to think.
If I had the chance
I'd ask the world to judge,
But I'm judging by myself.

"Correct punctuation, spelling, and grammar," observed Dinah, "although his thoughts seem to be a bit disorganized."

"What do the monetary figures mean?" wondered Ferguson.

"Is he bombing them because he's dissatisfied with their outreach to poor people?" added Sinclair.

"His last note called the church hypocritical and thieving," pointed out Dinah. "Are those lyrics, to end the note, or a poem he's written?"

Sinclair narrowed his eyes as he read them. Finally, he said: "If the bomber is continuing with the Billy Idol theme, these could be lyrics he's changed to suit his own purposes. It sounds like it could be the song 'Dancing with Myself,' only he's changed the words to 'judging by myself' instead."

"Why would he do that?" Dinah wondered.

There was nobody to answer their questions. Only the perp knew, and they didn't yet know who he was.

"Am I to print the letter again?" Haywood wanted to know.

"Yes, but only its existence," said Ferguson. "As we did last time."

"I can see a great editorial about this story," continued Haywood. "Can I ask you some questions?"

Ferguson glared at him. "No, you cannot. We're not talking to the media about this case — particularly since it seems our perp craves attention. Now, how did this letter arrive?"

"It was hand-delivered, by a courier," said Haywood, somewhat deflated.

"Excellent," said Ferguson. "The courier had to pick it up from somewhere. Where is the delivery note?"

Picking up his phone, Haywood ordered a minion to bring the note to his office. The courier company used was a seven-day operation, offering cheap rates and fast delivery.

Sinclair immediately got on the phone to find out the details of the delivery and quiz the driver.

As Sinclair paced around the room, Ferguson asked Haywood, "Have you received any correspondence regarding the first letter? Any strange phone calls?"

Haywood shook his head. "Not specifically. We've received plenty of correspondence about the bombings; people want to know what the police are doing about it and so on. Nothing to do with the letter itself, though."

Dinah continued to study the letter. She was intrigued by the monetary amounts given. Was it simplistic to assume that three bombings equaled the three amounts? It couldn't have to do with the damage inflicted; it would cost vastly more than $24,950 to repair the Catholic church, for a start. Could it have something to do with their charity programs, which the bomber seemed so disgusted with? Was he naming and shaming them with their donations to the poor? Was that why he was so angry with them?

Sinclair hung up his phone and appeared irritated. "The courier picked up the envelope from a locker in the baggage area at Union Station," he said. "There was another envelope with cash to cover the delivery fee."

Ferguson sighed. "So we have no idea where the letter came from?"

"Nope," said Sinclair.

"Are you sure the perp hasn't phoned the paper?" Ferguson asked of Haywood again, frustration obvious.

"I'm sure," he said, palms up as a peace offering. "We monitor our calls carefully."

Finally, the three investigators left and stood in the humidity outside the *Post* office. Dinah scanned the horizon for any signs of a thunderstorm that might break the oppressive heat, but the sky was clear.

"If you have time, can you keep working on tracking down thefts of the pre-made ANFO slurry?" Ferguson asked Dinah. "We're going to take this letter up to the lab."

"Sure," said Dinah. "I'll see you tomorrow."

As Ferguson lumbered away, Sinclair quickly whispered, "Are you free tomorrow for dinner?"

Dinah felt the thrill squirm in her heart and was about to agree when she suddenly realized that tomorrow night was her home group meeting.

"Uh . . . I can't," she said. "The following night?"

He nodded and winked at her, slipping away gracefully to catch up to Ferguson.

Dinah could do nothing but stand rooted to the same spot on the sidewalk, waiting for her hammering heart to calm down.

* * * *

The staff meeting seemed to drag interminably, and what dragged the most were the thinly veiled political speeches about who deserved tenure. Isabelle could barely keep her mind on the agenda, thinking instead of her mother's recent phone call.

Rosa was having trouble reaching Michael on his cell phone, and her concern was bordering on hysteria. Isabelle rolled her eyes and thought that a break from their mother was an infinitely sensible idea. "He's a grown man, Mom," she said, for the hundredth time. "He can go away for a week or work hard for a week or even visit friends."

"Without calling me?" wailed Rosa.

"Yes, believe it or not," said Isabelle. "He's not a kid anymore."

"He's just lost his father," responded Rosa. "It's not right for him to isolate himself. He needs his family!"

"Maybe he prefers to sort it all out in his own mind, in his own time," suggested Isabelle.

"Nonsense!" Rosa declared, who hadn't done anything under her own steam for a long time.

Isabelle usually finished such phone calls with her mother feeling exasperated, but this time, she couldn't help but share a niggling worry about her brother. He was reticent at the best of times; perhaps now *wasn't* the best time for him to be alone. She would never concede this to her mother, though.

Her own calls to his cell phone went unanswered. She sent him text messages too, asking him to let her know that he was okay. Compulsively, she checked her phone throughout the staff meeting, but it remained silent. Michael wouldn't have done something stupid, would he? *Listen to me,* Isabelle thought wryly, *I'm worried about him hurting himself — something I do to myself as often as I can.*

"Isabelle?"

With a jolt, she realized that the staff meeting was finally over and that her colleagues were packing up and leaving. Isabelle smiled and said goodbye, then checked her watch as she left the building.

With a cold stab of fear, she realized that it was 7:30. How had the meeting dragged on for over two hours? If Scott was home and saw that she wasn't, he would be furious. In the car, driving as fast as she dared, Isabelle prayed that tonight would be one of the occasions when he didn't come home until late — if at all.

When she pulled into the driveway, her heart sank like dead weight. Scott's car was parked there and lights blazed in the house. Isabelle gathered her bags with clammy hands and tried to muster some courage. In truth, she wanted to stay in the car and drive away, somewhere far away from her husband, her mother, the memories of her father, *all* of it. She could change her name and start a new life. Perhaps that's what Michael had done. If so, she envied him fiercely.

She opened the front door and pretended to be indifferent to the fear and dread that engulfed her. "Hi, I'm home," she called cheerfully. "Sorry I'm late. The staff meeting went on *forever.* I thought I'd never escape!"

There was no reply. Isabelle walked into the kitchen and found Scott sitting at the table, his face a mask of fury.

"Oh . . . there you are," she said lamely. "How was your day?"

"Do you know what time it is?" he asked, eyes like chips of ice.

"Yes, I had a staff meeting that seemed like it would never end." She moved around the kitchen, getting out ingredients for dinner, keeping her shaking hands busy.

"In this house, I expect to come home and have dinner prepared," snapped Scott. "Is that too much to ask?"

"No, but. . . ."

"I've told you that if your job interferes with your duties as my wife, then you must quit your job." Scott's words were tight and fast, like tiny bullets that found their way directly to her heart.

She stared at him, dismayed. "You're not. . . !"

"Yes, I am. Tomorrow, you will quit."

"No, Scott, please don't," she pleaded, her hands stilled. "I love my job!" *It's the only time I feel normal, where I'm in control, where I'm not anxious that I've said the wrong thing, where I'm free!*

"I'll do it for you, if I must."

Isabelle's eyes filled with tears. "No, please! Next time, I'll just skip the staff meeting. It'll never happen again!"

A thought struck her: he couldn't phone in her resignation for her because he had no idea who she reported to or what her work numbers were. She had never directly defied him, but he'd never threatened to take something so dear away from her. With new resolve, her tears dried up. "I'm not going to resign, Scott." She began chopping garlic and onion.

He froze. "Excuse me?"

"I'm not going to do it. I love my job." She spoke with courage, but she couldn't meet his gaze. "I'm here for you almost every night. I make dinner for you even though you often don't bother coming home. You don't call me when you decide not to come home. I won't let you take away the only thing that gives me stability."

"How dare you speak to me like that," said Scott, standing up and stalking slowly around the island bench. "I am the leader of this house! It's not your place to question my activities but it sure is my business to know what you're doing and who you're with."

"Is that what this is about?" Isabelle asked, surprising herself. She'd have normally backed down by now. "You think I was with someone tonight?"

"I can't imagine anyone else who would want you," snarled Scott. "Who would want a wife who doesn't take care of her husband and spends her free time mutilating herself?"

Isabelle took a deep breath at the onslaught of his words. She could think of nothing to say that would make the situation better — except to accede to her husband's demands — and that she just couldn't do.

Suddenly, Scott was next to her, reminding her that his size and strength were far superior to her own. "You *will* resign," he said, fists balled at his side.

Isabelle focused on quartering snow peas. "I will not," she replied quietly.

Scott yanked her arm with surprising force, spinning her to face him. "Do you really want to do this?" he shouted. "You really want to defy me?"

"I'm not going to resign." She just couldn't look him in the eye, where cold fury had replaced all reason.

"This is your last chance," he warned. He raised his fist, and Isabelle was starkly aware that he was capable of violence.

Almost unable to hold herself upright such was the terror pulsing through her veins, she showed him the kitchen knife in her other hand. "Don't do it," she said very softly.

They froze, like two combatants in the boxing ring. Scott seemed to be weighing up whether his wife would use the knife. Isabelle wondered if she possessed the resolve to defend herself.

"This is a big mistake," Scott finally said, letting go of her arm. "You will regret this every day for the rest of your life."

"I already am," Isabelle said, though she was talking about something very different. As she watched him stalk away, she dropped the knife into the sink with a clatter and collapsed, a shaking mess, onto a chair. When would this nightmare end? Deep in her heart, she knew the answer was *until death do us part.*

* * * *

One of the lovely ladies in her Bible study had brought homemade chocolate chip cookies, and the smell permeated the air as Dinah rushed into the church building. She was usually the last one to arrive at the meeting, punctuality not being her strongest trait.

"Hi, sorry I'm late," she said, sitting down and grabbing a cookie in one fluid motion. "Hope you haven't been waiting long."

The four other women watched her with amusement.

"Well, Dinah," said Ruth, the recognized leader of the group, "there is something different about you tonight. What's going on?"

"Yeah," chimed in Alicia, the youngest woman in the study. "You look really happy."

"What?" Dinah asked. "What do I look like normally?"

"Well . . . just not quite so elated," said Alicia. "What's happened?"

Dinah looked around the group, wondering what to say. They were godly women, offering wise counsel. She would be foolish not to seek their opinions.

"Uh . . . well, I sort of met someone," she said awkwardly.

Sara, a mother of four, clapped her hands together excitedly. "Tell us all about it!"

"Well, I met him at work," said Dinah, her cheeks burning. "He's an FBI agent. We're working on the bombing case together."

"What's his name?" Alicia wanted to know.

"Aaron."

"Have you been out with him?" Deborah, a well-dressed ambassador's wife, asked.

"Yes, we had brunch together yesterday," said Dinah, unable to keep the smile from her face.

"Is he good-looking?" Alicia asked, with an infectious giggle.

Dinah's entire face burned. "Well, I think he is."

Ruth touched Dinah's arm and asked gravely: "Is he a Christian?"

Dinah was taken aback. She recalled their discussion about church: he hadn't directly said he wasn't a Christian, but he had preferred to go running instead of to a service. "Uh . . . you know, I don't know."

Ruth nodded. "Dinah, you are a new Christian so you shouldn't feel bad, but the Bible is very clear about the types of romantic relationships we allow ourselves into."

"It is?" Dinah hadn't known that.

Ruth flipped open her Bible. "Specifically, the writer of 2 Corinthians, chapter six, verses 14 and 15 talk about this issue. It says,

'Do not be yoked together with unbelievers. For what do righteousness and wickedness have in common? Or what fellowship can light have with darkness? . . . What does a believer have in common with an unbeliever?' "

"What the passage is saying is that you are now on Christ's team," added Deborah. "It would be foolish to yoke yourself to someone who is not on Christ's team. Would he come with you to church? Would he support you doing Bible study? Would he be a source of temptation, to do things you know are wrong? How could he be a godly husband if he's not a Christian? Would it pain you to know that he is not saved for eternity?"

Dinah blinked. "I hadn't really thought about it, to be honest. I mean, it was just one date."

"Do you intend to go on more dates?" Sara asked.

"Well, yes."

"And you really like him, don't you?"

Dinah cleared her throat, embarrassed. "Yes."

"Then you need to think carefully about what God says," said Sara. "Marriages between a Christian and a non-Christian can often be very painful. Sometimes the non-Christian spouse can lead the other away from faith or make decisions that are the opposite of what God would want."

"There is also the issue of dating itself," added Ruth. "Society has welcomed premarital sex as being quite normal and acceptable. God says, in the Bible, that sexual relations are for the marital bed only. Would he be likely to pressure you into conforming to the world's standards instead of upholding God's standards?"

Dinah felt stricken. "I . . . don't know. I haven't thought about it. I didn't really know." She took another cookie and jammed it into her mouth so she couldn't speak.

"It seems like we're ganging up on you," said Deborah gently. "But I can't stress how important it is to enter into a relationship with prayer; to search God's Word to find out what God wants you to do. Your relationship with God and your belief and faith in His commands must come before all else."

Dinah leaned back in her chair and swallowed the last of her cookie. "Wow. I must seem pretty dumb, but I truly didn't know any of that."

"You are far from dumb," said Ruth, squeezing her arm maternally. "One of the best things about being a Christian is that we never stop learning. I have been a Christian for 15 years and I am still learning new things about my relationships with others and deepening my faith. It is a lifetime journey, perfected only once we're in heaven."

"So what should I do?" Dinah asked. "Aaron asked me to go out with him tomorrow night."

"I would take it as an opportunity," advised Deborah. "You can be completely honest with him about your Christianity and how important it is to you. Explain that if he chooses to be a non-Christian, then you can be friends only."

"It's a great way to witness to him," added Ruth. "You can offer to take him to church or answer his questions about Christianity."

"Just make sure he understands that an intimate relationship is something you'll only consider with another Christian," chimed in Sara.

"Okay, I see." Dinah nodded, but inside she felt conflicted. *What if he hates me? What if he laughs in my face?*

They opened their Bibles to the times of King David, and began to immerse themselves in the study. Dinah found it hard to concentrate, but having heard their counsel, she knew they were right. If Aaron laughed at her or walked away from her because she was a Christian, then a relationship with him would be doomed from the start. On the other hand, perhaps he'd be interested and want to know more.

God, she prayed, *please take control of this situation before I lose my mind. Help me to do what is right in Your eyes and the rest I give over to You.*

A Dinah Harris Mystery

* * * *

Sussex 1 State Prison
Waverly, Virginia
Prisoner Number: 10734
Death Row

Today, Dinah's not messing around. She's all business.

I know I can't leave her in the dark for much longer. She knows how I built and detonated the bombs; she wants to talk about why.

I'm tired — I want to sleep until this whole death row thing is over.

"Tell me where this hatred of churches comes from," she wants to know. "You sat in the third church you bombed without feeling any remorse for the people you were about to kill and injure."

How can I explain that they are not people to me? I looked around that church and I saw greedy pigs getting their fill at the trough of life — more than their fair share.

"What does the Bible say about the poor and oppressed?" I ask her. Without waiting for a reply, I answer myself: "It says not to deny justice to poor people in lawsuits, doesn't it?"

"Yes, I believe it says that in the Old Testament," agrees Dinah.

"Exodus," I affirm. "In Psalms, it instructs us to defend the cause of the weak; to maintain the rights of the poor and oppressed."

"Yes, it does," agrees Dinah.

"Proverbs says that he who oppresses the poor shows contempt for God," I continue. "How do you think the churches are doing?"

"I don't know," says Dinah. "But I know there are many churches that care greatly about the poor, and provide services to those who wouldn't otherwise be able to access them."

"Not the churches I bombed," I inform her.

"Okay, so you're angry with churches because they have a bad record of helping the less fortunate?" Dinah asks, taking notes furiously.

"Among other things," I say, "they seem to be very good at ignoring the commands found in their own Bible."

"So you grew up in a church?" Dinah asks shrewdly.

"Yes, but I stopped going as soon as I was allowed to make my own decision."

"What would you classify yourself as now?"

"I'm a secular humanist," I say. "I don't believe in anything supernatural. Nature is all that exists."

"I see. And how did you decide that that's what you wanted to be?"

"Let's just say that I grew tired of answering to a God who didn't seem to care," I say. "Humanism appealed to me because it discounts anything supernatural. Humans are ultimately responsible for their own destiny. There was something significant missing from the church I attended," I add. "Compassion."

Dinah nods thoughtfully. "So when you looked for something to fill the void of church, you found something that teaches compassion?"

"The sixth entry of the Humanist Manifesto 2000 — our Ten Commandments, if you will — is a commitment to preserving human rights and enhancing human freedom and dignity," I say. I have memorized the Manifesto.

Dinah purses her lips. "Do you see that it's ironic — your desire for compassion and your hatred and subsequent murder of church parishioners?"

I frown at her. "What do you mean?"

"Well, those who are of a humanist way of thinking often espouse the need for tolerance of all people," continues Dinah. "You just said that the Manifesto specifically mentions that humans ought to be afforded freedom and dignity."

"Right," I agree.

"Yet you are guilty of murdering those who practice Christianity and your humanist brothers and sisters actively deny Christians the right to practice their religion in public. For example, humanists have had some success in banning nativity scenes and prayer in public buildings. I would argue that this is in fact intolerant, which means that humanism is just as hypocritical as you say Christianity is."

Dinah says this without heat or venom in her voice — just lucid logic. When she finishes, she waits for my reply, looking at me.

If I wasn't on death row — if my brain was working properly — I would have the answers for her. However, my habit of sleeping for 14 hours a day due to sheer boredom seems to have detrimentally affected my ability to think.

"I'm aware," she continues, "that more specifically, your church didn't help you when you needed it. That's where the hatred started, isn't it?"

I glare at her. She was recalling a conversation we'd had under the most arduous of circumstances. There were some things that I just hated to bring up. I can't bring myself to talk about it calmly. It's a story best told when emotions get the best of me — fear or anger.

Abruptly, she changes the subject. "How did you manage to hide your hatred for so long? I mean, you held down a job and had good relationships with your family and others. Most people who knew you can't believe that it was you who detonated those bombs."

"I guess I just became good at it," I say, glad to be on a different topic. "Like anyone who leads a double life. I was good at faking an acceptable personality and good at lying. I never let anyone get too close."

Dinah seems to be thinking long and hard about this. Perhaps she is thinking of her own experiences — her double life as a former alcoholic and the lies she once told.

Don't we all have a double life? Even those who go to church compartmentalize their lives into things that are public and things are hidden away in the darkest parts of the soul. People are capable of hiding so much behind closed doors: the way they treat their children, the way they speak to their spouse, their business dealings, the taxes they cheat on, their affairs, the drug that helps them cope, their temper. The list is endless.

Most people think they would never be like me. I am the lowest kind of person; barely human at all. But if you have a secret life, you are more like me than you know.

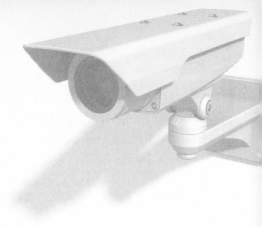

The owner of the boutique strip mall next to the bombed cathedral in Kalorama Heights had given the FBI closed circuit television footage taken from his premises, and they had spent the night reviewing it. Now Ferguson and Sinclair wanted to talk to the owner, and Dinah wanted to see the footage for herself. Dinah met Ferguson and Sinclair at the mall, at an hour that seemed inhumanly early. Dinah couldn't park close to the mall, given the entire area had been closed off by the Metro Police and the FBI, and so she walked by the wounded church and marveled at its melancholy atmosphere. The absence of people in a place that should be so vibrant; the building's mortal wounds; the air that seemed to be heavy and listless all added to the somber undercurrent.

When she saw Ferguson and Sinclair waiting for her at the mall's entrance, her heart did a familiar skipping dance, this time tinged with confusion. She couldn't deny her attraction to Sinclair — who was handsome, funny, and smart — but she knew in no uncertain terms that she couldn't enter into a relationship with him unless he was a Christian.

With a sigh, she resolved to think about it later and smiled at Ferguson and Sinclair as she joined them. "Good morning," she said.

Sinclair winked at her. "Hi."

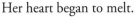

Chapter 12

Her heart began to melt.

"Morning," said Ferguson. He waved over another man, a middle-aged, balding man with heavy eyebrows and dark eyes.

"This is Usman Fahja," Ferguson introduced the man. "Special Agent Sinclair and Consultant Harris. He is the owner of this mall and has given us the CCTV footage." He gestured at Dinah. "Our consultant hasn't yet seen it — can we look over it again?"

Fahja nodded at them. "Come to my office," he said. "You'll be able to see it there." They followed Fahja to the back of the mall where his small office was located. A square security TV had an image frozen on the screen.

"I installed cameras after a few burglaries," explained Fahja. "A lady was also mugged in the parking lot. So the cameras I installed survey the shops and the entire parking lot."

Dinah felt a sense of excitement. "The bomber parked his vehicle in the parking lot."

Fahja nodded and they all stared at the small screen, dated from the previous Sunday. It was a normal scene — the cafe doing brisk brunch trade. The parking lot was perhaps half full and there was no sense of the tragedy that was about to unfold. The camera shot changed to show the parking lot in its entirety. The side of the lot that directly abutted the church wall could be clearly seen.

"Can we stay on this camera angle?" Ferguson asked.

The time stamp on the footage showed that it was about an hour and a half before the explosion. They hit the jackpot within the next half hour of footage. A large red Ford Expedition parked in the space from which the bomb had been detonated.

Dinah held her breath. They were watching the bomb arrive — but would they see the person responsible?

A man climbed from the Expedition. He was dressed smartly, in a button-down shirt and chinos. He had a military-style buzz cut and was tall and broad. His facial features were unremarkable.

"That's why no hair fibers were found in the baseball cap in Manassas," whispered Sinclair. "He barely *has* hair."

Dinah nodded her agreement, amazed for the hundredth time that the person capable of killing and maiming others looked so ordinary.

The bomber strolled toward the mall, and Fahja quickly changed the camera so that the store fronts could be seen. The bomber sat down at an outdoor table at the cafe and had a coffee. From Dinah's estimation, she thought he was facing the church, watching his prey as they assembled.

The bomber finished and left the cafe, walking in the direction of his bomb-laden car. The camera angle changed again and the four watched him walk past the Expedition into the grounds of the church.

From there, the bomber disappeared from view. About half an hour later, the cameras captured the explosion and there was silence as the Ford disintegrated into a flash of fire and smoke.

"Have you seen that man before?" Sinclair asked the owner, breaking the stunned silence.

"No," said Fahja. "The guy who runs the cafe told me he is not a regular; he didn't recognize him either."

"Listen, we'll need to take the tapes," said Ferguson.

Fahja nodded. "I thought so. I made copies for myself."

"Thanks for your help," Sinclair added. "You may have helped identify the bomber."

Fahja shrugged. "My motives aren't completely clear," he admitted. "This bomber has ruined trade in the mall — our customers can't shop here until the scene is cleared up. The store owners will all fall behind in their rent, but I've still got mortgage payments to make. The sooner the guy is found, the better for all of us."

In the listless air outside, Ferguson gave the tapes to Sinclair. "We need to release the footage to the media immediately," he instructed. "Someone out there knows who this man is. He must have family, friends, work colleagues, neighbors, *someone* who will recognize him."

"If only the walls could talk," murmured Dinah, staring at the silently dignified cathedral. They stood in silence, Dinah thinking of the moment in which the Expedition had unleashed its fury on the unsuspecting parishioners inside.

Then Ferguson said triumphantly, "This guy has made a major mistake. If he thinks there isn't a person out there who will recognize him. . . ."

"Do you think he didn't see the closed circuit television?" Dinah asked, thinking out loud. "Sure he didn't do this on purpose?"

"What for?" Ferguson asked. "To taunt us? Because he wants to be caught?"

"I don't know," she admitted. "It was just a thought."

They stood in silence again, all lost in a separate reverie until Ferguson finally said, "Let's go. We gotta get these tapes to the media."

* * * *

Isabelle had woken to an ominously quiet house.

She'd barely slept at all, her anxiety at the evening's confrontation growing with each passing hour. She'd dug into her hairline and ripped her fingernails to the quick in an attempt to quell the fear. Finally, after an exhausted few hours' sleep near dawn, she woke and crept into the kitchen, filled with dread.

A solitary empty coffee cup in the kitchen sink led to waves of relief washing over her. Scott had risen early, had his morning coffee, and left for work. That meant she didn't have to face his wrath this morning, and for that she was grateful.

She sat at the kitchen table with a steaming mug and stared, unseeing, at the blank television screen. She imagined a normal family, gathering for breakfast around a similar table: kids talking over each other and starting fights, Dad trying to listen to the news, Mom making breakfast, pouring coffee, and mediating between the kids at the same time. With a kiss planted squarely on each proffered cheek,

Dad leaving for work. Mom trying to organize school bags, lunches, and ensure homework has been done.

In that family, fear would live outside the front door, too scared of the love that bound that family together to darken its doorway. Anxiety would be felt *for* each other — a hard school exam, a worrying phone call from the doctor, job security — rather than *because* of each other. Venomous words were not designed to intimidate and crush the spirit, but instead were spoken thoughtlessly and apologized for quickly. Control was not exerted with the ruthlessness of Stalin; rather, loving boundaries enforced.

Isabelle had long harbored her happy family in her heart, wondering what it would be like to live in one. As a child, she'd promised herself that she would never make for herself a life identical to her mother's. She would be free, independent, free of fear. Yet look at how she lived — under threat, in danger, and at the point of causing herself physical injury to block out the immense emotional agony that existed within her.

Isabelle glanced at her watch and saw that it was time to get ready for work. Despite the confrontation with Scott last night, she was determined to hold onto this last vestige of independence, no matter what it cost her.

Showered, freshly made-up, and ready, Isabelle dug around in her purse to find her keys. After a few moments of rummaging, she realized that they weren't there. With a frown, she tried to think where she'd left them. Had she taken them out for some reason? She thought back to yesterday, when she'd last used the car, and she remembered putting the keys back in her purse.

Isabelle conducted a quick search of the house and couldn't find them anywhere. With a sigh of frustration, she decided she'd have to catch a cab to work.

Her cell phone, usually resting safely in the front pocket of her purse, was not there. She suddenly felt a stab of dismay. She ripped open her purse. Every single credit card and her ATM card were missing. There were no notes or coins left in her purse.

Pieces of Light

What is going on? Have I been robbed?

When she discovered that the two cordless phones for the house landline were missing, and the computer's modem had also disappeared, it became clear.

Her husband had sent her a message: *Do not mess with me.*

She had no doubt that her keys, cell phone, credit cards, modem, house phones, and cash were all in Scott's car or with him at work.

He had effectively isolated her from the rest of the world. She couldn't contact work to let them know she couldn't make it; she had no money to hail a cab or even a bus for that matter. She couldn't call a locksmith to cut her a new key for her car — she had no phone and no money. She couldn't send an SOS to her family — she had no cell phone and no computer.

Realizing the futility of her situation, Isabelle collapsed into the living room couch, too stunned to cry.

Why am I so stupid? How could I have let this happen?

This was all her fault, that much was obvious. If only she'd skipped last night's staff meeting and arrived home at the normal hour. Why did she think she could bend Scott's rules so far? She should have known better!

Furthermore, she'd defied him when he asked her to resign from her job. Wouldn't it have been better to acquiesce to his demand and find a job with no after-hours staff meetings? Didn't her family come first?

What was I thinking? I've messed this up totally!

He was her husband, after all, and he had the right to decide how the family would operate. She had openly refused to obey him, and his punishment was swift and severe. She just felt lucky that Scott was not like her father, who had made his point with his fists.

Isabelle tried to gather her thoughts together. It was clear she wouldn't be doing much today, except waiting for Scott to get home. That thought caused so much apprehension to immediately course through her veins that she realized it wasn't really an option at all. She had to think of something to do with herself.

She still had her legs, she realized. While she didn't have the money to even use a pay phone, she could visit someone who would let her use the phone for free. The closest person was her mother, but once she heard what had happened, she would freak out. It would make a stressful situation even worse.

She didn't have any close friends; anyone she knew socially had been Scott's friend first. She didn't know them particularly well, and she knew she couldn't trust them.

That left her brother, Michael. He was the farthest but was the only person she could totally trust.

Several minutes later, with shorts and sneakers on, the spare house key in her pocket and a bottle of water, Isabelle set off for her walk.

The unrelenting sun beat down on her head and she resolutely thought of anything except her marriage. There would be plenty of time for that later.

* * * *

The news media began their breaking news footage at lunchtime, and replayed it every hour on the hour throughout the afternoon. Tensely, Ferguson and Sinclair waited for the phones to ring, while at her own home, Dinah waited for news.

It didn't take long for various assorted prank calls to come through, and the FBI agents' frustration levels rose with each new call.

The phone call came at four o'clock that afternoon. A parishioner from the bombed Episcopalian cathedral recognized the man.

Ferguson and Sinclair picked up Dinah on the way to the man's house, only a few blocks away from the bombed cathedral in Kalorama Heights.

"How does he recognize the bomber?" Dinah asked in the car.

"He says he was part of the congregation," said Sinclair.

"What?" Dinah hadn't been expecting that response. "*Part* of the congregation?"

"That's all I know," said Sinclair.

Dinah was intrigued, and for some reason, Ferguson insisted on driving as sensibly as possible. *Come on,* she encouraged him. *Put your foot down and get this car moving!* She ground her back teeth together to stop herself from making a sharp comment.

Finally, they arrived to a beautiful, turn-of-the-century manor house, covered in creeping ivy and surrounded by manicured lawns. A man in his fifties appeared on the front porch and waved them through the gates. He was completely bald, dressed casually in Armani and holding a Blackberry in one hand.

"I'm Simon Browning," he introduced himself, as the three investigators climbed out of the car. He spoke quickly and efficiently, much like he conducted most of his life, guessed Dinah. "Please, come in," he added, before they'd even had a chance to introduce themselves.

Browning led them into a formal living room lined with book shelves and furnished with leather reading chairs. On cue, a young man brought drinks and food on a silver tray — pastries, complicated-looking cookies, and prepared fruit.

Ferguson managed to eventually introduce himself, Sinclair, and Dinah, and evidently decided to take control of the conversation. "Thank you for calling the FBI, Mr. Browning," he began. "I understand you saw the footage broadcast by the news media this afternoon of the bombing suspect and that you recognize him?"

"Indeed I do," agreed Browning, swirling mineral water garnished with a slice of lemon. "In my business, attention to detail is the most important factor."

"What is your business?"

"I own an escrow agency," said Browning. "Essentially I wire money between parties conducting business transactions, into the hundreds of millions of dollars. We must follow the instructions perfectly, down to the last penny. There is no room for error. As a result, I've developed over the years a clear eye for detail."

"Tell us how you identified the suspect," suggested Ferguson.

"I'm a regular parishioner at the cathedral," explained Browning. "I'm there three out of every four weeks, I'd say. I've been going there for over 20 years, so I know all of the regulars. That day, a man I'd never seen before appeared. I'm pretty outgoing by nature, so I decided to welcome him to the church and strike up a conversation with him. That man was the suspect in the footage."

"What did the man do, from the time you noticed him?" Ferguson asked, while Sinclair wrote in a notebook furiously.

"I was already sitting down, but I was turned sideways, facing the other pews. You know, seeing people I knew, saying hi, and so forth. I saw this man walk through the doors and sit down right behind me. I knew at once he wasn't a regular — I'd never seen him before."

"You then tried to talk to him?"

"Right. I think I was friendly enough, asking him how he was, was this his first time here, what he did. All I got was yes/no answers. He made it pretty clear he didn't want to talk to me."

"How did that conversation end?" Ferguson asked.

"Well, eventually he just gave me a stare that was hard to describe. It was full of contempt and irritation, I suppose. I got the message, turned around, and stopped trying to talk to him." Browning speared a pastry with a toothpick and took a bite.

"Did the suspect interact with anyone else in the church?"

"No, I don't think so."

"Where did he sit, exactly?"

"I was on the opposite side of the church to the wall that was bombed," explained Browning. "I only got a few minor skin burns. He was right behind me, but he sat as close to the unaffected wall as possible."

"Or, in other words, as far away from the bomb as possible," interjected Dinah.

"Do you remember what happened during or after the explosion?" Ferguson inquired.

Browning spent several moments in thought. "I remember the force of the bomb smashed me against the wall. I was kind of dazed for a while, then I started trying to help get people out of the church. I don't remember seeing him afterward, but I'm pretty sure he wasn't significantly injured. I would have remembered seeing that. In fact, most of the parishioners on the same side of the church as me weren't hurt."

Dinah wrote a sentence down in her own notebook: *Why did he want to experience his own bombing?*

"How was the suspect dressed?"

"Well, that's another thing I noticed," Browning said. "I won't lie to you — our church is pretty financially comfortable. Our regulars dress pretty well. This guy, in comparison, looked pretty ragged. Not in a homeless way; more that his boots were worn and scuffed, his pants were faded, his shirt washed a few too many times. You know what I mean?"

"So what exactly was he wearing?"

"Black boots, dark blue chinos, a black button-down shirt." Browning seemed lost in thought for a moment.

"Apart from not wanting to engage in a conversation with you," continued Ferguson, "did he seem nervous, anxious, jumpy?"

Browning considered. "No. He seemed pretty calm to me. Only. . . ."

They let Browning compose his thoughts, but the silence dragged on interminably. Dinah wanted to shake the man and scream, *What? Only what?*

"Only, he seemed to exude waves of anger," Browning said at length. "He struck me as being very, very angry. Not in the sense that he'd lose his temper, but in a cold, calculating kind of way."

"If I suggested that the bombing were in part motivated by revenge, would that seem strange to you?" Ferguson asked.

"Not at all," said Browning immediately. "That definitely fits with the anger I sensed in the man." He paused. "Revenge? Is that what the bombing was about?"

"No, it's just a theory," said Ferguson quickly. "I don't suppose you ever found out the man's name?"

"Sorry, I can't help you there."

Dinah underlined the sentence she had written in her notebook. A coldly calculating bomber, intent on punishing churches, had borne witness to his own detonation.

But why?

* * * *

Senator David Winters had turned his back to his desk and sat staring out the window in his Senate Office Building. He had a view of the Lower Senate Park and he stared at the green lawns, deep in thought. In fact, he was so deep in thought that when there was a polite cough behind him, he almost jumped out of his skin.

Carefully, he regained his composure before swinging his chair around to face Connor Eastleigh, his latest intern. The young man stood awkwardly with a sheaf of papers in his hand.

"Why are you skulking around here like a bandit?" Winters demanded bad-temperedly.

Connor flushed. "I thought you heard me knock and come in, sir."

Winters ignored that, knowing full well that he should have heard the young man. He had been a Special Forces commander and his senses had once been finely tuned. Apparently not anymore, he mused sulkily. "What do you want?" he asked.

"Well, you asked me to get you some information about case law regarding separation of church and state?" Connor said. "It's ready."

Despite himself, Winters did want to hear the information that Connor had gathered.

"Sit down and tell me," he commanded.

"Okay, *Hein v. Freedom From Religion Foundation,* in which the FFRF sued on behalf of taxpayers the funding of conferences which help religious organizations apply for federal grants, under President George W. Bush's Faith Based and Community Initiatives Program. The basis for the lawsuit was that FFRF claimed the conferences promoted religious community organizations over secular ones. The district court dismissed the case, while the appellate court reversed the decision. The Supreme Court ultimately granted review of the case in 2006, in which the opinion majority held that the taxpayers had no standing to challenge the use of discretionary funds." Connor took a breath and paused.

"So we lost that one," said Winters, starting hard at the young man.

"Right. In Pennsylvania, 2005, *Moeller* v. *Bradford County*, the ACLU filed a lawsuit on behalf of taxpayers and a former inmate of the Bradford County jail. It was alleged that a religious vocational training program run within the jail, which was funded almost entirely by both federal and local governments, proselytized to inmates and that inmates were forced to take part in prayer. The case was eventually settled with Bradford County, wherein agreements were made that the county severely restrict the use of public funding to aid religion, and that any faith-based organization is intensively monitored to ensure compliance with those restrictions."

"So we won that one," mused Winters.

"Yes, sir. You might be interested to know that the vocational training program no longer operates and has not done so since the legislation."

"How interesting!" Winters allowed himself a smile.

"In 2000 in the case *Padreira v. Kentucky Baptist Homes for Children*, the ACLU filed suit in the federal district court challenging the state's funding of the home, in which children under the care of the state were living. The district court dismissed all claims and an appeal was lodged with the Sixth Circuit appellate court. In 2009 the appeal was upheld although the case is now pending on the result of a similar case."

"So it looks like we'll win that," summarized Winters.

"In 2010 *Arizona Christian School Tuition Organization v. Winn* was filed challenging a statute which allows residents to direct part of their tax payments to organizations which provide scholarships to students, the majority of whom go to religious schools. The plaintiffs argued that allowing residents to direct tax payments is the same as providing cash grants. The district court dismissed the case and the appellate court reversed that decision."

Winters nodded. "It would appear the appellate and Supreme Courts are more generous toward our side."

"It does appear so, sir." Connor shuffled paper. "Would you like to hear more?"

"Let's hear one more," said Winters, thinking of his Supreme Court justice pal, Maxwell Pryor.

"In *Freedom From Religion Foundation v. McCallum*, a lawsuit was filed challenging the state of Wisconsin's funding of a drug and alcohol treatment center, called Faith Works. Faith Works is a religious organization and it was claimed that participants were indoctrinated with religion. At issue were two payment streams: fixed grants and per capita funding. The district court found that the fixed grants were unconstitutional but the per capita funding was allowable. This decision was upheld by the appellate court."

"So a win for both parties there," said Winters. "Although I'd imagine the case cost the center the majority of their funding. So what do you think we can expect from our lawsuit?"

"I wouldn't be surprised if the district court dismisses your case," replied Connor confidently, "and the appellate court reverses that decision. The Supreme Court, should it get that far, will almost certainly uphold your claims."

Winters felt absurdly pleased with his young intern. "Well done, young man," he said, rare praise indeed.

"Thank you, sir," said Connor, flushing bright red. "Can I ask a question?"

"Sure, go ahead," said Winters magnanimously.

"Broadly, I understand what's going on here," said Connor. "Christianity shouldn't receive special treatment or funding from the government, nor should they be allowed to force their beliefs down other people's throats. But . . . aren't you imposing *your* beliefs down other people's throats instead?"

Winters went very still and thought he might have to rethink this young intern. "In what sense?"

"Well, these lawsuits are stripping away any remnant of Christianity, and in their place stands atheism or humanism, which are religions themselves."

Winters' eyes glittered. "Where did you get that notion, son?"

"Both have rejected God, and therefore one could say they have no belief in a supernatural religion," said Connor, oblivious to the look on the senator's face. "However, in its place is a religion based on human understanding and reason. An atheist or humanist views evolution as much more than mere science, but rather as ideology which has its own meaning and morality. Richard Dawkins, the prominent atheist, admits that atheism is the logical extension of believing in evolution. Furthermore, evolution has, like every other world religion, provided one explanation for the origins of life, for death and suffering, for why humans exist and what will happen to humans in the future. It also provides for a new kind of morality, where one is no longer answerable to God but only to oneself. If that isn't the very definition of religion, then I don't know what is."

Winters had gone ominously quiet. Finally, he said through gritted teeth: "Who has been telling you these lies, Connor?"

"Just my initial impression," Connor said naively.

Winters controlled his temper, telling himself that the boy didn't know any better. "We're just after freedom from religion, son. Nothing sinister about it."

Thus appeased, the intern left his office and Winters vowed to keep a closer eye on Connor Eastleigh.

Dinah left Ferguson and Sinclair frantically fielding calls from thousands of citizens who supposedly knew the man in the CCTV footage. That was one part of the job she didn't miss at all.

On the way home, her cell phone rang with a familiar number.

"Andy? Is that you?" she answered.

"Hi!" Andy Coleman replied brightly. He and his wife Sandra had first met Dinah during the Smithsonian case, a mystery in which a good friend of theirs had disappeared and subsequently been murdered. It had been Sandra who'd recognized Dinah's descent into alcoholism and interrupted her suicide attempt, and who had eventually led Dinah to the Lord. Andy had founded an apologetics ministry based in Cincinnati, Ohio, called the Genesis Legacy, which sought to protect and defend biblical authority in a society quickly losing sight of its Christian heritage.

"Are you going to be home in a few minutes?" Andy asked.

"Yes," said Dinah. "Are you in town? I'd love to catch up with you." Already at the point of speeding, Dinah had to be careful not to exceed the limit as she rushed home.

Andy and Sandra were waiting for her, leaning on their car in the sweltering late afternoon. He was a tall, lean man with shaggy gray hair that never looked properly cut. His dark eyes were sharp and keen, and he always wore a few days' stubble on his face. His wife was shorter and rounder, with curly blond hair and large blue eyes and an Australian accent that hadn't changed despite the length of time they'd lived in the States.

After greeting her friends, Dinah led them up to her apartment and busied herself fixing drinks for her guests. "So what brings you to D.C.?" she asked, once they were all comfortably seated in the living room.

"Schedules, to be blunt," said Andy with a laugh. "I still spend a lot of time touring around the country, speaking at churches and conferences, and summer is a busy time for conferences. The lawyer for the Genesis Legacy seems to do an awful lot of traveling himself. This was the only time and place that we could find to meet together."

"Your lawyer?" said Dinah. "Is everything okay?"

"You would think I'd be used to it by now," said Andy, "but we've been named in a lawsuit and I need to make sure the lawyer's got it all under control."

Dinah was intrigued. "What's the lawsuit about?"

"Well, have you heard of the Ark Experience?" Andy asked, his face lighting up with excitement.

Dinah shook her head.

"We've acquired some land near Cincinnati and we're going to build a Noah's ark themed attraction," explained Andy, "including a full-size ark, according to the dimensions stated in the Bible, using the materials that would have been available to Noah. We're going to show how the animals would have fit on the ark and answer lots of questions people have about whether Noah's ark could have been real. There'll be lots of other exciting things to do and see there too, but the main one is the ark."

"Wow!" said Dinah. "That's amazing! I would love to see that."

"So would millions of people, according to our research," said Andy. His entire face was animated.

"So, the lawsuit is to stop you building the ark or something?" asked Dinah.

"No. The attraction is going to be built in Kentucky, and there are some there who are convinced that taxpayer money is going to be used to help fund it," said Andy, his exhilarated expression dying. "There are groups of atheists, humanists, civil libertarians, and the like, all across the country, who think that government spending on religious organizations is a direct violation of the First Amendment — supposedly separation of church and state."

A spark flashing, Dinah jumped up and tried to find the lawsuit that had been mailed to her by Senator Winters, among the other papers she had on her desk. "Keep going," she said. "I'm listening."

"They're wrong on a few levels," continued Andy. "First, the Ark Experience will receive no funding from the state whatsoever. Patrons who choose to attend the attraction will pay sales tax as part of the ticket price. We will apply to receive tax incentives as part of the state's Tourism Development Act, to receive partial refunds on the sales tax collected by the attraction. By the way, such incentives are available to anyone who opens an attraction designed to draw tourists into the state of Kentucky. Whether they're religious tourists or not is irrelevant, frankly. Furthermore, I have to point out the obvious — we will employ hundreds of people, all of whom will pay taxes; plus we will generate city and county real estate tax."

Dinah found the envelope containing the lawsuit and pulled out the thick wad of paper.

"That hasn't stopped a humanist group from filing a federal lawsuit in which we are named, albeit among hundreds of others, as violating the First Amendment," Andy explained. "Apparently any financial intervention by the state government violates the First Amendment. This is patently untrue. The Tourism Development Act of Kentucky is non-discriminatory, which means by law they can't discriminate against us *because* we're Christian. Virtually any tourist attraction can apply for incentives regardless of the message. Legally, the threat against us is a waste of time."

"So, clearly I'm not up-to-date on the latest church and state separation legislation," said Dinah. "But it would seem to me that if you don't like the idea of a religious tourist attraction, you just wouldn't go. Right?"

"Common sense doesn't apply." Andy grinned. "Atheists and humanists are not happy to leave it there. They object to *anyone* going to the Christian tourist attraction, because they want to completely eradicate Christianity from our country."

"Is the lawsuit by any chance filed by Elena Kasprowitz, supported by the American Humanist Cooperation and the Secular Humanists of America?" Dinah asked.

"Yes, why?" Andy looked surprised.

"My old friend Senator Winters sent me a copy of the lawsuit, for some reason," said Dinah. "Is that what the lawsuit is about? Government funding religious organizations?"

"Yes, erroneously," said Andy. "Unfortunately the interpretation of the First Amendment by the courts and liberal commentators is very different from the intentions of the Founding Fathers. The whole idea of separation of church and state was supposedly established by Thomas Jefferson, who wanted to build a secular state. However, the facts tell a very different story.

"For one thing, this concept of separation of church and state being enshrined in the Constitution is completely false. Jefferson mentioned it in a letter he wrote to a group of Baptists, and the primary concern was that the federal government would try to impose a state religion. Jefferson himself was not a Christian, but he recognized the great need to protect religious freedom. Therefore, he fought for the right of freedom *of* religion, not freedom *from* religion. Can you see the difference there?

"Jefferson, and the Founding Fathers, wanted to protect the *church* from the *state*. The current interpretation is that the state requires protection from the church. Jefferson actually believed that the government ought to have no power to interfere with freedom of religion. He had witnessed the tendency of government to encroach upon the free exercise of religion — precisely what is happening in modern-day America today. In those days, many of the pilgrims who found their way to America had been persecuted for being of a different religion than the reigning monarch of the time. One could be summarily executed for being a Protestant if the king happened to be Catholic, for example.

"Thus he, together with the other Founding Fathers, believed that the First Amendment had been enacted *only* to prevent the establishment, by decree of the state, of a national denomination.

"Furthermore, their intentions were that the government ought never to interfere with traditional religious practices outlined in the Scripture — including public prayer, public acknowledgment of God, and so on. Yet what do we see all around us today? We have lost the freedom to pray in public, to talk about God in public, to even look at a picture of the Ten Commandments."

Dinah could sense Andy was only just getting warmed up to his subject.

"Furthermore, Jefferson himself declared that the power to prescribe any religious curtailment must rest with the States. Yet the federal courts take it upon themselves to ignore this, and misuse his separation phrase to strike down dozens of state laws which encourage or maintain public religious expressions."

Dinah chewed her lip. "So basically, the way in which courts apply the separation of church and state is almost the exact opposite of what it originally meant?"

"Right," said Andy. "What does that mean practically? It means that *my* right to practice religious freedom has been sacrificed on the altar of the religion of atheism. Make no mistake about it, what these humanist groups are seeking to do is not just eradicate Christianity but evangelize their own religion. What modern-day America is experiencing is not freedom of religion but the enforced secularization of church and state."

Dinah could see plainly the deep love and concern Andy held for his country etched intensely on his face. Then he said softly, "If the foundations are destroyed, what can the righteous do?"

* * * *

Isabelle was hot, tired, and grumpy by the time she arrived at her brother's house. Her shirt was plastered to her body, and sticky strands of hair were tucked behind her ears. The farther she walked, the angrier she became with her controlling husband.

How dare he! she raged to herself. *This is his fault! If he hadn't tried to control me, if he'd just let me live my life.* She wouldn't dare say anything like that to his face, of course. In fact, she didn't even really believe it herself. Deep down she knew that it had been her fault for defying Scott's wishes. The heat and exhaustion she was already feeling just made her grumpy, and so she yelled at everyone she knew inside her head.

When Michael opened the door, he did a double take. "What on earth?" he exclaimed, as he ushered her into the house, which was only marginally cooler than the vicious sun.

In the small kitchen, Michael poured her a tall glass of cold water, which she gulped down too fast, resulting in an unpleasant ache in her head.

Her brother waited, despite the fact that he was obviously dying to ask her what was wrong. After the second glass of water, he finally said, "So what's going on?"

"Um . . .," said Isabelle, wondering briefly how honest she should be. Then she decided Michael knew her so well that he'd be able to tell if she was lying. "Well, Scott took away my keys, money, and phone because I refused to resign from my job," she explained succinctly.

Michael raised his eyebrows. "What?"

Isabelle told him the full story, of the staff meeting running late, Scott's wrath at her being late, and his subsequent demand to quit her job.

Michael shook his head. "You didn't agree, did you?"

"No, for once I actually stood up to him," she admitted. "I thought he was going to hit me. In fact, he almost did. He stopped when he saw I had a kitchen knife in my hand."

Michael grasped his sister's hand. "Good for you!"

"Yeah, I felt pretty good until I woke up this morning and figured out that Scott had taken all my money, my credit cards, my cell phone, my keys, and even the house phone and modem."

"So I guess he's expecting you to wait at home for him like a good wife," said Michael, pouring himself a glass of water.

"Yeah, I guess. I just couldn't, though," said Isabelle. "I can't be alone for that long with my own thoughts."

Michael nodded and took a long drink. "What are you going to do?"

She sighed. "I don't know. If he goes home tonight and I'm not there, he'll probably kick me out of the house."

"Is that such a bad thing?"

"You mean apart from Mom flipping out because one of her kids is getting divorced?" Isabelle said dryly. "I take marriage seriously. I don't want to throw it away because of one stupid argument."

"I know I'm an outsider," said Michael after a lengthy pause, "but do you think this is a marriage worth saving?"

"Why? What makes you say that?" Isabelle felt oddly insulted.

"He puts you down, he calls you names, he doesn't come home sometimes," began Michael. "He controls you, he isolates you. He takes your money and phone and keys when he's unhappy with you. Come on, you must realize that you. . . ."

"Don't say it," Isabelle blurted. Somehow, if the words weren't spoken, they lost their power.

"You married our father," insisted Michael, raising his voice over her.

"That's ridiculous!" Isabelle felt the heat in her face rise. "For one thing, Scott has never raised his hand against me. . . ."

"Only because you happened to have a kitchen knife in your hand at the time," Michael swiftly interjected.

"But he's never hit me or touched me in anger," asserted Isabelle. "He doesn't lose his temper, the way Dad did. He's the very opposite, he gets very quiet when he's angry."

"Yet he still puts you down and hurts you with his anger, doesn't he?"

"He doesn't get drunk around me," continued Isabelle.

"He doesn't need to," rejoined Michael. "The man is a sociopath — he is capable of cruelty stone sober."

"He provides a nice house for me. He doesn't mind what I buy," she added, somewhat lamely.

Michael just stared at her. She felt like she was fighting a losing battle. "What?" she said, when the silence had dragged on for too long and her brother's gaze had disconcerted her.

"Why haven't you had children with him?" he asked quietly.

Isabelle didn't want to go to that place. Not that dark, cold place. She knew very well why she hadn't had children with Scott but refused to admit it to her own heart.

"You know if you had kids with that man," said Michael, "that they would grow up devoid of a father's love. They would be damaged. Like me. Like you."

"No," said Isabelle, barely more than a whisper.

"What is this, then?" He pushed her long sleeve up her arm, exposing the scars on the underside of her wrist. "Are these the marks of an undamaged person?"

Defensively, she whipped her arm away from him and pushed down her sleeve. "It's nothing. I'm just an anxious person; I worry too much."

"Oh, I know you worry," agreed Michael. "All you can think about is the sound of Dad coming up the stairs, wondering whether it'll be you who bears the brunt of his frustration tonight. You think about all the lies Mom told the emergency room doctors. You think about the stark reality of loneliness, when you realize there is truly nobody in the world who will protect you."

Stricken, Isabelle didn't want to hear her brother's words, as right as he was. "Well, what about you?" she snapped. "You seem to have turned out okay!"

"Don't be so naive," Michael said in a voice so harsh it shocked her. "You grew up thinking that you deserve to be treated badly by men. You think you deserve the abuse that Scott dishes out. You know what I fear? I fear that I'm going to become *that* abusive man! I fear that the first time I lose my temper at a woman, I'm not going to be able to control my fists. I fear I'm going to take out my anger on a person weaker than myself. How do you think that makes me feel?"

"You are not that person, Michael!" cried Isabelle, tears forming in her eyes. "I know you too well!"

Michael looked at her with pity. "You don't know me at all," he said softly. "You don't know the things I've already done."

Isabelle felt tears spilling onto her cheeks and she closed her eyes, unable to look into the suddenly strange, burning eyes of the brother she thought she knew.

* * * *

Dinah got up to put on a pot of coffee, while Andy and Sandra swapped positions on the soft couch. When Dinah brought back three cups of steaming coffee, Andy said, "Our culture today reminds me of a Bible passage in Joshua 4. Joshua had been a great leader and commander of Israel, leading them into the Promised Land. After they crossed the Jordan River, God instructed Joshua to pile up 12 stones as a memorial to the crossing. The 12 stones were meant to be a reminder so that future generations would know that the Lord God had allowed the Israelites to cross the river on dry ground and that His hand is powerful, so that they might fear the Lord God forever. Yet it was only one generation later that the Israelites had forgotten what the 12 stones meant and did evil in the eyes of the Lord. In Judges 21:25, the Bible says that in those days there was no king and everybody did what was right in their own eyes. Do you know why the next generation turned their backs on God?"

Dinah, still a new Christian, had yet to explore much of the Old Testament in particular. She shook her head.

"The previous generation neglected to teach their children the significance and importance of the monument," explained Andy. "That's exactly what has happened in modern-day America. Our president has said many times over that we are no longer a Christian nation, but he doesn't say exactly what we've become: a secular nation. The *Free Inquiry* magazine, published by the Council for Secular Humanism, proclaimed that the First World — America, Canada, Europe, England, and Australia — is entering the Secular Age where science and knowledge dominate. Perhaps more accurately, they should have said that the First World is coming under the domination of the new religion, atheism."

Sandra raised her eyebrows at Dinah. "Now you've started him, he's not going to stop."

Dinah laughed. "I don't mind. I'm always guaranteed of learning something new when Andy comes to visit."

Andy was waiting impatiently. "If you two are finished," he said, "can I go on?"

"Who will stop you?" joked Sandra.

"We need to understand how we got to this point," continued Andy, poking his wife in the side in mock outrage. "We begin by removing from our culture references and reminders of our Christian heritage. In 1962 the Supreme Court ruled that prayer in public schools was unconstitutional. In 1963 the Supreme Court ruled that Bible reading in public schools was unconstitutional. In 1985 erecting nativity scenes at Christmas in public offices was deemed to violate the separation of church and state. Do you see what's happening?"

"In one generation," mused Dinah, "we've started to lose our Christian references."

"It continues at a rapid pace today," added Andy. "Our current president ceased funding abstinence-based education in public schools. At a speech he gave at Georgetown University, his staff asked that an emblem symbolizing the name of Jesus Christ be covered."

Andy stood up to pace the room. "You know, when a group tries to change a culture, the smart thing to do is start with kids, right? If you can influence the next generation, you have great power. Under the flawed interpretation of the First Amendment's separation of church and state, atheists and humanists have succeeded in driving out Christianity from our public schools, and replacing it with their own religion. Their prophet? Darwin. Their Bible? *Origin of the Species.* Their creed? Naturalism."

"Surely if they *really* embraced free inquiry," said Dinah, thinking out loud, "they'd embrace and discuss all explanations for the origins of life. After all, Darwin wasn't actually there and his theory cannot be proven in a science laboratory."

"Well, you'd be wrong," said Andy. "Actually, there is only one acceptable explanation, and that's the one taught to children in our public schools. Atheists and humanists claim that education ought to take a neutral position. They say that education ought to be free from religion. Yet they will not take responsibility for the fact that atheism *is* a religion and that in fact, they are forcing *their* religion down the throats of every child who attends public school. They have also managed to usurp Christian morality with their own brand."

"What do you mean?" Dinah asked.

"Where does the concept of right and wrong come from?" Andy asked rhetorically. "It comes from the Bible — from God very clearly showing us the standards of behavior He expects from us. However, if God is rejected, then His commandments about behavior are also rejected in favor of humans' own decisions about what is right and wrong. But who decides? Society has a code in place, the law, for setting standards of behavior. Much of the American code of law comes from the Bible, by the way: do not kill, do not steal, for example. However, an atheist is being illogical if he professes to believe in the concept of right and wrong because he no longer believes in an absolute authority. Therefore, their morality can only be relative to their own experiences and biases. If I decided to kill you, is that wrong? Perhaps in your eyes, but not in mine. I'm simply adhering to my own code of morality."

"What if morality could be what the majority thinks it should be?" suggested Dinah, playing devil's advocate.

Andy laughed. "Let me just say that Hitler was able to convince a majority of his people that his actions were right. Of course, the majority of people would now disagree. So this concept of majority is fluid and arbitrary in its own right."

"If this is what they're teaching in schools, they've been successful," commented Dinah.

"Yes, they have. And they *have* succeeded in influencing an entire generation," agreed Andy. "They taught kids that they are no more than animals, random accidents in a very big picture, that nothing matters except brute survival. They are taught to be respectful and honest, but why? Outside of the Bible, there is no basis for exhibiting this behavior. It is simply one person's opinion — and is it any more valid than another opinion which suggests that we should look after ourselves first? There is no right and wrong. Each individual decides what is right or wrong for themselves. The consequences are far-reaching. For example, when a student in Finland took a gun to school and killed nine people, he posted a video on YouTube stating that he was a natural selector who could eliminate all those who were unfit, who were a disgrace to the human race, and who were failures of natural selection. He also says that he is just an animal, putting natural selection and survival of the fittest back on track. That's pretty scary, but I can't fault his logic."

"They are becoming much more aggressive in their beliefs, too," added Sandra. When Andy threw her a quizzical look, she said, "What, I don't get my two cents' worth, too? Atheists and humanists are actively evangelizing. . . ."

"Something that Christians are increasingly not allowed to do," interjected Andy.

"Right. You have probably seen the billboards and advertising on buses."

"And I've seen the television ads they rolled out as part of this lawsuit," chimed in Dinah.

"They've built a great foundation with our kids in public schools," explained Andy. "And now they're going for the jugular."

"They're capitalizing on our failure," Sandra said. "We failed to influence the next generation, and we're paying the consequences now."

"Christianity in America in some ways is like the contaminated salt Jesus talks about in Matthew 5:13," said Andy. "The verse says: 'You are the salt of the earth. But what good is salt if it has lost its flavor? Can you make it salty again? It will be thrown out and trampled underfoot as worthless.' I think that's a pretty accurate description of what we've allowed our Christian heritage to become — worthless."

Dinah contemplated this in silence. Her new Christian faith to her was more priceless than a rare jewel. Her relationship with the living God had saved her not because she needed a crutch, not because she was weak, but because it gave her hope. It had given her hope for a life filled with purpose and meaning, knowledge that perfect love *did* exist, and the joyous anticipation of eternal life.

To consider that worthless was an outrage to her.

* * * *

The quiet of the stiflingly hot afternoon was disturbed by the chirping of her doorbell. Dinah frowned. She wasn't expecting anyone.

The voice on the intercom was familiar, though.

"Hi, Aaron. Come on up."

Her heart started thudding faster, racing like storm-chased clouds traversing the sky. When she opened the door, she started to feel sick. How was she going to have this difficult conversation with a guy she liked so much?

Dinah introduced Aaron to Andy and Sandra, flushing red when the other woman flashed her a quizzical look.

"Maybe we should go," said Andy, standing up.

"No, no," said Dinah. "You've only just arrived. Please, sit down."

"Sorry," said Aaron. "I didn't realize Dinah had visitors. I'm sorry to interrupt."

"We'll go for a quick walk," suggested Dinah, glancing at Aaron, who nodded quickly. To Andy and Sandra, she said, "Please, stay here and make yourselves at home."

Outside, in the suffocating humidity, she asked, "How are the phone calls going?"

"Every lunatic in the city has rung, convinced that they know who the person in the CCTV footage is," said Aaron, still managing to sound cheerful about it. "In fact, I'm in personal receipt of three confessions."

"Well, case closed then!" joked Dinah. More seriously she added: "No identifying call yet?"

"Nope," said Aaron with a sigh. "Listen, I'm sorry, I didn't realize you had visitors. I came here to ask you out to dinner."

"Oh," said Dinah. "Uh . . . yeah, well, tonight's out."

"What about tomorrow night?"

Dinah glanced sideways at him and caught a flash of his brilliant blue eyes. "Uh . . . "

She felt his gaze boring into her.

"Something wrong?" He suddenly sounded guarded.

"Well, it's complicated," Dinah said, marveling at her own inability to have important, meaningful discussions.

Aaron stopped walking and grasped her arm. "Tell me what's wrong," he said.

Dinah forced herself to look at him and drank in his features — those striking eyes, the strong jaw, the sculpted cheekbones.

"There are lots of things you don't know about me," she began, hoping to muster some courage as she talked. "There are many things I am that make this very difficult."

"Dinah," said Aaron gently, "I know about your past. I know. . . ."

"That I'm an alcoholic?" Dinah challenged him. "That I tried to commit suicide?"

Aaron took a deep breath. "I know that you were an alcoholic. I didn't know about the suicide."

"Aaron, I *am* an alcoholic," she corrected him. "I will be for the rest of my life. There is no cure except to stop drinking altogether."

"Okay," said Aaron. There was a long pause. "Do you think that would scare me away?"

"Do you want a relationship with someone who struggles with a temptation like this?" Dinah asked. "Wondering if I've had a drink?"

"I don't know," said Aaron honestly. "But I'm willing to find out."

"That's not the biggest issue we've got, anyway," said Dinah, staring at the hazy horizon.

Aaron waited her out.

"The major reason I'm no longer drinking, and that I no longer want to die, is because I'm a Christian," explained Dinah quietly. "I'm only new at it, but it's the most important thing in my life. Something that's part of my faith is to be careful about getting into a relationship with someone who doesn't share my beliefs."

Aaron was completely silent for such a long time that Dinah felt as if she'd aged a decade or so.

"Is that the main problem?" he asked. "It's not me, then?"

She suddenly became aware of vulnerability in him that she'd never seen before. He'd been worried that she was rejecting *him*!

"Aaron, I like everything about you," she said, a lump rising in her throat. *Don't cry now, for Pete's sake!* Her voice cracking, she continued, "You're the first person since my husband died who I could actually see myself in a relationship with. I think you're so gorgeous I can't believe you even noticed me. I like how easy it is to be with you, and talk to you."

Aaron took both of her hands in his and stared deep into her eyes, beyond her eyes, to her soul. "Then why are you doing this?"

"Because, as much as I like you, my relationship with God comes before everything else," Dinah said. "I know what's right and wrong, and I know what God expects of me."

"You're serious about this?" Aaron stated, almost a rhetorical question. "You'd only date me if I became a Christian?"

"Aaron, I'm sorry. That's the way it has to be," Dinah whispered.

Aaron dropped her hands from his and they suddenly seemed ice cold. "Don't be upset," he said gently. "That's the way it has to be."

Tears sprang to her eyes as she sensed him leaving, both physically and emotionally. "Aaron," she said desperately. "If you change your mind . . . I'll be waiting for you."

He nodded. "Goodbye, Dinah."

He turned and walked away, and Dinah watched him leave. The wellspring of emotion inside her rose and destroyed the thin veneer of control she had struggled to maintain. Tears streamed down her face as she suddenly realized that this level of emotion didn't come because she merely liked him. She was falling in *love* with him.

And before it could even start, she had to say goodbye to him. Unable to face going back to her apartment, she sat on the gutter, put her head in her hands, and let the tears fall. She didn't care who walked by and saw her.

When she finally lifted her head, she wiped her cheeks and tried to compose herself before facing Andy and Sandra, who were waiting in her apartment.

This is really hard, God, she prayed. *Please help me say goodbye to him if that's what I need to do.*

Back at her apartment, Andy and Sandra took one look at Dinah's red eyes and blotchy face and chose to say nothing.

Sandra decided to make some dinner for all of them — Dinah not being much of a cook — and Andy decided to watch the evening newscast on television.

Dinah had never been so glad that her friends knew to leave her alone, and she decided to read through the lawsuit Senator Winters had sent her.

She watched the top story: the familiar CCTV footage of the bomber as he prepared to wreak destruction on the beautiful cathedral. Then she went back to reading.

It took a long time — taking a break only to eat dinner, when again, the Colemans didn't ask her about Aaron — but she suddenly discovered something interesting. In making the argument for the state's inappropriate involvement in religion, the plaintiff had listed individually the organizations that had received federal funding as defendants. A few pages later, Andy's Ark Experience was also mentioned, though not directly as a defendant but rather as an example of state violations of the First Amendment.

Chapter 14

Dinah read through the list of direct defendants several times to make sure she was correct. Every church that had been bombed was listed in the lawsuit. Was that a coincidence?

Dinah read through all of the defendants again. The lawsuit didn't just deal with churches — there were charities, vocational programs, education programs, and family programs that were all independent of a church but still religious in their structure. There were five churches mentioned in the lawsuit — three of which had been bombed. That just couldn't be a coincidence.

There was also something nagging her, in the back of her mind. Something she'd read in the body of the lawsuit that triggered a memory. She couldn't quite dig at it. What was the connection between this lawsuit and the bombings?

Dinah picked up her phone and started to dial Aaron, before she realized that that was no longer an option. So she rang Ferguson instead.

He sounded seriously peeved. "What?" he barked into the phone.

"I'm fabulous, thanks for asking," replied Dinah. "Really, your concern for my well-being is just too much."

"Shut up, Harris," growled her boss. "You don't know what I've had to put up with today. I have never talked to so many disturbed people in all my life!"

"I'm sorry," said Dinah seriously. "Asking the public for help is always a big gamble."

"So what can I help you with?" Ferguson said, sounding slightly less grumpy.

"I've just found all of our bombed churches appear in a lawsuit," said Dinah.

"What? What lawsuit?"

"It's a long story as to how I came to have a copy," said Dinah. "It's a lawsuit filed by a group of secular humanists against religious organizations who receive funding from the government."

"Right, separation of church and state or whatever," said Ferguson.

"Yeah. The bombed churches are all named as defendants in the lawsuit. There are only five churches named as defendants. There are other religious organizations also named, but the bomber so far seems to be only targeting churches."

"You thinking it's too much of a coincidence?"

"Yes — three out of five?" said Dinah. "Out of all the churches in this city?"

"Yeah, I hear you," agreed Ferguson. "Who has access to the lawsuit?"

"It was filed a couple of weeks ago, so anybody who cares to look," said Dinah.

"Did the first bombing occur before or after the lawsuit was filed?"

That was an interesting question. Dinah was silent for a few moments as she worked out the chronology. "The first bombing happened *before* the lawsuit was filed," she said.

"Excellent, that's what I was hoping. That means our perp had access to the lawsuit before it was filed somehow," said Ferguson. "He must have been involved in putting it together."

"That makes sense," agreed Dinah. "I'll start chasing that down. There are two humanist groups acting as plaintiffs. He could have been active with either of them."

"Good, I'll have Sinclair assist you with that."

Dinah swallowed nervously.

"I'll stick by the phone, I suppose," said Ferguson, sounding discouraged again.

"You're a great boss, you know that?" said Dinah. "Most bosses would make their inferiors work the phone."

Ferguson laughed. "Have you heard Sinclair's phone manner, Harris? He's worse than you!" With another guffaw, he hung up.

Dinah allowed herself a wry smile. She started to read the lawsuit again, trying to figure out what the niggling in the back of her mind could be. It hit her, two-thirds of the way through the stack of paper.

The bomber, in his last communication, had used three figures: $24,950, $88,400, and $55,000.

Those very same figures appeared in the lawsuit, right next to three corresponding churches.

Our Lady of Mercy Catholic Church — $24, 950.

First United Methodist Church — $88,400.

The Heights Episcopalian Church — $55, 000.

The federal government was currently funding charity programs within these churches, and the figures amounted to the annual government funding. This was the funding the lawsuit sought to cease.

Okay, thought Dinah, leaning back in her chair. *I've figured that out — but what does it mean? What significance does it have in the overall picture?*

A loud crash from the kitchen startled Dinah, and she suddenly realized that her guests were now washing the dishes in the kitchen, having been completely ignored by her for the past couple of hours.

"I'm so sorry!" she cried, rushing into the kitchen.

Andy and Sandra just laughed at her, and Dinah was once again thankful for these wonderful friends God had provided for her.

* * * *

The restaurant catered to high-powered politicians and business people, and discretion was assured. Senator Winters commanded the best table when he arrived and immediately ordered the most expensive bottle of imported red wine on the menu.

His old friend Maxwell Pryor, Chief Justice of the Supreme Court, slipped in about five minutes later. The waiter appeared instantly to fill the tall man's glass and then vanished just as miraculously.

"How are you doing, buddy?" Winters asked jovially.

Their friendship had started out as one of convenience — they'd both been trying to achieve the same objective when they met during the Smithsonian case. Where Winters was ruthless, Pryor was more likely to stick his head in the sand. Yet he knew when a problem had to be dealt with — even by murderous means — and he always supported the senator's plans.

Now it seemed likely the Supreme Court justice would be doing him a favor.

"Just fine. How are you?" Pryor asked, tasting the wine and apparently approving of it.

"Just great. Trying to change the world, one step at a time," laughed the senator.

"And you need my help?" Pryor asked, raising an eyebrow. The two powerful men didn't meet for small talk. Usually they got right down to business.

The waiter took their order, and then Winters started to explain. "I'm supporting a lawsuit filed here in D.C. in the federal court," he told Pryor. "It involves the government funding religious organizations who expressly proselytize. It's a clear violation of the First Amendment."

Pryor nodded slowly. "The district court will probably not rule in your favor," he opined. "Most district judges seem to leave the serious lawmaking up to the appellate courts."

Ouch, thought Winters. "My research would seem to support that view," he agreed. "Of course we will appeal."

"Where it is likely you'll win," said Pryor. "What do you need me for?"

"I'm hopeful I won't need you," said Winters. "But I can guarantee you that the defendants will submit a writ of certiorari to the Supreme Court. They don't want precedents being set on this matter against them, if they can help it."

A writ of certiorari was a plea to the Supreme Court, asking for their case to be heard. It was filed by the party that had lost in the appellate courts. The Supreme Court didn't accept every request that was filed; indeed, they usually chose cases that had broader implications for the law.

Pryor nodded. "So you need me to ensure the Court accepts the writ of certiorari, and rules favorably upon it."

"I guess it's a lot to ask," conceded Winters. "But I can assure you the reward would be great."

Pryor had dealt with Winters enough to understand that by "reward," the senator meant money. He lived for nothing else, except perhaps power.

Pryor thought about this quickly. "You understand, of course, that my fellow judges are *all*, without exception, very sharp, independent, and serious-minded individuals. I simply cannot try, or be seen to, unduly influence any decision they might make."

"Let's start with the Court granting the writ of certiorari," suggested Winters. "There would be reward in itself for that."

"I think I can deliver on that," Pryor replied. "I'm the Chief Justice. They hold my opinion in some degree of high regard. In any case, most of the justices are extremely interested in interpreting constitutional law. I only need the agreement of three other justices to grant cert, anyway."

"Excellent." Winters poured another glass of wine without waiting for the attendant. "The second request is the most challenging, I understand that. I'm sure you have a good understanding of whether justices tend to lean to the right or left."

"Certainly," Pryor agreed. In fact, he could usually predict the verdict in any case that was controversial — death penalty, human rights, or the Constitution. The conservative judges tended to vote conservatively, while the liberal judges tended to judge liberally. The side that won the verdict depended on whether the justices were in the majority liberal or conservative. At the moment, it was split. There were three conservative judges, three liberal judges, and Pryor, who would usually vote liberally. The remaining two prided themselves on being moderate, and therefore open to influence by either side in the debate. Pryor knew he'd only have to convince one of them to vote his way to ensure the Supreme Court decision was favorable to Winters. As Chief Justice, he certainly wielded enough power and respect to make a compelling argument — but he would never be able to guarantee a certain outcome. Justices of the Supreme Court of the United States were not appointed because they were gullible, easily influenced, or open to bribery.

Pryor explained this to Winters.

Senator Winters didn't want to tell his friend that part of his *own* reward money depended upon the Justice succeeding. For one thing, it wouldn't impress Pryor, and for another, it wouldn't advance the outcome for which he was looking.

All he could do was hope that Pryor's greed became more pressing as the possibility of receiving such a windfall improved.

In all likelihood, it would take about three years for the Supreme Court to receive the petition for a writ of certiorari, in a best-case scenario. In the meantime, Winters had to fervently hope the Chief Justice didn't have a heart attack or get hit by a bus.

"Precedent set in other areas of First Amendment law seem to be favorable," said Winters at length. "By both the Supreme Court and district appellate courts."

"Indeed," agreed Pryor. "I can't foresee much of a problem, except if the current mix of judges is interrupted in any way."

That was a scenario outside of Winters' control, much to his disgust. He started to feel a surge of anger toward Cartwright for making demands upon him over which he had little power. Winters, onto his third glass of wine, decided his fee had just increased.

They ate, talked about the prevailing Washington, D.C., gossip, and drank some more. Winters may once have commanded a platoon of Rangers, but it seemed his powers of observation and paranoia were beginning to fail him. He didn't once see the slight figure of Connor Eastleigh, his new intern, sitting behind him, pretending to eat dinner but in reality, listening to every word.

* * * *

Dinah reluctantly bade farewell to Andy and Sandra, who would remain in the city for several days, and then left the apartment herself to meet Ferguson and Sinclair at the nearby Starbucks. She took the thick wad of paper that made up the lawsuit with her.

They were both waiting for her, somewhat impatiently. Instead of flashing her a deep, azure gaze, Sinclair stared solemnly at the table.

Dinah took a deep breath and commanded herself to act normally. "So our bomber has hit three of the five churches mentioned in this lawsuit," she explained, after coffees to keep them awake for several hours yet had been ordered. Thankfully, the belligerent sun was sinking, and the air cooled with every passing minute.

"What's the link?" Ferguson asked, mostly for Sinclair's benefit, who was showing little interest in the case at the moment.

"The case is essentially suing for violations of the First Amendment, namely separation of church and state. All three of our bombed churches are named as defendants, because they run charity programs which attract government funding."

"What programs?" grunted Sinclair, as if he were just waking up from a deep sleep.

"Uh . . . the Catholic church runs a phone domestic violence counseling service; the Methodist church in Manassas runs a prison vocation and parole advocacy program; and the Episcopalian church offers professional services, like lawyers and accountants for free to people who wouldn't otherwise be able to afford them."

"They seem like worthwhile programs," commented Ferguson.

"That doesn't seem to matter," replied Dinah.

"Who are the remaining two churches?" Sinclair asked.

"Sixteenth Street Baptist Church and Calvary Holy Church," said Dinah. "The Baptist church runs a literacy class for homeless and transient adults, and the Calvary church runs a vocation program out at Waverly, Virginia."

"Doesn't seem to be much of a link between the programs offered," said Ferguson. "They're all varied. Which church do you think he'll hit next?"

"There doesn't appear to be an order, at least going by the lawsuit," mused Dinah. "The Catholic church that was hit first is listed right in the middle of the document, for example."

"We can't take any chances," said Sinclair. "We need to send officers to both locations on Sunday, which" — he glanced at his watch — "is only one and a half days away."

"All right, let's go for a drive," suggested Ferguson. "Talk to the fine fellows in charge of these churches."

Ferguson drove, and Dinah had the backseat to herself, for which she was thankful. The awkwardness between herself and Sinclair was growing at a supercharged rate.

Sixteenth Street Baptist Church was located, as the name suggests, on Sixteenth St., and it didn't take long for them to arrive. The Friday night youth program was in full swing, the church lit up with floodlights and the sound of excited laughter spilling from the doorway.

Pastor Bobby Spring was supervising events, which looked like an obstacle course designed to wear out energized teenagers.

When Ferguson showed him his badge, he left the youth group in the capable hands of the youth pastor and showed them to his cramped office. "Can I offer you a drink?" he asked, showing them to a corner, where he intended to sit on a desk chair, and the only remaining seating was a long couch. Ferguson declined on behalf of all of them, and the race to find the most comfortable position on the couch began.

Unfortunately, Dinah was wedged between the bulk of Ferguson and Sinclair, and although he steadfastly refused to look at her, she was distracted by the lean heat of his arm, which pressed against hers, and the sheer closeness of his presence.

"We're here because we believe your church may be under threat," began Ferguson.

"By whom?" Pastor Spring asked.

"You may have heard of a domestic terrorist targeting churches in the greater D.C. area," said Ferguson. "There have been three churches bombed, unfortunately resulting in loss of life and injury."

Spring looked both horrified and shocked. "And you think we could be next?"

"I'm afraid so," said Ferguson. "We've received some new information that leads us to believe it's a distinct possibility. We'd like to send officers to each church service you hold on Sunday. It'll cause disruption to your day, and I'll apologize in advance for that. However, I'd prefer a little inconvenience if it saves the lives of your congregation."

Spring seemed to be having trouble processing this new information. "Of course, Special Agent. If you think it's really necessary, I'll happily comply. I . . . I just don't know why we'd be a target."

Ferguson seemed to be debating within himself how much to tell the pastor. Finally, he said: "We believe it has to do with a charity program. You run literacy classes for homeless or transient adults?"

Spring nodded. "Yes. You don't think a homeless person . . . do you?"

"No," said Ferguson. "At this stage we don't believe it has anything to do with someone who's been through your program."

Leaving the pastor to contemplate the sudden change in circumstances for his little church, the three investigators climbed back into the car and drove south on the I-95 to Richmond, Virginia. The interstate was pretty clear at this time of night, but they didn't arrive until after ten.

The Calvary Holy Church was dark and quiet, any evening activities having long since finished. Sinclair rang the pastor's number, who invited them to his house, only two streets away.

Pastor Dan Rockwell was middle-aged, round, and cheerful and asked them into his living room, which thankfully had plenty of individual seating.

This time, the investigators all gratefully accepted coffee, and then Ferguson explained the reason for their visit. "The bomber has not struck outside the city of D.C. yet," acknowledged Ferguson. "But new information would lead us to believe that it's not the physical location of the churches that inspires our bomber."

"Why would he choose us?" Rockwell asked.

This seemed to be the most common question, one Dinah intended to ask the bomber herself.

"It seems to have something to do with a prison vocation program," explained Ferguson.

"One of the inmates was released?" asked Rockwell, wide-eyed.

"No, we don't believe so," said Ferguson with a frown, though in all honesty none of them had thought of this as a possibility.

Again, they left the pastor more disturbed than they'd found him — but at least the safety of both congregations was somewhat ensured.

The drive home into the dark, warm night was quiet, with each lost in his or her own thoughts. Dinah tried to think of the case, but her mind kept returning to one thought, annoyingly playing over and over: *How can I give up the only man I've come close to loving since my husband?*

* * * *

The night drew late, but neither Michael nor Isabelle wanted to go to bed — or to go home, in Isabelle's case. She wondered what Scott was doing — whether he would appear at Michael's house, knowing that that's where she was likely to go. However, she thought he was probably quite cheerfully depositing her possessions on the curb and changing the locks.

Michael's cell phone buzzed, for the umpteenth time. He glanced at it and deliberately pressed the CANCEL button.

"Who is it?" Isabelle asked curiously.

"Who do you think?" said Michael with a wry smile. "Mom."

"Oh, she mentioned to me that she was trying to contact you," said Isabelle. "She was upset because she wants to be able to talk with you every day."

"Yeah, well," said Michael, "there are times when I just can't deal with her *drama.*"

Isabelle sighed. "What do you think she'd say if I told her Scott decided to divorce me?"

"She'd flip out," said Michael immediately. "Marriage is for life, you know that."

"I don't disagree, but what if there is abuse within the relationship?"

"You're asking the wrong person," explained Michael. "Mom was punched, shoved, and kicked on a weekly basis, but still played happy family at church on Sundays. You probably couldn't get a better excuse for divorce than the stuff she went through, yet she didn't leave him."

"And by default, what *we* went through," added Isabelle, her mood darkening.

They sat in silence for several moments. Michael's phone rang again and he turned it off, the screen fading to black.

"Why don't you just talk to her?" Isabelle suggested. "She's probably ringing my phone after you. It must be bugging Scott no end."

Michael smiled. "Then I'm glad. Let her keep ringing him."

"You really don't like Scott, do you?"

Michael considered his older sister, still so naive and eager to please in many ways. "Let me put it to you this way. I spent my childhood watching the finest bully on earth wreak havoc in our family. I swore to myself I'd never let myself be bullied when I became old enough to do something about it. Hence my unsurprising intolerance of bullies." He paused for a moment. "Honestly, did you grow up in the same house I did?"

Isabelle laughed. "Yes, but I think our reactions to our father were different."

"Why do you say that?"

"It made you stronger," explained Isabelle. "More determined to do the right thing. It made me weak, accepting of bad behavior, and clearly crazy." She pulled her sleeve up momentarily to display a scar.

"I'm not stronger," said Michael quietly. "If Dad was alive and slapped Mom in front of me, I'm not sure I'd still be able to stand up to him."

"What did you think about — you know — during the beatings?" asked Isabelle.

There was silence for several long minutes.

"I just imagined that one day I'd have the pleasure of doing the same to Dad," said Michael. He stared at his hands. "I fantasized about walking up to him and telling him that this was it, no more violence, and that if he laid a hand on any of us again, I'd kill him."

Isabelle nodded, her eyes fixed on a point outside. The sun had disappeared a few hours ago, but light had only just given way to night. They hadn't bothered to turn on the lights and sat in the murky shadows of the kitchen.

"What did you do?" Michael asked.

"I figured there had to be something I could do to make it better," said Isabelle. "Be a better daughter. Get better grades. Be quieter. Stop making mistakes. I guess I always thought it was my fault."

So what's changed? You think by being a good wife you'll stop Scott from hurting you? By becoming a gourmet cook? By being home precisely when he wants you to be? By resigning from your job?

As if taking over from the voice in her head, Michael continued: "So you pushed the pain down, as far as it would go, and hoped it wouldn't surface. Yet it always did, and it was so immense that you had to distract yourself with something that was somehow worse. And not much is worse — except the sudden pain of cutting yourself. It gives you some feeling of control, of power over your pain, if only for a little while."

Isabelle stared at him with eyes that were hot and wet. "Are you a psychiatrist now?"

"It's simple: I know how you feel," said Michael. "Instead of hurting myself, I hurt others."

"I've never seen you hurt anyone!" she protested.

"I always hurt women before they can get too close," said Michael, by way of explanation. "I have been cruel so that they wouldn't get too close. I've burned friendships by being closed and uncaring. Look at the relationship I have with my own mother."

Isabelle almost didn't want to ask the next question, but she knew it was important. "Michael . . . is that *all* you've done?"

She could plainly see he was deeply conflicted, but finally he said honestly, "No, it isn't. I can't tell you," he said, unfolding his tall frame and pacing in the small kitchen.

"Come on, Michael," she said encouragingly.

Michael stood in the doorway, a silhouette that was suddenly frightening.

"You want to know what I've done?" he said softly. "Come here."

"What do you mean?" *How well do I know my own brother?* All at once this question seemed vital.

Michael used a remote control to turn on the television. "Come here and watch this. Then you'll see what I've done."

"What are you talking about?" Still, Isabelle was inexplicably drawn toward the screen now flickering in the dark room.

"Watch this. You'll see what I've done," said Michael as the newscast began.

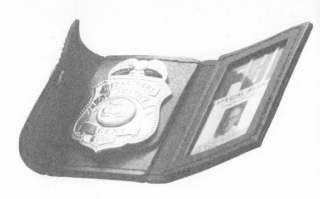

It was past midnight, and Isabelle had watched the news in horror, unable to believe her own eyes. Over and over, the image burned into her brain, she saw her brother walk casually from a car laden with explosives into a church, knowing full well he was about to kill some people therein. "Michael . . ." she said finally, "what have you done?"

"I don't know," he said miserably. "I don't know."

Isabelle leaned back in an armchair, unable to take it all in. "*You're* the bomber?" she asked. Her own problems paled in comparison. "But *why?*"

"I told you I can't control it," he said. He spoke slowly, weighing his words carefully. This was the first time he'd spoken out loud of the dark things that had always been kept close to his heart. "I'm a bad person."

"You're not!" protested Isabelle, instinctively. "Look at all the things you've done for me: you stand up for me against Scott, you're loyal, you try to protect me! Those are things a *good* person does."

"A good person does not kill people in a church with a bomb," said Michael flatly.

That was true and hard to argue.

"So tell me why," said Isabelle. "Why do you want to kill people in a church?"

Chapter 15

Michael stood and paced the dark room. "I look at them, and I see hypocrites. I see people concerned with their own happiness, their own prosperity. They didn't care about me when I was a kid, and they don't care about me now."

Isabelle nodded. "Okay. But you killed people you didn't even know."

"Luckily for the people I *did* know," muttered Michael darkly. "Look, I can't explain it well. Maybe I should put it in these terms. You feel pain and anger from our childhood, right?"

"Of course. It doesn't go away," admitted Isabelle. "Somehow you have to learn to live with it."

"Right. In your case, when you feel your emotions getting to be too much, you turn inward and cut yourself," said Michael. "Apparently quite common among females. But me . . . when I feel the anger, I just want to hurt somebody. It sounds awful, but it's the truth."

"Why didn't you just visit Dad when he was still alive and ask him to fight you or something?" Isabelle asked. "You could've taken out your anger on the person who truly deserved it!"

"I wish I could have," agreed Michael. "Somehow, I could never shake the fear of him. It was like I was always a little kid around him."

They fell silent. Isabelle knew how that felt — she'd been the same. Even as an adult, her father losing his temper had reduced her to a quivering, helpless, frightened child. She had barely begun to understand what Michael had done: her brain simply couldn't process it. It felt surreal to be sitting in his ordinary living room, discussing the most extraordinary situation. She felt like she was looking through a haze, a fog of incomprehension. "Why did you wait until Dad died to start doing . . . this?" she said at length.

"I have been planning this for a long time," said Michael. "But I'd always hoped that when Dad died, the hatred and anger would die with him. I hoped that I would finally begin to heal once he was dead. But it didn't work. In fact, I felt worse."

"So why not Mom, then?" Isabelle asked. "She should have protected us, and she didn't. You would have a legitimate anger toward her."

"Perhaps," agreed Michael. "But then, she suffered as much as we did. She didn't escape the abuse."

"So you saw churchgoers as a legitimate target, then?"

"I can hardly call them legitimate," said Michael. "But it made the most sense to me. I *knew* I was going to be violent. I could feel it build up inside me to a point where I could no longer control it. But I didn't want to be random about it. I thought if I did it in a measured way, with a message, that people would understand."

Isabelle sighed. "People aren't going to understand, Michael! You killed innocent people on a personal vendetta!"

Michael started out the window moodily. "I knew this day would come," he said. "They're going to come for me."

Isabelle now tried to wrap her mind around this truth. They would come, with SWAT teams and sniper rifles and stun grenades. If he made one false move, they would shoot him — and they would mean to kill him.

"They're going to kill me, Isabelle," said Michael, his voice echoing her thoughts.

"No. If you cooperate with the authorities, they won't kill you," she said. "You just have to. . . ."

"They'll kill me with a gun or by lethal injection," said Michael. "It doesn't matter. Either way, I'm dead."

Isabelle was suddenly seized with fear. She couldn't lose her only brother, her protector, the only person who'd ever tried to keep her from harm. He'd done something awful, something mind-bendingly shocking, but he was her brother and she loved him. She couldn't let him die! "It doesn't have to be that way," she said desperately. "We can get a good defense attorney and. . . ."

"Don't you see?" Michael interjected. "I'm already dead."

Isabelle stared at him in horror as his words hit home. He had started to die the very first time Reginald McMahon had left a bruise on his small body. His spirit had withered in an environment of fear and brutality. Who he could have been was slowly and methodically extinguished.

How was she any different? She vented her pain on herself, enjoying the power pain gave her. But when she finally made a cut too deep, too far, and her very life began draining down the bathtub, she would be no different from Michael. She, too, was the walking dead.

Neither had known what it was to live. They were biding time until death claimed them. No light had ever pierced the darkness that surrounded them, and she suddenly understood the desperation in which Michael lived.

"I understand," she said quietly. "I'll stay with you, until the end."

He reached over and grasped her hand. "Thank you."

* * * *

Very early the next morning, Dinah was jerked from a deep, dreamless sleep by the shrill chatter of her cell phone.

"Yes, what . . . hello?" she mumbled into the phone, not certain of where she was or what time it was.

"Harris, wake up," ordered Ferguson. "We've just received a phone call from a relative of our bomber."

That shook the final sleepy cobwebs from Dinah's head. "What?"

"The bomber's mother has contacted us. We're picking you up in 15 minutes."

Dinah showered quickly, dressed, and spent several moments vacillating over whether to wear makeup. Finally, she gave up — she no longer wanted to impress Sinclair, and he was clearly no longer impressed.

Ferguson and Sinclair screeched up to Dinah's block, and she jumped in the back seat. Sinclair handed her a small tape recorder, and didn't meet her eyes.

"Listen," ordered Ferguson, as he accelerated down Dinah's block.

The conversation taped was between Ferguson and a woman who claimed to be the suspect's mother.

"Hello, FBI," rasped the familiar voice of Ferguson over the tape.

"Yes, hello? I'm calling about the footage on the news," said a quavery female voice. She sounded like she was at least middle-aged, possibly older.

"Yes, ma'am." Dinah could detect a trace of frustration and impatience in her boss's voice.

"The bomber? The footage of the bomber? I know who he is," said the woman.

"And how's that, ma'am?"

"He's my son."

There was a tiny pause, and then Ferguson suddenly sounded very interested. "What is your name, ma'am?"

"Rosa McMahon. It's my son. His name is Michael McMahon."

"Are you sure?"

"You think I don't know my own son?" Here, Rosa McMahon dissolved into a flood of tears.

"We're going to visit you this morning," said Ferguson. "What is your address?"

That's where they were headed — the tidy, scrupulously neat home of Rosa McMahon. It exuded a cottage charm: though small, the porch was decorated with hanging baskets of flowers and a shabby rocking chair, the garden beds were well-tended with a deliberate overgrown feel, and the lush green lawn was spotted with stone bird baths.

Rosa McMahon, a small woman in her sixties, was waiting anxiously on the porch, wringing a handkerchief in her hands. She led them into a living room, decorated with floral carpet and heavy drapes. It was dark and cool, giving the investigators some respite from the muggy weather outside. She gave the detectives a recent photo of Michael, a young man in his late twenties with a rather expressionless face. It was, without doubt, the bomber in the CCTV footage.

"What can you tell us about Michael?" Ferguson asked gently. Rosa McMahon, they could see, was teetering on the edge of hysteria. *How would you even begin to process the fact that a child of yours is a mass murderer?* wondered Dinah.

"He was a good boy," said Rosa. "A lovely child, so quiet, never in any trouble. I started to lose him in high school."

"Lose him?"

"He refused to come to church with us anymore. He told me that church was full of hypocrites. He started exploring other religions and philosophies," Rosa remembered. She looked haggard in the dim light; she probably hadn't slept at all the previous night. "He stopped talking to me. He distanced himself from all of us."

"Did he get into trouble as a teenager?" Ferguson asked.

"No. He never got into fights or drugs or trouble with the law," said Rosa. "In fact, he continued to get good grades. He just stopped doing the things I asked of him."

"What sort of philosophies did he explore?" asked Dinah, thinking of the last case on which she'd worked. A killer had wholeheartedly believed in eugenics, the science of improving the human race, and considered it a favor to humankind to kill those he deemed unworthy of life. Having a dangerous set of beliefs could easily lead to extreme violence.

"He started with Buddhism, if I remember correctly," said Rosa. "He also tried Hinduism and some old, African animism-witchdoctor type of thing. Eventually, he declared that all the religions' gods were the same and that he didn't believe in God at all."

"What church had you been going to?"

"We're Catholic," said Rosa. "I was deeply shocked when he told me he didn't believe in God."

Dinah exchanged glances with Ferguson. The first church bombed had been Catholic — was that symbolic of something Michael felt for that denomination?

"Did something happen as a teenager to make him start questioning his beliefs?" asked Dinah.

Rosa stared at her hands miserably. "It wasn't just one thing. It was all my fault. I'm the one who drove him away from the Church."

"Why do you say that?"

Rosa wept silently for a few moments and then tried to pull herself together. "I was married to a violent man," she said. "Their father would beat me and the kids for any slight infraction, or for no reason at all. My kids grew up in fear and it changed them forever."

Dinah nodded. Domestic violence often perpetuated a vicious cycle through the generations, of continuing violence and abuse.

"Yet we pretended everything was normal at church on Sundays," continued Rosa, her voice betraying the heartbreak she felt inside. "Even though I'd turn up with a black eye or busted lip. I'd make up some excuse and everyone believed it. Reginald — my husband — was so charming and likeable that they probably didn't want to believe he was capable of violence."

Rosa wiped her eyes with her sodden handkerchief. "I know as they grew up my kids probably wondered why I stayed in the marriage," she said. "But they didn't understand that divorce isn't an option. I tried to protect my kids from the worst of it, and I failed miserably."

Dinah pressed her lips together. "Do you think Michael resented the fact that the church turned a blind eye to what was happening in your house?"

"Yes, he probably did. He told me on a number of occasions that he couldn't correlate the 'love-thy-neighbor' message on Sunday with the reality of life on every other day. I know he certainly resented me."

"Is your husband still alive?" asked Dinah.

"No, he died just over four weeks ago," said Rosa.

Dinah carefully filed this away. The dominant, violent patriarch of the family had died four weeks ago, and the son — possibly full of resentment, rage, and hatred — had commenced bombing churches only a week later.

"How did Michael take his father's death?"

Rosa sighed. "It's hard to say. He doesn't show much emotion and he doesn't speak to me about anything more than superficialities. I didn't think he felt grief; I think he was relieved."

"What does Michael do for work?" Ferguson asked.

"He's a paralegal for a legal firm here in D.C., and he's also a freelance writer," said Rosa.

Ferguson cleared his throat. "Mrs. McMahon, we need your son's address and phone number. We'll be going over there to visit him with a warrant for his arrest. You need to be prepared for that."

Large tears fell from Rosa's eyes. "I have already prepared for that. I've just turned in my own son. No matter what happens to him, he'll never forget that I betrayed him, one last time."

* * * *

A makeshift office was set up in the car outside Rosa's home. Ferguson started the car and began driving with reckless abandon toward headquarters. Sinclair, on the phone to the first judge they could think of, began his quick argument for a search and arrest warrant. Ferguson, on his own cell phone, one hand to his ear and one hand on the wheel, began notifying the SWAT team leaders of their intention and set up meetings for later that morning.

Dinah felt quite helpless until her own cell phone rang. "This is Dennis Flynn," a man introduced himself. "I'm returning your call."

Dinah had no idea who Dennis Flynn was or why she'd wanted to talk to him. "I'm in my car," she said apologetically. "So please jog my memory — where are you from?"

"I'm from Vermont Stone and Granite Company," he explained. "I'm the site foreman on a granite quarry up here in Vermont. You called wanting to know if we'd had some problems with some explosive slurry being stolen." Dinah suddenly remembered. After she'd explained her theory to Sinclair that the ANFO slurry had been pre-mixed, she'd called around a dozen or more mines, trying to discover where the ANFO explosives had been sourced.

"Right. So have you had any problems?"

"The only problem we had was when there was one particular employee," explained Flynn. "He came to work in munitions and was mostly responsible for setting the charges in our granite quarry. Unfortunately, he was also responsible for ordering supplies."

"That's how you mine granite, I understand?" Dinah asked. "You use explosives to dislodge it and then transport it to be cut and polished?"

"Right. We had a few munitions guys working for us," said Flynn. "But this one guy was in charge of stocking the explosives. There was always a problem with an order — a bag missing here, some dynamite missing there. It was always a very small discrepancy that was explained away. The supplier had sent the wrong amount, or the order hadn't been entered properly."

"How were the explosives packaged? Did they come pre-mixed or did you mix the ammonium nitrate and fuel oil on site?"

"No, we didn't mix anything. We bought the stuff pre-mixed, in these big, heavy bags. All we had to do was attach the primary explosives, fuses, and timers."

"And those bags started to go missing?"

"Right. Just a couple at a time, over a long period of time," said Flynn. "We called the police, of course — we're talking about explosives, after all. But we never caught anyone red-handed. I could never substantiate my suspicions. And when the guy left, the thefts stopped."

"How many bags were stolen in all?"

"Maybe 25?" *Enough for five bombings,* thought Dinah.

"And what was the guy's name?"

"Michael McMahon."

Another piece of the puzzle fell into place. Dinah thanked Flynn for getting back to her and relayed the news to the front seat.

Ferguson screeched into the parking lot of the J. Edgar Hoover building and explained to Dinah that the meeting with the SWAT teams was about to begin. "You want me to be there?" she asked, referring to her long and painful history with the Bureau.

"Yes," said Ferguson, panting a little at the pace Sinclair set in front of them. "Anyone got a problem with it, they'll have to get over it."

Inside a nondescript conference room, the bulky forms of an FBI Hostage Rescue Team and a SWAT team sat at attention, ready for their next mission. Ferguson had called in the HRT because they were experts in dealing with terrorism and could begin negotiations with the bomber, and the SWAT team for their ability to storm the building as the need arose.

Tersely, Ferguson began: "We have identified the perpetrator responsible for bombing three churches in the greater D.C. area and we have obtained his home address, where we believe he is currently located. We intend to travel to his residence and we have been granted arrest and search warrants this morning."

Sinclair nodded confirmation that the warrants had been granted.

"The residence to which we'll be going is located in Parkview," continued Ferguson. "The first thing we all need to keep in mind is that there is a high likelihood of explosives in or around the residence. It'll be a small, bungalow-type residence that is single-story. We've already sent two agents to the location to ensure that the target is there, and to scope out vantage points. Once we get there, any further decisions will be made in the field. Any questions?"

"Do you think he'll have hostages?" one of the team leaders asked.

"We don't know at this stage. We'll have to assess the situation when we get there."

That was enough for the HRT and SWAT; they were eager to begin their mission. Testosterone charged through the air as guns were checked and body armor donned. Ferguson beckoned to Sinclair and Dinah to follow him back to the car. Once they were on the way to Michael McMahon's house, Ferguson glanced over his shoulder.

"I can't give you a weapon, Harris," he said. "But we'll give you a vest."

"I understand," said Dinah. She could feel the nervous tension charging the air — all of them were feeling anxiety, fear, excitement, and a great desire to apprehend the bomber.

To keep her hammering heart under control, she looked out the window and saw a typical Saturday morning unfolding for the people on the street. Moms pushed strollers with towheaded toddlers in them; young people hurried to retail jobs; cab drivers waited in the warm air for their next fare.

She could see the dark head of Sinclair as he stared out of the front passenger seat window. She felt her heart surge again. *Stay safe,* she told him silently. *I could not bear to lose you, too.*

* * * *

Senator Winters had been dragged into a weekend meeting of the Committee on Armed Services, a position he held by virtue of his previous service in the Rangers. As a result, his offices were quiet — his secretaries, aides, and interns were all enjoying a rare day off.

When Connor Eastleigh let himself into the darkened offices, every sense was hyper-alert. He strained his ears for footsteps and his eyes swiveled constantly, checking for people who shouldn't be there.

When he was satisfied that he was alone, he carefully crept down the carpeted hall toward the senator's office. If he was caught, the ramifications could be explosive. But if he completed his mission, the results would be catastrophic — for Winters.

Connor felt nothing personally for the senator — he wasn't motivated by hatred or revenge. He was simply doing what he'd been told to do. In a city where the weak were routinely destroyed, it was just another fact of life.

Really, he thought, there was little difference between street gangs and the gangs in Capitol Hill. Both had a code of unwritten rules with brutal consequences for breaches.

Inside Winters' office, Connor knelt down behind the desk so that should anybody walk by, they couldn't see him. Using a long, thin tool, he carefully picked the lock on the filing cabinet.

From there, he quietly and methodically looked through every file in the cabinet. Most of it was generic, senatorial office paperwork that would ruffle nobody's feathers. He finally found it in a file buried at the back of the cabinet, appropriately misnamed. When he found the documents he'd been looking for — the smoking gun — his pulse quickened.

He stood up and checked the hallway again. It was all clear, and he quietly walked to the open office area, where the photocopier was located. This was the most dangerous part of his mission — should he be caught here, he'd probably go to jail. Actually, he'd been warned that if Senator Winters caught him, he'd probably end up dead.

The hairs on his neck stood on end as he waited in a vulnerable position for the photocopier to finish running. When it was done, he carefully replaced the documents in the filing cabinet and locked the cabinet. Then he took out a cloth and polished every surface he'd just touched.

Finally, he left the senator's offices and walked down the street. He expected to hear a yell behind him, the footsteps of a security guard demanding to know what he'd been doing. The hairs on his neck stood on end as chills raced each other up his spine. He finally managed to get to a Starbucks, where he ordered a grande and dialed a number on his cell phone. "It's done," he said tersely.

"Well done. What did you find?"

"I found financial documents confirming our suspicions," said Connor, looking over the documents again.

"Excellent, excellent. I always knew that forensic accounting degree would come in handy for you, son."

Connor smiled. "Why do you want to take this guy down so badly?"

"It's a long story, son. Suffice to say he's not a nice guy and he's had it coming for a long, long time. He's hurt a lot of folks."

"Is politics always this dirty?"

There was a bark of laughter. "Politics is *usually* a dirty business. The sooner you learn that, the better. And some people become so obsessed with power they'll do anything to get it — or keep it."

Connor glanced around the Starbucks, still not feeling safe. He eyeballed the other patrons, trying to decide if any of them looked suspicious. There were no men in dark suits and sunglasses, no shifty glances, no one who looked even remotely interested in Connor or what he was doing.

"Are you sure he won't come after me?"

"We're gonna take him down for good, son. He won't be able to come after you. I promise."

Connor hung up and finished his coffee, starting to relax.

Outside in the balmy spring air, Connor walked in the opposite direction to where the Capitol dome was lit up in the night. As he walked, he marveled at this great city of contradictions: promises of transparent, honest government made against the backdrop of back room deals; the manipulation of power; the intensity of personal gain. It reminded him of a shiver of sharks, all circling in the same small tank. The smaller ones inevitably are eaten by the larger ones, until there is none weak enough left to eat. Those left take any sign of weakness as an opportunity to destroy an opponent.

He arrived at the designated safe house and dropped the documents off. From there, another photocopier whirred into action and several people worked late into the night, putting together the story of the decade. Then the documents were sent to a regulatory authority, where a contact was ready and waiting for the information.

Slowly but surely, the downfall of Senator David Winters had begun.

* * * *

Sussex 1 State Prison
Waverly, Virginia
Prisoner Number: 10734
Death Row

Last night I dreamed that I was free from prison, but the tradeoff was that I had to live in my father's house again, enduring the beatings and abuse. This raises an interesting dilemma. Would I trade one torment for another?

I think about how I survived as a child, always leaving my body behind and floating to a fantasy land where I dreamed of exacting revenge on my father. Somehow, I blocked out that physical pain and ramped up for myself alternative emotional agony.

I lie awake for most of the night, mostly wondering why I had been chosen to be born into that family. Why did it have to be me who grew up with long, skinny scars on my back? Did blind bad luck seal my destiny as I was born? What person would I have become if Reginald McMahon hadn't been my father?

I can still taste the fear, as coppery as blood, flooding into my mouth when the front door opened, heralding his arrival. I can still hear my mother's lies at the emergency room: he fell down the stairs, he fell off his bike, he jumped off the porch. I can still hear the deafening silence when we walked into church, Mom sporting a black eye, and everyone looked the other way. I can still see the starburst of vivid colors that exploded in front of my eyes after a particularly vicious blow, and the feeling of falling, falling into a crevice where nobody could hear me scream.

I may as well have fallen into a crevice, I think, as I get up to prepare for my meeting with Dinah Harris. Nobody did hear me scream, nobody wanted to hear me scream.

My lack of sleep gets Dinah's attention. "You look awful," she observes, eyes darting from my gray skin to my red eyes to my puffy face. "Are you okay?"

"Couldn't sleep," I mumble.

"Thinking too much?" she asks sympathetically.

"Remembering too much," I reply.

She knows some of what I went through as a kid. She's never heard the full story, but she can hazard a guess as to what I mean.

"You look haunted," she says.

"Why wouldn't I be?" I challenge her. Today I feel exposed, vulnerable. I hate that feeling, so I get defensive and angry. "The past is full of pain, I have no hope for the future, and the present is barely better than torture. Is there anything in my life that could possibly be worth living for?"

"I wondered the very same thing myself less than a year ago," says Dinah.

I wasn't expecting that reply. I thought she'd offer platitudes about how I should live for the people who loved me, that I could make myself a better person here on death row. I just stare at her.

"I even went as far as purchasing the alcohol and pills I was going to take," she continues. "I wanted to go to sleep and never wake up."

Perhaps that's what lethal injection is like, I think wryly.

"Why?" I ask simply.

She nods. "I'd lost my husband and son in an auto accident. I wasn't handling the grief and I turned to alcohol. I messed up at work and I was fired from the Bureau, even though they'd given me a second chance. Believe me, I know what it's like to have no hope for the future."

She stares at the table for a few moments, and then lifts her head to look at me. Her eyes are bright and shining. "That's changed for me," she says. "I have hope now, and into eternity. I have a purpose for my life. Life takes on far greater meaning when you know that you're loved unconditionally."

"How?"

"I discovered that I was created by the hand of God, that He knows my name and that He loves me more fiercely than I can imagine," says Dinah. "I knew that I was a failure, a broken person, but God accepted me as I was and changed me into a new creature. I discovered that even while I denied God, Jesus died on the Cross in my place, as punishment for my sins. He defeated the death that had been reserved for me, and offered in its place salvation. I accepted and now have the rest of my life and beyond to look forward to understanding more about God."

I was ready for the religious talk, but I wasn't ready for the raw emotion in Dinah's voice. I have comebacks, retorts, put-downs for every religious argument. I don't have any answer for the deeply personal, loving way in which she speaks about God. It's like God is a beloved family member, like she actually has a relationship with Him.

It's a far cry from the distant, unknowable God of my youth who seemed to demand rituals and ceremonies and mindless devotion.

"Let me put it another way," Dinah adds. "Jesus walked into the cell, sat down on your bunk, and told you to leave. He'd spoken to the judge and the prosecutor and the warden, and they all agreed that even though you're guilty as charged, you're free to go as long as Jesus remains in your place. Jesus went into the execution chamber in your place, and died in your place. You are free, as if your crimes were never committed. No criminal record, no conviction, just a free slate. Would you be so crazy that you wouldn't take that gift?"

If that was here and now, of course I'd take the gift. But she's speaking in the abstract about an event that supposedly happened two thousand years ago.

"I'd take the gift," I admit.

"You'd take it even if it meant you only lived out the rest of your days on the earth," says Dinah. "But what if you got life on this earth plus life eternal? This life is just a precursor to what comes next. You decide in this life which eternity you want to choose — with God, or without Him. He'll honor your choice."

The guard raps on the metal door and it startles me. "Time!" he yells, as he marches in to re-shackle me and take me back to my cell.

"Think about it," calls Dinah as I leave the room. "Which eternity will you choose?"

ONE YEAR EARLIER

Michael was haggard and gray when he woke Isabelle up. He looked like he hadn't slept, and Isabelle had crashed for a few hours on the couch. He handed his sister a mug of hot, black coffee. "They're going to come for me today," he told her.

"Okay," she said uncertainly. She didn't know what this would mean; her mind flashed with images from the movies.

"I'm not going to surrender," he added. "You might want to think about leaving now."

He stood up and walked back into the kitchen. Two bombshells, dropped in rapid succession, left Isabelle reeling. Her blurry, sleep-deprived brain took several moments to process this.

"What? *What?*" She raced after him. "What do you mean, you're not going to surrender?"

He regarded her, almost with amusement. "Come on, Isabelle. What do you think will happen to me if they capture me? I go on trial, am convicted of killing people, sentenced to death, and sent to death row. There I await my state-sanctioned death for years in a tiny cage.

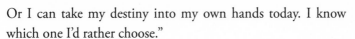

Chapter 16

Or I can take my destiny into my own hands today. I know which one I'd rather choose."

"You might not get the death penalty," argued Isabelle desperately. "You might only get a life sentence or. . . ."

"A life sentence? Somehow, that's even worse," interrupted Michael.

"So . . . what are you planning? Suicide?" Isabelle could barely spit the word out.

"Not technically," he replied. "If I don't surrender, it's likely the FBI will use lethal force to capture me. I probably won't survive."

Isabelle was beyond appalled. They were sitting in the kitchen, calmly discussing Michael's likely death, as if it had no more consequence than what they planned to eat for breakfast. Then there was the matter of Michael's next bombshell.

"I'm going to come back to this subject, but in the meantime, what do you mean I should leave? I thought we'd already discussed the fact that I want to stay with you."

Michael sighed. "I don't want to subject you to the lethal force, when it comes. You must understand you could be killed or hurt, too."

"What's the alternative? Leaving you here to face this on your own?" Isabelle shook her head stubbornly. "I won't do it. I have to stay."

"Isabelle, I created this situation on my own, and I know I have to face the consequences. Please, I don't want you to have to face them, too," pleaded Michael.

"I have never abandoned you, Michael," said Isabelle. "I'm not about to start now. You'll just have to deal with it."

Michael absorbed this information and nodded. "Then you should know there's been a black car parked outside the front of the house since four o'clock this morning," he told her. "They've been watching the house. The cavalry will be here soon. Just thought you might like to know."

"Okay." Isabelle stood and walked into the front room. Michael had drawn the curtains, and she peeked through the crack into the morning light. A black vehicle with no obvious markings was parked on the opposite side of the street, two men sitting in the front seats. They made no attempt to hide the fact that they were watching the house using binoculars.

Isabelle was overcome with a sense of foreboding that was almost calming in its intensity. It was a feeling much the same as when her father's footsteps would sound heavily up the stairs. It was perhaps the knowledge that she had no power to change the outcome. That she had always been powerless and would always be — she had been with her father and she had been with Scott. Here she stood, powerless against the might of the FBI, coming to take her brother away.

For the next hour, they sat in the kitchen, eating Cheerios and trying to pretend that on this last normal morning together, things would be okay. Isabelle tried to memorize the good things she knew about him, rather than the shocking revelations that he was responsible for the deaths of innocent people.

She remembered that he'd always tried to protect her from their father, that he'd never let her suffer alone. Even if all he could do was hug her as tightly as his little body would allow. He had lied for her, when someone had asked her how she broke her arm. He had stood up to Scott when she was being treated harshly. He had tried to protect her from Scott's insidious emotional abuse.

Michael was restless. He stood to look through the crack in the curtain once again.

"They're evacuating the street," he announced.

Isabelle took a look for herself. Very quietly, with a minimum of fuss, several men in dark suits were knocking on doors and shepherding the neighbors down the street.

And still, it looked like a normal Saturday morning.

She heard Michael's cell phone ring, and he answered. Several moments later, he appeared in the living room, his face even paler.

"What is it?" she asked

"It was Mom," he said, his voice faint. "She called to let me know she was the one who turned me in to the police."

Isabelle was stunned.

"Good old Mom," he said. "Throwing me to the pack of wolves yet again."

"Is that why she's been ringing you every five seconds?" Isabelle asked, wondering if her own cell phone — whereabouts currently unknown — had also been ringing off the hook.

"Yup. She wanted to know what was wrong with me. Like she doesn't already know," said Michael bitterly.

He was glassy-eyed and spoke in a monotone. Isabelle recognized his defense mechanism, withdrawing into himself, to the dark place where his anger festered and grew, feeding on itself.

"Listen," she said encouragingly. "Don't think about it. Does it really matter? You knew that it was only a matter of time before the FBI came. That's a minor detail now."

But she couldn't get through to Michael, who was changing before her eyes. Gone was the calm, lucid brother and in his place was an angry, volatile man with murder in his eyes.

When he reappeared in the kitchen with a semi-automatic gun and a cell phone she'd never seen before, it seemed that her heart momentarily stopped.

"What are you doing?" she gasped.

"Isabelle, it's time to get serious," he said. "If you're determined to stay here with me. . . ."

"Yes, I am," she interjected.

"Well, they'll see you as being a hostage," Michael continued. "The only other option is that you're an accessory, which I refuse to allow you to do. So if you're a hostage — I have to look the part, don't I?"

Isabelle swiftly grasped the finer details of the point Michael was making. "Can we do without the gun?" she pleaded.

"We'll see," said Michael. "We play by my rules."

He heard something and got up to investigate. He came back with a strange look on his face.

"They've come for me," he said. "It's time."

* * * *

In Parkview, the street on which Michael McMahon lived had been evacuated by the time Ferguson, Sinclair, and Dinah arrived. Behind them the Hostage Rescue Team and the SWAT team swarmed like black flies over the scene.

It was dull and overcast today, and the humidity was vicious. Dinah took off her jacket as Ferguson set up a mobile command center from the back of the SWAT team's SUV.

The team leader of the HRT was named Roger Strauss, and he approached Ferguson with the team leader of the SWAT team, Rudy Carroll. They were virtually imitations of each other — as wide as they were tall, the bulk of it muscle. Both sported buzz cuts and a ferocious appetite for breaking down doors to nab a bad guy.

Carroll spoke first. "My team has checked out the southwestern perimeter of the location," he reported. "There is one back door and several small windows to the rear of the property. I have located two possible sniper points — one on the roof of the nearby garage and one behind a grouping of trees in a neighbor's yard. Both points have a direct view into the suspect's house."

"Did you see the suspect?" Ferguson asked.

Carroll shook his head. "Windows are closed and curtains are drawn."

Strauss took over. "We scouted the front of the property and found no usable sniper points. There is a front door and two large bay windows through which we might gain entrance. The house is closed up and curtains drawn."

"Would there be any cover if our teams attempted forced entry?" Ferguson asked.

Both men shook their heads. The yard surrounding the bungalow was sparse.

"I'm somewhat reticent to send men anywhere near the garage," Ferguson said. "We know a suspect can build bombs and it wouldn't surprise me if there was a bomb in there waiting for us." He paused for a moment, thinking.

"Do we know the approximate layout of the house?" he asked.

"The front consists of a long living room and entry to the left of the front door," explained Carroll. "To the right are two bedrooms. Facing the rear of the property are the kitchen, dining room, bathroom, and bedroom."

Strauss and Carroll didn't reply but simply nodded in unison.

"What would you do, if you were in charge?" Ferguson asked. Dinah knew this was a question he asked to find out more about the team leader's style. Men who were anxious to send in the armed cavalry immediately were considered to be a little too enthusiastic to commit violence. Ferguson wanted to see whether both men would agree to a more measured, planned approach with violence as a last resort.

Unfortunately, their replies didn't instill a lot of confidence.

"I'd use stun grenades," said Strauss. "Cover the entry with sniper fire and immobilize the suspect as soon as possible."

Carroll nodded his confirmation.

Ferguson raised his eyebrows. "You don't know if there are hostages in there," he said mildly.

Carroll and Strauss glanced at each other and shrugged.

Ferguson caught Dinah's eye before he said firmly, "We're going to try negotiation first. We need to discover who is in the house and his state of mind before we go charging in. Where is your hostage negotiator?"

"On maternity leave, sir," said Strauss.

Ferguson compressed his lips until they were white. "I see. Sinclair, you've done some negotiating, haven't you?"

The other man nodded. "Sure, a little bit."

"Okay, you're on."

Dinah stood back as Sinclair was given headphones and a stalk microphone with which to make a call into the house. The entire conversation would be recorded by a device hooked up in the back of the SUV.

Ferguson sent both tactical units to their assigned locations with binoculars. No one had yet caught sight of the suspect inside the house or garage, and the FBI agent-in-charge wanted to know he was before contact was made.

The little house was closed up tighter than a crypt, and there was no report of movement. It was as still and silent as death.

Finally, Ferguson shook his head and said to Sinclair, "Okay, we've got no choice. Call him up and try to work out his location in your conversation."

Sinclair dialed the number and they waited, still as statues, for a reply.

Finally, there was a click: "Hello?"

"Hello, is this Michael?" Sinclair asked, infusing his voice with warmth to ensure the suspect remained calm.

"Yes. Who is this?"

"My name is Aaron. I guess you probably know that the FBI is here."

"I've seen them. Are you with the FBI?"

"Yes. I'd like to work out a way to resolve this situation as peacefully as possible," said Sinclair.

"What situation?"

"Well, we'd like you to come out of the house so we can talk."

"About what?"

"It's really best if we talk in person," said Sinclair. "That's why we'd like you to come out."

"So you can shoot me?"

"No. As I said, we'd like for it to be as peaceful as possible. We just want to talk."

There was a harsh laugh. "Somehow, I don't think so. How many guns you got pointed at me, Aaron? I'll bet there are a couple of snipers just itching to pull the trigger."

"That's the worst possible case scenario, Michael. Let's not let it go that far."

"Well, let me give it to you straight. I'm not coming out."

Sinclair pursed his lips and glanced at Ferguson. "Why do you say that, Michael?"

There was a long silence. Sinclair frowned. Dinah knew the feeling: that the situation was slipping out of control.

"Michael? Is everything okay?" Sinclair asked.

"Yes, it's fine. Look, I just can't come out, okay?"

"Can you tell me how you're feeling?" Sinclair tried a gentler approach.

"I'm not coming out. My sister and I have agreed. We're staying here, understand?"

The phone abruptly went dead.

* * * *

Isabelle stared at her brother as he hung up.

"What's going on?" she asked urgently.

He wasn't talking. His eyes were wild and he got up to check the curtains and doors for the thousandth time. He didn't let go of the gun but cradled it close to his chest as he darted between windows.

Isabelle was starting to get a panicky feeling in her own chest, and it didn't have anything to do with the armed men waiting outside. It had more to do with this side of her brother that she hadn't seen before, and it was scaring her.

Michael sat down, and Isabelle saw the beads of sweat standing out on his forehead and upper lip.

"She couldn't call the cops when we actually needed them," he continued. "Like, I don't know, to *protect* us. But when it comes to betrayal, she knows just what to do."

Isabelle pursed her lips as she suddenly saw a flash of insight into Michael's mind. She could plainly see that the only way she could get Michael out of this situation alive was to somehow persuade him to surrender. She had no training in psychology — how on earth was she supposed to accomplish this?

"You know," she said, at length, "I totally understand what you mean, but don't you think now that we're adults we should try to . . . forgive?"

Michael stared at her, his eyes as hard and glittery as diamonds. "What are you talking about? Which part do you want me to forgive exactly? My father for beating me? Or my mother for lying about it? My mother for failing to protect me from that beast?"

"Michael, I know," said Isabelle pleadingly. "I was there, remember? I *know*."

"What you're asking me," Michael said, "is impossible. I can't do it. It's too late."

"We can try to make this right. We can start now."

Brooding, Michael checked the doors and windows.

They were both startled by the phone ringing. Michael snatched it up and turned the speaker phone on.

"What?"

"Hello, it's Aaron," said the FBI agent calmly. "Is everything okay in there?"

"Why wouldn't it be?" snarled Michael.

"Yes. Well, that's good to hear. How is your hostage?"

Michael flashed a painful smile. "She's just fine."

"You got anyone else in there? We really care about the welfare of everyone in that house," said Aaron.

"There's just the two of us," said Michael. "What are you planning out there, Aaron? You got snipers in the trees? Planning an assault on the house?"

"Now, we just want this to end peacefully," said Aaron soothingly. "If you'd just come out. . . ."

"I'm not coming out!" yelled Michael, making Isabelle jump. "Get that through your thick head! And if you're thinking of sending in the troops, you'd better think again. This whole house is wired to the roof with explosives. It won't just take me out, you understand? It'll take out the houses on either side *and* your entire post out there on the street."

There was silence on the other end of the phone, and then Aaron said, in a somewhat strangled voice: "Okay."

"So call off the dogs, Aaron. Personally, I don't care if I get blown up — maybe that's what I've always wanted. But I don't think my sister deserves it, and I'm sure you don't want to be either."

"Michael . . . okay, I hear you," said Aaron. There was a strange muffled noise in the background. "What is it you want out of this situation?"

Michael didn't answer but hung up.

Isabelle didn't think she could be any further shocked, but Michael was proving her wrong with every passing second.

"Is that true?" she whispered. "About the bomb?"

He pointed at the cell phone, sitting harmlessly on the kitchen table. "That's not for making phone calls, Isabelle."

Isabelle shifted her chair away from it unconsciously. How could such a harmless-looking instrument wield so much power?

"Why would you do that?" she asked. "Would you really try to take everyone out with you? You would kill more people?"

"No, I really don't want to," he said. "I'm not a complete monster. But it's a negotiating tool, okay?"

"Michael . . . but what do you really want?" Isabelle said. "I know you said earlier that you want to . . . end it, but is that truly what you want?"

Michael sighed. "You know what? None of this is what I wanted. I don't know how it got so out of hand."

Isabelle watched him and waited.

"I just want people to know that what was done to me as a child is wrong," he said, pain infusing his voice. "It changed me for the worse.

Yet it's happening to thousands of kids all over the country every day. This is what it turned me into — that's what I want people to know."

Isabelle nodded. What he said made sense, and she didn't disagree.

Michael, the D.C. bomber, was the tragic outcome of a violent father and a passive mother and a society that turned a blind eye. Michael bore the full responsibility of his actions, Isabelle knew, but if only someone had stepped into their family, shown some love and affection, maybe things could have turned out so differently.

Her heart broke afresh for her sad, dysfunctional family.

* * * *

When Sinclair hung up the phone, he looked dejected. Everyone heard what had been said and silence reigned in the command post.

Ferguson scratched his eyebrow. "Well," he said, at length, "I guess that dashes our hopes of the suspect coming out peacefully."

Dinah glanced at those gathered in the small, hot space: Ferguson, who was in charge; Sinclair, Strauss, and Carroll, none of whom looked happy. A perimeter had been set up at either end of the street, and Dinah could see the media vans parked en masse as close as possible. She remembered what it was like to be a rookie FBI agent assigned to keeping the media under control: in many ways, they were harder to reason with than a criminal.

"All right," said Ferguson. "Let's hear your opinions. What do you think we should do?"

"Forced entry," said Strauss immediately. "We know there is only one innocent in there; I think we can contain collateral damage. The location is reasonably easy in which to maneuver."

"And what of the bomb supposedly wired in the house which could take your entire team out?" demanded Sinclair, raising his eyebrows. "I think we should continue to negotiate further. Everyone has a pressure point, something that'll convince him to surrender. I don't think we should try violence except as a last resort."

"I agree with Strauss," said Carroll. "Though if you're worried about the house being wired, we can set up the snipers."

"Yeah," said Strauss, nodding. "I like that. We can get the sniper a great angle and take him out. Then we'll worry about the explosives."

"Well, I still don't like it," said Sinclair. "We should be considering killing a suspect as a last resort, where the suspect is threatening lethal force. Our suspect is doing nothing lethal: he's just noncompliant."

"Oh yeah?" challenged Strauss. "What about his hostage? Taking a hostage isn't lethal?"

"Plus we know he's got a weapon," chimed in Carroll.

"I'm not convinced she's a legitimate hostage," said Sinclair with a frown. "She's his sister. You've been getting body heat readings from the house — you know they're both sitting at the kitchen table. We haven't seen any violence from him toward her."

"Any suspect who is noncompliant is fresh out of chances in my book," muttered Strauss. He glanced at his buddy.

"Yeah," said Carroll. "This is not your garden variety wife-beater with the brains of a jellyfish. In case you've forgotten, this guy is responsible for *murdering* people. You can't really get much more lethal than that, can you?"

"I still think if he sees a sniper getting into position, he's gonna blow up," said Sinclair. "Pardon the pun. You really want to take the risk of detonating this entire street?"

"Well, negotiating hasn't exactly worked, has it?" snapped Carroll.

"All right, calm down," said Ferguson. He rubbed his temples. "I'm not entirely comfortable with exercising lethal force either, I have to say."

Strauss and Carroll glanced at each other and rolled their eyes, a gesture that was not lost on Ferguson, who glared at them.

"The suspect has demonstrated his ability and willingness to use explosives," he snapped. "If there is a possibility he's got a bomb in that house, then I'd prefer to check that out before we send a dozen men to their deaths. So now we're going to talk about negotiation. If you don't have anything useful to add to the conversation, you can leave the command post."

Carroll and Strauss glowered, but both decided to leave the command post, such as it was. Sinclair sighed. "Okay. Suggestions on how to find this guy's pressure point?"

"He has a point to the bombings," said Dinah, who'd been silent up to now. "We know that much from the communications he sent to the media. He has done everything for a reason. We just need to know what that reason is and use it."

Ferguson nodded thoughtfully. "He's very angry about something; I assume something to do with churches. How can we capitalize on that?"

"We just need to talk to him," said Dinah. "We need to win his trust. We can't do anything until then."

Sinclair nodded. "Okay, so up to now we've asked him to come out. We've made some demands on him. Maybe it's time to back off, find out what he wants."

"That's the thing," said Dinah. "I'm not sure he knows what he wants. If you think about most hostage situations, the suspect wants something: money, freedom, a guarantee of something. Our guy hasn't asked for anything — yet."

"It'll just be a matter of time," said Sinclair. "He'll want something."

Dinah pursed her lips. "Have you thought about the fact that he might want to end this on his own terms?"

"What do you mean?" Ferguson asked.

"Well, if he just wants to die," explained Dinah, "he would just sit there and wait for the SWAT team to come after him. Why would he bother with the bomb if that was the case? It doesn't make sense. Plus, I really don't think he wants to hurt his sister. He wants *something* from us, and then I think he'll be ready to die."

Ferguson asked, "Suicide by cop?"

"Yeah. That could account for his noncompliance," said Dinah. "Once he gets what he wants, he'll probably walk through the front door with a gun, knowing that the nearest sniper will take him out in a millisecond."

"I'm sure Strauss and Carroll would like nothing better," muttered Sinclair.

"That's not happening on my watch," said Ferguson firmly. "A gun battle is the last thing we need, especially with the media down there viewing the whole thing."

"I have an idea," said Dinah. "You know I used to be a negotiator, right?"

"Right," said Ferguson.

"I was pretty good at it, right?" Dinah continued. "I mean, I was working with very hostile subjects. This guy is a walk in the park in comparison."

"What are you getting at, Harris?"

"I could go in there and talk to him," suggested Dinah. "Just me and him, shooting the breeze. I know how to build trust with a suspect and I know I can end this thing peacefully."

"No way!" declared Sinclair immediately. "It's too dangerous! You're not an active agent, you don't have a weapon or a badge, and we don't know what this guy could do to you."

Dinah felt a little surge of warmth toward Sinclair — did he not want her to go in because he cared for her?

Ferguson was looking at her thoughtfully. He hadn't immediately discounted her plan, and that meant she had a chance.

"You want to go in there and talk, huh?" he mused.

It was a risk, Dinah knew, but she was up to the challenge.

The morning newspaper was waiting on Senator Winters' desk when he arrived in his office; admittedly he was a little late this morning, but then he'd had a long night.

His secretary, Trixie, watched him walk into his office with large, scared eyes. He frowned at her. "What's wrong?" he demanded.

She looked at the floor. "Uh . . . nothing. Good morning, sir."

He rolled his eyes and shut his office door behind him. He stretched a little before he sat down, closed his eyes, and buzzed Trixie to get him a double-shot coffee.

When he opened his eyes, his gaze fell on the day's edition of the *Post*. His heart stopped beating and he stopped breathing. His face was plastered across the front page of the newspaper, with the headline SENATOR IN CAMPAIGN FUNDING SCANDAL!

Winters didn't recall feeling this out of control since being outnumbered in Vietnam in the middle of a tropical storm, his platoon assaulted on all sides by Vietcong bullets and grenades. But he forced himself to read the article.

Chapter 17

It has been revealed that Senator David Winters harbors ambitions greater than his current office, evidenced by the sudden inflow of money into a campaign fund. Documents sourced show that the senator has received a large donation from an entity in the last month totaling $500,000. The source of the funds proves to be most troubling, with traces showing every cent of the donation originating offshore.

The FEC regulations surrounding campaign finance strictly prohibit campaign finance from foreign nationals. The Federal Election Campaign Act prohibits any foreign national from contributing, donating, or spending funds in connection with any election in the United States.

This serious violation of ethics will surely derail any ambition Senator Winters may have had for the presidency, with sources on Capitol Hill suggesting he could face a disciplinary ethics committee hearing over the scandal. He may also face a backlash from his electorate, with many American citizens fed up with political corruption and cover-ups. He will most certainly be required to return the funds to their source.

One thing is for certain: Senator Winters, once the golden-haired child of liberal politics, faces an uncertain future with an irrevocably tarnished reputation.

Senator Winters let the newspaper drop to the ground as Trixie crept into his office with his coffee. Winters could see that she had already read the story and was now fearfully awaiting the fallout.

"Trixie," he said very quietly, "do not take any phone calls. Do not let anyone into this office. Do not make a comment to anyone. Do you understand?"

She nodded and backed out quickly, clearly wanting to be out of the room when he inevitably erupted.

Winters strode to the bar and poured himself a double shot of bourbon. He drank it in one gulp, and he was glad for the burning in his throat as it went down. It sharpened his thoughts. *How could this have happened?* he wondered relentlessly. He covered his money trails impeccably. He was very careful about what money was deposited where, and how long it stayed there. It was obviously the money sent by Cartwright, who'd promised to wire it through a legitimate American organization. Winters realized that he had not checked the source of those funds, and that he'd trusted Cartwright.

I'm slipping, he marveled, *I'm really slipping. What was I thinking?*

In the filing cabinet at his desk, Winters feverishly searched for the documents that showed the money trail. He studied it. It was perfect, as usual. In fact, Cartwright had done as he had promised: funneling the money through various legitimate American organizations. It looked like a completely genuine campaign donation.

How had the media been tipped off?

Winters knew that someone very smart had dug very deep into his financial affairs to discover the truth. Someone who had knowledge of how to trace money.

Suddenly, Winters froze. He spent several moments, his brain in overdrive. Then he snatched up his phone and buzzed Trixie.

"Yes, sir?" she said tentatively.

"Where is Connor Eastleigh?"

"I don't know, sir. I haven't seen him for two days."

"Try to contact him. It's urgent. Don't give up!"

Winters dropped the phone and remembered his very first conversation with the young intern: *I suppose you have a degree in political science? Yes, sir, and in forensic accounting.* Who better to understand the complexities of a money trail than a forensic accountant, a person trained to find money after the fact?

Winters cursed and threw his document to the floor, then hurled the tumbler from which he'd drunk bourbon across the room. It crashed into the opposite wall and smashed into a million pieces.

Winters found it immensely satisfying. He looked around for another glass to throw.

His phone buzzed. It was Trixie, calling to let him know that Connor Eastleigh was not contactable and, indeed, seemed to have fallen off the face of the earth.

Winters spent some more time raging around the office, destroying anything he could get his hands on. He simply couldn't believe that there was someone out there, brash enough, confident enough, and stupid enough, to double-cross him! Didn't they know who he was and of what he was capable? Winters had killed good men for much more minor infractions.

When I find you, he promised Connor Eastleigh, *I am going to make you beg for death. I am going to make your final living hours so unpleasant that death will be a release for you. I will find you, my friend, if it's the last thing I do.*

Unfortunately for Senator Winters, Connor Eastleigh was long gone, his task accomplished, his name and identity shed like the old skin of a snake.

* * * *

Sinclair said vehemently, "She can't go in there! She has no authority with which to negotiate!"

Dinah would have been insulted by his lack of support had she not sensed that his entire body was thrumming with anxiety.

"Sinclair, Dinah was indeed a very good negotiator in her day," said Ferguson. "Probably the best we had. If there is anyone I would send into that house, it'd be her."

"She's not a Bureau employee," argued Sinclair. "If something happens to her in there, it'll be your butt getting kicked from here to Leningrad!"

"I'm happy to go in under your obvious and clear disapproval," said Dinah. "Would that make you happier?"

"Not really," muttered Sinclair.

She turned to Ferguson. "I know I can get through to this guy. I just have a gut feeling that I can find out what he needs. I don't think he's done anything for the sake of inflicting violence upon people. I believe that he is desperately trying to send a message and he's run out of options. I think if I can somehow let him know that his message will be honored, that he'll surrender."

"You think it's that simple?" Ferguson asked skeptically.

"Think about the bombings. He built small bombs — he could have made them much larger to inflict more damage. He could have potentially killed more people. He could have loaded the bombs with nails or ball bearings to inflict maximum injury."

"He could have not bombed anyone at all, Harris," insisted Sinclair. "It takes someone with violent tendencies to carry this plan through. After all, he had to make the bomb, steal the car to put the bomb in, drive there, and detonate it. It was all done in cold blood."

"I know that," Dinah said. "I'm not denying that. I'm simply suggesting that his behavior was nonetheless somewhat regulated, and that's a person I can work with."

"You know I can't send you in there with a weapon," said Ferguson.

"You can't be serious!" exclaimed Sinclair.

"I know," said Dinah. "I want to go in as non-threateningly as possible."

There were several moments of silence, and then Ferguson said: "Okay, you're going in."

Sinclair threw his hands up in the air and shook his head angrily.

"Here are the conditions," said Ferguson. "I want you to call us every half hour, to let us know the situation is stable. If you miss a call-in, I'm sending in the SWAT teams. If the situation suddenly deteriorates, you need to send us a message."

"Your guys have body heat–reading binoculars, right?" Dinah said. "I'll put my hands up, like he's going to shoot. If you see that, come right in."

"Sinclair, call the suspect and let him know Dinah's coming in," ordered Ferguson.

Sinclair glared at them both and made the call.

"Yes?" Michael answered.

"It's Aaron. How are you guys doing in there?" Sinclair said warmly.

"Just fine. Don't you guys have anything better to do?"

"No, actually we don't. Listen, I'd like to run an idea by you," said Sinclair.

"What?"

"We want to send in a person, to talk to you."

"Why?"

"As a gesture of good faith," explained Sinclair. "We want to prove to you that we're not keen on escalating the situation. If we send one of our own in, you can be assured that we won't assault your house while she's in there. She can find out from you what you need."

There was silence, and then Michael said, "Will she come alone?"

"Yes."

"Unarmed?"

"Yes. But I must stress that we need her to be free to call us every so often, so that we know everyone is safe."

Michael laughed. "You think I'd hurt her?"

"Your track record isn't so hot," said Sinclair bluntly.

"I'm not going to hurt her. Send her in. But she better be alone and unarmed. And if I sense that she's even so much as hinting at calling in the troops, I'm not going to hesitate to push the button and blow this place sky high. You get what I'm saying?"

"Yes, I hear you loud and clear. Her name is Dinah, and she's coming to the front door."

"I'll send my sister to get her, so make sure you tell your snipers to stand down," added Michael.

Dinah was preparing herself to go into the house. Ferguson gave her a cell phone so that she could call in. Otherwise, she was taking nothing else to protect herself.

"I have implicit faith in you, Harris," said Ferguson. "But if the situation starts to get out of control, you need to get out of there. I don't want to have to live with the idea of you martyring yourself on my watch, okay?"

Dinah laughed. "I promise not to do anything stupid." She glanced at Sinclair. "Well. I'm ready to go."

She began the walk across the street toward the house in which Michael and his sister were ensconced.

Sinclair, standing in miserable indecision, suddenly rushed after her and grabbed her arm. "Dinah," he said, his voice a husky growl. "Dinah. Please be safe in there."

Dinah breathed in the sensation of being close to him and looked into his glorious eyes. "Aaron — please trust me. I know what I'm doing."

"I can't lose you," he said desperately.

"It'll be okay," she replied. *I have to let you walk away if you won't share my faith.*

When he gripped her arms, she felt the worry for her coursing through every vein and muscle in his body. "God is with me," she whispered.

He looked like there were a thousand things he wanted to say but couldn't say any of them. Finally, he simply said, "Just be safe. Don't take any chances. Promise?"

"I promise," she said quietly.

He leaned down and very softly, like a feather on a breeze, brushed her lips softly with his own. Then he turned and walked back to the command post, his fists clenched with tension.

Dinah stared after him with wonder, her heart conflicted. She faced the house and walked toward it — alone, unarmed, unprotected. Just a woman, and her God.

* * * *

When Dinah knocked on the door of the little bungalow, she felt as though she had entered another time zone or another planet. The house was so normal looking, and yet so extraordinary. The door opened a crack and a sliver of a woman's facial features became apparent. "Are you alone?" she hissed.

"Yes," said Dinah.

"I'm going to stand behind the door while you come in," said the woman. "Michael has a gun ready to shoot if anything funny goes down, okay?"

"Okay."

The door swung open a little bit more, enough for Dinah to slide through sideways. The woman slammed it shut when she was barely through, ramming the deadbolts home. A tall man, partially hidden in a doorway, aimed a semi-automatic pistol at her. Dinah said calmly, "It's just me. I have no gun or weapon. You can search me if you like."

They waited in the thick atmosphere of tension, Michael obviously expecting a trick. Finally, he lowered his gun and beckoned them both to the back of the house, where he'd been sitting at the kitchen table.

Dinah followed them carefully and sat down at the table. "I'm Dinah," she said. "You must be Michael."

"Right, and this is my sister Isabelle," he replied.

Dinah tried to observe them as casually as possible. Both looked tired and dispirited. Michael was tall and built like an athlete — wide, powerful shoulders, a narrow waist, and strong legs. He had shaved his hair very short and his wide face showed the competing emotions that afflicted him. Isabelle was smaller and thinner, with brown eyes that seemed perpetually worried, and quick, nervous gestures.

"Are you guys doing okay?" Dinah asked. "Are you hungry or thirsty?"

"We're okay," said Isabelle. "There's food and water in the fridge."

"Great. Isabelle, can I ask if you are here by choice or being held against your will?" Dinah asked. *Nothing like getting straight to the point.*

"I'm here by choice," the other woman declared. "I'm not abandoning my brother. He needs me." Dinah filed this away carefully. Outside, the SWAT teams had assumed the lady was a hostage — but she wasn't.

"Sure, I can understand that," said Dinah with a smile. "So Michael, can we talk about the bombs?"

He shrugged. "Knock yourself out." There didn't seem to be an ounce of struggle or violence left in him. He appeared to be thoroughly dejected, waiting for an outcome over which he had no control.

"Where did you learn to build bombs?" she asked casually.

He looked steadily at her. "You didn't find out during your investigations?"

"Well, I only know a little," said Dinah. "I understand you worked in a granite quarry in Vermont?" From Isabelle's posture, Dinah saw that she was just as interested in the answer.

"Right. I was responsible for sourcing and setting up the ANFO," said Michael. "It was brought into the mine in plastic bags, pre-mixed. All I had to do was add the primary explosive."

"That's what you did when you bombed the churches?"

Michael nodded. Dinah continued, "So you worked there about three years ago and you started stealing the pre-mixed ANFO back then? Did you have a plan for these bombings?"

Michael glanced at Isabelle as if he was afraid of her reaction to his answer. "I always fantasized about this, you know."

"About bombing churches?"

"Well, just about my church for a while there," said Michael. "Then I guess it expanded to include other churches."

"So you always had a plan to do this?"

Michael considered. "Not in concrete, but since I was fantasizing about it, I saw the opportunity."

Dinah nodded. "Okay." She glanced at her watch. "I have to call my boss and let him know we're all okay. I'm going to put my hand in my pocket and get out my cell phone, okay?"

Michael nodded and watched her carefully.

Dinah called the saved number and Sinclair answered, almost frantically: "Dinah?"

"We're all okay," she said calmly. "Having a really good talk."

"Okay, okay," he said, sounding relieved.

Dinah hung up and smiled at Michael and Isabelle. "I really appreciate that you're talking to me so honestly. I understand this can't be easy for you."

Isabelle expelled a rush of air, as if to say, *You're telling me.*

Michael looked hollow-eyed. "What else am I gonna do?"

Dinah catalogued this: he appeared and spoke with a defeatist air, as if he'd already given up. She wouldn't have been at all surprised to learn he was planning to die in this house.

"So how did you choose the churches?" she asked. "It looked random, but I know it couldn't have been."

Michael smiled. "No, it wasn't random. I found them in a lawsuit."

Dinah pretended to know nothing about the lawsuit. "Really? What lawsuit?"

"I'm a paralegal," explained Michael. "The firm I work for donates hours to the American Humanist Association and they needed a draft of a lawsuit written. That's how I came across the churches."

"The lawsuit targeted three churches?" Dinah asked.

"No, there were other organizations," admitted Michael. "But when I researched them all, the churches stood out to me. They made me angry."

"Why?" Dinah pressed.

Michael clenched and unclenched the muscles in his jaw. "Because they're protecting abusers."

Dinah processed this. "Abusers?"

"Men and women who abuse children," hissed Michael. "That's who they're protecting. That made me angry!" He was suddenly agitated and he stood up. "I hate them!" he snapped. "They are self-serving and hypocritical! They don't care about the welfare of children!"

Dinah sensed him spiraling out of control and backed off.

Michael paced into the living room to check the curtains and doors.

Dinah looked over at Isabelle, a question in her eyes.

"He hates abusers," said Isabelle, "because we were the victims of one. Our father was an abuser."

Dinah took the opportunity to call the command post again and let them know they were all okay. During that time, Michael had sufficiently calmed down enough to return to the kitchen table with a can of soda.

"How were these churches protecting abusers?" Dinah asked in her gentlest tone.

"Well, take the Catholic church," said Michael. The nervous tension in his body made it impossible for him to sit still. He flicked at the soda can while he spoke. "They ran a phone domestic violence counseling service."

"Right," said Dinah. "Isn't that a good thing?"

Michael gave her a withering look. "It's a counseling service for *men*, Dinah. Not for the abused, but for the *abusers*."

Dinah nodded and chose her words carefully. "Okay, but what if those men are seeking help to stop abusing their wives and children? What if they're reaching out for help?"

Michael made a noise of contempt. "You think the abused wife and children don't need help more than the men?"

"I don't know," admitted Dinah, not wanting to upset him again. She steered away from the topic. "So that's why you chose the Catholic church — because they were offering help to men?"

Michael nodded.

"And what about the Methodist church at Manassas?"

"They run a prison vocation service and parole advocacy at Waverly," said Michael. "In case you don't know, Dinah, Waverly is a maximum security prison for murderers, rapists, and abusers of the worst kind. Oh — who just happen to be men."

"I see," said Dinah. "So again, this prison advocacy group exists to help men who have been violent." *I can see a pattern emerging here.*

"Yes."

"What of the Episcopalian church?"

"Free legal and financial advice," explained Michael. "Including free representation in court for those pesky assault charges and restraining orders."

Dinah chewed on her lower lip thoughtfully. "Did you ever intend to bomb the Sixteenth Street Baptist Church or the Calvary Holy Church?"

He looked perplexed. "No, why?"

"Just wondering," she said vaguely. They sat in silence for a little while, both Isabelle and Dinah using the time to think about what he'd said.

"Michael, you are very angry with your father, aren't you?" said Dinah, at the risk of stating the obvious.

He glared at her. "You think?"

"Did bombing those churches satisfy your anger?"

Michael sighed. "No."

"Is your father still alive?"

"No."

"Did you ever think about having a conversation with your father about what he did to you?"

Michael laughed, but it was not a happy sound. "You tell her, Isabelle."

Isabelle, who was looking more wilted with every passing moment, said, "You don't understand the power the man held over all of us, even as adults. We didn't question him or challenge him. We tried to make sure he was always happy. We never, ever provoked him. It was like living with a rabid dog."

Dinah briefly touched the other woman's hand. "Okay, I understand. So Michael, did you target the churches just because of the charity programs they were running?"

His foot bouncing on the floor underneath the table, he said, "No, I've managed to nurse quite a healthy hatred toward churches without any help from anyone else."

"Why is that?" Dinah sensed she was getting to the crux of the matter, where what Michael needed to end this siege would be revealed.

"It reminds me of the church I had to go to as a child," he mumbled.

"What happened, Michael?" Dinah asked. She thought of his mother, skirting around the issue of Michael leaving the church and pronouncing that there was no God.

"My father, if I may use the term so loosely, didn't try to hide the marks he left on us," said Michael, through clenched teeth. "Mom would turn up at church with a black eye. Isabelle would have a broken arm and a completely implausible story as to how she'd broken it. I'd have a broken nose. Do you think one person at that miserable church bothered to find out if we were okay?"

"I'm guessing not," said Dinah quietly.

"Don't get me wrong — Dad was a very charming man when he wanted to be. You see, nobody wanted to believe that he would do such a thing, not when he was such a pillar of the community. They didn't want to believe it was happening, so they didn't."

Isabelle hunched even further into herself, if that were possible, as if to protect herself from the memories being conjured by Michael's words.

Dinah had to check in with the command post, so while Michael checked the curtains and doors, she phoned in.

"Is everything okay?" Sinclair asked.

"We're all perfectly fine," said Dinah, smiling at Isabelle. "Nothing to worry about."

"Okay, good. Have you felt fearful for your safety at all?"

"No, not once."

"Okay, keep us updated."

Dinah hung up as Michael came back in. He looked haunted and worried. "When are you sending in the troops?" he asked.

"Don't worry," said Dinah. "They're all well back. They won't come while I'm in here."

He nodded and stared in the distance.

Dinah had a thought and said, "Michael, getting back to those churches you bombed. Have you thought about the fact that all three of those charity programs being run by the churches could have helped *you?*"

"Oh, yes," said Michael, with a smile that was more a grimace. "I have thought about that."

"Yet you've reacted with such hatred toward them? Why would you hate something that could be beneficial to you?"

"Isn't it obvious, Dinah? Because I hate myself."

While Dinah continued to talk to Michael and Isabelle, and win their trust, outside the troops were getting edgy. It was a given that the Bureau never agreed to terrorists' demands. Therefore, the SWAT teams reasoned, there was nothing the suspect inside could ask for that the FBI could deliver. Why, then, were they wasting time with talk?

Ferguson and Sinclair knew better. The key to a peaceful outcome was not caving in to the suspect's demands but reaching a point where he no longer *had* any demands and surrendered peacefully. It was easier to achieve such an outcome through negotiation than brute force.

Strauss and Carroll were unhappy that they'd been told to back down. They were keyed up on adrenaline and testosterone to do their job, and they didn't want to wait. That's why they convened a secret meeting well away from the command post, under the guise of checking their weapons.

"This is nuts," said Strauss bluntly. "We have a guy in there who blew up three churches, killed innocent people, and hurt dozens more. Why are we treading so lightly here?"

Carroll agreed. "Not only that, they sent in a civilian to negotiate!"

Chapter 18

"She's a civilian?" Strauss was shocked.

"Used to be FBI, but that doesn't matter," explained Carroll. "She's not FBI now, yet *she's* who they trust to solve this scenario."

He didn't need to elaborate on what he meant by "they": it was implied to be Ferguson and Sinclair.

"It's a small house," said Strauss. "Uncomplicated layout. We could assault the building before the subject could locate the button he needs to push to blow the joint."

"Right," enthused Carroll. "We know he spends most of his time sitting at the kitchen table. I think we should begin with stun grenades. He's not going to be able to detonate anything in that environment."

A stun grenade, also known as a flash-bang, was a non-lethal grenade that used the bright light of burning a small amount of explosives — the flash — and a very loud sound — the bang — to confuse and disorient targets. It gave the SWAT team the element of surprise, and therefore the upper hand. They only needed several seconds of lead time to capture and neutralize the suspect before he could reach his gun or detonate the bomb.

"Could the stun grenade detonate any explosives in the house?" asked Strauss. Neither had to explicitly say it, but they were formulating a plan of attack, both fully intending to carry it out.

"They can ignite volatile fumes," said Carroll. "But ANFO is reasonably stable and has to be contained — within a barrel or bag for instance — to work. It also requires primary explosive to detonate it, and flash-bangs aren't powerful enough to set off a primary blast."

Strauss nodded. "The suspect keeps his weapon on his person at all times," he observed. "I propose an assault to his rear will provide the best outcome, as he'd have to swing around 180 degrees to defend himself. That'll buy us a few seconds, even assuming he's not incapacitated by the flash-bangs."

"What about the friendlies?" Carroll asked, referring to Isabelle, who was technically a hostage, and Dinah, who represented law enforcement, however loosely.

"We could potentially warn Harris," said Strauss. "But we'd have to communicate that through the phone to her, and to do that, we'd need to have *their* support."

"Which is unlikely," chimed in Carroll.

They fell silent for several moments. Both knew there was virtually zero chance of an assault taking place while Dinah Harris was in the house. She was clearly a favorite of Ferguson's and had some kind of special relationship with Sinclair. Yet she was unlikely to come out unless the situation deteriorated badly, by which time the SWAT teams would have no advantage over the suspect. In fact, they would be disadvantaged, because they'd be reacting to a situation they hadn't created.

It seemed that the choice came down to sacrificing Dinah Harris, or sacrificing the SWAT team troops. By every greater good argument, the troops won due to their numbers. It was better for one to be injured than a large number.

"How are we going to get authorization?" Carroll asked.

"We need to go over their heads," said Strauss, thinking out loud. "We need to somehow imply that the chain of command has broken down, and that he's not capable of making decisions."

"Without actually saying that," added Carroll. They both knew that such a conversation would be taped, and if the situation deteriorated badly, they needed to ensure that their butts were covered. If the idea to overrule Ferguson's authority came from a superior, rather than from Strauss or Carroll, they would be okay.

It would be a delicate conversation to frame, but Strauss thought he knew how to do it. They had an ace up their sleeve: Ferguson had sent a civilian into the house to negotiate. Even worse, he'd sent an unarmed and unprotected civilian into a house where they knew the suspect was armed and could have wired the house to explode.

"What if the worst happens?" Carroll asked, trying to think of every contingency. "What if we receive the order to go in, but Ferguson commands the troops to back down?"

"My team is wholly loyal to me," said Strauss. "If I give an order, they'll follow. It'll be up to me to defend my decision to give the order."

Carroll nodded. "Good. My guys will follow me in, too, no questions asked."

"We need to head off that situation before it happens," said Strauss. "I think we should quietly tell Ferguson that we've received authorization from a superior and to argue with him. In the meantime, we can carry out the order."

They both nodded and left their unspoken thoughts close to their chests.

There would be collateral damage, they knew that. It was likely to be Dinah Harris and Isabelle.

There would be a price to pay — as long as they or their men didn't have to pay it.

* * * *

"You know we talked to your mother," said Dinah.

Isabelle moved around the kitchen, her movements jerky as though she was forgetting how her arms and legs worked. She had offered to make them all a cup of coffee.

Michael scowled. "Yeah, I know."

"She was very worried about you," continued Dinah.

She watched him roll his eyes. "She also intimated that something happened at the church while you were in your teens."

Isabelle stiffened in the kitchen and turned around. Michael also suddenly looked disturbed.

"What did she say?" he asked.

"Nothing specific," said Dinah. "Enough that I know it was *something*. Enough to make you leave the church. Enough to make you hate the church, even."

Michael stood up and skulked around the house, checking the doors and windows. When he returned, Dinah was waiting for him. He didn't look at her.

"Look," she said. "I understand this is tough to talk about, but I really think it'll help you."

"How is it going to help?" he demanded. "It's not going to change the fact that your troops out there want to kill me, or that even if I make it out alive, I'm going to jail for the rest of my life. Maybe I'm happy to die right now, in this house, on my terms!"

Isabelle gasped and turned white. The coffee was forgotten.

"Michael, everything you're telling me is important," said Dinah. "I can be your advocate, if only I can gain some insight into your actions. If you just let me in, I can be your greatest ally."

Michael glared at her suspiciously for a moment. "When I was 15, I went to see the pastor at our church," he said, his tone expressionless. "I was desperate for someone to help us. Dad was getting worse, and I really thought he was going to kill one of us."

Isabelle slipped into the seat beside her brother and touched his arm briefly, in encouragement.

"I explained to the pastor everything that had been happening," Michael continued. "Everything, over all the years. I reminded him of the times Mom had come to church with a black eye, and of the times we had turned up with a broken limb."

Dinah nodded, afraid that if she said a word he would clam up.

"I had never told another soul about our family. It took all of my courage to go to the pastor. I was afraid of what would happen if my father found out." There was a long pause as Michael struggled with the emotions the memories caused.

"The pastor looked at me for a long time," Michael said at length. "I was just a skinny teenager, sobbing in front of someone from outside my family for the first time. I had never been so vulnerable in all my life."

Isabelle's eyes filled with tears as she remembered.

"Then he said to me, 'Son, it's a grave sin to dishonor your father.' I had no idea what he meant so I didn't say anything. He then said, 'Are you familiar with a verse from Proverbs that says, "A wicked man listens to evil lips; a liar pays attention to a malicious tongue"?' I shook my head. I still didn't understand what he was talking about. Then he asked me if I wanted to make a wicked man of him? It was slowly dawning on me that he didn't believe a word I'd said. He went on to tell me that a father is a great blessing from the Lord, if only I would think about all the kids out there who didn't even have a father. He told me to lie about my father like that was a very serious sin. He listed all of the wonderful things my father had ever done for the church. Finally, he told me I should go home, repent of my sin, and ask both my father and God for their forgiveness for my lies."

Dinah was shocked. Such a profound betrayal at an early age would have damaged Michael even further.

"I walked out of that church and vowed that I'd never return," finished Michael. "I have never set foot in a church again until last week."

"That's why you hate churches?" Dinah said, still trying to process what he'd told her.

"Yes, but not only for that one man's betrayal. *All* of them turned a blind eye, pretended it wasn't happening. They were happy to listen to sermons about loving one another, caring for the weak, et cetera, et cetera, as long as it was an abstract concept. When it came to the reality of loving one another, they weren't interested."

Michael's voice was steeped in bitterness.

"Why did you take it out on churches you'd never been to?" Dinah asked gently. "The churches you bombed could have been very good at practicing love, for all you know."

Michael shrugged. "I doubt it. Christians are well known for their hypocrisy. Every time I turn on the news, another pastor or evangelist or well-known Christian admits to having affairs or being a drug addict or embezzling funds from their own organization. In any case, I decided on that day that God had also betrayed me and I stopped believing Him."

Dinah nodded. "Michael, I can't tell you how sorry I am that all of these things happened to you. I am particularly saddened that your pastor didn't believe you or help you in your hour of need. What happened when you got home?"

"What do you think?" Michael said with a grimace. "The pastor had phoned ahead to inform my father of what I'd done. He was waiting for me. I spent the next two days in the hospital."

* * * *

Strauss and Carroll decided to use a cell phone to call the deputy director of the FBI, James Wakefield, the man to whom Ferguson reported and the only man who could authorize an assault without Ferguson's agreement.

Carefully, they rehearsed what they were going to say.

"It has to be his idea," Strauss cautioned. "We have to be sure we don't bring it up. All we can do is strongly recommend a certain course of action."

"Right," agreed Carroll. "And you have to make sure it sounds like there is no other option."

Strauss and Carroll looked at each other. "I guess *I'm* making the call?" said Strauss.

Carroll nodded. "You're better at this than me."

Strauss dialed the number and tersely explained to Wakefield's assistant a brief rundown of the situation. He was immediately patched through to James Wakefield's office.

"What's up, Agent Strauss?" Wakefield asked, his deep voice booming. He had presided over making changes to the "new" FBI, a Bureau that was seen to be more caring, more generous with their information, more interested in preserving life. He had achieved the massive cultural achievement with a will of iron. He was both respected and feared in the Bureau.

Strauss planned to capitalize on the deputy director's deep aversion to negative publicity.

"We have a situation, sir," said Strauss. "We currently have a hostage situation with the terrorist who bombed the three churches."

"I'm aware of it," said Wakefield. "Has there been loss of life?"

"I don't believe so, sir. The situation as it stands is that there is one hostage, and the terrorist is refusing to leave the house. He is armed and claims to have built a bomb big enough to inflict major damage on the entire street."

"It would seem he's capable of building such a bomb," said Wakefield. "I'm inclined to believe him. How are the negotiations going?"

"Well, sir, that's what I wanted to talk to you about," said Strauss. He hoped he sounded empathetic and concerned. "That's not going well, at all."

"How so?"

"The terrorist refuses to negotiate and has made no demands. He simply does not want to come out of the house."

"Made *no* demands?" Wakefield said. "That's unusual."

"Negotiations failed quickly," continued Strauss. "He doesn't want anything, and so there is nothing we can promise him to entice him to end the siege peacefully. I then suggested that we mount an assault on the house, as per our procedures."

"An assault on a house with a bomb?" Wakefield said skeptically.

"It's believed to be an ANFO bomb," explained Strauss. "A primary explosive must be detonated to in turn detonate the ANFO. If the terrorist is unable to send the signal to the primary explosive, there is no danger."

He had glossed over a few things there, Strauss thought, as he listened to the deputy director's silence.

"I suggested using stun grenades to disorient the suspect," said Strauss, "thereby rendering him unable to send the signal to the primary explosive. We have body heat readings from the house and we know where he is located. We also have snipers positioned to take him out."

"I see. What's the problem, then?" Wakefield asked.

"The agent-in-charge does not want to mount an assault," explained Strauss. "He has decided to continue with negotiations."

"That seems reasonable, if that's what he thinks," snapped Wakefield. "Again, what's the problem?"

"He has sent a civilian into the house to negotiate on the FBI's behalf," said Strauss.

The silence that followed was priceless. Strauss could almost imagine the expression on Wakefield's face.

"He did *what*?" the deputy director eventually managed to choke out. "Put him on this minute. I want to talk to him."

Time for an outright lie. "Well, the thing is, he's not here."

"What do you mean, not there? Isn't he in charge?"

"Well, yes, but I'm not sure where's he gone. He seems to have a lot of faith in the civilian."

"Where is this civilian now? In the house itself?"

"Yes. She is unarmed and ill-equipped to deal with this situation," said Strauss. A few more half lies, but what did it matter? "In my view, sir, we have just added another hostage to the situation."

Then Wakefield asked a question that Strauss had been hoping for: "Does the media know about this?"

"No, sir. They've been cordoned off at the end of the street, for their own safety. However, they'll be all over this story if something goes wrong."

"You don't need to tell me," grumbled Wakefield. "This is disastrous!"

"Sir, my men have lost confidence in the leadership of the agent in charge," continued Strauss. "They can no longer be sure that his decisions are sound and are reluctant to take orders from him."

"This situation needs to be dealt with quickly," said Wakefield. "Do you think you can send an assault team in and achieve a positive outcome?"

This was Wakefield's way of saying: *Can you sort this out without anyone finding out?*

"Yes, sir. I believe the use of stun grenades will be sufficient to take down the suspect," said Strauss. "We will have backup from the snipers."

There was more silence from Wakefield. He was not a stupid man — the idea of storming a property with a bomb was highly risky. He had to weigh up the risks of potentially detonating a large bomb with the risk of the media finding out that a civilian had been sent into negotiations.

"All right," he said at last. "I'm giving you the order to mount an assault on the building. I want minimum injury and loss of life, Captain. Minimal damage to property. Get in and out as quickly as you can."

"Yes, sir!" said Strauss, giving Carroll the thumbs-up.

Dinah didn't know it, but the biggest threat to her life now lay in the hands of Strauss and Carroll, who began to prepare their teams to assault the house.

* * * *

Senator Winters should have gone home but thought that if he attempted to leave his office he would be chased all the way by the media.

He sent Trixie and all other staff members home. Before she left, she looked at him with some sympathy and said, "You probably should call a press conference."

Winters knew that but he needed to get his strategy right first. Campaign finance violations were enough to sully a political career, but not finish it. He would probably be investigated by the Senate Ethics Committee and could even face a reprimand. His biggest concern was whether his broader corruption would be discovered.

If Cartwright had indeed disappeared, then this was probably a good thing for the senator. The last thing he needed was Cartwright blabbing on CNN how he'd paid Winters to achieve a certain outcome in the Supreme Court. Justice Maxwell Pryor would certainly not open his mouth about it; he stood to lose just as much as Winters if the truth was discovered.

Winters slammed his fist on the desk. Under the rules of engagement, he knew he needed to get rid of Cartwright and that brat Connor Eastleigh. He couldn't abide knowing that two enemies who could at any time ruin his career and send him to jail were free.

He poured himself some bourbon. He couldn't believe he'd been so trusting. He had always been a man who'd ruthlessly eliminated enemies and the competition like their lives were worth nothing more than an annoying mosquito. He tied up loose ends and left nothing to chance.

He could see now that he'd been played by Cartwright. The man had capitalized on Winters' greed and hatred of Christianity to perjure himself. Winters had played right into his hand. In hindsight, he could see now what Cartwright had done.

Why pay money to a senator for the outcome of a trial in the Supreme Court that wouldn't end up there for years? It didn't make any sense; Winters could see that now. But his greed had blinded him. It had been a great opportunity to set the senator up and then make him take the fall.

Winters cursed his own stupidity. Cartwright probably didn't care about the lawsuit at all — he just wanted to get rid of Winters. *Why?* mused Winters. *What will he achieve if he gets rid of me?* He drank the bourbon in one gulp, just as a knock at his door sounded. "I thought I told you to go home!" he yelled, thinking it was Trixie.

Instead, two dour-looking officials opened the door: a woman with a severe black haircut and a man with a permanent frown.

"We're Clarke and Mowbray from the Federal Election Commission," the man said. "We're here to talk to you about some alleged campaign finance violations."

Winters sat down at his desk and decided he would run with ignorance. "I've only just discovered these violations myself," he told them, adopting a grim tone. "I assure you, I will ensure my treasurer will be held accountable."

The man, whose name Winters assumed was Clarke, frowned deeper. "I believe this to be your signature, sir?" he said, holding up a document.

Winters compressed his lips. It was indeed his signature, accepting payment via a wiring company for the money from Cartwright to be accepted.

"I suppose so," he admitted. "But I didn't know where the money was coming from. My treasurer explained that it was legitimate."

Clarke and Mowbray spent the best part of an agonizing hour, producing documents left and right inculpating Winters. It didn't take long for him to realize that his ignorance defense probably wouldn't fly. So he simply answered questions with sentences as short as he could make them, being as obtusely unhelpful as possible.

Clarke and Mowbray departed with the stern warning that he would be referred to the Senate Ethics Committee based on the information they had obtained.

Once the door closed behind them, Winters' smile dropped from his face. He had work to do. He had to eliminate the threat of a corruption investigation, which most certainly would ruin his career.

The sound of an e-mail being received in his inbox momentarily distracted him. However, it gained his full attention when he saw that it was from Cartwright.

Resign by Monday.

A simple message, but one that made Winters' heart almost stop beating. Stunned, he stared at it, willing it to change. Finally, he typed a reply. *Why?*

Cartwright was quick. *We have evidence of your corruption. We'd rather you resign quietly than be indicted and sent to prison.*

Winters frowned, and again typed: *Why?*

It took a little longer this time.

We don't want an investigation any more than you do. We prefer to remain anonymous. However, we have much less to lose than you in the event of an investigation. Therefore, we encourage you to take this opportunity to end it quietly.

Winters pondered this with another shot of bourbon. Finally, he typed: *Who is "we"?*

And why do you have it in for me? he asked silently. What was their agenda?

Does it matter? You have your choice. We hope you make the right decision.

Winters cursed loudly. He had to find Cartwright and eliminate him, one way or the other. It would be an impossible task to achieve by Monday. He was sure Cartwright was no longer in the United States.

He had worked so long and so hard to get to this position of power, and he only had one more step to take to the ultimate job — the White House. It was all about to be undone by one man with whom he'd had a handful of conversations.

Winters didn't once blame his own greed or hatred for the position he was in; it was squarely the fault of others. So he spent the next hour venting his anger in his office.

Cartwright was right. He didn't really have a choice — if he left his fate in the hands of a corruption investigation, he would not only lose his job, he would also lose his reputation and be sent to jail.

At least if he resigned quietly now he could dedicate his life to hunting down Cartwright and Connor, and ensuring that they could never implicate him. Then he could find some other way of influencing Washington. You didn't need to be a senator to have enormous power in D.C.

Winters began the slow, painful task of realizing that by Monday, he would no longer be a United States senator.

Michael," said Dinah. She desperately searched for the right words, wishing Andy or Sandra could have been next to her advising her on what to say. "I'm really sorry to hear about your experiences, both at the hands of your father and by the church. That was terribly unfair."

Michael shrugged. "Well, it made things pretty clear to me. I no longer believe in God. The church seems to me to be irrelevant, mired down in rituals and regulations. I'm just glad I discovered that early in life."

"Well, you're not the only one," said Dinah, thinking about a book she'd read recently. "Did you know that two-thirds of young people who were brought up in the Church are walking away because they begin to doubt the Bible?"

He made a snort of contempt. "What a surprise. Why bother teaching what the Bible says when none of them bother following it anyway?"

"Fair point," conceded Dinah. "The problem is that young people, who are by no means stupid, are continually being taught about evolution, the big bang, and the age of the earth at school, which contradicts what the Church teaches on Sunday. Yet when they ask their pastor or elder or teacher about the discrepancy, they are unable to defend their faith or uphold the Bible as true. As a result, kids become disillusioned and doubtful that anything the Bible says can be trusted, and begin to drift away from the Church."

"Sounds about right to me," commented Michael. "I should have guessed you were a Christian."

"Well, I think one of the reasons the Church didn't protect you and your family is because the teaching of the Bible wasn't being followed," explained Dinah. "I'm not a Bible expert, but I try to read it every day. For example, I know that Titus says in chapter two that men are to be self-controlled, sound in faith and love. The same passage tells all men and women in church to live self-controlled, upright, and godly lives. Further, it commands the leaders of the church to rebuke those who don't follow this teaching."

"What's your point?" Michael demanded.

"I think your church failed to rebuke your father for failing to show self-control," suggested Dinah. "Venting one's anger and frustration on women and children is, at a basic level, a complete lack of self-control. Furthermore, he was clearly violating the law of the land. However, the leaders of the church didn't rebuke him. And Jesus quite clearly tells us we have to care for the poor and the oppressed."

"No arguments from me there," said Michael.

"Well, I just wanted to say that it's not supposed to be that way," continued Dinah. She felt like a blind woman, trying to feel her way through a completely foreign environment. "The Bible is God's inerrant Word. When we start to treat it as any less, the consequences are great. The consequences include men continuing to beat their wives and children, or young people walking away from the Church because they start to doubt whether the Bible is true. The Church ought to stand on the authority of the Bible without compromise."

There was silence for several minutes.

"I guess what I'm encouraging you to think about is that you had a bad experience in church, but that not every church is like that and it certainly shouldn't be. It would be a terrible shame if you decided all of Christianity is the same. It's not; we're not."

"Actually, I don't agree," said Michael. "One of the things I do know about Christianity is that some of the major Christian seminaries and professors in this country have publicly said that they teach the Bible is not inerrant. Many reject biblical truthfulness altogether, and have started reinterpreting the Bible. Isn't that true? So why should I believe anything a Christian says or anything the Bible says? You can't just pick and choose the bits of the Bible you like and say that those are from God, and completely ignore other parts."

Dinah thought about that quickly. "I totally agree," she said. "I think you need to have an all or nothing approach. I believe *the entire* Bible is God's Word, and therefore inerrant. That's not a blind belief, though: there are reasons I believe it to be true. One is that recently discovered biblical texts, such as the Dead Sea Scrolls, show that the Bible today is virtually the same as when it was written thousands of years ago. The scrolls were written more than a century before Christ's birth, meaning that many of the prophecies contained therein about Jesus had to be written before He was born. There are over 60 prophecies in the Old Testament written specifically about Jesus — and *all* of them came true! Even ones over which He would have no control, such as the place of His birth and the actions of other people on the day of His death. The Dead Sea Scrolls show that the Bible was copied very accurately from generation to generation, and so there aren't any copyist errors, but also that it was written prior to Christ's birth. Therefore, we can claim that the Bible is ultimately trustworthy and accurate."

Michael raised his eyebrows. "Does it matter, though? You might believe that the Bible is true, but you might not live that way."

"Sure," agreed Dinah. "But don't make the mistake of assuming Christians ought to be perfect. We're prone to sin and mistakes, like any other human being."

Michael got up to check the windows and doors again. When he returned he said, "Tell me, Dinah, why do you care?"

"Outside of this particular situation?" Dinah said with a wry smile. "Because there is no neutral position. God tells us plainly that we're either for Him or against Him: in James chapter 4 verse 4, it says that anyone who is a friend of the world is an enemy of God. It also states in Romans 8:7 that the mind set on the flesh is hostile to God, for it does not submit to God's law; indeed, it cannot. You are either on God's team or you are not. There is no sitting on the fence. I care that you are an enemy of God."

"Gee, thanks," said Michael, rolling his eyes.

"Michael . . . you've just said you are happy to die in this house on this day," said Dinah gently. "Yet you have no concept of what happens after death. So yeah, I care."

Michael laughed bitterly. "I can't imagine any concept of heaven accepting *me*," he said. "I'm a mass murderer!"

Isabelle flinched, as if she hadn't quite come to terms with what he'd done.

Dinah leaned forward. "That's the beauty of it," she said urgently. "Heaven is perfect. Who on earth would get in? None of us are perfect."

"Well, I'm sure you're a little more perfect than I am," he said.

"Let me tell you something," said Dinah. "For a long time, I carried on my heart the burden of causing the deaths of three people. Does that sound perfect to you? I used to work with gang members, extracting them and safeguarding them in exchange for information. One night, I drank so much alcohol that I forgot a promise to a gang member to meet him in a park and take him to a safe house. His body was found the following day, and gangs who discover snitches within their ranks ensure it's a not a quick and painless death."

Dinah had to pause for a few moments to gather her thoughts. It was still painful to think of the young man she'd betrayed so horrifically.

"Not only that, but the last time I saw my husband and son alive, I screamed at both of them. I yelled at my baby son to shut up. Nice, huh? You think they accept people like me in heaven?"

Michael seemed to be looking at her in a new light. "Maybe," he said. "It's not like you intentionally hurt any of those people."

"Still, what about alcoholics? That's what I am," added Dinah.

Maybe Michael was thinking of his own father when he said, "No, I don't think so."

"Yet I can say with one hundred percent certainty that I'm going to heaven when I die, and there is nothing I can do to change that fact," continued Dinah. "And the same could be true of you, too. The reason is that there is *nothing* you can do to make God reject you."

Michael raised his eyebrows sardonically.

"All of us are unworthy to be in God's presence," she said. "There are no categories of sin, you know. Hate is just as bad in God's eyes as murder. So none of us deserve anything from God, let alone the promise of heaven. I can speak with confidence only because God provided a solution to this problem, out of His great love for us. He requires punishment for the sin in the world, but rather than visit His wrath upon us, He sent a perfect replacement. His Son, Jesus Christ, who was without sin, died in our place, enduring the wrath of His Father, so that we don't have to suffer eternal separation from God. All we have to do is receive this free gift and repent of the things we've done wrong."

Dinah tried to think of how she could express the deep feeling inside her. "It's total freedom, Michael. Freedom from the guilt and shame of the past. Freedom from worry for the future. Freedom from the burdens of this world. There is such liberty in knowing that your past wrongs have been erased. And it's not just release in this world, but hope for the next one. I have no fear of dying."

Michael stared at her with red-rimmed, exhausted eyes. "I wish I could say I had no fear of the future, or of dying. My future is so depressing! I have the rest of my life in jail with which to deal."

"I understand," said Dinah gently. "But let me tell you this. You can have the hardest life here on earth, and still have the hope of heaven. But if you decide to end your life now, then that decision is final. There will be no second chance. I implore you, please start thinking of life as worth living, even if it's in jail. There is so much more to look forward to, I promise."

Michael glanced at Isabelle, as if to gauge what she thought. Regardless of whether she thought Dinah was a crackpot or not, the ex-FBI agent knew that Isabelle wanted her brother to live.

"Please take her advice," said Isabelle, her voice urgent. "I will never abandon you, Michael. Even if you go to jail, I'll always be here for you."

"I have to know that there's a good reason," said Michael. "I don't want my story to go to jail with me, you know? I was not the only kid abused by his father, and grew up to be a crazy adult. We can't ignore the epidemic of child abuse. The consequences are too far-reaching."

Dinah nodded. "Is that what you were trying to say when you sent the letters to the newspaper?"

"Yes, in a roundabout way," admitted Michael. "Without giving myself away."

"Listen, I think I can help," said Dinah. "I'm going to write a book, about my experiences at the FBI and now that I'm a consultant. I could write about you and your life in my book."

Michael suddenly looked energized. "Really? You would explain everything about my father? How it affected me?"

"Yes," said Dinah. "I happen to agree with you, Michael. There are so many things that went wrong: too many people refusing to see the truth."

She glanced over at Isabelle. "But if I agree to that, Michael, I need you to put down your gun, disarm the bomb, and leave this house without a fight. I promise I'll stay with you every step of the way. I won't let any harm come to you. I need you to let go of the notion of dying today."

Michael took a deep breath. "If you promise me that I'll be in your book, Dinah, I'll come out peacefully."

Dinah let out a big breath of relief and reached across to shake Michael's hand. "It's a deal," she said with a warm smile.

* * * *

Sinclair appeared by Ferguson's side like a ghost and startled the big man. "Do you have to creep around?" Ferguson demanded. His good temper had vanished a while ago, and his concern for Dinah permeated every thought.

Sinclair didn't crack a smile. "We've got a problem," he said in a low voice.

Ferguson tensed, expecting the worst. "What? Is something wrong?"

"Yes, but as far as I know Dinah is fine," said Sinclair, reading the other man's thoughts. "The problem is here on the outside."

Ferguson drew his eyebrows together in a frown. "What?"

"The two team leaders of the tactical units, Carroll and Strauss, want to mount an assault on the house and take down the suspect," explained Sinclair.

"Yeah, I know," said Ferguson. "I told them no way, not while Dinah is negotiating in there."

"Right. Well, they don't agree with you. Apparently, they consider her to be collateral damage."

"They're going to defy my orders?" exclaimed Ferguson, aghast.

"Not quite. They've gone over your head and obtained orders from the deputy director to mount an assault." Sinclair was pale. "They told him that you'd sent a civilian into the house to negotiate."

"She's hardly your average citizen!" raged Ferguson. "How do you know this?"

"I was eavesdropping," admitted Sinclair. "I overheard it all. Well, they're getting their teams ready to go. Here's what I think we should do. You speak to them and delay them. Get into a big argument if you need. I'll get the deputy director on the phone and explain what's going on. Hopefully, he'll rescind those orders."

Ferguson nodded briskly. "Good plan," he said. In the bright sunlight of the afternoon, he could see the black-clad figures of the tactical team, moving around purposefully and setting up their weapons. He marched over to where they were assembled as he heard Sinclair say into the phone, "The deputy director, please. Hurry, it's urgent!"

Ferguson was both tall and big, and he was thankful he towered over the blocky forms of Strauss and Carroll, who both looked formidable in their body armor. "What do you think you're doing?" the boss demanded, turning the full force of his glare on each of them in turn.

Strauss sighed. "It's nothing personal, sir. We felt uncomfortable with the direction the negotiations had taken and sought the counsel of your superior."

"By uncomfortable, I guess you mean you didn't want Harris going into that house," snapped Ferguson.

"We don't send civilians to do the Bureau's job," said Carroll stiffly.

Ferguson rolled his eyes. "Do you have any idea who Harris is? She was an FBI agent for many years, working in the Gangs unit. She negotiated the release and protection of high-ranking gang members. She is one of the very best negotiators I have ever known! She's hardly a civilian."

"She's not with the Bureau anymore, though," said Strauss. "If the situation deteriorates, the FBI is put in a bad position, having to explain her presence in the house. We know that the suspect refuses to negotiate. Given that we know the layout of the house and who is in the house, including the precise movements of all three, a tactical assault seems to us to be the only option."

"With Dinah and a hostage in there?" Ferguson exclaimed. "Are you insane?"

"We know what we're doing, with all due respect," said Strauss, his tone becoming cold. "We will take a no-fatalities strategy."

"You have no way of knowing how this will go down," snapped Ferguson. "You can't mix a volatile suspect, who is both armed and in control of a large bomb, with two tactical units who are heavily armed, and expect it to work out smoothly. What if he panics and shoots Dinah accidentally? What if he presses that button and the street is blown to smithereens? That hardly sounds like a low-risk option to me."

"Well, how are the negotiations going?" snarled Strauss. "Doesn't look like much movement to me. With the media attention on us down the street, you really want this to drag on?"

"I'd prefer it to having to explain how lives were lost," replied Ferguson.

"Well, sir, I'm afraid we have orders from the deputy director himself," said Strauss smugly. "So we are going to execute the assault in" — he glanced at his watch — "about 60 seconds."

"I know what you told the deputy director, and it was a bunch of lies," said Ferguson angrily. "He's based orders on your false statement. How's that going to look when I tell him why he's got blood on his hands?"

Carroll's eyes widened, as if he were shocked that they'd been overheard. It was all Ferguson needed to confirm Sinclair's account of what had happened. "I am expressly forbidding an assault on that house," he said, in a low tone that brooked no argument. "Do you understand me? Just so we're clear: if you go into that house, it shall be considered a direct violation of my orders."

Strauss didn't look away. "I'm sorry you feel that way, sir. We have orders from the deputy director."

He turned away from Ferguson and called to his men: "Ready, Team One!"

"Ready!" came a chorus of somewhat nervous voices.

Ferguson was almost apoplectic with rage, his face turning a deep purplish red.

"Ready, Team Two!"

"Ready!"

"Snipers, in position!"

"Roger," came the reply through the radio.

"Here's how we'll assault," continued Strauss. "I want. . . ."

"You might *want* to stop right there!" called Sinclair in ringing tones. He waved his cell phone in the air.

Strauss would have bared his teeth at Sinclair and growled had he been any angrier. "What are you doing?" he snapped.

"I have fresh orders from the deputy director," said Sinclair. "The order is *not* to attack the house and to stand down. In fact, he's on the phone and wants to talk to you right now."

Strauss looked like his head was about to explode, amid a harmony of disgruntled mutters from the tactical units. He snatched the phone from Sinclair's hand and listened, a peculiar mixture of dread and disgust on his face.

"I'm not at all happy that you misled me," snapped Wakefield. "The negotiator is hardly a naive civilian, is she?"

"I understand, sir, but technically, she is still a civilian," protested Strauss weakly.

"Oh, for crying out loud," exploded Wakefield. "You also mentioned that Ferguson had lost control of the situation and that he'd left the location! All of which was patently untrue!"

"Uh . . . well," stammered Strauss.

"You and your crony better start thinking of some alternative career plans," continued Wakefield. "There is nothing more dangerous in the field than a team leader who deliberately goes over the head of his superior, endangers the lives of countless people *including* civilians, and lies about it to me! You understand what I'm saying?"

Strauss gave the phone back to Sinclair.

Ferguson waited, watching him with a triumphant expression on his face.

Finally, Strauss looked at his men and snapped: "Stand down! Wait for further orders."

"Well," said Ferguson breezily. "I'm glad this all got sorted out, aren't you? Guess I'll go back to running this operation now, if you don't mind." He marched off, leaving the two team leaders, both of whom looked dangerously close to emptying the contents of their stomachs under the nearest tree, to exchange a worried look and start thinking about a new career.

Ferguson and Sinclair returned to the mobile command center and watched the glowering tactical team leaders mutter under their breath.

"Well, that was a colossal waste of time," said Ferguson. "Now, what's happening in the house?"

"I know what's *not* happening," said Sinclair with a frown. "Dinah hasn't rung in for an hour."

"*What?*" Ferguson glowered at the phone, as if it were at fault.

Sinclair lifted a pair of binoculars to his eyes, which had body heat lenses attached. "And I can see movement in the house. They've all moved from the kitchen into the front room, near the front door."

"Maybe he's letting the hostage go?" Ferguson suggested, taking up a pair of his own binoculars. He found his radio and barked into it.

"SWAT Teams A and B, be alert! We have movement in the house near the front door!"

With expressions that clearly said *I told you so*, Strauss and Carroll sprang into action. Their black-clad teams formed a protective ring around the front perimeter of the property.

Collectively, every law enforcement agent tensed as the front door swung slowly open. Ferguson prayed there were no trigger-happy rookies in the squad today.

The person silhouetted in the doorway was Dinah Harris. She stood with her hands in the air, in the accepted no-threat position. "We are all walking out slowly and calmly," she called, her voice clear in the still afternoon air. "None of us are armed or have access to weapons of any kind. Isabelle will come first, then Michael, then me. The suspect has assured me that he does not pose a threat to anybody."

This didn't seem to soothe the tactical team members, who seemed to tense over their weapons even further.

Ferguson used a megaphone to ensure his instructions were heard. "Isabelle — please come out of the house with your hands on your head. Armed officers will approach you but do not be alarmed. They will lead you to safety if you follow their instructions."

A woman in her early thirties appeared, her face a mask of fear and uncertainty. With her hands on her head, she stiffly walked out of the house and cringed as the officers approached. They gave her a quick pat down to ensure she wasn't hiding weapons then led her to the command center, where paramedics waited.

The SWAT teams moved in closer as Michael appeared in the door, his hands on his head. It took only a few seconds for him to be lying prostrate on the ground, five automatic weapons aimed at his head. After a search, he was handcuffed and hauled to his feet. Ferguson and Sinclair breathed a sigh of relief each, exchanging glances.

Then Dinah appeared, calm and composed. She left the building and searched the crowd with a steady gaze as SWAT teams rushed into the house to secure it and locate the bomb. Her eyes didn't rest until they landed on Sinclair, who was watching her with a smile on his face.

Dinah really wanted to run to him, like they did at the end of cheesy movies, and throw her arms around him. Instead, she approached the command center.

"That was some nice work," said Ferguson admiringly. "I knew if anyone could talk him down, you could do it."

"Thanks," said Dinah. "As usual, it was just a matter of finding out what his terms of release were. Once I'd built up enough trust, he was ready to tell me."

"What were his terms?" Ferguson asked.

"He wants people to know that he acted out of an anger that began many years ago, when his father would abuse him mercilessly. The anger grew exponentially when he asked the priest at his church for help. The priest didn't believe him and he was punished so badly by his father that he was hospitalized."

"Ah. That explains why he was so angry with the Church," said Sinclair. "But why didn't he take out his anger on his father — or even men who represented his father?"

"Even as an adult, he was too scared," said Dinah. "The man had a truly impressive psychological hold over his children. He did choose churches he felt were protecting or helping violent men, though. If you look at the charity programs the churches ran, you'll see they often catered to imprisoned or paroled men."

Sinclair shook his head. "What a sad turn of events. But for his father abusing him, he may have grown up to be a normal human being and we wouldn't have to investigate the deaths of innocent people doing nothing more than going to church."

"What about the humanism angle?" Ferguson asked.

"He got the names of the churches from a lawsuit he helped draft," explained Dinah. "He became an atheist after the aforementioned church incident and joined the American Humanists Association, where his healthy hatred of churches was encouraged. That certainly didn't do his state of mind any favors. Nor did the fact that he was also encouraged to develop his own moral code, outside of supernatural influences. Given his past suffering, his moral code was skewed and he felt perfectly justified in bringing justice upon churches he felt deserved it. And that is the danger of moral relativism."

Ferguson gave the all clear for Michael to be taken to federal prison, and they began dismantling the mobile command center.

"What do you mean by moral relativism?" Sinclair asked curiously.

"It's what many Americans believe is the right thing for our society," said Dinah. "Each individual decides for him or herself what is right and wrong. A moral code is subjective if invented by a human being, upon their own experiences. Michael's moral code was built upon a childhood of brutality and the absence of love, and it colored his view in life accordingly. If you believe in moral relativism, you couldn't seriously argue with this position. It seems only logical that such an individual would want to exact revenge."

Ferguson took a few minutes to update the deputy director on the outcome, and while he was gone, Sinclair said, "I've never been so happy to see you as when you came out of that house."

"I've never been so happy to see *you* when I came out of that house," admitted Dinah, a flush working its way up her face.

"I'd like to take you to lunch," suggested Sinclair. "You can tell me all about your beliefs and why they mean so much to you."

Dinah smiled. "Tomorrow is Sunday. Why don't you come to church with me in the morning and then we'll go to lunch afterward?"

Sinclair shrugged. "Sounds good to me. It's not like I have to worry about being blown up anymore."

Dinah pretended to be shocked and socked him lightly on the arm. Inside, her heart felt light, as if it would fly free from her chest in sheer joy.

The press room was packed to capacity, and as Senator Winters walked into the room, there was a dazzling bombardment of flashing bulbs following his every move. He was joined by his lawyer, a discreet man who could be trusted to keep his mouth shut.

Winters stood at the podium and glanced through his prepared notes. Almost unable to believe what he was about to do, he began speaking. "Good morning. You will by now know that I've been accused of receiving improper campaign finance donations from a foreign source. I'd like to vehemently deny those accusations. I believe I am the victim of deception, designed to smear my reputation."

He stared straight into the eye of the news camera. *This one's for you, Cartwright.*

"I will not rest until my name is cleared and those responsible for this deception are revealed. However, in the meantime, because I care a great deal about personal integrity, I wish to announce my resignation as the United States senator representing the state of California. I wish to avoid any appearance of impropriety while the investigations are undertaken by the FEC. When my name is cleared, I will consider my options."

Chapter 20

Light bulbs flashed blindingly as reporters fired their questions at Winters.

"One at a time," snapped Winters, barely able to conceal his irritation.

"Why are you resigning? Many politicians before you have been investigated by the FEC for campaign finance violations but haven't resigned. It seems to be a drastic move," suggested an intense young man.

You're absolutely right, Winters thought. *It's called blackmail.*

"I don't feel it's appropriate to continue holding office when there are charges of dishonest conduct pending," he said. "That would violate my own personal code of ethics. I am confident that my name will be cleared, at which time I may consider running for the Senate again."

"What will you do in the meantime?"

"I'll return home to the fine state of California," said Winters, thinking, *I'm going to hunt down Cartwright and Connor and personally kill them both with my bare hands.* "I'll take a break and then vigorously defend my character."

"I understand the Senate has established a House Ethics Committee investigation of your conduct in addition to the FEC investigation?" a pinch-faced woman asked.

"I believe so," said Winters coolly. "But I have no doubt both investigations will find me innocent."

"Who do you suspect of trying to tarnish your reputation?" This question came from the back of the room.

"I'm confident I will find that out," said Winters, again staring at the camera.

"*Why* do you think someone would deceive you in this manner?"

"Perhaps I made some decisions that weren't liked," said Winters. "Perhaps I said something that ruffled some feathers. However, I'm sure that this, too, will come to light eventually."

Actually, this question disturbed Winters most of all. He had no idea why Cartwright had betrayed him and he didn't like that one bit. He had thought the Englishman had been a colleague, not an enemy. Why did Cartwright want him out of the way? What could he hope to achieve with Winters out of the Senate? He knew better than anyone that Winters was able to be bought. That was priceless in the world of politics. Winters did not like the feeling of helplessness one little bit.

"Are you saying there is a conspiracy to cause your career to be ruined?" the pinch-faced woman asked.

"At this point, we simply don't know," said Winters. "I'm confident we'll find out."

Abruptly, he decided he'd had enough. He thanked the press with more graciousness than he felt and left the room. As he did so, his cell phone buzzed.

"What?" he barked.

"Senator, I just watched your press conference," said a familiar voice.

"Dinah Harris," said Winters with a scowl. "I should've known you'd call to gloat."

"Actually, that's not why I called," said Dinah mildly. "I called to thank you for helping me solve a case."

Winters stood at a window and watched dark thunderclouds bank up on the horizon. "What are you talking about?"

"I realize you've been occupied with other things," said Dinah, "but recently, there's been a bomber targeting churches in the D.C. area. We just solved the case, and if it wasn't for that lawsuit you posted me, I may not have put all the pieces together as quickly."

Winters glared at his own reflection. "Why would the bomber be interested in that lawsuit?"

"He helped to draft it," explained Dinah. "What he read in the lawsuit fanned an already angry and violent nature. He picked his targets directly from the pages of the lawsuit."

Winters shook his head. Was there no end to the craziness of this day? "I had no idea about that," he said.

"What are you going to do now that you've resigned?" Dinah asked.

I want to go on a murderous rampage, thought Winters. "Watch the press conference again," he snapped. "I already answered that question."

"Well, you know, I still pray for you," said Dinah. "Maybe one day God will soften your heart and open your eyes."

Winters rolled his eyes. "Are you done? I certainly am." He hung up and slipped the cell phone into his pocket. Dinah's call did nothing to improve his mood.

Winters left the building and made his way to his expensive town house in Alexandria Old Town, where only those who could afford the pricey real estate lived.

Alone, he poured himself a bourbon and sat in the den. It was time to make a plan.

* * * *

While Winters sat brooding in his home, a luxury private jet streaked across the sky above the cobalt Atlantic Ocean. Cartwright and his protégé Connor were flying back to London, having accomplished their goals in the capital city of the United States.

Cartwright leaned his tall frame back in the reclining leather seat. In front of him, an early gourmet dinner had been served with a glass of expensive French wine. "Well, old chap," he said to Connor, "I'd like to propose a toast to a job well done."

He held up his glass. Connor clinked it with his own. "To a job well done," he echoed. "It seemed so easy, in retrospect."

"That's an important lesson," said Cartwright. "When dealing with corrupt individuals, it often *is* easy, providing their paranoia doesn't get the best of them. You must always appeal to their strongest desire — greed, pride, lust for power."

Connor ate some gnocchi stuffed with cheese. "I'm a little concerned that Winters won't go away."

Cartwright agreed. "I suppose we could have come up with a more permanent solution," he said. "But it's very risky trying to eliminate a United State senator. The risk for reward ratio was too high. In fact, this whole operation cost us nothing. We made an initial upfront payment of half a million dollars, knowing full well that the FEC would require the senator to return the funds once he'd been caught. I'm pretty happy that we not only took Winters down, but we also got our money back."

"Perhaps now that he's no longer a senator, it could be done?" Connor asked.

Cartwright laughed. "You are a bloodthirsty creature, aren't you? Perhaps we could think about creating an unfortunate accident. In the meantime, we'll leave him alone. We have other things to do."

They sat in companionable silence for several moments.

"So now that Winters is gone, how does that help us?" Connor asked, trying to get his mind around intricacies of the older man's plan.

"We know that Winters was liberal in his political views," explained Cartwright. "In many cases, that does us a favor. However, he shared a similar view with many of his Congress and Senate buddies with regard to illegal immigration."

"He's considered soft on illegal immigration," said Connor, nodding.

"Right. In fact, he and his liberal colleagues had suggested that tough illegal immigration laws were likely to do nothing to stop the influx of illegals pouring across the Mexican border. They suggested assisting illegals already in the country with health care and access to welfare, for example. Winters in particular supported a civil rights movement which advocated for the rights of illegal immigrants." He stopped talking to take a bite and wash it down with a sip of wine.

"Now, Winters hails from California, a state which has a major illegal immigration problem. Were he successful in relaxing illegal immigration laws, his state in particular would be affected."

"Now why is that a problem?" Connor asked, puzzled. "We'd have more aliens entering the country than ever before."

"Ah yes, but those aliens would now have *rights*," said Cartwright. "We want the illegals to have *no* rights, so that they have no choice but to remain under our control. There is an extraordinary amount of money to be made through illegal immigration. The rules of supply and demand work in that arena as well as any other — when you relax laws so that supply is made easier and cheaper, prices fall as the demand is met. You really want laws to be tightened so that supply is restricted, demand soars, and prices rise as a result. If you happen to be in control of supply, you make a preposterous amount of money."

"So we needed to get rid of Winters because he wanted to relax immigration laws," said Connor thoughtfully, "in favor of someone who is going to take a hard-line approach?"

"Right. When the border is sealed up, fewer immigrants can cross on their own steam. But we can help them, for a fee, of course." Cartwright looked immensely satisfied with himself.

Connor gazed out of the window for a moment. "What you're talking about, of course, is not illegal immigration but human trafficking," he said.

Cartwright shrugged. "Call it what you want. As long as there are people desperate enough to cross the border illegally, I see it as an opportunity to make money. A *lot* of money."

"I guess you have a plan for state and local government?" Connor asked. "After all, a federal senator whom we can use for our own purposes is one thing, but he has no control over state and local law."

"Just another piece of the puzzle," said Cartwright, his face inscrutable. "This is not a plan that can be executed overnight. We've achieved the first goal; the next is to work on the governor of California. You work with what you've got — bribery, blackmail, extortion — whatever their breaking point happens to be."

"And if they don't have a breaking point?"

"We get rid of them," replied Cartwright immediately. "Election campaigns are ridiculously easy to manipulate. If we have to do that, we can."

Connor finished his meal. "I see. You know, I always knew it was going to be interesting working with you."

Cartwright smiled. "You're learning from the best, son."

The private jet continued to hurtle through the sky while its inhabitants plotted and schemed. In the United States, the person who had once been known as Cartwright had ceased to exist and there was no record of him ever being in the country. His name was not and had never been Cartwright.

Similarly, the existence of a person named Connor Eastleigh had been erased as if he'd never been born. If anyone tried to trace the whereabouts of that young intern who'd worked in Senator Winter's office for a month or so, they'd find that the trail went cold very quickly.

Cartwright chuckled to himself as he settled back for a quick nap. Senator Winters had had no idea who he was really dealing with. Had he known that Cartwright was a prince in one of the world's largest and most powerful cartels, which dealt in everything from drug trafficking to human trafficking, he would have had a heart attack.

That was the simple beauty of it.

* * * *

The following morning, a gloriously mild Sunday that hinted that cooler weather was on its way, Dinah took Aaron to church. It was with great thankfulness in her heart that she sang the final song: *Lead me to the Cross/Where your love poured out/Bring me to my knees/ Lord I lay me down.*

It was clear Aaron hadn't been to church in a long time, but he listened intently. He didn't seem to mind when he was surrounded by Dinah's friends after the service, all of whom were very interested in Dinah's new companion.

Finally, they managed to leave church and made their way to Dinah's favorite deli for brunch. Dinah drank in the sensation of simply being with a man for whom she cared so deeply.

"Well, I hope you didn't find that too confronting," she joked, once coffees had been served.

"Not at all," said Aaron. "You know, I'm not anti-Christian or anti-God. I just . . . don't really know much about it all. My parents were not into church, and I can count on one hand the times I've ever set foot in one."

"I'm a little similar," admitted Dinah. "I grew up in much the same circumstances. I didn't encounter God until I'd made such a mess of my life that I actually wanted to end it." It was hard to be so honest. Speaking about her past with such brutal candor was a little frightening.

Aaron nodded. "So what made you decide to become a Christian?"

Dinah thought for a few moments. "I suppose because it was the only thing that made sense. My world was chaos; God offered order. I was hurting; God offered peace. It was more than that. It was as if I'd stumbled across what I knew to be the truth after all these years. As soon as I heard it, I knew in my heart of hearts that it was the truth."

"So what *is* Christianity then?" Aaron asked. The waiter arrived to take their order. Dinah didn't reply until they'd both ordered.

"It's an understanding that I was born with a sin nature," she explained. "That I'm an imperfect person. I can try to live up to God's expectations through being good, but I'll always fail. God created a perfect world, where we could have a perfect relationship with Him. But the human race rejected God and asked for independence. God calls us into a relationship with Him, but even if we wanted to, our sin makes that impossible. God is a completely just and holy God, and He can't excuse or tolerate sin. Really, He could have completely wiped us from the face of the earth — we'd completely rejected Him, after all. Instead, because of His great love, He chose to offer us a way of entering into a relationship with Him. He created a scenario where He could punish all of mankind's sin once and for all, using the sacrifice of a person who'd never sinned and was perfect. That sacrifice was His own Son, Jesus, who came to live on earth as a man. He suffered not only a physical death, but a spiritual one that we all deserve, as God heaped upon Him the wrath for the sin *we'd* committed. Only Jesus defeated death because He wasn't just a man — He is God, too — and was resurrected from the dead on the third day."

Their food arrived and Dinah took a moment to sample her eggs Benedict. "All we have to do is recognize what Jesus did for us, and accept His offer of forgiveness and salvation. In doing so, God no longer sees our sinful hearts but hearts made clean and fresh. He also offers life with Him after death, for eternity."

She paused again to gather her thoughts.

"You see, Christianity is not about always doing the right thing or saying the right thing or performing the right rituals. It's about the state of your heart: recognizing your own sinfulness, your own need for God, understanding what Jesus' death on the Cross actually means, and receiving salvation. It's about leaving your old life behind and living a new one dedicated to Jesus. It's about your personal relationship with God."

Dinah took a sip of coffee. "It's also about having hope for the future, and that your own existence has a purpose. We are not random accidents of nature — we are created in the beloved image of God. Bad things happen — because it's no longer a perfect world. When you have faith in God, you can endure the bad things, knowing that life on this earth is simply a prelude to the next life."

She smiled. "I'm not afraid to say that I do have a personal relationship with God. I talk to God through prayer, and God talks to me through the Bible. That's why I take what the Bible says seriously."

Dinah sat back, realizing that she'd been talking nonstop and hadn't allowed Aaron to get a word in. "Sorry," she said. "Please, ask questions or make comments. I didn't mean to hog the conversation."

Aaron just laughed. "I liked listening to you," he said. "I can see that you deeply believe what you're saying and that you're passionate about it."

He spent several moments collecting his thoughts. "I admit, I was distraught when my sister Carmen died. I couldn't see the reason in it. I couldn't understand the casual cruelty of life. Listening to you, I can start to understand more about the meaning of life, as clichéd as that sounds."

"Right," said Dinah.

There was a silence as Aaron processed his thoughts. "Dinah, I won't lie to you," he said. "I don't know if I want to become a Christian. I don't know enough about it. I just know that I'd like to learn more . . . and I'd like to be your friend."

Dinah couldn't help but smile. "Aaron, I'd be happy to be your friend, but you must understand that I cannot offer you anything more than friendship at this point."

Aaron rolled his eyes playfully. "Yes, you've made that very clear."

"I can introduce you to my pastor," suggested Dinah. "He can help you to learn more and understand what it is to be a Christian."

Aaron nodded. "It's a deal," he agreed.

They spent several hours together, talking and laughing, simply enjoying each other's presence. Whether Aaron would prove to be the man God had set apart for her — Dinah didn't know. She did know that God cared about even the tiniest detail of her life. Whatever His will was for her, she would follow with praise in her soul.

Her world had once been tinged with loneliness, despair, and grief. Now it was fragranced with hope, joy, and the promise of the future.

* * * *

Sussex 1 State Prison
Waverly, Virginia
Prisoner Number: 10734
Death Row

I have been set free.

Not literally. I'll live the rest of my drastically shortened life in this metal box, until they put a needle in my arm.

However, I have come to see that I can be free even when caged in the most extreme circumstances. I have come to understand that true freedom is not found in a physical sense or a mental sense, but in a spiritual sense. I can see now that I was just as much a prisoner when I set those bombs as I am now in prison. I was a prisoner to hatred, anger, despair, and evil. I allowed my heart to be chained and shackled with my selfish desires.

I can see now that I am no better than my father.

Wow. It's taken me a long time to realize this, and it's a blow to my very soul. The man whom I vowed I would never be, somehow caught up with me and morphed into me. I opened myself up to evil. I can admit my wrong now; I know fully that my actions, which led to the death and suffering of many people, violated man's law and God's law.

I look out at the patch of blue sky when I'm allowed out of my cell. I stare at the pieces of light that fall my way. I imagine my soul flying free through the bars, soaring like an eagle. I imagine my world hasn't shrunk to a steel cube the size of a postage stamp.

I have hope; my family has hope. Isabelle has moved in with our mother, after Scott refused to let her back into the house and sent her divorce papers. They are trying to heal many wounds, many inflicted by me. They come to see me when they can, and perhaps one day all that's gone between us will fade into forgiveness.

I think about how I stand at the foot of the Cross, mesmerized by the wonder of what was accomplished there. The power of the Cross washed away my guilt, eliminated my shame, and restored my life. There is nothing I can do — or have done — that can defeat the victory won there on that day. I am a human being so low that my society sees fit to lock me in a cage and one day execute me. Yet for me, the lowest of the low, He died!

It is precisely as if Jesus walked into this prison, told the guard that He had committed the bombings and murdered those people, and that I was to be set free from all punishment. In my place, He lies down on the cold, steel table and takes the needle. He dies the death reserved for me.

Pieces of Light

How could the God of everything, the One who created everything with His word and His breath, the powerful King who holds the world in His hand: how can it be that He should die for me?

That is why I do not fear today or tomorrow. I do not fear the black inkiness of the night. I feel no terror when others scream and thrash violently in their sleep. I have no despair at the thought of endless days stretching before me with nothing to do but read and sleep. I feel only peace when I think of that final day, the day they come for me to end my life. There is nothing in this world that can defeat the glory for which I now live.

I see only streets of gold, a place where there are no tears, no pain, no sorrow, and no death. I see an eternity of glory where I can feast my eyes on the One who saved me. I see indescribable joy, unspeakable delight, and stunning wonder when I peer into my future.

Into this dark prison, where men die slowly each day, where hope is snuffed out like a candle in the breeze, where spirits are crushed and sanity lost, there streams brilliant pieces of light. It streams into my soul and feeds my spirit. Its source is unquenchable, its bright fire pure and cleansing.

I have been set free from the prison in my blackened heart.

JULIE CAVE

Julie has loved books all her life and began writing at the age of 12. At the age of 15, she heard a creation science speaker at her church which ignited her interest in creation science and sparked an enthusiasm for defending the Bible's account of creation. It wasn't until she was in her mid-twenties, after re-dedicating her life to Jesus, that she began thinking about combining the two as a Christian ministry. In the meantime, she obtained a university degree in health science, worked in banking and finance for ten years, and is currently completing a university degree in law. Julie is married with one daughter and lives on the east coast of Australia. Her interests include reading, writing, and spending time at the beach.

Keep track of Julie's latest writing projects through:

- her blog at juliecave.com
- her tweets on twitter.com/julieacave

DON'T MISS OUT

on the first two books of this thrilling fiction series!

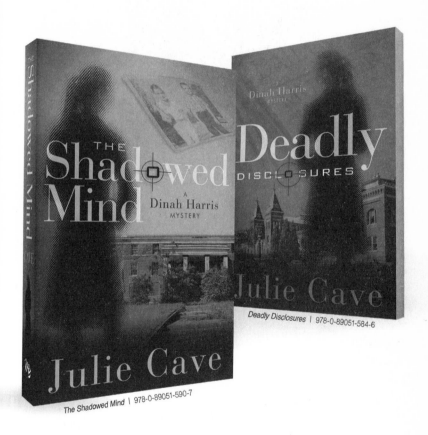

The Shadowed Mind | 978-0-89051-590-7

Deadly Disclosures | 978-0-89051-584-6

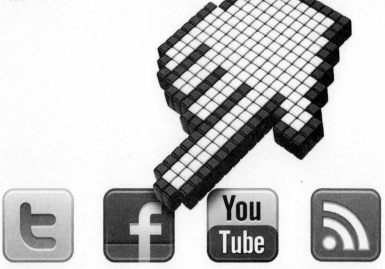